NIGHTINGALE

JENNIFER ESTEP

Nightingale

THE BIGTIME SERIES
by Jennifer Estep

Karma Girl

Hot Mama

Jinx

A Karma Girl Christmas (holiday story)

Nightingale

Fandemic

NIGHTINGALE

by

JENNIFER ESTEP

BOOK FOUR IN THE BIGTIME SERIES

To all the fans of the Bigtime series who wanted more stories,
this one's for you.

To my mom and my grandma—for everything

And to Lucky, one of the best dogs ever.
Nineteen years wasn't long enough.
We'll always love and miss you.

PART ONE

NIGHTINGALE

CHAPTER ONE

Sometimes, I really hate parties.

Especially engagement parties.

I hate the nose-watering flowers. The overpriced food. The endless champagne toasts. The hours-long parade of pomp, circumstance, and well wishes. The mushy exchanges of *I love you* that fail to last through the night, when the bride-to-be catches her fiancé in the broom closet with her best friend.

Most of all, I hate the unending crises surrounding any party—especially those of the rich and socially elite in Bigtime, New York.

Too bad I make my living planning such events.

A ragged breath cut through my dark reverie. I stood in a small antechamber deep inside the Bigtime Convention Center and Orchestra Hall. A woman dressed in a sequined, scarlet gown slouched in a chair in front of me, her head almost to her knees.

"This…is…wrong…Abby," Olivia O'Hara wheezed. "This…is a…mistake. We're doing this…for…all…the wrong…reasons."

Another night, another debutante, another cosmic meltdown ten minutes before the party started. This scenario had played itself out so many times before I could have calculated it down to the second, although most folks waited until their actual wedding day before panicking. Debutantes. They were even more temperamental than the superheroes and ubervillains who populated the sprawling city of Bigtime.

"It's not a terrible mistake." I raised my green eyes heavenward, asking for patience. I'd given this pep talk more than once too. "You care about Paul, don't you?"

Olivia hesitated. Her eyes dropped to the teardrop-shaped diamond on her left hand. She nodded again, stronger this time.

"As long as you care about him, it's not a *terrible* mistake. And if it is, well, that's what divorce lawyers are for. Just ask Joanne James. I'm sure she knows some good ones. Now, breathe into the bag before you start hyperventilating again."

She stuck her nose and mouth back into the brown paper bag I'd given her two minutes earlier. Olivia might be having a nervous breakdown, but she took care not to smear her perfect makeup. That alone told me she was going to walk into the party right on schedule.

Of course, Olivia O'Hara wouldn't smear her makeup anyway. Her family owned Oomph, one of the biggest makeup companies in the city. She'd been born with a mascara wand in one hand and lip liner in the other.

Still, if Olivia wasn't being so careful of her face, or worse, started pulling the diamond-studded clips from her hair, well, then I'd be worried.

Soft jazz music drifted in from the main auditorium. I checked my watch and nodded in approval. The band started right on time. Olivia couldn't hear the music. Nobody could have from this distance, unless they had superhearing—like me.

Don't get me wrong. I'm not a superhero. Not like the Fearless Five, Debonair, Swifte, or any of the other dozens of heroes who call Bigtime home. I don't dress up in formfitting spandex. Don't wear a mask. Don't call myself by another name.

2

And I *definitely* don't go around fighting crime. I have enough trouble handling the crises at my events.

A couple of years ago, though, I just happened to have acquired supersenses, thanks to a spilled amaretto sour and an over-electrified amp at a karaoke bar. Enhanced eyesight. Supersharp hearing. A heightened sense of touch. Souped-up taste buds. A nose that can smell cheeseburgers a mile away. I got the whole shebang, thanks to a couple thousand volts of electricity surging through my body.

Olivia kept wheezing, shooting looks at the closed door in front of us. I checked my watch again. Seven minutes and thirteen seconds until Olivia was supposed to make her grand entrance with Paul. Time to bring out the big guns.

I unzipped a pocket on the vest covering my upper body. The khaki mesh didn't quite go with the black pants, silk camisole, and jacket I wore, but I didn't care. My vest was better than the fanciest gown because the multiple pockets, zippers, and hidey holes contained my supplies. Today, I'd stocked it with my party gear. Bobby pins, glue, extra panty hose, clear nail polish, bandages, antacid, smelling salts, and a little pharmaceutical help—all of which were perfect for dealing with anxious, drunken, and unruly partygoers.

"Here." I shoved my brown hair off my shoulder and pulled a white pill out of one of the upper pockets. "Take this."

"What is it?" Olivia asked, staring at the tablet with suspicion.

"Something to help you relax. You want to relax, don't you? After all, this is your big night—the only engagement party you're ever going to have."

Probably.

"If you say so, Abby."

I checked my watch. Six minutes, thirty seconds. "I say so. Now take the pill."

I pulled out a small bottle of water from the side of my vest and handed it to her. Olivia swallowed the pill, washing it down with the water. Really, the pill wasn't all that potent, only having the effect of one good, stiff drink, but just the act of taking it helped most people, including Olivia. Her tight face relaxed, and her brown eyes softened. The nervous edge melted away. She'd be all right now.

I gave it another thirty seconds just to be on the safe side, then moved toward the door. "Are you ready? Paul is waiting for you."

Olivia stood, smoothing the wrinkles out of her dress. "I'm ready."

I opened the door.

Octavia O'Hara, Olivia's sister, paced outside, while Olivia's fiancé, Paul Potter, slouched in a chair. With black hair, deep brown eyes, and crimson lips, Octavia was a slightly older, sultrier version of her sister. Paul wore square glasses, and his pale, thinning, blond hair flopped over his forehead, no matter how many times he pushed it off his face.

"Is she okay?" Octavia asked. "Has she finally decided to come out? Or do I need to remind her how much money we've spent on this?"

I nodded. "Olivia's fine now. She just needed someone to calm her down. You know how jittery brides-to-be can be."

Well, she probably didn't. Octavia ran Oomph and was one of the most respected businesswomen in the city. I'd never seen her get jittery, nervous, or upset about anything, even when her father, Otto, died last year in a boating accident on Bigtime Bay. I'd planned his funeral, and Octavia had been the proverbial rock. I hadn't even seen her cry—not once. Olivia, on the other hand, had been a hysterical, weeping basket case.

Octavia nodded. "Thank you, Abby. I'm glad you were able

to get the door open and we didn't have to resort to more extreme measures."

I gave her a modest smile. "That's what I'm here for. To see to these little crises."

Olivia had only locked the door. All I had to do was dig through my vest pockets until I found the master key to the convention center, which I kept handy for just such emergencies. If Olivia had done something more difficult, like move a dresser in front of the door, I would have had to get some of the custodians to help me break it down, creating another headache. Morris Muzicale, the director of the Bigtime Symphony Orchestra, hated it when I broke something in his auditorium.

Olivia stepped into the hallway, fiddling with her engagement ring. Octavia hurried to her sister's side, and I was immediately forgotten, as usual.

I checked my watch again. Four minutes, three seconds.

I looked over at Paul. "Are you ready? It's almost time."

Paul continued to slump in the chair, staring at nothing in particular. I had to repeat myself, putting more bite into my words, before he looked at me, sighed, and heaved himself to his feet.

Octavia kissed her sister's cheek, smoothed back Olivia's hair, and murmured into her ear. "What were you thinking? Pull yourself together. *Right now.*"

Though she spoke in a harsh whisper, I heard Octavia loud and clear, thanks to my superhearing.

"It will all be over soon," Octavia continued, "and you can go back to your incessant shopping and partying and pretend like everything is fine."

Olivia dropped her gaze and didn't look at Octavia.

Those weren't the kindest or most reassuring words to say to your sister, but who was I to judge? I'd learned a long time ago that spouting sunshine rarely got the job done. This wasn't the first dysfunctional family dynamic I'd seen, and it wouldn't be the last. This whole incident was rather tame in comparison to some of the things I'd witnessed. Bitch slaps, hair pulling, stabbings, the occasional shooting. I even had one bride take a hot curling iron to her mother's face because she found mommy dearest screwing her intended. Yeah, the O'Haras ranked pretty low on the Richter scale when it came to family feuds.

Octavia patted Olivia's cheek and stepped aside so Paul could squeeze into the picture. He offered Olivia his arm. She gave him an uncertain smile and took it, her brown eyes a bit glassy. Olivia was feeling no pain now. Ah, relaxidon, the anti-anxiety wonder drug.

I pulled my cell phone out from another pocket on my vest. Thanks to the video cameras I'd hooked up earlier, the phone screen showed me the inside of the auditorium. Flowers, decorations, and five hundred invited guests crowded into the space. In addition to hosting an engagement party for her sister, Octavia intended to announce Oomph's buyout of Polish, the lip-care company Paul's family owned. This was definitely a *merger* in every sense of the word.

I hit a button on the phone, and the screen flicked to another camera. The band members were clustered together at the foot of the stage, having just finished a number and preparing to play the entrance music. The guests had turned toward the doors, waiting on Olivia and Paul. I checked my watch. Fifty-seven seconds.

I activated the headset clamped to the side of my head. "Talk to me, Chloe."

"We're a go," Chloe Cavanaugh, my right-hand woman, chirped in my ear. "The band's ready, and everyone's eager to get a glimpse of the happy couple."

I glanced at the screen once more. The house lights dimmed, until only candles flickered in the auditorium. As I watched, a spotlight appeared on the doors where Olivia and Paul would make their grand appearance.

Satisfied everything was as perfect as it was going to get, I signaled to the two waiting ushers to open the doors.

"All right," I told Chloe. "Here they come."

Olivia gave me another soft, dreamy look before she and Paul stepped inside. Gasps, claps, and murmurs of appreciation swept through the crowd.

I nodded. Another job well done—so far.

Olivia and Paul moved through the throngs of guests with Octavia watching their every step. I headed for the concrete stairs leading to the second-floor, balcony level of the auditorium.

I emerged onto the landing, and Chloe turned at the sound of my footsteps. Chloe was a petite woman in her late twenties with black hair, hazel eyes, and olive skin. Like me, she wore a simple black pantsuit. Unlike me, she didn't have a vest on over the top of it.

I'd offered to buy Chloe a vest when I'd hired her six months ago, but she'd politely refused. She thought she could get by with what she had stuffed in her pint-sized purse. Rookie. Chloe hadn't been through the disasters I had. She'd learn, though—if she lasted that long. Most of my employees tended to burn out after a few months. They couldn't handle the pressure I put on them—or myself.

"How is everything?" I asked, moving to stand beside her.

Chloe swept out her hand. "See for yourself."

I peered over the metal railing to the floor below. Earlier today, workers had removed the auditorium seats and had them replaced with thick, padded benches. Balloons shaped like enormous red lips, Oomph's logo, bobbed up and down at the ends of the benches, while faux ivory columns ringed the area. The columns held up a sheer silk netting embossed with more lips and filled with red roses, ivy, and baby's breath. Lights entwined with the roses made the velvet petals glow. I'd been worried about the heat from the lights igniting the flowers, but everything seemed to be okay—for now.

Olivia and Paul made their way to the middle of the

auditorium, where they shook hands and kissed cheeks. If the relaxidon didn't take Olivia's mind off her worries, maybe the constant attention would. She'd barely have time to breathe for the next thirty minutes.

From this distance, Olivia and Paul resembled two delicate figures on top of a wedding cake, surrounded by an army of moving, glittering frosting. At least, they would have to most people. I could see them as clearly as if they stood right in front of me. I might not care for some of my supersenses, but the enhanced eyesight was a perk—most of the time.

Chloe shook her head. "You've done it again, Abby. I can't believe you planned this party on a week's notice. It looks like it took months."

I couldn't believe it either. I might be *the* professional event planner in Bigtime, but even I had difficulty throwing together a high-society soiree in five business days. But Octavia had insisted. Her baby sister's engagement and the Oomph and Polish merger had to be announced simultaneously by mid-January in the most lavish manner possible. Olivia freaking out right before the party had been the least of my problems. Given the time crunch, I'd had to beg, badger, and berate everyone from the caterers to the florist to the band. Well, more so than usual. But somehow, it had all come together at the last minute.

My critical gaze moved from one thing to another. Decorations. Flowers. Lip balloons. Olivia. Paul.

A sense of accomplishment, of pride, filled me. I might sometimes hate parties and the crises that went along with them, but nothing satisfied me more than a job well done. Chloe was right. Everything was perfect. Just the way it should be.

Just the way I'd planned.

CHAPTER TWO

The engagement party kicked into full swing. Olivia and Paul kept smiling and shaking hands while the band played jazzy music. The guests sipped champagne as they waited their turn in the receiving line.

But my job wasn't done yet. In addition to wanting her sister to announce her engagement in the richest manner possible, Octavia had demanded the accompanying sit-down dinner—focusing on the merger of the two companies—be just as marvelous, which meant more work for me.

"You stay here and supervise," I said. "I'm going to the dining hall to make sure everything's set up there."

Chloe nodded.

I moved down the stairs to the ground floor of the convention center, stopping a moment to twist my neck from side to side. I was rewarded with a slight *pop* as my tension-filled bones found a bit of relief. January usually was one of my slowest months, but this one had been nonstop action. I'd done five weddings in as many weeks. With Valentine's Day only a month away, I was already hip deep into planning couples' dinners and romantic rendezvous. On the big day, I wouldn't have a moment to myself—I'd be too busy overseeing everyone else's happiness.

Did I mention I hate some holidays too?

I checked my watch. The two-inch-wide silver timepiece was more like a small computer. It boasted three separate black faces, each one showing the minutes and seconds remaining until the next events were supposed to start. Four minutes, twenty-nine seconds before the dining hall doors opened. Fifteen minutes before the food would be set out. Thirty minutes until Olivia, Paul, and the rest of the guests entered the dining room.

Satisfied everything was on schedule, I set off down the corridor.

The Bigtime Convention Center had more square footage than almost any other building in the city. I'd planned and overseen so many weddings, parties, and fundraisers here I knew the layout blindfolded. I used my master key to open a door marked *Staff Only* and entered another hallway.

The twisting corridor was the belly of the beast. It ran the length of the center, a secret passage offering access to every part of the building. At first, the dimly lit hallway with its faceless concrete walls had creeped me out, but I'd gotten used to it. I couldn't afford not to.

More than once, I'd stashed some drunken best man down here so he could sleep off his buzz rather than tell his buddy the groom that he was secretly in love with the bride. Sometimes, I thought I should give up event planning and just start blackmailing people. I had enough dirt to bury several of Bigtime's high rollers.

I closed the door behind me, stepped onto a strip of gray carpet, and walked on. The concrete floor used to be as bare as the walls, and you could hear someone's footsteps ring out the entire length of the hallway. Since my karaoke accident and subsequent acquisition of supersenses, loud, sharp noises aggravated me—and echoing footsteps almost always guaranteed a killer migraine. So, I'd convinced Morris Muzicale to put some carpet down here, along with a couple of cots, blankets, and pillows for my under-the-table party guests. I'd also brought in my own supplies—bottled water, protein bars, relaxidon, and a spare vest, all of which were stashed in my locker. Now, the convention center was like a second home.

I reached a door marked *Dining Hall 5*, used my key to unlock it, and stepped through. A six-foot-high potted palm tree partially obscured the entrance. I shut the door behind me and wiggled past the green leaves.

The dining hall looked similar to the auditorium, with its netting of roses and lights. But instead of benches, round tables large enough to seat eight people each ringed a parquet dance floor. A projector screen hung down one wall behind a podium flanked by two long tables. The happy couple and miscellaneous family members would sit there, and Octavia would announce the merger from the podium later. More Oomph lip balloons were tied to various columns. A banner stretched across the front of the podium read *Olivia + Paul, Oomph + Polish = Two Matches Made in Heaven*.

Lip-shaped crystal bowls sat on every table, each filled with samples of Oomph cosmetics. The guests would take the samples with them, instead of more traditional party favors.

Waiters bustled around the dining hall, lighting the candles on the tables and popping the corks off champagne bottles. One of the waiters stepped through a door leading to the kitchen. With my supersense of smell, it was easy to distinguish among the various aromas. Red-pepper-crusted chicken, garlic mashed potatoes, Parmesan-dusted asparagus, warm pumpernickel bread.

Olivia and Paul had forgone the typical bland dinner fare of baked chicken and fish in favor of more unusual dishes. Or rather, Octavia had. She'd insisted all of the food be red, white, black, or green—Oomph's corporate colors. It wasn't the strangest request I'd gotten. Nothing could top Milton Moore's desire for strippers wrestling in a pit of strawberry gelatin at his ninetieth birthday party. Still, I'd tried to point out how limiting color-coordinated food could be, but the customer was always right—and Octavia always got what she wanted. Besides, she was paying me enough to do whatever she wanted, whenever she wanted—short of sleeping with her. Even then, I might consider it.

But right now, I had a caterer to talk to.

"Where's Kyle?" I asked one of the waitresses.

She jerked her thumb over her shoulder in the direction of the kitchen. I pushed through the swinging double doors. A dozen chefs wearing food-spattered aprons and tall, white hats crammed inside, chopping vegetables and yelling out instructions. More waiters scooped and arranged mounds of potatoes and pounds of chicken onto plates. Kyle Quicke stood in the middle of it all.

A tall guy with a very lean figure, blue eyes, and a mop of sandy hair, Kyle owned Quicke's, his family's restaurant. Thanks to some secret recipes, Quicke's served up the best food in the city. Everybody loved it, and it was my go-to restaurant for catering events. Kyle hadn't blinked an eye when I'd told him I needed five hundred pounds of chicken in less than a week. It took a lot to ruffle Kyle, who took everything in stride.

"Abby Appleby." Kyle smiled. "I was wondering when you were going to show up. Are you okay? You look a little tired."

I was tired. I'd been working eighteen-hour days for the past week to make sure this party went off without a hitch, but I wasn't about to tell him. If there was one thing an event planner could never do, it was show weakness. People expected you to be cool, calm, and in control—and more or less awake—always.

"Well, here I am. You know what I was wondering, Kyle? Where my lip-shaped cake is. It's supposed to be outside when the guests come into the dining hall. A big visual reminder of the merger. We talked and talked and *talked* about this."

Actually, I'd done most of the talking. With a touch of berating. Maybe it was the perfectionist in me, but I tended to get a little worked up at my events. All right, a lot worked up. Most of the time, I was able to get things done just by politely asking, but the rougher the going, the louder my voice got. My customers paid me to deliver the best, to make sure every detail was seen to, no matter how small, trivial, and inconsequential. Perfection was what I'd built my business, my reputation, on, and I liked to deliver. Molding chaos into birthdays, parties, and weddings to remember gave me a sense of accomplishment, satisfaction, and pride.

I pointed to a table where the cakes sat—five of them, courtesy of Bryn's Bakery. Four chocolate layer cakes, and one monstrous, red, liplike behemoth with seven butter cream-filled layers. I thought the giant lips looked a little garish and creepy, but that wouldn't stop Bigtime's finest from digging into the cake—provided it made it outside on time.

"Abby?" Chloe's voice crackled in my ear. "A few folks are leaving the auditorium, and Olivia and Paul have just started posing for the photos. Everyone should be headed your way in about ten minutes."

"Thanks, Chloe."

I turned back to Kyle, but he'd already moved to the other side of the kitchen, despite the fact that his chefs blocked the aisles. Kyle was stealthy. He always managed to slip out of reach whenever my back was turned. He has excellent survival instincts.

"I know, I know, get the cakes out pronto, or you'll have my guts for garters," Kyle said, still smiling. "Relax, Abby. You worry too much."

I really must be tired, because I was getting a little too predictable. I'd have to come up with some new threats for Kyle Quicke.

Kyle and the waiters placed the cakes on the dining hall tables a scant twenty-seven seconds before people started filing inside. Everyone made a beeline for the desserts, just as I'd predicted. By the time Olivia and Paul arrived, the first round of food and drinks had been served, and guests had consumed three of the chocolate cakes.

Waiters brought in the chicken entrées, and everyone drifted away to their tables to eat. I stationed Chloe behind a column next to the stage so she could see to the needs of Olivia, Paul, and their family members while I took up a position next to the kitchen to make sure the food and drinks kept coming.

Nothing much happened during dinner, and finally, Octavia got up to toast her sister and soon-to-be brother-in-law—and announce the merger of their companies.

"This is not only a joining together of two terrific people but of two visionary businesses," Octavia said.

A spotlight fell on Olivia and Paul. Maybe it was just the glare, but the two of them weren't exactly smiling—more like cringing.

"With Oomph's recent acquisition of Polish, we will continue to bring you not only the finest makeup but also the best lip-care products on the market," Octavia continued.

She raised her champagne glass, and everyone applauded. Octavia's speech soon drifted into the land of stock speak, the way these things always did. I tuned most of it out.

A few minor crises occurred during the evening, most notably Paul's father, Peter Potter, getting drunk and trying to wrest the microphone away from Octavia. But I muscled Peter into the bathroom, shoved his head under the sink, and got him sobered up enough to return to the party.

At least no superheroes or ubervillains decided to crash the dinner. I worried about that with every event. A villain might decide to hold everyone hostage—or worse, take all of the food and booze with her. The fear was greater now, since a museum benefit I'd recently helped to plan had ended in disaster just that way—not once, but twice—with Berkley Brighton, the richest man in the city, getting killed in the crossfire.

Speaking of rich people, more than a few were in attendance tonight. The O'Hara-Potter engagement and merger were big news, as both families were worth a couple hundred million. Sam Sloane, Devlin Dash, Wesley Weston, Grace Caleb, and dozens of other business tycoons populated the room. The society and other reporters for the newspapers and TV stations had also come out to cover the event, including Carmen Cole with *The Exposé* and Kelly Caleb of the Superhero News Network.

I spotted Joanne James in the crowd, talking with Bella Bulluci. Joanne was hard to miss with her mane of black curls, lithe body, and sharp tongue. Bella, meanwhile, was a quiet, curvy, petite woman with frizzy hair. The two couldn't have been more different, but they'd recently become good friends.

Joanne and Bella had been at the museum benefit the second time ubervillains had struck, and they'd both been kidnapped. Although they'd survived, Joanne's husband, Berkley, had been killed. I'd planned his funeral a few months ago. It was one of the hardest jobs I'd ever done, mainly because I had only a couple of days to pull together what amounted to a state funeral.

But Joanne had seemed pleased with my efforts, enough to hire me to coordinate some of the other events accompanying Berkley's passing, including all of the dedications and ribbon-cuttings his benefactors were holding. The whiskey mogul had been worth billions, and he'd spread his wealth to dozens of

Bigtime charities. Pretty soon, Berkley Brighton's name would be on just about every building in the city.

I waved to Joanne and Bella, trying to catch their attention, but the two women were deep in conversation—one I could hear, despite the ambient noise in the room.

"I still can't believe Jasper is your brother," Bella said, "and that the two of you don't speak."

"Are you on that again?" Joanne snapped. "I told you Jasper and I don't have the same cozy relationship you have with your brother, Johnny. We never have."

"I'm just worried about you. That's what friends do. They worry about each other."

Joanne rolled her eyes, but she linked her arm through the younger woman's. "There you go again, being all sugary sweet and concerned and making my teeth hurt. Don't worry, Bella. I'm fine. Or as fine as I can be with Berkley gone."

The two women started talking about other things, including Bella's significant other, Devlin Dash. I waved again, but Joanne and Bella didn't see me, didn't even look in my direction, didn't even know I was alive. Nobody saw me at events. I faded into the background, just like the Invisible Ingénues did. Oh, people knew I was around, but they didn't actually *look* for me—unless they needed something. In addition to having supersenses, I was an invisible woman—whether I wanted to be or not.

So, I quit listening to Bella and Joanne and went back to work. I stood against the wall, eyes flicking around, ears open wide, using my superpowers to make sure every single thing was still perfect.

By the time we got through the toasts, dinner, and dancing, it was almost midnight. I shifted on my aching feet. I would have loved to leave hours ago, but I always stayed until the bitter end. The one time I'd left a wedding before the reception ended, the maid of honor had tossed champagne on one of the groomsmen just as the waiter served the baked Alaska. One thing had led to another, until the Bigtime Fire Department had to be called out to save what was left of the church. So, I didn't take any chances now.

"Oh, Abby?"

I jumped at the sound of Octavia's voice. She stood beside me, propping up a very drunk Peter Potter. Superhearing or not, I'd been so preoccupied I hadn't even heard them approach. Good thing I wasn't a superhero and they weren't ubervillains. I might have been in serious trouble then.

"Yes, Octavia?"

She murmured in my ear. "I'm afraid Peter still isn't…feeling well. Do you think you could take him someplace and get him to lie down for a while?"

In other words, could I stash the embarrassing relative out of the way so everybody else could keep having a good time. I might call myself a professional event planner, but I was really just a glorified shrink, pharmacist, and babysitter rolled into one.

Before I could respond, Peter's stomach rumbled. His round face paled, and I could hear his rapid heartbeat and ragged breathing even over the music. All the signs of a man about to be violently sick.

I stepped back but wasn't quite quick enough. I doubted even the superhero Swifte would have been with his superspeed. Peter lurched forward, bent over, and puked all over me. The hot, sour stench of booze hit my nose while warm, squishy things I didn't want to think about splattered onto my shoes and pants.

Oh, yes. I *definitely* hated engagement parties.

CHAPTER THREE

Thankfully, only a few stragglers saw Peter upchuck all over my shoes. I fished a ginger tablet out of my vest and gave it to the businessman to help his queasy stomach. By the time I put him in a limo home, went to the bathroom, and cleaned myself up, everyone else had left.

I walked back to the dining hall to find it deserted. Thanks to the convention center's staff and Kyle and his army of workers, the decorations and dirty dishes had already been cleared away. The area had been returned to its usual, empty, pristine shell, just as Kyle had agreed to in the contract. I might not care for his lackadaisical attitude, but Kyle always was efficient.

Because everything had been taken care of, I trudged back to the hidden corridor and made my way to the staff break room. A couple of vending machines hunkered inside the windowless area, flanked by several plastic tables and rows of metal lockers. A man wearing gray janitor's coveralls sat at one of the tables, drinking a soda and chain smoking while he flipped through a hunting magazine.

"Hey, Colt," I said, moving to my locker and spinning the combination lock.

"Hey, Abby. How was the party?" Colt Colton asked, taking another drag off his cigarette.

"Not too bad, except for the guy who puked on my shoes."

Colt leaned over and stared at my black pumps, which weren't quite so black anymore. "That's messed up, Abby."

"Tell me about it."

He started to reply, but his cell phone rang. He tapped the screen and started talking.

I threw my puked-upon shoes in the trash. Digging some wool socks and my snow boots out of the locker, I plopped down in one of the chairs and pulled them on. Colt finished his call, crushed out his cigarette, and swallowed the rest of his soda.

"Duty calls." He folded up the magazine and stuck it in his back pocket. "Later, Abby."

"Later, Colt."

The custodian left the break room. The second the door shut behind him, I reached into my locker, pulled out an industrial-sized can of air freshener, and sprayed a liberal amount. Cigarette smoke always aggravated my supersenses. It never failed to make my eyes itch, nose twitch, and skin crawl. Unfortunately, Colt had a two-pack-a-day habit, and the break room always reeked of smoke.

I put the air freshener back into the locker, grabbed my black coat, and shrugged into it. A black toboggan went on my head. I glanced at my watch. Just after one in the morning. I thought about calling Piper Perez, my best friend, to see if she wanted to get a drink, but it was too late to go to The Blues, the karaoke bar we still frequented despite my unfortunate accident there. So, I buttoned up my coat, pulled on my gloves, wrapped a scarf around my face and neck, and headed out.

The party guests had long deserted the convention center, leaving the long, wide hallways still and silent. Thick, crimson carpet stretched across the floor, while sheer, matching fabric covered the walls. Gold threads arranged in paisley patterns in the fabric shimmered under the low glow of the house lights. More gold glinted on the Renaissance-style paintings, while murky shadows sprawled across the floor and crept up the walls. I made a right and entered the lobby, with its hundred-foot-high ceiling, elegant chandeliers, and gold-leaf crown molding.

Eddie Edgars, the college-age guard who manned the front desk, waved at me, then returned to his reading. Even though I was about fifty feet away, I could see the cover. Eddie was engrossed in a comic book by Confidante that chronicled the latest adventures of the Fearless Five, Bigtime's most powerful and popular superhero team. Each of the members—Striker, Fiera, Mr. Sage, Hermit, and Karma Girl—was featured in a heroic pose on the cover. I waved back to Eddie, pushed through the revolving doors, and stepped outside.

A hard spurt of wind slapped me in the face, chilling my cheeks through my scarf. It had snowed while I was inside, and several inches blanketed the street. A cold front had been stalled over Bigtime for a week. Every day, it snowed a little more, adding to what was already on the ground. The forecasters were calling for an actual blizzard tonight.

I reached through a slit in my coat and turned on the pocket-sized heater hidden in my vest. The machine clicked on, and warm air rushed across my chest, fighting back the cold. Let Chloe scoff all she wanted. There were advantages to having a vest of many things.

I stuck my gloved hands in my pockets, tucked my chin down, and walked on. I'd recently moved to a loft in the city so I could be closer to my office. My building was only a few blocks from the convention center, but the snow made it slow going.

Quiet cloaked the streets, along with the snow. Only an occasional puff of wind whistled at the icy silence. I enjoyed the tranquility after the clang, clatter, and conversation of the party. I'd learned to tune out much of the noise that aggravates my enhanced hearing, but I still ended up with killer headaches after some of my more boisterous events. Tonight, I'd been lucky; I had only a dull ache in my temples.

I'd just passed an alley on Thirteenth Street when a strange noise broke the cold quiet. It sounded like a large zipper being drawn down. A soft sound, no louder than a whisper, I wouldn't have heard it at all if everything else hadn't been so still.

I continued on my way, but when I heard a different noise, like metal scraping together, I stopped and concentrated, trying to find the source of the sounds. They seemed to be coming from deeper in the alley. I stepped inside a shadow at the far end and reached for my stun gun.

The alley ran about a hundred feet straight back before curving to the right. A few Dumpsters sat against the brick walls, and shadows pooled around them like blood. I looked—*really* looked—toward the end of the alley where the shadows were the darkest. Most people would have seen nothing but blackness ringed with snow, but I wasn't most people. Not anymore. My vision was just as good at night as it was during the day.

The sound of metal clanged together again. A black zip line uncoiled at the end of the alley, and a figure slid to a stop, his booted feet crunching into the snow-covered ground.

His back was to me as he undid a buckle securing him to the line. He held up something that resembled a gun and pressed a button. The line, which had a silver hook attached to the end, zipped into the gun, like a tape measure being drawn into its case, and he stuck the weapon in a leg holster. He turned then, and I got a look at the noisemaker.

He wore a cobalt-blue leather costume that outlined his muscular body. In a darker shade of blue, a fierce-looking bird with outstretched wings spread across his chest. But the most prominent parts of the bird were its talons, which appeared ready to erupt from the costume and slice you with their sharp, curved edges. A harness around the man's right thigh held a gun topped by what looked like a small crossbow, while the one on his left leg contained the gun with the grappling hook I'd just seen him use. A belt studded with crossbow bolts encircled his lean waist. A cobalt toboggan covered his hair, probably to protect him from the cold, while a wide, blue-tinted, wing-shaped visor wrapped around his face, obscuring most of it from sight.

It was Talon, one of Bigtime's many superheroes. Talon was a bit of a Robin Hood. He frequently robbed the rich to give to charity. At least, he robbed the rich drug dealers and gangsters who populated the city. Unfortunately, there were almost as many of those as there were ubervillains.

Talon also wasn't your typical hero in one other respect—he didn't have a superpower. At least, none I knew of. Most of your Bigtime heroes and villains fell into one of two categories. They were either Ps or Gs—powers or gadgets. That was how I thought of them. Superheroes like Fiera, the member of the Fearless Five who could form fireballs with her bare hands, were Ps. Heroes like Talon, who relied on complicated weapons and other gizmos, were Gs. I admired the Gs much more than the Ps. Anyone with a power could be a hero. It took someone with a lot of guts to be a hero without any superpowers.

There was a finesse to Talon's gizmos, a cool cleverness I appreciated far more than the brute strength some of the other heroes used to fight evil. The crossbow-topped gun on his thigh could do everything from shoot darts to morph into a quarterstaff, and his grappling hook gun had a myriad of functions as well. At least, that was what my friend Piper said. She knew everything there was to know about Bigtime's superheroes and ubervillains.

Talon slid something small, skinny, and silver into a slot on his belt. I shrugged and turned, ready to get to my warm, cozy loft, when another odd sound caught my ear. It sounded like more zippers—a lot more zippers.

A second later, six men dressed in dark clothes rappelled down into the alley.

"There he is!"

"Get him!"

"Don't let him get away!"

Talon whirled to face the men as they ganged up on him, but he more than held his own. In addition to being a gadget guru, he was a solid street fighter. The superhero punched, kicked, and took down one man after another. I just stood there and watched, too awestruck to do anything else.

Talon had just dispatched the last man when a gun burped orange fire from the other side of the alley. A bullet pierced Talon's left shoulder, and he cried out in pain. Clutching his shoulder, he stumbled back. The bullet kept going. It hit the wall behind him and exploded, spewing a black gas in Talon's face. The superhero screamed, as though the gas burned him. I shrank back against the alley wall.

A figure eased out of the shadows where the bullet had come from. He looked like a bad guy from some old spaghetti western movie. He wore a long, black leather duster and cowboy boots, complete with silver tips and jangling silver spurs. Black hair hung loose to his shoulders, while a black-and-white, paisley bandana covered the bottom half of his face. A black, ten-gallon hat was pushed low on his forehead. He held a silver revolver, except it was much larger than your typical gun. I knew who he was too—Bandit, one of the city's ubervillains who was known for his two six-shooters. The handguns fired a variety of unusual projectiles, in addition to bullets. Bandit was a gun for hire, so to speak, an ubervillain who pimped himself out as a mercenary and enforcer to anyone who could pay his price.

Gun drawn, Bandit moved in front of Talon, who slumped against the alley wall, clutching his wounded shoulder. The other men limped to their feet, forming a semicircle around the injured superhero.

"Tycoon wants what you took from him," Bandit said, drawling out each and every syllable. "Now."

Tycoon was mixed up in this too? A whole smorgasbord of heroes and villains had come out to play tonight. Tycoon was Bigtime's most notorious mob boss—and one of the most secretive. He'd never been photographed, and only two or three of his most trusted lieutenants even knew what he looked like or who he really was. More info gleaned from Piper. She paid attention to such things.

Tycoon could have been an ubervillain for all his secrecy. Yet somehow, he managed to run an empire of gambling and prostitution—and never get caught. Lately, the rumor mill and news outlets buzzed about him branching out and dealing in euphoridon, a very dangerous, very addictive radioactive drug with all sorts of nasty side effects.

"Tycoon…can go…to hell," Talon said. "And you with him."

Bandit raised his gun and leveled it at Talon's heart. "Fine. Dead bodies are always easier to search anyway."

I couldn't believe what I was seeing. Talon with a bullet wound in his shoulder—and about to be killed by an ubervillain. I might know a thing or two about handling drunken businessmen, anxious debutantes, and carefree caterers, but this was beyond my area of expertise. By the time I called the police, Talon would be dead, and Bandit would have whatever he was after.

I decided to improvise, something I was pretty good at. Through the slits in my coat, I patted the various pockets of my vest, searching for something useful. I'd once saved the mayor from embarrassment by spray-painting red polka dots all over her white suit after she'd sat down in a puddle of ketchup at a restaurant opening. Surely, I had something that could help save a superhero. Gum, breath mints, tissues, hairspray, more relaxidon pills…

My fingers closed over my cell phone. I whipped it out and turned it around, shielding the screen's light from the goons in the alley. They probably couldn't see me anyway, but I didn't want to take any chances.

I tore off my glove and scrolled through the various ring tones until I came to the one I needed—the police siren. I'd used it before to sober up wasted frat boys and sorority girls at college mixers.

I called up the sound file and pressed *Play*. Half a dozen sirens erupted from the phone. It didn't sound like the real deal to my supersensitive ears, but it should be good enough to fool Bandit and his gang of thugs. At least, I hoped it was. Otherwise, there would be one less superhero in Bigtime.

Bandit's head whipped around to the end of the alley where I stood. I forced myself not to shrink back into the shadows. I didn't think he could see me, because I wore black from head to toe, but I wasn't going to draw attention to myself by moving. You never knew what ubervillains would do—or what they were capable of.

"Bandit! Let's get out of here!" one of the men said. "The cops are coming!"

I cranked up the volume, trying to add to the illusion.

Bandit kept staring in my direction, probably looking for the red and blue flash of the oncoming police cars. A small *click* rang out above the roar of my cell phone. Somehow, during the commotion, Talon had managed to straighten up—and he now had his crossbow gun pointed at Bandit's back.

The ubervillain looked over his shoulder, then back in my direction. I turned up the volume on the phone as loud as it would go, hoping it would be enough to save Talon.

"This isn't over, Talon," Bandit snarled. "Tycoon wants you dead. We'll be back for what you took."

Bandit spat on the snow, swiveled on his booted heel, and stomped through the right side of the alley. The other men limped along behind him. Talon held on until they left. Then, he let out a low groan and fell to one knee. Blood dripped from the wound on his shoulder, staining the white powder a harsh crimson.

I waited to be sure Bandit and his men weren't coming back before I scurried to the end of the alley. "Are you all right?"

Talon paid no attention to me. Instead, he clawed off his visor and scooped handfuls of snow onto his eyes. The superhero had his back to me, so I couldn't see his face.

"It burns," he said to no one in particular. "Damn, that burns."

I assumed he was talking about the gas that had erupted from the bullet Bandit had shot him with. My foot snagged on something in the snow, and I grunted and yanked it free. Talon froze. Then, he sprang into action, searching the ground around him. His fingers closed over his visor, and he slipped it on his face before turning toward me.

"Is someone there?" he asked.

I opened my mouth to respond when I realized Talon wasn't looking in my direction. I was less than six feet away, but his head was pointed off to the right, as if I was standing over there. But there was no way he could have avoided seeing me. Even I wasn't that invisible.

Unless…he *couldn't* see me.

Maybe he couldn't. The gas must have penetrated his visor, gotten into his eyes, and blinded him. I wondered if the effect was temporary—or permanent.

"Is someone there?" Talon repeated, moving into a low crouch, his hand tightening on his crossbow gun.

I could tell by the sharpness in his voice that he was worried I'd seen him—that I knew who he was. I didn't know what to do, so I played dumb. I waited a beat, then scuffled around in the snow as if I'd just arrived.

"What happened?" I asked, playing the part of the upstanding citizen.

Talon gestured at the blood trickling down his shoulder. "I got shot."

I started to open my mouth to respond but thought better of it. From the way I was stating the obvious, you would have thought I was the one who was blind.

"That. Right. Let me call the police."

He frowned. "They're almost here, aren't they?"

I looked down and realized my phone was still on and still blaring out the sound of sirens.

"Oh no," I said, shutting it off. "That's just one of my cell phone ring tones. I heard a strange noise and clicked it on. It's something I do whenever I'm nervous."

Talon cocked his head to one side as if I was spouting nonsense. Maybe I was. So much had happened in the past few minutes. It was a lot to process.

"But you're hurt. Let me call the cops for real. They'll bring an ambulance and take you to the hospital—"

"No!" he said. "No cops, no ambulance, no hospital. I'll be all right. Just give me a minute."

"All right? You have a bullet wound in your shoulder. How is that *all right?*"

The wet, coppery stench of his blood made my stomach twist. That was the bad thing about having supersenses—I heard and felt and smelled bad things that much *more*. These days, being exposed to even a bit of blood was more than enough to make me light-headed.

Talon reached out and fumbled at my hand, the one holding the phone. His fingers closed around my wrist. Good grief, the man had a strong grip, even though he'd just been shot.

"I can't just leave you out here," I said. "You're bleeding, and it's snowing again. You'll get hypothermia in no time."

His fingers tightened on my wrist. The palm of his hand was rough and cold, his fingers hard and calloused, but a hot tingle traveled up my arm at his touch. A small rush of interest, of attraction, I hadn't felt in a long time. I wasn't into superheroes, not like Piper, who could recite obscure facts about every hero

27

and villain in town, but I found myself very curious and very drawn to Talon.

"No. Promise me you won't call the police. They can't protect me. Bandit will come to the hospital and finish the job, and I won't be able to stop him. Not now. And a lot of innocent people could get hurt if they get in his way."

"But—" I protested.

"No, no police."

I drew in a breath and opened my mouth to argue when I caught a whiff of his scent. He smelled like snow mixed with mint—crisp, cold, sharp, clean. A wonderful aroma, even if it was tinged with blood.

I looked up into his face. I couldn't see his eyes, of course. The blue, wraparound visor hid them from view, but he had a strong, square jaw. Talon wasn't really handsome, not like Debonair or one of the other suave superheroes, but he had a rugged look that appealed to me.

He was Talon. A superhero. A larger-than-life G-man who went around the city making things right.

And I found myself nodding in total agreement, as if it was a perfectly reasonable plan, instead of the dumbest thing I'd ever heard.

"All right. I won't call the cops."

"Good." Talon smiled. "And let me thank you. If it wasn't for you, I wouldn't be breathing at the moment. Now, can I ask you to do one more thing for me?"

"Anything," I asked, mesmerized.

"Help me stand up."

I scooted closer to him and put my shoulder under his left arm. He was heavier than I expected—much heavier than Peter Potter had been. Then again, Talon was all leather-clad muscle, whereas Peter had been all portly businessman. I made sure my boots were steady beneath me, then rose to my feet. I'm sure there were some women in Bigtime who would have gracefully guided Talon to his feet, who would have been strong and solid while still maintaining elegance and girly-girl mystique. Not me. I grunted like a noisy tennis player from the effort of hauling the superhero upright.

But I managed it, and we stood there, like lovers in a heated clinch, my face pressed against his chin. A bit of dark stubble scraped against my skin, and I breathed in, enjoying his crisp, cold scent. Talon was a couple of inches over six feet but seemed larger, stronger in the dark night. I'd never paid much attention to superheroes, but I was definitely intrigued by the man before me. Even if he was bleeding all over my coat. Good thing it was black. At least I couldn't see the stains easily, even if I could smell them.

Talon slid his arm off my shoulder and took a step back. His boots skidded on the snow a moment before he found his footing.

"Are you sure you're okay?" I asked, still worried.

Talon's face was pale, despite the stubble darkening his chin. Beads of cold sweat glistened on his forehead, and his breath puffed out in ragged gasps—all signs of someone about to pass out, superhero or not.

"I'm fine," he said. "It's just a flesh wound. Now, I'm sure you want to get in out of the cold. So, it's time for me to go."

Talon grabbed at his leg harness, fumbling around until he found his grappling hook gun. Finally pulling it free, he raised it over his head and squeezed the trigger. The hook arced up into the night sky before clanging onto the roof above our heads. Talon clipped himself to the line and gave it a tug to make sure it was anchored on something solid.

"Thanks again for the rescue," Talon said, looking off to the left instead of at me. "Tonight, you're my hero."

Talon started to press a button on the side of the grappling hook gun, but his finger slipped off the gadget. He tried again, with the same result. The third time, he dropped the gun entirely. The superhero teetered from side to side, his legs crumpled, and he pitched forward, face-first into the snow.

I stared at his unconscious form. Snow drifted down from the black, winter sky, covering his cobalt-blue costume one white, crystal flake at a time.

I rubbed my aching head. I had a wounded, unconscious superhero who'd made me promise not to call the police and not take him to the hospital. Bandit and his thugs could come back any second, and the weather was going from bad to worse.

I was used to dealing with crises, but this was a doozy even for me.

What was I going to do now?

CHAPTER FOUR

Even though my headache throbbed toward full-blown migraine, I didn't panic. I never did, not even when the cruise ship I'd rented out for a bar mitzvah capsized in the middle of Bigtime Bay with two hundred people on board. I hadn't panicked then, with the threat of mass casualties and the end of my career as an event planner staring me in the face, and I wasn't going to now.

Instead, I thought about things, the snow still falling around me. I looked at my phone. I could call the cops. I *should* call the cops. They could help the superhero, make sure he got the medical attention he needed. But Talon didn't want me to. And he'd been right about something. If Bandit came after him while the superhero was in the hospital, he'd be dead—and other people would get caught in the crossfire.

Besides, I'd promised the superhero I wouldn't. I always kept my promises—even when I had to plan the perfect party in less than a week's time.

So, no calling the police.

I could hail a cab, but I doubted any were running at this hour, especially with the snow picking up speed. Even if I did find a cab, the driver would just take Talon to the hospital, and the police would get involved there.

So, no hailing a cab.

But I had to do *something*. I couldn't leave the superhero in the alley in the cold. Talon would freeze to death—or Bandit would come back and finish him off. I massaged my temples, trying to think of some anonymous place where the superhero would be safe, warm, and hopefully stop bleeding.

The convention center. The public library. Quicke's. Oodles o' Stuff. Paradise Park. I ticked off the downtown locations in my head, discarding them all. Every place was either already closed or there'd be too many people asking too many questions.

I glanced over my shoulder toward the deserted street. I should have just kept on walking instead of stopping to investigate some strange noise. Damn superhearing. It always got me in trouble. I could have been at home in bed in my loft right now, instead of out here, freezing my ass off—

Wait a minute. My loft. I could take Talon to my loft. It was safe and warm and free of ubervillains. Better yet, it was only a few blocks away.

It was the best plan I could come up with—the only plan. Now, all I had to do was figure out how to get him there. I didn't think I could carry Talon. At least, not more than a few feet. I looked back toward the end of the alley, hoping Fiera, Wynter, or some other superstrong superhero would just happen along to help me move Talon—or better yet, take him off my hands altogether.

But, of course, it didn't happen. That was another reason I didn't pay much attention to superheroes. They were never around when you *really* needed them. Like during my water-logged bar mitzvah. I'd expected, even hoped, for Cap'n Freebeard and his Saucy Wenches to show up and take everyone off the sinking ship, but the pirate and his psychedelic party barge had been nowhere in sight. We'd had to wait for the Coast Guard to rescue us.

So I was on my own—like always.

That's why I wear a vest crammed full of emergency supplies. Saving a bleeding superhero from freezing to death wasn't the sort of emergency I usually handled, but if I could strong-arm Bigtime's wealthiest citizens into behaving, however badly, I could figure out some way to get Talon to my loft.

I unbuttoned my coat and patted the pockets on my vest, going through a mental inventory of everything stuffed inside. Nail polish. Tissues. Bobby pins. Hairspray. Breath mints. Garbage bag—

Garbage bag—that might work.

I unzipped the appropriate pocket and pulled out a large, black, plastic bag—one of several I carried around in case somebody at one of my events made an enormous mess. They also were good to give to folks like Peter Potter when they'd had a few too many.

I looked at Talon's long torso. Good thing it was a heavy-duty, supersized bag, because he wasn't a small man. I unrolled the bag on the snow next to him and tied two knots in the end. Then, I got down on my knees and pushed and strained and heaved, rolling him onto the bag, face-up.

During my shoving, a silver flash drive slipped out of a slot on Talon's belt. I picked it up. The gizmo looked like your typical flash drive—except for the letter T embossed on the glossy surface. I wondered if the T stood for Talon or something else. No writing or labels were stuck on it to tell me what information it contained, but I slipped the drive into my coat pocket. I'd give it back to Talon later, when we were both warm and conscious. I also plucked his grappling hook gun out of the snow, unbuckled him and the gun from the zip line, and slid the weapon back into the holster on his leg.

The superhero's shoulder wound had stopped bleeding,

probably because he'd been lying in the cold snow for several minutes. Talon's leather costume looked fairly thick and weatherproof. I hoped it would keep him warm enough until I got him to my loft.

Once I had Talon more or less arranged on the bag, I brought the edges up and tied it around him. By the time I finished knotting the plastic together, the superhero resembled a mummy swathed in one big, shiny, black bandage.

Talon didn't move or stir during the ordeal. I was glad he couldn't see me like this, grunting, sweating, and flailing in the snow. I wasn't naturally graceful anyway, not like Piper, but I was being clumsier than usual. My normal awkward self and then some. Not that Talon could see me anyway with the gas Bandit had sprayed him with. Or that he'd ever noticed me before. Few people did.

Then again, I'd never really been up close and personal with a superhero either. It wasn't like I was one of the folks in the *Slaves for Superhero Sex* group. *SSS* was one of the city's more infamous organizations, filled with people who did extremely stupid things like handcuff themselves to railroad tracks in hopes of being saved by a hero or even a villain—and showing their gratitude with their bodies afterward. But I couldn't scoff too much at the group. The members had been smart enough to hire me to plan their Valentine's Day dance this year.

Once I had Talon wrapped up, I grabbed the two knots I'd tied at the end of the bag, using them as handles. I turned toward the front of the alley, my back to Talon, took a step forward—and almost yanked my arms off.

The bag didn't come with me, didn't budge an inch. I was lucky the plastic hadn't ripped. But this was the plan I'd come up with, so I tried again. Still, the bag didn't move.

I tried again. Nothing.

Finally, I hunkered down, dug my boots into the snow, and surged forward with a fierce growl that would have drowned out

Yeti Girl. This time, the bag moved—five whole inches. Well, it was five inches closer to my building.

"You're heavy, you know that?" I groused.

Talon didn't respond.

I wiped the freezing sweat off my forehead and tried to quit wheezing. It was times like these when I wished I'd gotten superstrength from my run-in with that overcharged amp. If you're going to almost get electrocuted to death, you should get *something* good out of it. But no, I'd wound up with supersenses instead, which were completely useless in this situation.

But Abby Alexandra Appleby was nothing if not persistent. Somehow, I grunted, heaved, and dragged Talon out of the alley. The snow made it easier, once I got going. If the ground had been bare, I never would have managed it. The bag helped too, sliding along the icy terrain.

Three minutes later, I reached the end of the alley. I looked up and down the street. Swirls of snow gusted here and there, splattering a fresh coat of the white stuff on whatever was in the way. I cocked my head to one side, listening—*really* listening. Silence. More fat, fluffy flakes cascaded around me, whipped sideways by a blustery breeze, like I was trapped in a snow globe someone kept shaking.

Once I got my breath back, I cracked my neck, gripped the bag handles, and plowed down the street. I managed to build up a bit of speed, mainly by ignoring Talon's body thumping up and down on the snow. I did stop when I lost my footing and banged the superhero into the side of a mailbox, but Talon didn't wake up, so I figured it hadn't hurt him too much. Besides, I was saving his life. What were a few bruises compared to that?

Normally, it would have taken me about five minutes to walk the remaining blocks to my building. Tonight, dragging an unconscious superhero behind me, it took closer to thirty.

By the time I reached my building, I was a sweaty mess. My toboggan had slid down into my eyes, along with my brown hair, and my scarf hung limp around my neck. My body ached from the strain of hauling Talon around, and my numb, stiff fingers wanted to stay permanently curled around the knots on the bag. Why couldn't I have run into somebody lighter, like Aria? The thin, petite superhero, who was fond of singing opera while she fought ubervillains, didn't weigh much more than a hundred pounds. Talon tipped the scales at almost twice that much.

My building didn't have a doorman, something I was extremely grateful for tonight. If someone had been around, he would have asked a lot of awkward questions, like *Why do you have a black bag wrapped around a superhero? Why are you dragging him through the streets late at night? Aren't you worried about his head flopping around like that?*

I let go of the bag and opened the door with my key. Then, I stuck one foot inside so the door would stay open while I dragged Talon through it. I'd never been fond of brown linoleum, but it was relatively easy to pull the unconscious superhero across the lobby floor.

Management had renovated the elevator a couple of months ago, so I didn't have to worry about how I was going to drag the superhero up five flights of stairs. I pulled Talon over to the gray metal doors, punched the *Up* button, and slumped against the wall, exhausted from my snowy workout.

The elevator's doors opened, but no *ping!* announced its arrival. I'd disabled the box weeks ago. There were some noises I just couldn't stand with my superhearing. Pinging elevators topped the list, along with roaring vacuum cleaners and chirping cell phones.

I hauled Talon inside and punched *5* for my floor. The elevator creaked and groaned, but slowly it started to rise. Gears churned and ground out ragged whispers, but I couldn't detect any other noises. I'd moved into the building six months ago for several reasons—including the fact that it was as still as a tomb. Most of the other residents were senior citizens. Nice, quiet senior citizens who didn't slam their doors or scream at each other and add to my migraines. Plus, the walls were very, very thick. I'd called up the building's architect and grilled him about that before I signed the deed.

The elevator door slid back, fronting a short hallway with a door at the end. I tugged Talon out of the elevator, opened the door to my loft, pulled him inside, and flipped on the lights. Then, I closed the door behind me and slumped against it, taking a much-needed breather.

My loft took up the entire fifth floor, but the space was empty, almost barren, mainly because I wasn't around enough to fix it up. Boxes full of clothes, books, and dishes lined one wall—the same spot they'd been in for months. The only thing I'd completely unpacked had been my collection of CDs and albums. Music was the one thing I couldn't live without—and the only loud noise that didn't automatically give me a headache.

Speaking of music, I needed some now. I shucked off my dripping boots and shrugged out of my coat. The coppery stench of Talon's blood on the black fabric made my stomach roil, and I made a mental note to drop the garment off at the dry cleaners.

I padded over to my stereo system, which took up the better part of one wall. I hit a button on my iPod, and a playlist featuring The Killers blared on. Maybe the pulsing rock beats would get me energized enough to get Talon into the bathroom so I could clean him up.

The superhero still didn't wake up, not even when I unwrapped the bag from around him. Talon was surprisingly dry, considering all of the snow I'd dragged him across and through, and he didn't seem to be any worse for wear from the bumps he'd taken during the trip—except for the wound in his shoulder. A small trickle of blood ran out of it, and the edges had turned purple from the cold. That didn't look good.

I plodded over to my desk and retrieved my executive-style chair—complete with rollers. Sweet, sweet rollers. I dug through one of the boxes marked *Towels* and put some black ones over the chair so the leather wouldn't get soaked with melting snow and blood. Then, I wrestled Talon up into the chair. From there, it was a breeze to slide him across my hardwood floor into the bathroom. I pumped the reclining lever on the bottom of the chair and tipped Talon over into the bathtub, which was sunk into the tiled floor.

I wiped the sweat off my face and cracked my neck to relieve some of the tension. I wouldn't have to work out for a week after this Fiera-like effort. I thought screaming at Kyle sapped my energy. Lugging a superhero around was worse.

But I wasn't done with Talon yet. Promise or no promise, I wasn't letting him die, which meant figuring out some way to see how injured he really was and warm him up at the same time. I crawled into the oversize bathtub with the unconscious superhero, propped him up into a sitting position, and placed a towel under his head.

Then I stripped him.

I started with his boots, yanking off the heavy, blue shoes and matching socks, before moving up and unbuckling the silver belt around his waist. The leg harnesses and grappling hook gun came next, minus the hook, since Talon had shot it away in the alley.

I put the weapon aside and moved on to the crossbow gun. I hefted that weapon in my hands, surprised by how light it was. The metal bow on top was the same cobalt color as the rest of Talon's costume. A bolt rested in place, the string pulled taut. All you had to do to fire it was pull the trigger mounted on the gun below. I peered at the bolt. The metal shaft led down to a clear, arrow-like tip that seemed to be made of glass. Something blue shimmered inside the bolt, and I jiggled the bow. The material sloshed around like liquid. Maybe Talon has his own version of blinding gas, just like Bandit did.

I curled my hand around the barrel of the gun, my finger on

the trigger. A row of buttons ran along either side of the barrel, just pressing into my hand. Each and every one of the buttons would probably make the weapon do amazing things. I didn't push any of them, though. I didn't need to shoot a crossbow bolt through the bathroom wall—or into my foot. I set the weapon down and continued with my superhero stripping.

I managed to peel Talon's pants down his legs and almost wished I hadn't when I realized he'd gone commando. But I needed to get him warm and cleaned up, and I didn't think he'd appreciate me soaking his costume in water. Next came the shirt—part of which was stuck to Talon's bloody shoulder. I tugged gently at first, trying to pry the leather off the crusty wound without causing him any more pain, but it wouldn't come free. In the end, I had to yank the stiff, sticky fabric away from the bullet holes in the front and back of his body. The superhero let out a low groan but didn't wake up. Probably for the best.

I also pulled Talon's toboggan off his head. I stared at his hair, a rich shade of chestnut shot through with maple highlights. He wore it short in the back and a bit fluffed out on top, or maybe that was because I'd yanked off his winter hat. For some reason, I'd always pictured Talon as more of a Nordic type, with shocking, white-blond locks and icy blue eyes to match.

I laid the toboggan with the rest of Talon's clothes just outside the door so they wouldn't get wet. The boots, pants, and weapons were fine, but the blood-soaked shirt was beyond help, especially with two bullet holes in the left shoulder.

I turned back to the naked superhero in the tub, my gaze examining his body from head to toe. Yeah, I knew it was wrong, but I leered at him. Only a little. Piper would never forgive me if I didn't. Believe me, Talon had plenty of assets to admire. Washboard abs, strong, corded arms, good pecs. I'd never believed in love at first sight. But lust? Certainly.

In addition to the hard body, Talon had plenty of scars; small, slightly puckered holes I took to be old bullet wounds; thin slashes from knives, swords, or other sharp weapons; even a burn mark that looked like a triangle on his right shoulder. Other nicks and scrapes dotted his torso like weird white freckles.

I traced my fingers over the triangle burn. Then, I laid my palm against his chest, right over his heart. Hot tingles surged up into my arm at the touch, and I sighed with pleasure. With my supersensitive skin, I was almost always cold, no matter how many layers I wore, but Talon radiated heat, even though he sat naked in my chilly porcelain tub. Good. That meant he wasn't suffering from hypothermia as I'd feared, although I still needed to get him cleaned up.

I moved my hand, examining the superhero's old wounds. I had some experience with first aid, having patched up numerous folks at my events. Kids, mostly, who'd gotten too enthusiastic about their playing and ended up with bloody knees. But the more I looked at the scars, the more I realized Talon wasn't just a G-man superhero. He was also a regular guy—one who'd gotten hurt more than once keeping others safe. One who was hurt right now. One who needed my help.

So, I quit leering. I turned on the tap, wincing as the faucets squeaked, and let the water get warm before stopping up the tub. I also put some Epsom salts into the mix. They always helped me relax after a long day at the office. Maybe they'd help Talon too—and hopefully drown out the lingering stench of blood clinging to his skin.

Now came the ultimate question—to remove the visor or not?

I stared at the visor covering Talon's eyes and most of his face. The cobalt lenses reminded me of a pair of wraparound aviator sunglasses more than anything else, although they were tall and wide. The design matched the bird on his suit, with its outstretched wings and claws. Right now, the visor was the only thing preserving Talon's anonymity. I'd stripped everything else away.

Piper wouldn't have hesitated. She would have yanked his

visor off first thing to see who Talon really was. She would have done it before she even thought about moving him out of the snowy alley. But I wasn't obsessed with superheroes like Piper was. I didn't particularly care who was who. I just wanted them to steer clear of my events.

But Talon had reacted violently to the gas spewed from Bandit's bullet. He'd clawed off the visor and scooped snow on his face as if his eyes were on fire, and he hadn't been able to see me afterward. I was betting his eyes were red and swollen—maybe worse. They needed to be cleaned and flushed, just like the wound in his shoulder. I'd rather remove Talon's visor and learn his secret identity than have him be blinded for life because I'd refused to act.

So, I reached for the visor—and was rewarded with a violent shock the second my fingers touched the smooth lenses.

BZZT.

"Ouch!" I yanked my hand back, shaking it. It shocked me! His damn visor had shocked me!

That was only the beginning. Tiny panels opened up where the lenses met the frames on either side, and two thin metal bars slid out. Awestruck, I watched as the bars wrapped around Talon's head and snapped together in the back with an audible *click*. I leaned back and realized that a small circular device had formed around the two bars, almost like a lock anchoring them together. My fingers crept out to touch it—

And a voice boomed through the bathroom.

Unauthorized user alert! Unauthorized user alert!

I screamed and stumbled back. After a moment, I realized the voice emanated from Talon's visor—a very mechanized, bossy voice.

Stop and desist your superhero unmasking immediately! Any further attempts to remove Talon's visor will result in increasing electrical shocks up to and resulting in death. This is not a joke. Repeat, this is not a joke...

The voice went on from there, chastising me for trying to

41

remove the visor and encouraging whoever was listening to dial 911 and/or the hot line for the Fearless Five and ask for the superhero on call. But only if Talon was bleeding copious amounts.

It took me a minute to realize what had happened—Talon's visor had some kind of automatic, self-defense mode to keep me from taking it off. I stared at the back of his head where the two bars had locked together. From the smooth texture of the metal, I was pretty sure the bars and lock were made of solidium, the hardest metal around. The stuff was virtually indestructible. You practically had to have a nuclear reactor to melt it down, which meant there was no way for me to get the visor off now. Not even a superstrong superhero like Fiera could have broken those bars. At least, not without a particularly heroic effort.

A visor with its own built-in defense mechanism to keep an unconscious superhero from being unmasked. Now *that* was clever.

I'd already been shocked to within an inch of my life once before, so I wasn't eager to repeat the process. I heeded the visor's warning and left it alone. I'd tried to help the superhero. That was all I could do.

I got out some clean washcloths and towels, along with some bandages and all the antibiotic ointments, healing creams, and painkillers I had. By the time I finished, a considerable pile littered the floor next to the bathtub.

After I'd been jolted into having supersenses, I'd tried every migraine drug on the market, trying to find some way to ease the constant pounding in my head. Even now, after I'd gotten a grip on my powers, a horrible headache manifested in my skull at least once a week.

Water filled the tub, and I turned off the faucets. Talon looked much better since I'd brought him in from the cold. The white strain had faded from his face, from what I could see of it, and his breathing was even and steady. I cocked my head to one side, listening—*really* listening. His heart pumped along with a steady rhythm.

My eyes went to his left shoulder and the small hole there. Now, it was time to get that disgusting, coppery blood off the superhero and see what else I could do to help him. I wet a washcloth and gently pressed it to Talon's injury.

The second I touched him, the superhero drew in a sharp, ragged breath.

Although I couldn't see them, I got the distinct impression his eyes snapped open. I didn't have any time to react or move. Talon jerked up and latched on to my wrist.

Then, he yanked me into the tub with him.

CHAPTER FIVE

I didn't just fall in. I plunged all the way in—fully submerged. Water forced its way into my mouth, my ears, and worst of all— up my nose. Water going up my nose was an excruciatingly painful and ticklish sensation now that I had supersenses, almost like inhaling liquid fire.

I flailed upward, breaking through the surface, coughing, sneezing, and sputtering water all over the superhero.

"Who are you? Where am I? What happened?" Talon demanded, thrashing around in the oversize tub.

Somehow, despite his injured shoulder, the superhero grabbed both my hands and pulled me toward him until I lay against his slick chest. Damn, he was strong, even for a mere G-man.

"You got shot by Bandit in the alley. I was there. You asked me not to call the police, remember?" I asked, trying to squirm free so I could push my wet hair off my face.

Talon's grip tightened on my wrists. "Bandit!" he hissed. "Do you work for him? Or Tycoon?"

"Of course not!" I snapped, trying to pull back again unsuccessfully.

It was more than a little strange to be trapped in a tub full of warm water, especially when I was not so gracefully straddling a very wet, very naked, very *excited* superhero. One with acres of muscles—everywhere. Muscles I could feel through my waterlogged clothes. I couldn't help but get a little *excited* myself. All right, a lot excited. Lust at first sight was a powerful, powerful thing.

"You got shot. Before you passed out, you told me not to call the cops, so I didn't. But since I didn't want you to freeze to death, I brought you to my apartment so I could clean you up and see how badly you were injured. That's all. I swear."

Talon stilled. The rest of the night must have come back to him, because he nodded and let go of my hands. I used the opportunity to scramble off his lap, careful not to knee him in the groin. I stumbled up out of the tub, water dripping out of my hair and pooling on the floor.

Talon reached up and rubbed his temple. His fingers stilled, and the superhero realized two metal bars encased his head— which meant I'd tried to take off his visor.

"I wanted to see how bad your eyes were," I said in a defensive tone. "That's why I tried to remove your glasses, not because I wanted to know your secret identity. Although from the shock I got, I'd say nobody takes off those glasses but you."

A faint smile curved Talon's lips. "That's the idea. They're programmed to accept only my DNA."

"Well, it's a good one. My fingers are still tingling."

My toes were too, but I think that had more to do with Talon being naked than with his electro-shock visor.

Talon chuckled. "Who are you?" the superhero asked, his voice now more curious than harsh.

I opened my mouth to respond but thought better of it. I'd wrapped a superhero in a garbage bag, dragged him down several city blocks, shanghaied him into my apartment, stripped him naked, and tried to take off his visor. This was awkward enough already. Did I want Talon to know who I really was? Chances were *he* was some rich businessman who did the superhero gig for kicks in his spare time. Some suave society playboy who'd be at the majority of events I planned. One who'd secretly think of me as a superfreak, while I had no clue who he was—or that he was laughing at me behind my back.

No. I was definitely *not* telling Talon my real name.

"Tell you what—why don't I just call you Talon, and you can call me..."

My eyes flicked around the bathroom, as if an anonymous name would magically appear in the steam on the mirror.

"Um..."

My gaze fell to the floor. No name there, just puddles of water.

"Um..."

I looked out the open door. Talon's clothes sat in a row in the next room. My eyes latched onto the winged bird insignia on the superhero's ruined shirt.

"Wren." It was the first thing that popped into my head. "Just call me Wren."

"Wren?" Talon asked. "Is that your real name?"

"Of course not. But it's a bird name. I thought you'd appreciate it."

"But why don't you just tell me your real name?"

I sighed. "Look, you're naked. In my apartment. I don't usually have strange, naked men in my apartment, especially not superheroes. You're not going to tell me your real name. Why should I tell you mine? It will probably be easier for both of us if we stick to anonymous names. That way, I won't wonder whether my mailman is thinking about the night I took off his clothes whenever he delivers my packages."

Talon threw his head back and laughed. The rich, throaty timbre rumbled through the room, almost like bass notes. The sound made me smile, despite the weirdness of the whole evening.

"Well, I can guarantee I'm not your mailman, but I get your point." Talon smiled. "So, Wren it is. You saved my life. That's all I really need to know. Nice to meet you."

Talon must have still been feeling the effects from Bandit's gas because he held out his hand about a foot away from where I stood. I leaned down and stuck my wet one in his.

"Nice to meet you too, Talon. Now, why don't we get you cleaned up?"

"I'd like that."

I spent the next half hour leaning over the tub, cleaning the wound in Talon's shoulder. The bullet had gone all the way through, which meant I didn't have to try to dig it out, like people always did in the movies. I don't think I could have, given how much smelly blood would have been involved. Looking at the two small, neat holes in his skin was bad enough.

Talon pressed a hidden button on the side of his visor, which started humming. A moment later, the mechanized voice delivered its diagnosis.

No vital tissue damaged in shoulder region. Flesh wound only. Recommended course of action is round of painkillers and bed rest...

"Your visor can tell how seriously injured you are?"

Talon nodded. "Yeah. I don't have superpowers, so I have to rely on my equipment more than most. I programmed the visor with a body scanner, basic medical information, and some other bells and whistles."

"That is too cool," I said. "A stun gun, a body scanner, *and* a medical encyclopedia. That thing's better than a Swiss Army knife."

The superhero laughed again. I liked the sound.

"You know, you have a very gentle touch," Talon murmured

as I rinsed off his shoulder. "I've barely felt a thing this whole time."

A gentle touch? Yeah, I supposed so, now that my skin was supercharged to feel even the slightest vibration up to ten feet away. That was one of the reasons I usually wore oversized flannel shirts, baggy cargo pants, and custom-made camisoles by Bella Bulluci and Fiona Fine whenever I was at home. I couldn't stand to feel anything but the softest, smoothest, silkiest material on my skin.

"Well, I'm trying," I said. "It's not every day I patch up a bullet wound."

Talon shrugged. "Don't worry. It's not that hard. I've done it several times."

I knew he had. Nicks and scars covered his body, the signs of old battles and the price of being a superhero—especially one without any regenerative capabilities. Unlike Striker, the leader of the Fearless Five who could heal instantly, Talon was more of a mortal superhero, a clever gadget guru who used his wits to get by, which made me like him even more.

"All right," I said. "It's as clean as I'm going to get it."

It was clean—squeaky clean. I couldn't smell any stench of infection, and the edges of the wound looked better now, if a bit jagged.

"I'm afraid it's going to leave a scar, though." I patted the wound dry and squeezed some superstrength antibiotic ointment into it, being sure to smear the grease on the front and back of his shoulder.

"That's okay. I've been through worse." His mouth tilted up into a smile. "Besides, chicks dig scars. Or so I've been told."

I laughed. Any chick who didn't dig him would have to be stone-cold dead. I didn't tell him, though. I didn't want Talon to think I was some weird *Slaves for Superhero Sex* groupie. I'd already stripped him naked. That was weird enough.

"Well, if chicks dig scars, they'll be swarming all over you when they get a load of this one," I replied, sticking a large, thick cotton bandage over the wound and taping it down. I repeated the process on his back.

"There. You're all patched up."

Talon grabbed my hand and gave it a gentle squeeze, his fingers even warmer than the water around him. "Thank you, Wren. You don't know how much this means to me."

"No problem." I pulled my hand away and ignored the hot tingles spreading through my body at his slight touch.

"Now, let's see what we can do about your eyes. Can you see anything? Anything at all?"

He shook his head. "Not yet. The blinding gas is something new Bandit's been using. The last time he hit me with it, I couldn't see for two days."

"But it's not permanent, then?"

"No," he said. "Just annoying."

I let out a quiet sigh. In other words, I was stuck with a superhero for the night.

I left Talon alone in the bathroom so he could take off his visor and flush out his eyes with some warm water. He opened the door ten minutes later. His visor still covered his face, but the two metal bars that had clamped it to his head were gone. I guess the superhero thought he could trust me not to lunge forward and yank it off his face. Or he just knew I didn't want to get shocked again.

Then came another problem—finding something for him to put on. I might be used to planning for every emergency, but having a naked, wounded superhero wearing nothing but a damp towel in my apartment was one even I'd never dreamed of.

My gaze traveled up and down Talon's body, taking in his

long torso, tight muscles, and white scars. Did this really qualify as an emergency? Because I could get used to this view—easily.

"I can just put my clothes back on," Talon said. "It's not a big deal. They've been dirty before."

I looked at the shirt. To my sensitive nose, it reeked of blood, metal, and gunpowder. The boots and pants weren't so bad. They just smelled like wet leather. But I shuddered at the thought of Talon putting that nasty shirt against his smooth, gorgeous skin—and clean wounds.

"Trust me. You don't want to put your clothes back on. At least not your shirt until I wash it."

"You can't wash leather," he pointed out.

"Oh. Right."

I knew that. I'd told Fiona Fine the same thing when she'd shown up wearing a white leather sundress at a barbecue I'd planned for Nate Norris. I'd warned Fiona her pristine leather probably wouldn't make it through the day stain-free, but the flamboyant fashion designer insisted dirt wouldn't *dare* stick to *her* clothes. Sure enough, ten minutes into the barbecue, someone jostled Fiona, causing her to spill a bucket of baked beans onto her dress—ruining it. I'd had to chew gum the rest of the day to keep from telling Fiona *I told you so*.

But something about Talon made me tongue-tied. Normally, I had no problem talking to people, even confronting them, no matter who they were, as long as it was in a professional capacity. I'd gone toe-to-toe with Joanne James, Johnny Bulluci, and all the other Bigtime wheelers and dealers. Maybe it was because he was paying so much attention to me, but I felt different around Talon. A little shy, a little uncertain, and not like myself at all. I wanted him to like me, and I wasn't quite sure why. Or perhaps it was just because he was rough and tough, and I was totally in lust.

"Maybe your husband or boyfriend has an extra T-shirt and some pants I could borrow?" Talon said.

"Sorry, I don't have a man of the house. It's just me."

The superhero looked at the wall where he thought I was. "You're not with someone?"

I shook my head. Then realizing he couldn't see me, I spoke. "Nope, afraid not. No pets either. It's just me."

"That surprises me," he murmured.

"Why?"

It didn't surprise me. I worked sixty hours a week planning event after event. What little free time I had I spent with Piper or at The Blues singing karaoke. Even when I was up on stage belting my heart out, it wasn't like men lined up to get my number. I wasn't exactly a knockout when it came to looks. My hair was long, straight, and brown. Not auburn, not caramel, not tawny. Just…brown. I had nice skin, if a bit on the pale side. My eyes were light too, a pretty but unspectacular green.

It all added up to a pretty average package. I was lucky if someone bought me a drink once a month. Even when I was on stage and supposed to be the center of attention, I always managed to fade into the background.

Don't get me wrong. I'd dated several guys over the years, including some of Bigtime's playboy businessmen, but things never jelled. I worked too much, and he didn't work enough. I couldn't cook or decorate, while he was a gourmand. I liked rock 'n' roll, while he preferred—heaven help us all— polka music. And with the playboys, I was never rich or thin or pretty or flamboyant enough to hold their interest for very long.

I'd given it my best shot with Ryan Rivers, the hotel heir. Ryan had been everything a billionaire playboy should be— charming, handsome, funny. So charming, so handsome, and so funny I'd been willing to overlook his love of the aforementioned polka music. Shudder. Things had gone great for about three months. Then, Ryan had grown distant. Canceling dates. Ignoring my phone calls. Never wanting to hang out. He'd delved to the depths of Abby Appleby and decided to move on to greener, richer, prettier pastures.

I hadn't wanted to have another failed relationship, so I'd resorted to desperate measures—and tried to mold myself into the sort of woman I'd thought Ryan wanted. I'd started dressing up, acting coy, and being as girly-girly as I knew how. Which, sadly, wasn't very. But the tighter I'd tried to hold on to Ryan, the faster he'd slipped away. He'd taken me out to Quicke's one night and given me the old *It's-not-you-it's-me* speech. Except I knew it was me and not him. At least, it was in his mind.

The day after he broke up with me, Ryan showed up at one of my events with a supermodel on his arm, looking happier than he'd ever been with me. Ryan didn't acknowledge my presence the whole night—or at any other event since. After that night, I vowed never to change anything about myself ever again. Especially not for some spoiled rich guy who thought he was better than me.

After Ryan, I'd concluded that relationships were messy and not worth the effort. Besides, I hadn't met a guy yet who wasn't turned off when he saw how I yelled at people to get things done. Or who didn't sneer and scoff at my vest.

Getting my heart trampled on by another Bigtime businessman and being tossed aside for a flashier model was a mistake I wasn't going to repeat—ever. My eyes went to Talon's obscured face. No matter how tempting it might be.

I shook my head. A relationship? With Talon? I barely knew the guy. Lust at first sight was one thing, but this was ridiculous. Forming an immediate emotional attachment to a superhero was something one of the *Slaves for Superhero Sex* groupies would do. I wasn't that much of a superfreak.

My eyes flicked over Talon's body again. It was the towel, I decided. Slung low on the superhero's hips, that damp, little towel revealed far more than it concealed. It was teasing me. Taunting me. Mocking me with brief flashes of Talon's impressive assets and reminding me how long it had been since anybody had rocked my world, so to speak.

"It surprises me you're not with someone because you're a remarkable woman, Wren," Talon said.

"Oh, I bet you say that to all the girls who save your life." I tried to keep my tone light so he wouldn't hear the longing in my voice.

He shook his head. "No, I don't."

"Well, I just haven't met the right guy yet."

It was my typical answer to end this runaway train of conversation. Some of my clients, especially the older society matrons like Grace Caleb, thought I would make an excellent blind date for their thirty-something grandsons. I'd gone on a couple of those dates and lost some clients when things didn't work out. Now, I had a strict, *no-dating-clients'-grandsons* policy.

Talon opened his mouth to say something else, but I cut him off. I didn't want to hear him expound on my virtues anymore. It only made me want things I'd given up on a long time ago. Love, tenderness, decent sex. Things I could never have—like him.

"Come on," I said. "Let's find you something to wear."

I rummaged through my unpacked boxes of clothes, but no man of the house meant no men's clothes. In the end, the only thing long enough to cover the superhero was my old, gray flannel robe—and it reached only to mid-calf. Still, I helped him slip into it.

"Soft," Talon murmured. "But not as soft as your touch."

My hands froze. He was temporarily blind so he didn't see the horrid blush screaming across my face, but I could feel each and every one of my pores turning tomato-red. If I didn't know how much blood the superhero had lost in the past few hours, I would have thought he was flirting with me—and been embarrassed at how much I liked it.

No, I decided, Talon would never flirt with me. Oh, he might exchange witty, sexually suggestive banter with the mysterious

Wren who'd saved his life. But he'd never engage in such activities with *me*. Not if he could see me for who I really was— good ole dependable Abby Appleby.

"Come on. I know you must be tired. I'll show you to the bed."

I took Talon's hand, ignoring the heat of his calloused fingers on mine, and led him farther into the loft. My king-size bed stood against the back wall, flanked by a line of floor-to-ceiling windows. Heavy, black drapes covered the glass, cutting off my view of the patio outside.

I turned Talon around, put my hands on his shoulders, and eased him onto the mattress. "There you go."

"I can sleep on the couch," Talon said. "I'm feeling much better now."

I didn't see how. If I'd been shot by Bandit, I still would have been whimpering like a baby, but Talon seemed positively cheerful. Maybe he still felt the effects of the adrenaline from the battle. Or maybe he just enjoyed the danger, like so many of the heroes and villains did.

"You'll sleep on the bed," I said in my best, no-nonsense, *I'm-the-boss-dammit* voice. "You'll be more comfortable, and besides, it's closer to the bathroom. I don't want you tripping over something and injuring your shoulder again."

Not that there was much to trip over. Besides the bed, my loft contained a sectional couch, a kitchen table with two chairs, my desk, and my entertainment center with its TV, enormous sound system, and stacks of CDs and albums. The rest of the space was open and empty, a hollow shell.

I helped Talon swing his legs up over the side of the bed and get settled under the covers. I smoothed the comforter and blankets down around him.

"I'll be right across the room if you need anything."

"Thank you, Wren," Talon said, catching my hand, "for everything."

I closed my eyes, savoring the slow stroke of his thumb against mine. He had such a soft touch and was so careful with his hands, as if I were made of the finest crystal. His gentleness, this simple show of courtesy, of affection, stirred something inside me I'd all but forgotten. Talon kept sliding his fingers over my hand like he never wanted to stop, and I didn't want him to. But he needed to rest, and I needed to get control of myself. So, reluctantly, I tugged my hand away.

"Good night, Wren," he whispered.

His voice sent tingles through my body, just as his touch had done moments ago.

"Good night, Talon," I whispered back.

CHAPTER SIX

A deep rumbling jolted me out of my sweet, sweet sleep. I sat straight up, eyes wide, heart pounding, breath caught in my throat. Was someone breaking in? What was going on? Why was I sleeping on the couch instead of in my own bed?

The sound rattled around inside my skull, the way all loud, unexpected noises did. I forced myself to listen to it, to focus, concentrate, and determine what it really was. With my enhanced hearing, a pin dropping twelve feet away could be as sharp, big, and painful as someone hammering a nail into the wall.

The sound came again, deep and even and sort of…phlegmy. And I realized what—or rather who—it was.

Talon. He was snoring.

Oh *no*. He was *not*.

If there was one thing I hated, one *noise* I detested above all others, it was the sound of someone snoring—I. Can't. Stand. It!

I need calm to sleep. Peace. Quiet. Dead freaking silence. Snoring is the antithesis of all those things—squared. An evil that should be eradicated, along with ubervillains. If someone's snoring, it means he's getting sleep—sweet, sweet sleep I am not getting. Instead, I'm the one awake, listening to a motorcycle roar through my head every time the snorer takes a low, slow, rattling breath. I had hated the noise before I developed supersenses. I absolutely despised it now.

I tried to ignore it, tried to block the snoring out of my mind and focus on going back to sleep. When that didn't work, I dug a pair of earplugs out of my vest and stuffed them in my ears. They muffled the noise but didn't completely block it. Now, it just sounded like Talon was in the bathroom instead of here in the main room. So I added a pillow. And a blanket. And the three sheets I'd put on the couch. Piling them all on top of my head.

Talon's snores penetrated my defenses, piercing them like Bandit's bullet had shot through his shoulder.

After an hour of tossing, turning, and muttering curses, I couldn't stand it anymore. I unwrapped the sheets from around my head, tossed the blanket on the floor, and dug out the earplugs. Then, I marched over to the edge of the bed. A shaft of moonlight slipped through the drapes, slicing across Talon's face. I didn't need it, though. With my eyesight, if there was even a hint of light in a room, I could see just as well as if it were noon.

The superhero was lying on his back, his good arm thrown up over his head. The sheet had slid down, bunching around his waist. For once I didn't leer at his toned chest. All I wanted was to stop that horrid, horrid noise coming out of his mouth. My gaze crept to the pillow next to him, and my fingers twitched. Suffocation would be one way to put an end to it. He was probably still weak from being shot...

I made my fingers unclench. No, I couldn't do that. So, I decided on a different course of action. If I wasn't sleeping, then neither was he.

"Hey!" I said, poking the superhero with my finger. "Wake up!"

I reached out to poke him again, when Talon sprang into action. He might not have any superpowers, but his excellent reflexes more than made up for it. He grabbed my wrists, yanked me down on the bed, and rolled on top of me before I knew what had happened.

"Hey!" I snapped, trying to squirm out from beneath him. "Watch who you're throwing around!"

"Oh, Wren. It's just you." Talon yawned. "What do you want? Is something wrong?"

"You were snoring," I accused, trying to ignore how hot his body felt against mine. He was a hundred times warmer than my microfleece sheets could ever be.

"Oh. Sorry. Did I wake you?"

I gritted my teeth. "You might say that."

Talon didn't let me up, though, and he didn't move away. We lay there on the bed, like a couple caught in the throes of passion—his thigh wedged between mine, his elbows just scraping the sides of my breasts. Talon's breath puffed against my face. He smelled of mint. How could the man have minty-fresh breath at five in the morning? Somehow, he did.

I couldn't see Talon's eyes behind the visor, but another part of him grew rather active against my thigh. Another loud *thump-thump-thump* caught my attention, and I realized it was his heart. Racing—just like mine.

For a moment, I thought of raising my lips to his, of indulging in this unexpected attraction I felt for the superhero, of being reckless and carefree and having what I wanted. Lust at first sight wasn't such a bad thing, was it? The people in *Slaves for Superhero Sex* had all sorts of sexcapades with the city's heroes and villains. College kids had one-night stands like they were going out of style. Bigtime's finest businessmen and women bed-hopped like it was an Olympic sport. Surely, one little kiss couldn't hurt—

Talon shifted his weight, breaking the lustful fog that had settled over me.

No—no, Abby, I chastised myself. Bad, bad idea. He'd been shot a couple of hours earlier. I wasn't going to take advantage of a wounded man, no matter how much my body screamed at me to do it. Besides, lust at first sight only led to early-morning regrets.

"Um, do you want to let me up, please?" I asked.

He let out another breath. "Of course."

Talon rolled away, taking the long, hard warmth of his body with him. I scrambled off the bed and hustled back to the couch.

"I'll try to keep the snoring to a minimum," Talon called out in a husky tone.

"I'd appreciate that," I replied, diving into my cocoon of cooling sheets.

"Wake me if it bothers you again."

"Sure," I said, even though I had no intention of getting within five feet of him for the rest of the night. I didn't trust myself—not now.

We lay there in silence. After about thirty minutes, Talon drifted back to sleep, but it was a long time before I followed, and Talon's snoring didn't have anything to do with it.

Well, not that much.

I woke up a few hours later. I didn't feel a hundred percent recharged but good enough to face the day and whatever it had in store—superheroes included.

I threw back the sheets and padded over to the windows. Talon was still asleep but, thankfully, not snoring now. I stared at him. The superhero had turned onto his right side, with his arm curled under his head. I didn't see any blood seeping through the bandages on his left shoulder. My nose twitched. I didn't smell any either. The G-man superhero was tough, even if he didn't have a power to help him battle evil and fight crime.

He looked so sexy sleeping that I reached out a hand, longing to brush the chestnut hair off his forehead, to see if it was as soft and silky as it looked. But I curled my fingers into a fist. Touching the superhero was a bad, bad idea. Besides, I didn't want to get shocked by his stupid visor again.

So I walked over to the windows, threw back the drapes—

And immediately closed them. The sun bounced off a thick layer of snow so white it pierced my eyes with its dazzling brilliance. I groaned, trying to ignore the migraine that popped to life inside my skull. In addition to loud noises, unexpected bright lights made my head ache.

"Wren?" Talon asked, stirring on the bed. "What's going on?"

"Nothing," I replied, peeking out through a crack in the drapes this time instead of yanking them wide open. "Except it looks like it snowed a couple feet last night. Nothing's going on."

I didn't see any cars in the street, except for the ones covered up past their wheels in the white stuff. None of the usual vendors populated the corner. No taxis, no one going to work or church. Even the city's numerous pigeons hunkered down in the eaves on the side of the building. I didn't see any tracks where a plow might have bulldozed through.

"Let's see what the news folks are saying."

I turned the TV to SNN. In addition to being devoted to all things hero and villain, the round-the-clock news channel was also the go-to source for information in the city.

"Can you turn it up?" Talon asked. "I can't quite hear it over here."

"Oh. Sure."

I cranked up the volume, wincing as the SNN theme music blared on and added to the ache in my skull. A news anchor with a tan face and a bad toupee smiled into the camera.

"Well, folks, this is one Bigtime snowstorm we've woken up to this morning. Heh, heh, heh. The city received almost three feet of snow overnight. Chief Sean Newman of the Bigtime Police

Department has ordered all businesses shut down for the day while plows clear the streets. We go out live now to Kelly Caleb, who's made her way to Paradise Park. Kelly, what's the situation?"

The camera cut to a blond woman wearing a fuchsia snowsuit, gloves, and a toboggan with a fuzzy ball on the end of it. She smiled, her perfect teeth whiter even than the dazzling snow around her.

"Well, Steve, I'm live in Paradise Park, which has become a winter wonderland today…"

Kelly talked about the record amount of snow the city had received and how everything was canceled because of it. I was grateful the O'Hara-Potter party had taken place yesterday instead of being scheduled for tonight. My next event, one of the Berkley Brighton memorial dedications, wasn't until Tuesday, which should be enough time for the city to dig itself out.

A noise on the TV caught my attention. A shimmering blur zoomed by Kelly, sending sprays of snow up around her before suddenly stopping. Swifte, another one of Bigtime's many superheroes, beamed into the camera. Usually, Swifte took center stage with his flashy white costume, but today he faded into the snowy background.

"Hey, Kelly, what's happening?" Swifte asked.

Kelly looked over her shoulder and ducked. A large snowball zoomed over her head and smacked into Swifte's chest.

A trilling laugh floated through the TV, and the cameraman swung his lens around to a woman wearing an ice-blue suit. A giant snowflake flashed like a strobe light on the front of her costume. Wynter. Another one of the city's heroes whose icy powers were just what her name suggested.

"Hi, Wynter." Kelly smiled at the superhero. "I thought we might see you out and about today."

"I do love this kind of weather," the superhero purred. "And I love snowball fights even more. What do you say, Swifte?"

The other superhero dusted the snow off his costume. "Sure. Just don't come crying to me when you lose."

Wynter held out her hands. Blue flames formed on her palms before turning into two snowballs. "Care to make a friendly wager on that?"

Swifte grinned. "Always."

The two heroes spent the next few minutes lobbing snowballs at each other while Kelly gave the play-by-play action. Swifte was faster, throwing the balls at the speed of light, but Wynter had an ace up her sleeve—her superpower. While Swifte lobbed fist-sized snowballs at her, she summoned a giant one on the hill behind him. Gravity did the rest. The ball bounced down the rise, picking up more snow with every roll. Swifte never saw it coming. The enormous mound landed on top of the superhero, picked him up, and kept right on going toward the park's Ferris wheel. All you could see of Swifte were his legs sticking out of the sides of the powdery mass. Winner, Wynter.

"Well, folks, as you can see, the superheroes are having just as much fun as the city's kids," Kelly Caleb said. "Speaking of kids, schools have already been closed for tomorrow, Monday, and could remain closed the rest of the week..."

She started listing the cancellations, and I clicked off the TV.

"I'm glad you came along when you did," Talon said. "Or I'd be another icicle out there."

I shrugged, even though he couldn't see me. "It was nothing, really."

"It was something to me, Wren." His voice was low and sexy. "It was really something."

The intense tone in Talon's voice rattled me, especially because he stared at the wall where he thought I was instead of looking at me.

"How about some breakfast?" I asked, changing the subject. "I know you must be hungry, and you really should keep your strength up."

"Breakfast would be great."

I'm not really a domestic type. Cooking isn't my forte, and I'd much rather eat out than make something for myself. In fact, one of my favorite guilty pleasures was getting barbecue and all the fixings shipped in from this restaurant called the Pork Pit down in Ashland. But I had enough food on hand to whip up some ham-and-cheese omelets, crispy bacon, blueberry pancakes, and apple juice.

While I cooked, Talon stumbled into the bathroom. Then, I helped him over to the kitchen table, put a plate of food in front of him, and slid some silverware into his hands.

Talon fumbled around with his fork, the metal utensil *screech-screech-screeching* against the stoneware plate every time he stabbed it instead of his omelet. After the fifth time, I took the plate away from him and cut up his food before handing it back. I just couldn't stand the noise.

"The pancakes are at three o'clock, the omelet's at six, and the bacon's at nine."

I wrapped my fingers around his hand and guided it to where the food was. More tingles shot through me at the feel of his skin on mine. I hesitated, enjoying the sensation, then pulled away. These *lust-at-first-sight* feelings were getting out of hand.

"Thanks," Talon said. "I'm usually not this clumsy."

"You're usually not blind either."

"My eyes are a little better today," he said. "Everything is gray now instead of totally black, and I can sort of make out blurry shapes. I should be able to see well enough to get out of here by tomorrow. I think that's long enough to impose on you."

Talon started eating his breakfast, but I put my fork down, troubled. Things would be different when his sight returned. I wouldn't be able to hide behind the name Wren. Talon would know exactly who I was while keeping his own anonymity intact. All the awkwardness and weirdness would return, and I'd be right back to wondering which rich playboy thought I was a superhero-stripping freak.

What exactly *would* Talon think when he could see clearly again?

When he could see the real me?

CHAPTER SEVEN

After breakfast, Talon took a painkiller and went back to sleep. Because I couldn't go to the office and leave the superhero alone, I used the opportunity to unpack my things, namely the few CDs that had gotten mixed up in the wrong boxes. Because Talon was asleep, I put a CD into the entertainment center and turned the volume down low, not wanting to disturb him.

As I moved around unpacking, I sang along. Most people sing only in the shower, but I do it whenever and wherever I can. It really helps me relax. My main guilty pleasure in life is doing a couple of numbers a few times a week at The Blues, the karaoke bar where I'd had my unfortunate run-in with that overcharged amp. As a way to keep me from suing her, Melody Masters, the owner, promised me free admission and drinks for life.

Cyndi Lauper launched into her classic rendition of "Time After Time," and I sang along, trying to make my voice, my tone, my pitch match hers. That was one good thing about having superhearing—it gave you a deeper appreciation for music. I'd always loved music, but now I did for another reason entirely—it was the only thing I could listen to really, *really* loud and not give myself a migraine. Something about the pounding beats soothed away the aches instead of adding to them.

Cyndi came to the end of the song, and so did I, letting the last note trail off. Claps sounded, and I turned. Talon sat up on the bed, staring in my direction.

"Wow. You have a beautiful voice. Absolutely amazing." The superhero smiled. "You should call yourself Nightingale instead of Wren."

I just looked at him, with his scarred body, gadget-filled visor, and all-around cool factor. He was a nightingale, a thing of beauty, mystery, and wonderment. I was nothing but a shabby little brown wren—one he'd never look at twice after he left my apartment. I don't know why that depressed me—but it did.

"Oh, I don't know," I said, trying to make a joke of things. "I think I'm more of a wren. Nobody ever pays much attention to me."

"Well, they should," Talon said in a firm voice. "They really should."

I couldn't stop the fierce longing that swept through my heart at his words.

Longing for him to keep on noticing me. Now, tomorrow…hell, forever.

We spent the rest of the day talking about everything—and nothing in particular. The weather, food, books, movies, sports. Small stuff, really. But somehow, it added up to a lot.

I felt like I could talk to Talon forever. We had so much in common. We were both ardent fans of the Bigtime Barracuda football team. Both wished we had more time to read. Both felt like we worked too hard but couldn't seem to stop ourselves.

Even more important than our similar interests was that I felt like I could talk to the superhero about anything. Bare my soul, my deepest, darkest thoughts to him, and have him be okay with it. That Talon would still like me, no matter what I said or did, what horrors I revealed. That was how I felt about him, I realized. That I would like him no matter what.

That I *did* like him.

"Come on," he said after lunch. "Tell me why some guy hasn't snatched you up already. I'm dying to know."

"Do I have to?"

"Oh yes," Talon said. "Aren't you tired of talking about sports? We can regale each other with dating disasters. That's what friends do."

"Are we friends?"

"Well, sure. Don't you think so?"

Talon was stretched out on the bed, an arm thrown up over his head, a leg cocked to one side, my old robe just barely covering him. I'd never seen a sexier pose, not even in Piper's *Bigtime's Sexiest Superheroes* calendar, and I was draped over the end of the sofa staring shamelessly at him. I just couldn't look away. I wouldn't describe my leering as exactly *friendly*, but I decided to answer his question anyway.

"No guy has *snatched me up* because I don't exactly advertise myself as being on the market."

"Why not?"

"Because I've had some bad relationships, including one that ended rather abruptly. I'm not anxious to get dumped again. I suppose I'm gun shy."

"Lies," Talon declared.

"Lies? How do you figure that?"

He grinned. "Because I bet you're gorgeous. A real heartbreaker. You probably have two or three guys on a string, all of them fighting over you."

I looked at my reflection in the mirror on the wall. Brown hair, green eyes, cargo pants, flannel shirt. "Gorgeous and I aren't exactly close friends. As for the guys, well, it's a nice fantasy."

"Oh, come on," Talon said in a firm voice. "You're gorgeous inside and out. I know it, and I'm sure other guys do too."

Gorgeous. He called me *gorgeous* again. Nobody ever called me that.

My heart fluttered, my hands trembled, and I wanted to sing and throw up at the same time. In that moment, in that instant, I realized I felt something for Talon. Something beyond lust at first sight. Something deep. A connection stronger than any I'd ever experienced. It wasn't sane or logical or rational, but it was there—a feeling I couldn't deny.

I wanted to go over to the bed. To touch Talon. To snuggle in the crook of his arm. To run my fingers through his hair (avoiding the damn visor, of course). To press my lips to his. To just let him hold me while we talked. But I couldn't do it. Images of Ryan and his supermodel flashed through my mind. I just couldn't take the risk.

"What about you?" I asked. "Why aren't you married with three kids?"

"Gun shy like you, I suppose. Haven't met the right woman. Bad experiences in the past. Et cetera, et cetera." His tone was cheerful, flippant even, but I heard a note of longing in it. The same longing that was in my own voice.

"And the real reason?" I asked, probing deeper.

Talon hesitated. "Maybe I'm a romantic, but I want the whole story, the fairy tale."

"The fairy tale?"

He shifted on the bed. "You know, the lightning, the magic, the fireworks. The desire to be with someone no matter what. To know this woman is the one for me. That's what I want. I just haven't found it yet."

Wow. I didn't know what to say, except to tell the superhero he was every girl's dream—including mine. My eyes traced over his long legs, his hard chest, his smiling face. I'd like to be the one to share in his lightning, his magic, his fireworks, his everything.

Talon grinned. "Don't tell anybody, though. Superheroes aren't supposed to be hopeless romantics."

"Why not? Don't you know chicks dig romantic guys? *Especially* if they're superheroes."

He just laughed.

The more we talked, the more I liked Talon. He was just…fun. Easygoing, carefree, and completely self-deprecating. Talon wasn't afraid to make fun of himself—or his supposed lowly standing among the superheroes in Bigtime.

"The Fearless Five rule this town," he said. "I'm just a second-string superhero, backing them up when they need it. Actually, more like fourth string. Swifte's the number two guy in town, and I'd say Debonair's number three, ever since he went over to the good side and started working with the art museum."

"I wouldn't say that," I protested. "I think you're one of the coolest heroes in the city. Certainly one of the cleverest, with your gadgets."

I cringed the moment the words left my mouth. I sounded like I had a fangirl crush on the G-man superhero, which I totally did—but he didn't need to know.

Talon grinned instead of seizing upon my fawning statement. "Well then, you need to buy some more of my action figures, because Striker is kicking my ass when it comes to sales."

"Well, I'll rush right out and buy one just as soon as Oodles o' Stuff reopens," I promised.

He nodded in satisfaction. "Good. Now, if you could convince about a hundred thousand of your closest friends to do the same, I might be able to move up to third string."

We both laughed.

Talon also wasn't afraid to parade through my apartment wearing nothing but my ratty flannel robe and a smile. It must have been *drafty* in certain areas, but Talon never complained, and he didn't ask me to trudge out into the snow to get him some decent clothes. Gentleman George, the superhero who paid more attention to his three-piece suits than fighting evil, would have been climbing the walls if his ascot had been the tiniest bit askew.

Just being with someone who didn't expect me to immediately see to his every whim was a refreshing, new experience. I liked it. Scratch that. I *loved* it.

Finally we got around to the make-or-break topic—music. Ever since I'd dated Ryan, the polka-loving playboy, I always asked guys about their musical tastes up front. It saved everybody a lot of time because I was *not* compatible with guys who liked rap, bluegrass, or polka. Shudder. I hadn't been before my accident gave me superhearing, and I definitely wasn't now that I could hear every painful note in crystal clarity.

"So, who's your favorite band?" I asked.

"Green Day," Talon said.

I liked Green Day too. My heart beat a little faster.

"The Pretenders are good."

I was cool with The Pretenders. So far, so good.

"And—" He cut himself off.

"And who else?" My eyes narrowed. "You were going to say somebody else's name. Whose?"

Talon turned away. He hadn't exactly been looking at me anyway; he still couldn't see, but now, the superhero totally averted his face. "It's sort of embarrassing…"

"Come on. Out with it. Who is it?"

"John Denver," he mumbled.

I snickered.

"Hey, hey," he admonished. "Quit laughing."

"John Denver?" I asked. "You, Talon, the rough and tough superhero who gives bad guys a hard time, like John Denver? The sensitive, soulful singer-songwriter?"

"Yeah, I do." His mouth lifted into a smile. "Besides, chicks dig sensitive stuff. But don't tell any of the other superheroes. I don't want to ruin my rep as a bad-ass."

I snickered again.

So, we listened to some Green Day and some Pretenders. I even dug out my CD of John Denver's greatest hits to appease the superhero's softer side.

"Why don't you sing something?" Talon asked after we'd finished listening to the CD.

We were sitting side by side on the couch now.

"I don't know," I said, fidgeting. "I don't really sing for other people, unless I'm drunk enough to do karaoke."

"You were singing before when you thought I was asleep. What was that song?" he asked.

"'Time After Time' by Cyndi Lauper."

"Sing that." Talon grabbed my hand and turned his head in my direction. "Please, Wren. For me?"

I stared at him, looking at his visor-covered face and scarred body that was more than a little visible beneath my robe. I wished I could have seen his eyes, seen what was in them, seen how he was *really* looking at me. Because I knew how I was staring at him—with my heart and with all these new feelings he stirred in me painted on my face.

"All right."

Against my better judgment, I sang it for him, once with the CD turned down low and once a capella.

"Wow!" Talon said when I finished. "Whatever it is you do, you should quit your day job and be a singer. You have a tremendous voice, Wren."

"Thank you," I said, glad the superhero couldn't see how impossibly red my cheeks were.

"No," he said. "Thank you. That was a musical treat."

He grabbed my hand and squeezed, his rough, calloused fingers dwarfing my own.

I squeezed back. This time, I didn't let go.

That afternoon, I made a dinner of tomato soup and grilled cheese sandwiches. Not the most glamorous or complicated of meals, but it was warm, filling, and soothing—just like being with Talon.

Afterward, the superhero and I sat together on the couch. SNN droned on in the background as Kelly Caleb did another story from Paradise Park. To my surprise, the power had stayed on, despite the wet, heavy snow blanketing the lines outside.

"You know, this has been the most relaxing day I've had in a long time," I said, sighing and sinking lower into the sofa.

"Really?" Talon said. "Why's that?"

"I don't get much time off from work, but it's my own fault. I'm a raging perfectionist."

"What kind of business are you in?" Talon said.

"No details," I chided. "Remember?"

"Of course," he said. "But let me help you relax a little more. It's the least I can do after everything you've done for me."

Before I could ask what he was up to, Talon reached over and fumbled around until he laid his hand on my neck. His hard, warm fingertips sank into my skin, gently kneading.

"Why are you doing that?"

"Because you've been cracking your neck all day," Talon said.

He kept right on massaging, his fingers pressing on the vertebrae in my neck. I sighed and leaned into his touch like a puppy. If I had a tail, it would've been thumping a hundred times a minute. My neck cracked in the most wonderful way, my bones popping from top to bottom. Pleasant tingles flooded my body, traveling from my spine into my arms and legs.

"You really are tense," he murmured.

Talon's hand slid lower, and he pressed his thumbs deep into the muscles of my back, loosening, soothing away my knots. I sighed in pleasure again, and Talon kept right on massaging me with his good arm.

I blinked. He'd stopped for some reason. I turned my head, and there he was next to me. I'd been so entranced by the massage I hadn't even felt him move closer.

"Nightingale," Talon whispered.

I opened my mouth to tell him my name was Wren, but I stopped. Instead, I lifted my fingers up to his face, laying my palm against his cheek. Stubble darkened his chin, and his sharp whiskers bristled against my sensitive skin. But I didn't mind the rough, prickly sensation. All I could think about was touching my lips to his, of giving in to these feelings, this rush of emotions I felt for the superhero.

So I did. And it was—*perfect.*

The kiss was perfect. Not because I'd planned or plotted or even imagined it—it just *was.*

Talon responded with just as much feeling. Maybe more, because he didn't stop there. He wasn't content to just steal a sweet kiss. Evidently, there were some things a man could do even when he'd been shot and temporarily blinded. Like put his hands up a woman's shirt.

He pushed aside my long, loose, flannel shirt with no problem or fumbling of any kind. My silk camisole confused him for a moment before he managed to slide his hand up under the band that bound my breasts. His fingers closed over my nipple, and I almost bucked off the sofa, the sensation was so strong.

"Do you like that?" Talon whispered, rolling the stiff peak between his fingers.

Like it? If he kept doing that, I was going to have an orgasm right then. I shuddered and tried to get a grip on the tingles racing through my body—tingles that turned into surges of hot, electric pleasure.

Talon pressed his lips to mine again. I grabbed his head with my hands and opened my mouth, my tongue meeting his. Somehow, despite the soup we'd had earlier, the man still tasted like spearmint, which was rapidly becoming my favorite flavor *ever*.

"I know this is crazy, that we don't even really know each other. But I want you, Nightingale," he whispered against my lips. "I want you so much. You make me smile and laugh and just *feel*."

I wanted him too. More than I'd wanted anyone in a long time. Ever, really. And I wasn't going to deny myself this. Not tonight. But I had to ask him one question first.

"Are you sure you're up to it?" I rasped. "Your shoulder—"

"Is feeling much, much better now. Let me show you what I can do with my hands," Talon teased, his fingers closing over my breasts and massaging them just as he'd done to my neck a few moments earlier. "See? I'm perfectly fine now."

If I should be a singer, then Talon needed to open up his own massage parlor. A whole chain of them. The man was that good.

"Then, hold on a minute," I said.

I scrambled away from him, crawling toward my vest, which I'd thrown on the floor in front of the TV last night. I yanked open one of the zippers and drew out a condom. Always prepared, that was me. I took birth control pills already, but it never hurt to have extra protection. Besides, you wouldn't believe how many times I'd had bridesmaids and other members of a wedding party come up to me and ask if I had any condoms they could have. So I'd taken to carrying them with me at every wedding—one for each bridesmaid and groomsman in attendance. It wasn't just limited to weddings. Recitals. Business conferences. Potluck dinners. I'd even had a soccer mom corner me at her kid's birthday party because she was getting back together with her ex—at least for the afternoon.

"What are you doing?" Talon asked.

"Getting a condom."

"Good idea," he said in a light, easy tone. "We'll get to that in a few minutes."

"And what are we going to do in the meantime?" I teased.

Talon stood, opened the robe he was wearing, and let it fall to the floor. Then, he put his hands on his hips and struck a pose that even showboat Swifte would have had a hard time copying. "I have some ideas," he said.

My eyes trailed down his body, stopping at his erection. "It certainly looks like you do."

"First things first," Talon said, holding out his hand.

I gave him the condom, and he tore open the packet and slipped it on. Evidently, that was something else a blind man could do quite easily. When Talon finished, I moved back into his arms. I thought about kissing him or running my hands up and down his chest. Instead, I just stood there. Hesitating. Truth be told, when I stopped to think about it, I always felt a little awkward and self-conscious during sex, because it was one of the rare times when a man's attention was focused squarely on me. And Talon was right. This was crazy, insane really. Lust at first sight gone out of control.

Talon didn't kiss me or try to undress me. Instead, he just stood there, running his hands up and down my body. His touch was light, surprisingly so, given how rough his hands were, but every soft fingertip he trailed up my shoulder and down my chest burned into my skin, making me ache inside. Overpowering all my awkward fears and doubts.

Finally, I couldn't stand it anymore. I grabbed his hands and held them tight against my chest. "What do you say we get naked?"

"I'm already naked," Talon replied, smiling. "But I'd be more than happy to help you."

He slid my camisole straps down one at a time, pressing sweet kisses along my arms and shoulders as the silk slid away. Then, he pushed the fabric down, exposing my breasts. His hands covered them again, kneading them as before. I couldn't stop the low groan escaping my throat. Talon leaned down, his mouth just brushing my nipple, his tongue just flicking out to tease it.

By this time, so many tingles rippled through my body I felt like I'd been electrocuted again. It was wonderful, but my skin was too sensitive, and I was too impatient. I drew back, unzipped my pants, and stepped out of them. My panties followed a moment later, then the camisole.

I put my hands on Talon's face and crushed my lips to his. He responded by yanking me toward him and pressing his fingers into my back, sliding them down my body, even as our tongues drove together. His shaft brushed my inner thigh. His fingers did too, before retreating. Again and again and again.

Exquisite torture. And I loved every second of it.

But I was in a frenzy. Too much pressure. Too much pleasure. Too many sensations.

"Talon," I said, my voice low and husky with need.

"I know," he said. "I know."

Talon picked me up. I locked my legs around his waist and buried my face in his neck, drinking in his minty aroma.

"Wall," he rasped into my hair. "Couch, table, chair, something, *anything*."

"Couch back and to your left," I murmured.

Talon swiveled around and took two steps forward. He reached out and touched the back of the couch. He laid me down on it. The fabric felt cool and scratchy against my bare back, but I didn't care. There was only one thing I wanted to feel right now—Talon.

He steadied himself, then slid into me. I opened my legs, taking him inside.

I'd had sex since my accident, so I knew what to expect with my supercharged skin and heightened senses—knew I'd feel everything more now. Feel his stubble scraping my cheek. Hear his voice rasping out my name. Smell his scent spreading over my skin. Taste his tongue in my mouth. See him moving over me.

But this pleasure was more intense than any I'd ever experienced. And it wasn't just physical. Hot emotions rushed through me as we kissed and caressed and moved back and forth together. I thought my supersensitive, supercharged body would explode as Talon thrust deeper inside me.

Then, it did, and we both did—together.

Afterward, we remained cuddled on the couch, wrapped in a blanket. I had my head pillowed on Talon's chest, while he drew small circles on my shoulder with his finger.

"I like being here with you, Nightingale," he said, his chest rumbling with every word. "You finding me in that alley was one of the best things that's ever happened to me."

"Why do you keep calling me that?" I asked. "I've told you a dozen times now my name is Wren."

"No it's not. Nightingale is your name," he said in a firm voice. "You're no drab wren. You could never be that."

Sure I could, I thought. *That's what I really am. You'd agree, if only you could see me.*

I closed my eyes as a horrific realization struck me. Talon *would* be able to see me, sooner rather than later. A few more hours, another day tops, and he'd get his sight back. He'd told me as much.

This cocoon we snuggled in, this perfect little bubble of easy happiness, would *pop!* as soon as Talon saw me. *The story*, as he called it, the fairy tale, would disappear as quickly as lightning striking the ground, leaving behind nothing but scorched earth—and the ashes of my heart.

He wouldn't want me anymore. He wouldn't want good ole Abby Appleby, who was practical, uptight, and occasionally yelled at people to get things done. He'd want his fantasy woman. Nightingale. The mysterious, clever, witty, gorgeous heroine who'd saved him.

I didn't know what Talon would do if he realized who I really was. How he'd react. Would he try to pretend he felt the same way about me as he did about Nightingale? Would he give me the *let's-just-be-friends* speech? Or the *it-was-great-but-it-was-only-one-night* talk? Or worse, would he be like Ryan—completely ignore me and pretend like this had never happened?

I didn't know, and I didn't want to find out.

"Would you like something to drink?" I asked, pulling away from him.

"Sure, that would be great."

"Just a minute."

I went into the kitchen and pulled a bottled water out of the fridge, but instead of handing it to him, I walked over to my vest, the one I'd worn to the O'Hara wedding, the one I'd gotten the condom from. I pulled a small, white pill out of one of the pockets and dropped it into the water, watching it fizz. When the pill dissolved, I moved back over to Talon and handed him the water. He sat up and took a long drink, draining half of it in one gulp.

"You know, I think Bandit's drug is wearing off," the superhero said. "The grayness is getting brighter, and I can see more shapes now. Like this bottle."

Talon looked at the bottle, and his head tilted to one side. He let out a slow breath. "Wren? I feel…strange. Did you…do…something…to me?"

"I'm sorry, Talon." I pressed my palm against his cheek. "I gave you a sleeping pill."

"But...why?" the superhero asked, his voice thick and slow.

"So you won't ever see the real me," I whispered.

The superhero's head dropped onto his chest. He slumped against the couch. The bottle rolled out of his hand and fell to the floor.

CHAPTER EIGHT

I stood there, holding my breath, but the pill, a combination of relaxidon and some other drugs, had already taken effect, and Talon slept peacefully—for now.

So, once again, I had an unconscious superhero in my apartment—and this time, I needed to move him before he woke up. Before he could see me for who I was—a superfreak.

I threw on some clothes and my vest, ignoring the treacherous, warm glow I still felt from being with Talon. Then, I redressed the superhero in his hat, boots, pants, leg harnesses, and weapons. I hesitated when I came to the bloody shirt. It went against all my supersenses, especially my nose, to put that nasty, smelly thing back on him, but I didn't have a choice. I couldn't take him out in the snow half-dressed.

The leather shirt had shrunk from being wet, and I struggled to get the stiff fabric onto Talon's body, but I managed by duct taping the leather together when I couldn't get the zipper in the back to close. The same thing went for his pants. First, I'd taken them off, and now I wrapped tape over certain sensitive areas to make sure they didn't get frostbite. I really was a superfreak.

Talon looked so calm, so comfortable, so sexy sleeping on my couch I almost changed my mind. Then I remembered how he kept calling me *Nightingale* and what would happen if he found out who I was. How disappointed he'd be. My resolve hardened.

Now I had another problem—where to take the G-man superhero. I wasn't just dumping him in the street. He'd freeze to death before the pill wore off. So, where could I stash him? The blizzard had shut down everything, even Quicke's restaurant, according to SNN.

I paced back and forth in front of the couch, zipping and unzipping the pockets on my vest, as if they held a space where a superhero could sleep off a pill and the lingering effects of a blinding gas. My vest held a lot of things, but that, unfortunately, was not one of them. My keys were in one of the pockets, and I pulled them out, spinning them around and around on their silver ring. I kept shooting looks at Talon, making sure he was unconscious, which was why I rammed my right knee into the kitchen table.

"Ouch!"

I put a hand on the edge of the table, catching myself before I did a complete nose dive, but my keys slid from my grasp. They smacked on the table before bouncing off onto the floor. I winced at the harsh *clang*. Cymbals clashing together in my ear couldn't have sounded any louder. But the jangling keys gave me an idea. In addition to the ones for my loft and office, the ring held another very important key—the one to the convention center.

That was where I was going to take Talon. It would be warm, and the superhero would be safe until he woke up. The center was only a couple of blocks away, and was big and anonymous. Talon would have no idea where he'd come from—or more importantly, who had taken him there.

One problem solved. Now, how to get the superhero out of my apartment and over to the center without anyone seeing us? I wasn't putting him back in a garbage bag and dragging him through the street, but I couldn't call a cab either. Talon would find a way to trace it back to me, if the cabbie didn't automatically lock the doors and drive my ass straight to the police station.

My eyes fell on my chair, the same one I'd used to maneuver Talon into my bathroom. No, I couldn't use that either. There was no way it would roll through the snow. I needed something that would glide. Something I could push or pull. Something like…a sled.

I frowned and looked over at the boxes lining one wall. They might have been twenty feet away, but I could read the small, white labels clearly. Piper had insisted we label every single box when she'd helped me move. She'd even brought her own label maker to ensure it was done to her satisfaction. My eyes traced over the boxes. *Dishes. Towels. Books. DVDs.* My gaze latched on to a label that said *Abby's Old Stuff.*

Because it was the biggest and longest, that particular box huddled on the bottom of the pile. Naturally. I marched over, shoved the other boxes off it, and ripped open the top. The cardboard box contained the assorted random stuff I'd stored in my mom's garage over the years. She'd foisted it off on me when I'd moved into the loft, but I hadn't had the time or inclination to unpack it. The box held junk, for the most part. Stuffed animals, old toys, tattered report cards, embarrassing childhood photos.

I pawed through the layers until I spied a bit of red plastic. I reached down, took hold of the plastic, and yanked. The animals didn't want to let it go, but I pulled out a small, plastic sled. In my younger years whenever it snowed, I'd trudge outside with the sled and spend hours climbing up and sliding down hills with Piper. I frowned. The toy seemed smaller than I remembered, only about five feet long and cracked down the middle. But it would do. It was going to have to.

I took the sled over to the couch and eased Talon onto it. It was a foot too narrow and more than a foot too short for the superhero. His chest hung over the sides, while his legs stretched out past the edge.

So, once again, I got out every woman's best friend—duct tape—and wrapped it around Talon, securing him to the sled. I also made sure I had a pocket knife in my vest, so I could cut him free later. Then, I went over to the windows and looked out. It was after nine now, darkness had spread its black blanket across the city. Nothing moved in the street below. Only a smattering of lights gleamed in the distance. Now was as good a time as any to go—and start pretending the past two days had never happened.

That Wren didn't exist.

That I'd never met Talon.

And that I didn't wish I really could be his Nightingale.

Dragging Talon out of my loft and into the elevator was simple enough. We rode down to the first floor in silence. The doors slid open, and I stuck my head outside. Everyone else had already gone to bed. No one haunted the lobby. So I grabbed the rope on the end of the sled and pulled Talon out of the elevator. I maneuvered him over to the front doors and peered through the glass.

I didn't see anyone out on the block. Then again, I usually didn't. This was a residential neighborhood, quiet except for the morning and evening rush hours. Only two other buildings populated my side of the street, and the block across from me was one enormous brownstone owned by a guy named Jasper.

Because the coast was clear, I opened the doors and dragged Talon outside. Kelly Caleb hadn't been exaggerating about the snow. The white stuff went up past my knees in some spots, but the plows had been out, and the snow on the streets had been packed down enough so you could walk on it, if you were careful.

Farther down the next block, a few kids sledded up and down the giant mounds of snow created by the city's plows. Their happy shrieks, giggles, and shouts carried through the still night air.

"Wheee!"

"That was awesome!"

"Let's go again!"

The kids were intent on their fun, and none of them gave me a glance. For once, I was happy to be the invisible woman as I pulled Talon out onto the street. Still, I turned away from the kids and walked fast, like I had somewhere important to be—and that it was perfectly normal to be dragging a body duct taped to a sled behind me.

The snow and the night fought for supremacy, reflecting off each other and making everything a dull gray. A rare, fresh tang hung in the air. I breathed in, and the cold burned my lungs. All I could smell was the thick, wet snow—mixed with Talon's clean scent on my skin.

I looked over my shoulder at the superhero, but Talon remained in the same position. Face-up, hands crossed and taped over his chest, a blanket piled on top of him for extra warmth. He wasn't even snoring.

I hurried on and made it to the convention center without incident. Darkness shrouded the massive building, just as it did every other one on the street. I went around to the alley, the one the caterers used for deliveries, and unlocked the side door. I'd go out through the front and smash the glass on one of the revolving doors. That way, Talon wouldn't wonder how he'd gotten into the convention center undetected. He'd just assume I'd broken in and dumped him there.

I dragged Talon inside and locked the door behind me. It was dark, but thanks to my enhanced eyesight, I didn't need a flashlight to make my way down the hall. The sled didn't glide as well on the carpet as it had on the snow, but I huffed and puffed my way to the service elevator and rode it up to the second floor.

I pulled Talon out onto the main balcony, flipped open my knife, and cut through the tape that bound him to the sled. Then, I grunted, heaved, and shoved him up into one of the cushioned chairs, making sure he was far away from the edge.

As I tried to make Talon as comfortable as possible, my hand brushed his visor. I tried to pull my fingers away, but I wasn't quick enough. The stupid thing shocked me again, even through my black fleece gloves.

Unauthorized user alert! Unauthorized user alert! The mechanized voice boomed out through the open auditorium, echoing back to me. Then, the bars shot out the sides, and the visor went into full-fledged self-defense mode.

I grimaced at the noise and wrung out my tingling fingers. I should have been happy this would be the last time I'd ever get zinged by that damn visor—but I wasn't.

I dropped to my knees in front of Talon. He slumped in the chair, head back, arms loose at his sides, like he was relaxing and ready to catch a show instead of sleeping off a pill. I leaned forward and pressed my palm against his heart, saying good-bye. Heat soaked into my gloves, reminding me of Talon's body moving against my own.

I dropped my hand, got to my feet, and turned away.

I reached down to pick up my pitiful red sled, and a creak of leather caught my attention. I looked up. Talon's head swiveled from side to side, as if he was looking for somebody—me. I froze. The superhero was waking up.

I quietly scooted away from him, abandoning the sled, and pulled my black toboggan farther down onto my head and my scarf higher up on my face.

Bandit's gas must have been wearing off as well, because Talon turned his head in my direction, drawn by my furtive moments.

"Nightingale?" he murmured, his words slurring together. "What's going on?"

"Just sit still." I kept backing away. "The drug will wear off soon. You'll be fine in a few minutes."

"Wait…" he called out.

It was too late. I'd already run down the stairs.

After smashing one of the convention center's front doors, I ran back to my building, if you could call falling, stumbling, and sliding along icy patches running. I didn't stop until I was back in my loft with the door locked behind me.

I pulled off my chilled clothes, trudged into the bathroom, and took a long, hot bath, trying to pretend like everything was normal. Trying not to think about how Talon had pulled me into the tub with him last night. Or how we'd spent our time together today.

After an hour, I got out, dried off, and put on my warmest, softest Bella Bulluci fleece pajamas. But the material didn't feel as smooth against my skin as it usually did. I doubted anything would besides Talon's hands. I wasn't likely to forget his touch anytime soon. That was another curse of having supersenses— everything got imprinted on my memory that much more. The good, the bad, the heartbreaking.

I shut the drapes, climbed into bed, and snuggled into my microfleece sheets. They, too, were the softest on the market, part of Bella's homeware collection. Normally I could go to sleep in a matter of minutes, drifting away into the blackness that waited. But tonight I couldn't—because my pillows and sheets were full of his clean, minty scent.

I buried my nose in one of the pillows and thought about Talon. I wondered if he'd left the convention center by now. If he had his sight back. If he was angry with me. Or just relieved I was gone. I felt panicked, confused, and sad about the whole thing.

Come on, Abby! I chided myself. There was no need to panic. Talon would never find out I was Wren. Even if the thought somehow crossed his mind, he'd dismiss it outright. Because I was good ole Abby Appleby. Not Wren, and certainly not someone like Nightingale.

There was certainly no need to feel confused, weepy, and sentimental about things. I'd slept with a superhero after an intense twenty-four hours of bonding. It happened to people practically every day in this city. All it meant was I could join the *Slaves for Superhero Sex* club now. Nothing else. Hell, the *SSS* freaks would applaud me for my *love-him, slip-him-a-sleeping-pill,* and *dump-his-ass-in-a-public-place* philosophy.

A one-night stand.

That was all it would ever be.

No matter how perfect it had been.

After a night of almost zero sleep, I got up early the next morning and peered out a crack in the drapes. The plows had worked through the night, clearing the streets. They'd cut what looked like a tunnel through the snow, pushing the heavy, wet stuff into five-foot-high banks and further burying most of the cars parked on either side of the road. Smaller plows had carved out paths on the sidewalks, which meant I could go to work. Good. I needed the distractions and crises today.

I opened the drapes a little more, letting cracks of sunlight into the loft. Then I padded over to the closet and slid back the door. Thirteen vests hung on the metal rack inside, along with the other clothes I'd unpacked. I flipped through the vests until I came to my Winter Wear one. The silver, down vest was equipped with the usual pockets and supplies, including a few extras, like hand warmers, a small can of de-icer, and tear-and-sip packets of hot chocolate.

I put on my usual black undies, along with some silk long underwear and a pair of heavy-duty waterproof cargo pants on top. A matching camisole covered my torso, along with a thermal turtleneck, a heavy, gray cable knit sweater, and a loose flannel shirt. I put on three pairs of wool socks, then stuffed my feet into my boots. A fleece hat went on my head, held down by a pair of earmuffs. I started to shrug into my black coat, when the rank odor of blood hit me. Talon's blood. Ugh. I wasn't wearing that until it had been cleaned. I grabbed a hanger and wrapped some plastic around the coat so I could drop it off at the dry cleaners.

I fished another coat out of the closet, a gray one that matched the vest, and finished off my weatherproof ensemble. I felt like a marshmallow, puffed up from the extra clothes, but I wanted to be warm. I also slid a pair of thick, black sunglasses on so the glare from the snow wouldn't bother me too much.

Once I'd properly equipped myself for the great outdoors, I grabbed my keys and the bloody coat and headed out. A guy wearing a gray trench coat and snowshoes trudged past me. The dark goggles wrapped around his face made me think of Talon. The superhero should be fine. The pill I'd given him should have worn off last night, and his eyes should have been fully recovered from Bandit's blinding gas by now.

I shrugged those thoughts away and started walking. Unlike my mad dash last night, I took my time this morning. Thinking. By the time I reached my office building, I'd convinced myself I was fine with being Talon's one-night-stand, mystery woman. That I didn't really care if I ever saw the superhero again. That everything was going to go on just as it had before. With no looking back and no regrets.

I rode the elevator to the thirteenth floor. The doors opened, but no loud, annoying *ping!* sounded. I'd disabled the sound in this elevator, too, and in every other building I frequented on a regular basis, including the convention center.

I stepped out into a typical office chamber. Chloe Cavanaugh's station, a round desk with a computer and several phones, stood in the middle of the open area. Three-foot-high silver letters on the wall spelled out the name of my business and motto. *A+ Events—When you want perfection, you want A+.*

Chloe wasn't at her desk, though. I checked my watch. Just after nine. She was probably having trouble with her car, given the massive amounts of snow that had been dumped on it in the past few days.

I swept past Chloe's desk and unlocked the door to my office. It was very much like my loft in that it contained a lot of open space—with little furniture. My desk took up most of the back wall, with its phone banks, two computers, two printers, and two monitors, and mounds of legal pads. Three leather chairs crouched in front of the desk, with a matching sofa shoved over in the corner. The sofa contained a fold-out bed I used for nights when I worked into the wee hours and was too tired to trudge home. A bank of windows behind my desk offered a view of the building across the street. At least, they would have if the black drapes hadn't been closed.

I put my keys down on the desk and shrugged out of my coat, earmuffs, scarf, and gloves. The red light on my phone blinked, and I checked my voice mail.

"Hi, Abby, this is Chloe. My car won't start, so I'm going to have to take the subway. I'll be there as soon as I can..."

I listened to the rest of her message, then hit the delete button, and moved on. A couple more missives from some of my favorite florists, caterers, and bands told me not to worry about various events. Right. I wouldn't stop worrying until they were over and done with.

I returned a couple of calls, but most folks were still digging out from the blizzard and weren't in the office yet. Around ten thirty, I'd finished calling everyone I could, so I took a break.

I drew the drapes back from the windows a little bit at a time until my eyes adjusted to the glare from the sun on the melting snow. Then, I pulled back one of the sliding glass doors and stepped onto the balcony attached to my office. The balcony was tiny and nothing like the sweeping observation decks over at the skyscrapers that housed *The Chronicle* and *The Exposé*, the city's two newspapers. But I liked it nonetheless, because I could sneak out here for a little peace and quiet when my clients and their insane demands got to be too much. I had a nice view of the street and some of the downtown landmarks, like the Ferris wheel over at Paradise Park and the giant F that marked Fiona Fine's fashion store. Plus, the balcony was high enough that I could breathe in air that wasn't completely smoggy. The height also muted the harsh cacophony of the streaming traffic below.

Faint scratches and twitters caught my attention. Being the kind person she was, Chloe had installed a bird feeder in the corner of the balcony. Given the cold, snowy weather, the feeder was quite popular this morning. Birds cheeped, chirped, and hovered around it, some perched on the lip of the balcony, all waiting their turn to get a beak full of precious birdseed.

I didn't know much about birds, but I spotted a couple of flashy red cardinals, as well some bossy, noisy blue jays. Another bird huddled among the bunch—a wren, its simple brown feathers and small frame overshadowed by the other bright colors around it.

A wren, not a nightingale.

Disgusted, I stomped back inside, slammed the door shut, and closed the drapes.

CHAPTER NINE

I'd just plopped down into my chair, determined to get back to work and forget about wrens, nightingales, and birds in general, when the phone rang. Normally, Chloe answered the incoming calls, but since she hadn't logged into the phone system today, they got routed to me.

"*A+ Events*. We make things perfect every single time."

"Hey, Abby," Piper Perez's warm, cheery voice flooded my ear. "What's going on?"

"Not much," I replied. "Just getting ready to call and nag at some more people."

"Is Kyle on your hit list?"

"Always."

"Well, how would you like to yell at him in person? I need to pick up some stuff for Fiona."

That was Piper's way of asking if I'd like to have lunch at Quicke's. The Fiona in question was Fiona Fine, Piper's boss and the main reason Quicke's stayed in business. The fashion designer's appetite boggled the mind, especially when you considered how svelte she was.

"Sure," I replied, even though I really wanted to be alone

right now. In the dark. Listening to music. Angsty stuff, punctuated with some angry rock here and there.

"Great!" Piper said, not picking up on my less-than-stellar mood. "I'll meet you there around one."

"See you then."

I hung up and swiveled my chair around to the window. Because the black drapes were shut, I couldn't tell if the brown wren had gotten its due at the feeder. Or if it still waited its turn, hidden among the other birds' colorful plumage. I pushed those thoughts away. Metaphors. Who needed them? Talon was out of my life. I'd never see him again, and that was for the best.

So, I turned back to the desk and reached for the phone, ready to make Flora of Flora's Fauna & Flowers a very unhappy woman.

Chloe showed up a little after eleven. She unwound her fuzzy, striped scarf from her neck and griped about having to walk a mile in the snow to catch the subway when her car wouldn't start.

"You should just get rid of that old clunker." I put some invoices that needed to be faxed on her desk.

"Well, I might be able to if somebody gave me a raise. Hint, hint. I'm ready to step up in more of a partner capacity." Chloe stared at me, her hazel eyes earnest and sincere. "You know I am, Abby."

I did know. Chloe had proven herself to be punctual, dependable, and capable of quick thinking during the months she'd worked for me. But I was a control freak. I always had been. In middle school, I was the annoying girl who planned the spring formal dance and tried to get everyone to color-coordinate their outfits to my balloons—or else.

People grumbled, but when they realized how well the dance turned out, I got a bit of grudging respect—and somehow got roped into planning all of the dances and school functions after that. The trend continued into my college years at Bigtime University. Event planning seemed a natural, lucrative fit for my perfectionist, anal-retentive skills, so I'd gotten my business degree and started *A+ Events*, building it up one event, one client at a time. Now, almost ten years later, I was *the* premiere party planner in Bigtime.

I didn't like to turn the reins over to anyone. Didn't trust anyone to oversee the details, put out the fires, and make sure every single thing was perfect. The only reason I'd hired Chloe was because I had to sleep *sometime*.

That hadn't stopped Chloe from bucking for a promotion, though. She was one of the few people who weren't afraid of me and my propensity to yell. She just let the noise slide off her, tuning me out until my voice fell back to its regular volume. Normally, when Chloe asked about a promotion, I told her *no* flat-out.

Maybe it was Talon and the longing he stirred in me to be noticed—or at least to have more of a life outside of work. Either way, I hesitated.

"I'll consider it."

You would have thought I'd handed her a winning lottery ticket. Chloe gasped. Her mouth dropped open, and her eyes widened. "Really?"

I nodded.

"Oh, Abby!" Chloe threw her arms around my neck, hugged me, and let out another shriek of happiness.

I winced as the sharp, girly-girl sound pounded into my skull. I'd give her the promotion right now just to stop her squealing in my ear.

Sensing this was as much as she was going to get today, Chloe let me go. But she kept beaming, her smile stretching from ear to ear. The phone rang, and she leapt to answer it.

"G-o-o-o-d morning! *A+ Events*. We make things perfect every single time! This is Chloe speaking! How may I help you?"

Grumbling, I turned and went back into my office.

By the time I finished calling people and making sure the upcoming Berkley Brighton memorial dedication would go off without any weather-related problems, it was almost one and time to meet Piper at Quicke's. I told Chloe where I was going and promised to bring her a Monte Cristo sandwich and piece of apple pie. I pulled on my layers, grabbed my bloody coat, and headed out.

More traffic crawled along the streets now, the cars and taxis moving at about a tenth of their normal, breakneck speed. A lone vendor stood on the corner hawking giant pretzels, but few folks were willing to wade through the drifts to get to him. In addition to the snow, jagged icicles decorated the roofs and eaves of the buildings. Soft *plop-plop-plops* of water fell from the sharp tips, splattering onto the sidewalks. Slowly but surely, the city was thawing out.

I trudged through the melting mess, dropped my coat off at Stan's Steamers Dry Cleaners, and made it to Quicke's a little after one. Even though it was early afternoon, the restaurant's blue, neon sign flashed on and off above the revolving door. Hot air blasted me in the face as soon as I entered the building, along with a smorgasbord of aromas. Fresh sourdough bread, steaming potato soup, hot marinara sauce, warm chocolate cake. I drew in a deep breath, and my stomach rumbled in anticipation. Everything always smelled and tasted good at Quicke's, so good that I didn't mind the noisy chatter of the crowd or the constant *clink-clank* of silverware that went along with it.

Kyle worked the podium at the front. He saw me and smiled.

"Abby, what's up? You're looking a little chilled," he joked, taking in my puffy layers.

"Well, I'm sure some of your amazing cuisine will be more than enough to thaw me out," I said. "So, how are we looking for the library dedication tomorrow night? Is the blizzard going to affect anything?"

He shook his head. "It's always business with you, isn't it?"

I crossed my arms over my chest.

"Well, I'm happy to say the answer is no. I had the supplies delivered right before the O'Hara party, and my workers have confirmed they'll be able to make it into the city for the event. So, we're good to go."

I opened my mouth but realized I didn't have any reason to berate him. At least, not right now. Kyle might be a pain in my ass sometimes, but he always came through—usually with surprising speed.

"Well, I guess I'll see you tomorrow night then," I replied.

"You will. Are you here to have lunch with Piper?"

I nodded.

"She's at her usual table next to the window." Kyle handed me two menus. "Tell her I said hello."

"You could tell her yourself," I suggested.

A sad smile flitted across Kyle's face, and his blue eyes wouldn't meet mine. He shook his head and looked over my shoulder, greeting the elderly couple in line behind me. I got the message. Subject closed.

Kyle and Piper had dated for a year, and she'd been totally, completely, madly in love with him. Things had been going so well she thought he was getting ready to suggest they move in together, but the bastard dumped her on their one-year anniversary a few months ago with no explanation. I thought it had something to do with the fact that Piper had been saved by Swifte from being run over by a bus a couple days before. Maybe Kyle had felt threatened. Piper had talked about the superhero nonstop after that. She'd even bought all of the Swifte merchandise she could get her hands on, adding it to her already significant superhero-ubervillain memorabilia collection.

Whatever his reasons, Kyle kept them to himself—and kept his distance from Piper. That was another reason I needled him whenever I could—payback for my best friend. She might be mature enough to eat in his restaurant without making a scene, but I wasn't above making his life difficult whenever I could.

Menus in hand, I headed past the podium. Folks of all ages crowded into the restaurant, having braved the snow in search of good food. Quicke's had some of the best in the city, along with speedy service, big portions, and reasonable prices. People also liked the restaurant's atmosphere; it was a shrine to Bigtime's superheroes and ubervillains. The Fearless Five, the Terrible Triad, Johnny Angel, the Mintilator. Posters and newspaper clippings of heroes and villains covered the walls, while toys, cars, action figures, and more decorated tables and the long, brass-railed bar running down one side of the restaurant.

Quicke's was neutral territory, one of the few places in the city where heroes and villains could hang out without fear of reprisals from one another or even the police. I spotted several bright splashes of spandex as I moved through the crowd. Wynter sipped something that looked cold and blue at the bar. A few feet away, Halitosis Hal and Pistol Pete, the two superheroes who were best friends, chowed down on double cheeseburgers, fries, and chocolate milkshakes. Another table next to them appeared empty, except for the glasses, plates, and forks floating back and forth across it. The Invisible Ingénues had to be sitting there. They were the only women in Bigtime who got noticed less than me.

I spotted Piper at one of the restaurant's prime tables in front of the windows looking out on the street. Kyle reserved the same spot for her every day, even after their breakup. The table was right under a poster of Talon holding his grappling hook gun. A poster of Bandit hovered next to it, both of his revolvers drawn and pointed at the G-man hero, as though the two of them were fighting just as they had in real life.

Piper Perez had been my best friend since forever. She also was one of the most striking women I'd ever seen. Her glossy, black hair framed her face like a silk waterfall, bringing out the dusky tones in her tan skin and highlighting her warm, brown eyes. The only thing distracting from her natural beauty was her nose—her very red, very swollen nose. Piper blew into a tissue. Several more littered her side of the table and clustered on the windowsill, along with her oversized purse.

"What's wrong with you?" I asked, unbuttoning my coat and hanging it on the back of my chair.

"Allergies." Piper sniffled. "They're killing me."

I wondered how her allergies could possibly be bothering her when every blade of grass in the greater Bigtime area was buried under three feet of snow, but Piper was hypersensitive. Dust, pollen, cat dander. *Everything* made her sneeze.

A waiter bustled over to take our order. Piper got a bowl of broccoli cheese soup with a baked potato and a basket of sourdough rolls, while I requested a salad with hot, grilled chicken and creamy blue cheese dressing. I also put in a to-go order for Chloe's sandwich and pie.

"And I need my usual carryout order, Ray," Piper told the waiter. "Times five today."

"Sure thing," Ray said, scribbling on his pad.

When he left, Piper turned her attention to me. She looked at me from top to bottom, and her dark eyes narrowed. Piper might not have supersenses, but she was just as observant in her own way.

"Spill it," she demanded.

"What?" I asked, trying to play innocent.

"Spill it. You're all depressed and moody. I could hear it in your voice over the phone this morning. Tell me what's bothering you, Abby."

I never could hide anything from Piper. Besides, I needed somebody to talk to about what had happened—and to tell me how crazy I was for wanting to see Talon again.

"Well, you know the O'Hara party on Saturday night?"

Piper nodded.

"Something strange happened after that…"

I told Piper everything from finding Talon in the alley to dragging him back to my apartment to having sex with him, then drugging him and taking him to the convention center. She listened intently through it all, making mental notes in her head. Piper had a mind like a supercomputer—she never forgot anything, especially when it came to superheroes and ubervillains.

"So you saved Talon, took him back to your place, and had your way with him?" Piper asked. "Sweet!"

"I wouldn't exactly call it *having my way* with him."

"Well, at least you got some action. Do you know how long it's been since I've seen a naked man?"

Piper's eyes drifted to the front of the restaurant. I didn't have to turn around to know she was staring at Kyle. Her dark gaze flicked to the poster above our heads.

"And with Talon. He's one of the coolest heroes in the city."

"I thought you worshipped at the altar of Swifte," I teased. "And the Fearless Five."

She waved her hand. "The Fearless Five are so passé. So over. Swifte too. Edgy independent operators like Talon are all the rage these days."

Piper was obsessed with superheroes, mainly because she kept getting rescued by them. She always seemed to be in the wrong place at the right time. If a building caught on fire, Piper would be stuck in the penthouse. If an elevator suddenly lost power, Piper would be trapped inside. She'd been almost mugged, almost flattened by a runaway subway train, and almost run over by more speeding cars than I cared to remember.

She'd been saved by everyone from Aria to Granny Cane to Wynter, and she had the autograph collection to prove it. Piper kept track of all the heroes and villains in the city, and she probably knew more about the superfolks than they did themselves. Sometimes I thought she ought to quit her job as the chief financial officer of Fiona Fine Fashions and go to work as a reporter for SNN. Piper could give Kelly Caleb a run for her money.

"So who is he?" Piper asked.

"I don't know."

Her mouth dropped open. "You had an unconscious superhero in your apartment, a *naked*, unconscious superhero, and you didn't look to see who he really was?" Her voice rose with every word, ending in a near screech.

I winced. "Keep your voice down. You know loud noises give me headaches."

"Sorry," she muttered. "But I have to say, I'm *very* disappointed in you, Abby."

"Well, don't be. I couldn't have found out who Talon was even if I wanted to."

I told her about the electro-shock visor and the metal bars that had shot out of it when I'd tried to take it off.

"Oh, yeah," Piper said. "Talon upgraded to a new visor about three months ago. I didn't know it had those sorts of capabilities, though."

Her chocolate eyes gleamed, and I could tell she was making more mental notes, probably for the hero-villain encyclopedia she was writing. Piper was such a fangirl she'd decided to pen the ultimate guide to Bigtime's superheroes and ubervillains, including all of their battles, rivalries, and costume changes over the years.

Ray brought our food, and we spent the next few minutes eating. My salad was wonderful, the way Quicke's food always was. Fresh, creamy dressing. Crisp vegetables. Chicken seasoned with tangy lemon pepper. But I didn't have an appetite; instead I pushed the greens back and forth on my plate.

"Do you think you're going to see Talon again?" Piper asked, tearing into a roll and slathering it with honey-cinnamon butter.

I shook my head. "No. He doesn't know who I am, and I don't know who he is. It's not like we swapped numbers or anything."

"But you sort of know who he is," she said. "You *have* seen him naked."

"I know, but I'm not sure I'd recognize him. I was a little freaked out by the whole thing."

"If you ever see him again, I think you'll know him. Especially with those supersenses you've got now." A wistful note crept into her voice.

Piper had been with me the night I'd received my supersenses. Her only regret was I'd gotten them and she hadn't. She'd always wanted to be a superhero, dreamed of becoming one ever since we were kids, but this time, I'd been in the wrong place at the right time instead of her.

We were at The Blues karaoke bar. I'd been doing my best impersonation of a diva, while Piper flirted with the bartender and sipped gin and tonics. I'd just finished my number when one of the amps beside the stage produced a screaming fit of static. I'd gone over to help Stanley Solomon, the bar's sound guy, fix it and started fiddling with some of the knobs.

Unfortunately, a giggly sorority girl chose that exact moment to spill her amaretto sour on the amp. The police said there must have been a frayed wire or something in the amp. Whatever it was, my hand was attached to it when it decided to pump out a couple thousand volts of juice. All I remembered was waking up in the hospital the next day screaming for someone to turn the volume down on their radio, only to discover it was the heart monitor beeping out my pulse.

Everything bothered me after that. The slightest noise. The softest touch. The faintest bit of sunlight. The migraines, oh, the migraines. Piper finally figured out what was wrong with me, after she'd gone to the Bigtime Public Library and checked out and read the few books on superpowers she didn't already own. Piper's theory was that the jolt I'd received had opened some closed part of my mind, giving me the ability to see, hear, taste, touch, and smell a thousand times better.

"Well, now that we've properly dissected your strange and curious love life, I need a huge, huge favor," Piper said. "Will you help me?"

"Sure," I said, pushing away my half-eaten salad. "What is it?"

"It's in my purse. Or rather, he is."

"He?"

Piper nodded. She leaned over and opened her bag. A ball of sandy fur nestled in a white blanket in the bottom. Fur?

I leaned over to get a better look, and a small whine greeted my ears. The ball of fur lifted up its head and stared at me with two liquid brown eyes.

"A puppy? Where did you get a puppy?"

"I found him wandering the streets right before the blizzard hit," Piper said, grinning. "He's the cutest thing, but you know I can't keep him because of my allergies. I can't even wear faux fur without sneezing for two hours afterward..."

Piper's voice trailed off, and she gave me a pointed, hopeful look.

"Oh no," I said. "Don't even *think* about it. No way. I can't keep him. I can't have a puppy around. I'm not home enough to take care of one."

She beamed at me. "But that's the beauty of this little guy. He's small enough right now to fit in a purse. Surely, you can hang him on your vest somewhere."

I looked down at the squirming ball of fur. "Hang him on my vest? He's not a water bottle, Piper."

"Listen, it's just for a few days until I can find him a good home. I just can't bear the thought of taking him to the pound. Please, Abby. *Please?*"

Piper looked at me with her big brown eyes—eyes very similar to the puppy's.

"All right." I sighed, knowing I was beaten. "But only for a few days. And you're buying the dog food. Got it?"

"Got it."

She reached down and petted the squirming ball of fur—and sneezed all over him. The puppy didn't seem to mind though, wiggling closer to her.

"Here." Piper shoved her purse at me. "Pick him up. Let him get used to you before we leave."

I put the bag on my lap. The movement excited the puppy, who stood up and put his paws on the side of Piper's purse. Sandy-brown fur covered his back, but his belly was pure white fluff. His big, triangular ears pointed up over his head and were rather large in proportion to the rest of him, like rabbit ears on an old TV.

"What kind of dog is he?" I shoved my finger into the purse so he could sniff it.

"A Welsh Pembroke corgi." Piper blew into another tissue. "They're supposed to be very intelligent."

The puppy certainly seemed smart. He was already trying to find some way to get out of Piper's purse, but his paws kept sliding off the slick fabric. I put my hand on him, and he calmed down. He nestled into the blanket, put his head on his paws, and went back to sleep.

"So does this furball have a name?" I asked, wondering how much this was going to complicate my life.

"No," Piper said. "I've just been calling him *dog* and *boy*. Why don't you name him? You're the one who's going to be taking care of him."

My eyes drifted back to the poster of Talon on the wall. That name was already taken, but another good one came to mind, one that made me think of the superhero.

"Rascal," I said. "Let's call him Rascal."

CHAPTER TEN

The waiter returned with our check. It was Piper's turn to pay, and I let her, particularly because she'd foisted Rascal on me. The waiter brought me Chloe's sandwich and pie, stuffed in a white bag bearing Quicke's logo—a winged, Hermes-like foot. Then, he went back into the kitchen to retrieve a large cardboard box for Piper. The waiter grunted as he set it down on the table.

I stared into the box, which contained dozens of containers of soups, salads, sandwiches, fries, drinks, and desserts. "Fiona must really be hungry today."

Piper shrugged. "She's *always* hungry. How that woman eats the way she does without blowing up like a blimp, I'll never understand."

Fiona had an appetite that would put a horse to shame—and a body a supermodel would envy. Blond hair. Long legs. Big boobs. A disproportionately small waist. She was a live, walking, talking doll.

Anytime Piper came to Quicke's for lunch, she took something back for Fiona—usually about half the menu. Today, Piper ordered enough lunch for ten people, but I knew Fiona would eat every single bite—and that Piper would be lucky if the enormous meal kept the fashion designer satisfied until dinner.

"You still think she has an eating disorder?" I asked.

"There's got to be something wrong with her," Piper replied, opening a container of creamy potato salad. "Now get Rascal out of my purse before you leave."

I grunted, reached inside, and grabbed the puppy. He barked with happiness at being out of the bag. A few of Quicke's other patrons shot me disapproving looks for having a dog inside the restaurant, but none of the staff batted an eye. Fiona—and by extension Piper—spent too much money in here for them to treat Piper like anything but a queen, even if she wasn't dating Kyle anymore. Piper could strip down, dance naked on the tabletops, and smash out every window in the joint, and they wouldn't lift a finger to stop her.

"All right, dog," I muttered, holding the squirming puppy with one hand. "Let's see how I can carry you back to the office without dumping you in the snow."

Piper was right—Rascal was small enough to fit inside a pocket on my vest, the big one I usually stashed my water bottle in. That compartment lies to the left side of my chest, which meant I could zip my coat up most of the way, and Rascal could stick his head out the front and breathe.

"Okay, guys, I need to get back to work before Fiona eats the furniture," Piper said. "Call me later, and let me know how he is, okay?"

"Sure, sure," I grumbled.

Piper gave Rascal a final pat, sneezed, grabbed the box of food, and headed outside.

"Well, I guess it's just you and me now, dog," I said, staring down at the furball.

Rascal licked the bottom of my chin with his wet, rough, stinky tongue. Ugh.

I'd walked about a block when I realized Rascal was going to be more trouble than all of my clients put together. The puppy barked at every single car and person we passed, his squeaky *yip-yaps* rattling inside my skull. He wiggled so much I finally put him on the ground. Rascal tried to hop over the snow without actually touching it. Evidently, the cold, wet sensation didn't feel too good against his tiny paws. After half a block, the corgi stopped, plopped down on his butt, and stared up at me, his brown eyes expectant.

"Come on." I walked a few feet ahead of him. "Let's go, dog. I have florists to badger."

Rascal barked. It might have been my imagination, but I thought there was a rather defiant tone to the sound.

"Come on. Come here, dog," I said, trying to get him to follow me.

That was what dogs were supposed to do, right? I didn't really know, since I'd never had one before. I'd never really had any sort of pet—or never one that lasted very long. The goldfish my mom bought me for my seventh birthday went belly-up the first time I changed the water in their bowl. The hamster she purchased for my eighth birthday ate his way through his plastic cage and got locked in a closet we rarely used. I found Scruffy two weeks later, toes up. The turtle I got the next year made it a month before I took him outside to play and let him wander into the path of an oncoming minivan, and Shelly got shellacked. After that, I didn't get any more animals as gifts, but my mom did make a generous donation to the Bigtime Humane Society in my name every year.

I plowed a few feet ahead, but Rascal didn't move. Instead,

he whined, so pitifully that an elderly couple walking down the street stopped to stare at us.

"I think he wants you to pick him up," the old woman said.

I opened my mouth to tell the lady I knew that already when I caught a glimpse of her face underneath her rose-colored hat. White hair, blue eyes, pink cheeks—Grace Caleb, one of the bastions of Bigtime society. More importantly, one of my clients. We'd worked together planning the doomed benefit for the Bigtime Museum of Modern Art.

"Oh, Grace, I didn't recognize you." I turned to the man standing beside her. "Or you either, Bobby."

Bobby was Bobby Bulluci, another bastion of Bigtime society and the grandfather of fashion designer Bella Bulluci and her brother, Johnny.

"That's all right, Abby," Bobby replied. His face was red and ruddy from the cold. "It's obvious you have other things on your mind. Like this little guy."

Bobby leaned down and held his gloved hand out to Rascal. The puppy sniffed it suspiciously for about half a second before he decided Bobby was friend material. Bobby responded by scratching Rascal's pointy ears. The puppy grunted with pleasure, his tiny tail sending up sprays of snow.

"I didn't know you had a dog, Abby," Grace said.

"He's not really mine. I'm just babysitting until I can find him a good home." I smiled at them. "What do you say? Would you like him? He's a very sweet dog."

Lying was another skill I'd perfected as an event planner. I'd had the puppy about ten minutes, but *sweet* wasn't the word I'd use to describe him. Rascal had proven himself to be stubborn, difficult, and demanding.

"Unfortunately not," Bobby said, straightening. "We're a bit busy to bring a dog into the house right now."

Grace nodded her head in agreement. "We're tied up almost every night."

"Literally," Bobby added.

They both chuckled, amused by some private joke.

Busy? Tied up? What did the two of them do at night besides attend society soirees? Go out on the town and fight evil? Jeez. It wasn't like they were Granny Cane and Grandpa Pain, the two seventy-something superheroes who suckered bad guys into mugging them before kicking their asses all the way to the police station. Grace and Bobby could have just told me no. They didn't have to make up some lame excuse about being too busy.

"We'd love to stay and chat, but we have a lunch date with Bella and Devlin," Grace said, referring to her grandson, Devlin Dash.

"Of course. Don't let me keep you."

Bobby held out his arm, which Grace took, and the two of them walked on. Rascal watched them go. When he realized they weren't taking him with them, his head swiveled back around to me—and he whined again.

"Fine," I muttered. "I'll carry you, you little con artist."

I picked up the dog and stuffed him back inside my vest. He wiggled closer to me, his scent filling my nose—an aroma my supernose particularly loathed.

"Now, you're wet. And you know what wet dogs do? They smell bad. Really bad. Especially to me."

Rascal just barked and licked my chin again. Ugh.

By the time I got back to the office, it was after two. The elevator whispered open, and I walked over to Chloe's desk and dropped her food bag on top of it. She looked up from her monitor.

"Thanks, Abby—a puppy!" Chloe yelled, catching sight of Rascal. "You have a puppy!"

I winced. First Piper, then the dog, now Chloe. Didn't anyone in Bigtime know how to modulate their voice? I plucked Rascal out of my vest and handed him to her. Chloe hugged the puppy to her chest, and he barked with happiness.

"When did you get a dog?" she asked, stroking his sandy fur. "I didn't think you liked dogs."

"About twenty minutes ago."

Chloe gave me a sideways glance. From the tone in her voice, you'd think I was a serial killer who mutilated small animals in my basement. I didn't *hate* animals—just the messes they made. I loathed planning any event that involved them. They were worse to work with than kids. Give kids enough sugar, and you could keep them happy, but animals were a wholly unpredictable lot. I still hadn't recovered from having a llama spit in my hair during Pistol Pete's Petting Zoo at Paradise Park last summer.

"He's not mine," I grumbled. "I'm just watching him until Piper can find him a good home. She found him wandering the streets before the blizzard."

"Well, he is just the cutest thing ever!" Chloe squealed in that high-pitched, singsong voice people use with their pets—the one that made my head pound.

I grunted. "Yeah, he's adorable."

Rascal seemed to know we were talking about him because he wagged his tail back and forth. He started squirming, so Chloe set him down. The puppy bounded along the floor, stopping every few feet to smell the carpet.

"Why don't you take him?" I suggested.

"I'd love to…"

Maybe Chloe would get that promotion sooner than she thought—

"But I can't."

Maybe not.

"My building has a strict, no-animals policy," she continued.

"Well, do me a favor then," I said, handing Chloe the hundred-dollar bill Piper had given me before we'd left the restaurant. "Run down to the pet store on Fifth Street and get him some food and one of those cushioned baskets to sleep in."

"Sure," she said. "I'll go as soon as I finish lunch."

I tried to get inside my office before Rascal could follow me, but he was strangely quick for a puppy. At least, he was on dry land. He bounded in just before I closed the door. I opened it back up, trying to shoo him outside where Chloe was, but Rascal trotted over to the couch, intent on jumping up on it, even though he was too tiny to hurdle the high cushions. He stared at the sofa, then at me. Then, he started barking, whining, and prancing around.

"All right, all right," I mumbled. "Here you go."

I put Rascal up on the sofa, and he yipped with gratitude. The puppy ran from one end to the other, sniffing the pillows and cushions.

"Now, you might be able to pull that *I'm-the-cutest-sweetest-most-adorable-dog-ever* stuff when we're out in public, but not with me. I have a lot of work to do. So, sit down and take a nap," I ordered.

Rascal dropped to all fours and put his head down on his paws, almost as if he understood exactly what I'd said. Then again, I didn't really know what dogs did and didn't understand.

While Rascal napped, I got back to work, fielding calls from various assistants wanting to know whose party I was planning for Valentine's Day. The answer? Pretty much everyone's.

Chloe came in around three with the basket and bowls of water and food for Rascal. The puppy hopped down off the sofa and tore into the puppy chow.

Crunch, crunch, crunch...

I heard every mouthful go down. With my superhearing, it was like listening to bones break.

After *oohing* and *aahing* over the puppy again, Chloe returned to her desk. A minute later, she buzzed me.

I pressed down on the intercom. "Yes, Chloe?"

"Hi, Abby. Wesley Weston is here to see you. He doesn't have an appointment but hoped you could squeeze him in."

Wesley Weston was another one of the society circuit's rich businessmen. Weston made his fortune through some computer gadget he'd invented, something he'd made smaller, better, and cheaper than the other guys, before selling the patent for several billion dollars. These days, he spearheaded a variety of companies under the helm of Weston Corp. Rumor had it Weston was a bit eccentric, buying and selling companies because they amused him and not necessarily to increase the bottom line in his portfolio. Then again, when you were worth close to fifty billion bucks, you could burn a significant amount of cash on mere amusements.

"Abby?" Chloe asked.

I glanced at my calendar. I didn't have anything else scheduled the rest of the day besides the usual round of phone calls. I might as well see what Weston wanted. I'd never done an event for him before. Maybe he'd finally realized he should hire *A+ Events* instead of leaving the planning to his army of underlings.

"Send him in," I said, getting to my feet.

Chloe opened the door, and a fresh, crisp aroma drifted into my office, overpowering Rascal's damp fur. Something about the smell bothered me, but I didn't have time to figure it out before he stepped inside. Weston was a little over six feet, although his boots gave him a few more inches. A royal blue trench coat hung down to his knees, flapping around his beige corduroy pants. A matching blue sweater peaked out just over his collar, contrasting with the faint stubble that covered his chin. His hair was a dark brown and spiked up a bit over his forehead.

The businessman wasn't particularly handsome, not like Sam Sloane or Johnny Bulluci. Weston's face was too rugged, his jaw too square. He reminded me of a boxer more than anything else—his face had the rough, hard look of someone who'd taken more than a few punches. Still, something about him nagged at me.

"Hi, Abby, I'm Wesley Weston," he said, extending a hand. His eyes, a warm, golden hazel, met mine. "I've seen you at several events, but I don't think we've been introduced."

Of course not. None of the society bigwigs ever bothered to introduce themselves to me—unless they needed something. Even then, they focused on what they wanted and how fast I could get it, rather than social niceties like first names and small talk. Or just saying *please* and *thank you*.

"It's a pleasure," I murmured, taking his hand in my own.

The second his skin touched mine, hot tingles flooded my body. His fingers were warm and hard and calloused. Exactly as warm and hard and calloused as the ones I'd felt glide along my body. The ones that had been more gentle and maddening than I'd thought possible.

I drew in a breath. His smell. The same sharp, clean minty aroma that had soaked into my sheets and pillows.

"Is something wrong?" Wesley asked.

His voice rumbled with a low, sexy timbre, the exact same one that had rasped out my name.

As much as they might annoy me, my supersenses didn't lie. They told me everything I needed to know. They told me who Wesley Weston was. Who he *really* was.

Talon—Wesley Weston was Talon, and he was in my office.

PART TWO

WREN

CHAPTER ELEVEN

He'd found me—*Talon* had found *me*. That horrifying thought slammed into my mind with as much force as one of Bandit's bullets.

"Is something wrong, Ms. Appleby?" Wesley repeated, dropping my hand. "Have I come at a bad time?"

"Of course not," I croaked, trying to keep him from seeing how shocked I was.

I just stood there, looking at him. Wesley glanced over his shoulder at Chloe, who hovered in the door and was just as confused by my glassy-eyed, slack-jawed stance. I didn't know what to do, what to say, what to *think*.

Rascal saved me. The puppy lifted his head from the sofa and barked with curiosity at the new person in the room. Wesley spotted the dog, and a smile creased his face.

While I gawked, Wesley strode over to the couch, dropped to his knees, and petted Rascal. For his part, the puppy rolled onto his back, giving Wesley access to his pudgy tummy.

Watching him pet Rascal gave me time to shake off my shock—and realize he hadn't found me. Wesley Weston didn't know I was Wren. If he did, he would have swooped into my office dressed as Talon to protect his own secret identity. Instead, he was here as Wesley Weston.

Wesley Weston, business mogul, had come to see Abby Appleby, event planner.

Not Wren—and definitely not Nightingale.

"I'm sorry about having the dog in here," I said. "A friend just gave him to me, and I haven't had a chance to take him home yet."

"No problem," Wesley said. "I like animals. Dogs, cats, birds."

Of course he liked birds. He'd named himself after part of one.

The businessman gave me a smile, the same sort of wry, self-mocking smile that had stretched across Talon's face, the one that made my heart pick up speed like a runaway train.

"Please," I said, snapping back to my senses. "Have a seat."

Wesley settled himself in the chair in front of my desk. I jerked my head at Chloe. She nodded, walked outside, and shut the door behind her.

Legs shaking, I plopped in my own chair and tried to pretend like everything was normal. Like my one-night, superhero stand hadn't just walked through the door in his street clothes.

"So what can I do for you, Mr. Weston?"

"Please, call me Wesley," he replied. "I need you to plan an event."

"Obviously."

"Obviously."

His eyes met mine again, and I noticed them—*really* noticed them. I marveled at their color. Technically, they would be classified as hazel, but *hazel* didn't tell you they were a shimmering gold, rich and jeweled and pure. Bright. Vivid. Intense. No wonder he hid them behind that visor. Supersenses or not, I would never have forgotten eyes like that.

I shook my head, trying to focus. "What sort of event is it?" I pulled out a legal pad so I could take notes. My fingers shook only a little.

"I understand you handled the engagement party and merger dinner for Olivia O'Hara and Paul Potter on Saturday night," Wesley said.

"Yes," I replied in a cautious voice. "But what does that have to do with your event?"

"I recently acquired Glo-Glo Cosmetics, and I want everyone to know the company is still a force to be reckoned with."

Another part of party planning meant reading the business pages—and listening to gossip on the society circuit. Glo-Glo was the other major cosmetics company in Bigtime—and Oomph's chief rival. In recent weeks, the two companies had been engaged in an intense bidding war to acquire Polish, the company owned by Paul Potter and his family. Industry insiders suggested whoever got Polish and its lip-care products would corner the makeup market—and brush the other company out of business. Octavia O'Hara had won that round, with the help of Olivia's engagement to Paul. More than a few folks had whispered the engagement was the *only* reason Weston Corp. hadn't acquired Polish—and that Octavia had hurried the two lovebirds' romance along to ensure that Oomph got control of Polish.

"What sort of event do you want me to put together?" I asked.

Wesley leaned forward. "A dinner announcing Glo-Glo's acquisition of Gelled. It's a lip-care company just like Polish. Gelled is much smaller, but it has great customer loyalty and the potential for major growth, which is a point I want to drive home."

I scribbled down notes, including one to remind myself to call Piper about all this. In addition to being obsessed with superheroes, Piper was rather particular about her appearance, having just about every makeup product you could imagine. She'd be able to tell me everything I needed to know about Polish, Gelled, Glo-Glo, and Oomph, including which colors and products were best for me. Piper was always trying to make me over, to get me to realize my *full potential*, as she called it. Like any good best friend, she thought I was prettier and more special than I really was.

"I'd like to start off with a formal sit-down dinner," Wesley said. "Followed by some talk about the new acquisition, then a night of drinks and dancing. But I don't want your usual business dinner. I want everything to be hip and young and fresh and cool. That's Gelled's demographic, and I want to show everyone how vibrant the company is."

"How many people do you want to invite?"

"Oh, I want to keep it small, say five hundred or so."

Small. Right. I made another note. "And when do you want this event to take place?"

Wesley hesitated. "Well, that's the thing, and the reason I came here in person. My secretary insisted on it after I told her what I wanted. I was wondering if you could pull something together for Friday."

I glanced at the clock on my desk. Just before four on Monday afternoon.

"Friday? You want me to pull this together by Friday night?"

He nodded.

Somehow, I managed to keep my expression smooth and even. "You want me to plan a hip, young, fresh, cool event, complete with a sit-down dinner, music, and dancing in less than a week's time?"

"I know it's asking a lot, but I'm willing to pay whatever fee you require to get it done."

Normally, I would have turned him down. I required at least two weeks' notice for events of this magnitude. Usually three. The only reason I'd done the O'Hara-Potter dinner was because Octavia had paid me through the nose—and suggested if I didn't, she'd never hire me to work for her again. I'd never worked for Wesley, so I wouldn't be losing his business if I told him no, but I wouldn't be gaining any either. And I desperately needed to rebuild my savings after sinking all my money into my loft.

But this was Talon sitting in front of me. The guy who'd noticed me, if only for a little while. The one who'd seen me, who'd made me feel interesting, witty, and vibrant. Who declared that I was gorgeous. The man who called me Nightingale.

So I quoted him a figure that was only four times my going rate, instead of five. I might be a freak for wanting to be close to my one-night superhero stand, but I wasn't stupid. This was going to be a lot of work in a short amount of time, and I wanted to be well paid for it.

Wesley didn't even blink. He drew a checkbook from inside his jacket. My eyes focused on his left shoulder, the one with the two bullet holes in it underneath his clothes, but Wesley showed no sign of pain as he wrote the check and handed it to me. His heart rate was fine, and he looked as though he hadn't done anything more strenuous than breathe the past few days. The G-man superhero really was a tough guy.

"I'll start calling my suppliers now to give them a heads-up and swing by your office in the morning to pitch you some ideas," I said. "Say around ten?"

"That will be fine."

I stood and extended my hand to Wesley. "I guess we have a deal, then."

He took it, his calloused fingers squeezing mine just as gently as they'd slid across my skin before. Treacherous, hot tingles spread through my body. Wesley's hand lingered on mine, his golden gaze sharp and probing on my face, as though he saw something unexpected in my green eyes.

For a moment, I wondered if he knew who I was—if he'd figured it out, just like I had. Because the attraction I felt for him was intense. Palpable. Undeniable. Like lightning surging through my whole body. But the smile he gave me was too bland and nonchalant. The notice he'd given me, the interest, had already melted away. He'd gotten what he wanted, gotten me to agree to plan his event, and I was all but invisible once more.

"Until tomorrow," Wesley said, dropping my hand.

"Until tomorrow," I replied, resisting the urge to massage the tingles out of my fingers.

He walked over to the couch, where Rascal perched, his brown eyes taking in everything. Wesley gave Rascal another pat, which the puppy happily accepted. Then, the businessman opened the door and left my office.

I stood until the door swung shut again. Then, I leaned over and braced my hands on my desk. My fingers tingled. My knees twitched. Tremors shook my body.

Fear was not a pleasant feeling, and I'd been so afraid he'd known. That he'd figured out I was Nightingale. That he'd finally realized I was nothing but a drab, brown wren.

Fear of disappointment, fear of rejection—those were two more reasons I didn't date much. I'd had more than my share of both. Ryan had just been the last in a long string of breakups. Each time, each experience, each failed relationship stacked another brick on top of the wall ringing my heart.

But Talon had soared over my defenses as easily as he'd defeated Bandit's goons. And I'd been thrilled by it—happy to fly up there with him, if only for one night.

But now it was time to come back down to earth. Back down to Bigtime, where things always seemed to work out for other people, instead of for me. Back behind my wall, where I'd be safe once more.

I breathed in, forcing the cool, stale office air into my lungs until I got control of myself. No matter what had happened between Wesley "Talon" Weston and me, it didn't change the fact that I had a major event to plan—and less a week to make everything perfect again.

I straightened and pushed the button on the intercom. "Chloe?"

"Yes, Abby?"

"Get Kyle Quicke on the phone. I need to order five hundred more pounds of chicken."

Chapter Twelve

I spent the rest of the day feeling like I'd been split into two people, like so many superheroes and ubervillains before me. Gentleman George. Captain Sushi. Caveman Stan.

First, there was Abby Appleby, who called Kyle Quicke and the other usual suspects to order supplies and book workers, space, and more for the Weston event.

Then, there was Wren, who kept remembering her time with Talon and comparing him to Wesley Weston—and found little lacking in either man.

"Abby?" Chloe said.

I jumped, startled by the sound of her voice. My assistant hovered in front of the desk, Rascal cradled in her arms.

"Did I scare you?" Chloe asked.

"Yeah," I said, letting out a breath. "You did."

She frowned. "But you always hear me come in."

With my superhearing, I could hear every move Chloe made, even when she was at her desk, the door to my office was shut, and I had music on. She was a good employee, only goofing off and playing computer solitaire late in the afternoon when she was killing time before she went home.

"I guess I was just distracted planning the Weston event."

Chloe nodded. "Well, I'm leaving for the day. Is there anything else you need?"

"No, because I'm leaving too."

She blinked. "You are? But it's only five. You never leave before seven, especially when you have a new client."

I shut down my computer. "Well, tonight I'm going home. I'll work on the Weston event from there."

Chloe's hazel eyes widened, and she stared at me like I'd sprouted blue fur. Maybe I should. People would probably pay more attention to me. Even Wesley might notice me then, at least until Yeti Girl arrived on the scene.

Chloe stared at me as I pulled on my hat, coat, scarf, and gloves. She handed Rascal to me, and I stuck him into the pocket on my vest. The puppy wiggled around until he got comfortable, then licked my chin with his wet, rough tongue.

"You ready to go home, dog?" I asked.

Rascal barked. To my surprise, he'd actually been good today, sleeping and amusing himself and not making too much noise. I scratched his ears. His tail thumped against my heart through the fabric of my vest.

I also grabbed the bag from the pet store containing the supplies Chloe had bought before turning off the office lights and heading to the antechamber. Chloe stood by the elevator, her finger on the hold button. She let go when I stepped inside, and the doors closed.

"You're *really* going home." From the awe in her voice, you'd think I'd just done some incredible feat, like climbing to the top of the Skyline Bridge and diving off into the waters of Bigtime Bay.

"Yes, I'm *really* going home."

We reached the ground floor, and the doors slid open. Chloe gave Rascal a final pat, and we said our good-byes. She crossed the street, her black hair swinging as she walked toward the subway. I turned the opposite direction and headed toward my building.

More of the snow had either been cleared or melted away, thanks to the plows and the superstrong salt the city workers used to coat the streets. Now, the wet stuff only reached up past my ankles. The winter sun painted the sky in dusky purples and twilight grays as it dipped behind the towering skyscrapers. The soft, pretty colors reminded me of a lovely painting I'd seen of a sunset at Cypress Mountain. The wind caressed my cheeks— cold, but not unbearably so. More people scurried on the streets, and cars rumbled through downtown, zipping by faster than they had this morning. Everyone was getting back to their usual snow- free routine.

Including Bigtime's superheroes and ubervillains.

A mob of people clustered at the end of the block next to a black van. I spotted a flash of silver, and smoke filled the air. That van, that silver color, that smell. It could only mean one thing—that the Fearless Five were here. More specifically, Karma Girl and Fiera.

I caught sight of the two superheroes. Fiera stood in the middle of the crowd, as eye-catching as ever in her skin-hugging, orange-red catsuit. She bench-pressed a fanboy over her head with one hand while his buddy took pictures. With her free hand, Fiera shot sparks up into the air, her trademark salute. Karma Girl leaned against the F5 van, signing an occasional autograph but mostly just watching Fiera show off.

I slowed down, threading my way through the milling mob. Unlike Piper and the other fangirls in Bigtime, I had little interest in superheroes, unless I needed them to do an appearance at an event.

A spark of blue caught my attention, and I turned my head. Karma Girl stared at me, her eyes glowing as bright as sapphires, almost like she could hear my thoughts. I waved at her. I knew Karma Girl better than some of the other heroes, and a few weeks ago she'd helped guard some toys for an annual Christmas charity drive that had been on display inside Oodles o' Stuff. Of course, a couple of ubervillains had stolen the toys and were going to sell them on the Internet before Karma Girl managed to stop them. It had been a close call—too close for my liking—but the toy giveaway had gone off as planned, thanks to Karma Girl and the rest of the city's heroes.

I looked at Fiera, then back at Karma Girl. She grinned and shrugged, as if to say *What can you do?* I shrugged back and walked on.

I'd gone about two blocks when I felt a series of vibrations under my feet that had nothing to do with the rush-hour traffic. I stopped, concentrating. The vibrations grew closer and stronger, as if something very large was headed my way. The vibrations traveled up through the street and into the surrounding buildings, until even the traffic lights swung back and forth from the force of them.

I looked over my shoulder. Through the gathering dark, something charged my way. Something big. Something blue. Something brawny.

I flattened myself up against the nearest building. A seven-foot-tall woman lumbered past. Blue fur covered her body, while her eyes glowed a milky white. She wore what looked like a blue toga and sandals, and her feet were big and bare with toes as long as my fingers. Yeti Girl. Another one of Bigtime's ubervillains. Sort of. Yeti Girl was a superstrong being who liked to smash things because the noise amused her. Every once in a while, she tore through town, flattening cars and leveling buildings before the cops and the nearest superhero managed to shoot her full of tranquilizer darts.

I'd just stepped back onto the street when I felt another series of vibrations—this time quick and smooth and churning. I sighed and put my back against the wall once more.

Swifte zoomed down the street after Yeti Girl, speeding by so fast he didn't even whip up any snow. A moment later, an SNN news van careened after him. The van took a turn on two wheels as the driver tried to keep up with the superfast superhero on the icy street. The squeal of tires screeched into my brain, and my temples throbbed with the beginnings of a migraine. Rascal barked, excited by the sudden action and wanting to follow the news van. No doubt the pint-sized puppy thought he could help corral Yeti Girl, even though she was twenty times his size.

"Sorry, dog," I said. "We're going home. I've still got work to do."

After making sure nothing else was coming out of the dark to squish me, I crossed over to the next block. It was quieter here, so quiet I didn't even see the figure dressed in black until I was about five feet from her. She wore black leather from head to toe as so many of the heroes and villains did, but what set her apart were the snakes—live snakes covered her arms like turquoise and coral bangle bracelets. A few more curled around her neck and shoulders, while still more dangled from the elaborate headdress she wore. Black Samba leaned against a bus stop sign, doing a little shimmy, her arms crossed over her chest to ward off the cold.

Rascal stuck his head out of my coat a little more, intrigued by this new person. I looked down at Rascal, then back at the superhero. She had snakes. Those were animals, albeit cold-blooded ones. Maybe she'd want another. It was worth a shot.

I marched over to the superhero, plastered a smile on my face, and tapped her on the shoulder in a spot that wasn't covered by a sleeping snake.

"Yes?" the superhero asked, turning around.

"Hi, Black Samba. Sorry to bother you. I'm Abby Appleby. I met you at the petting zoo last year at Paradise Park."

She nodded, the snakes in her headdress bobbing up and down. "I remember. You were the one who got the mice to feed to my babies."

Contributing to the genocide of small mammals hadn't been

one of my finer moments, but it had kept the superhero and her snakes happy. "Yeah, that was me. Anyway, I was wondering how you feel about dogs."

"Dogs?"

I pointed at Rascal. "Yeah, dogs. I'm trying to find him a good home."

A bus screeched to a halt in front of the stop. Black Samba stared at Rascal, who let his tongue hang out, showing off his happy, goofy, puppy face.

"He's cute, but the snakes don't do so well with other animals," she said. "Sorry."

"You're not the only one," I muttered.

Black Samba leapt up onto the hood of the bus. She waved at the driver, then climbed onto the roof of the vehicle. The superhero tapped her foot on the metal, signaling the driver that she was ready to go. She started dancing again as the bus pulled back into traffic.

Rascal barked, and Black Samba waved good-bye to us.

"I just can't give you away, can I, dog?" I said.

Rascal barked again.

I made it back to my loft without running into any more heroes or villains. I put Rascal down and shrugged out of my coat while checking my messages. There was only one from Piper, asking how Rascal was doing. I put some food and water out for the puppy, slipped a Green Day CD into the player, plopped on the couch, and called her back. I told Piper that Rascal was doing just fine. Then I revealed exactly who had come into my office this afternoon—and his alter ego.

"You're kidding me!" Piper squealed. "Wesley Weston is really Talon?!"

I held the phone out until Piper got control of herself—and her voice. "I'm positive it's him. His hands felt the same. He smelled the same. His voice was the same. It *has* to be him."

"How exciting!" she said. "So what are you going to do now?"

"What do you mean what am I going to do now? I'm going to plan his event."

"And?" Piper prompted.

"And what? I'm not going to tell him who I really am, if that's what you're thinking." The thought made my stomach churn with fear.

"Abby—"

"No, Piper," I cut her off. "I'm not going to tell him. There's no point in it. It would just make things weird. Well, weirder. It was a one-night stand, and now, it's over."

"It's not over," she said in a firm voice. "It's just getting started. This is destiny, Abby. Destiny with a capital D. She's tapping on your shoulder and saying *Hey, this great guy is for you. Do you really want to ignore her?*"

I rolled my eyes. In addition to being a total fangirl, Piper was a hopeless romantic. She believed in destiny, true love, and karma, despite her breakup with Kyle.

"You said the same thing when I got fried by that amp at The Blues. That me getting struck dumb with supersenses was destiny. That I was going to do great things with my new powers. All I've done is see the world in high-def and hear it in surround sound. Frankly, I've had enough of destiny and the migraines that go with it."

Because I wasn't answering destiny's call, Piper tried another avenue. "The sex, Abby. Think of the sex. Wouldn't you like to have more of that?"

As badly as an ubervillain wanted world domination. But I wasn't going to admit that. It would only make her more determined.

Piper argued some more, but I didn't budge. She might be a romantic, but I was a realist—and more stubborn. She finally agreed to let me handle Wesley my own way, even though she told me I was making a terrible mistake. She also made me promise to give her hourly updates, if the situation warranted. Like if I somehow tripped and found myself naked in Talon's arms again. I only wished I could be that clumsy.

I ignored the mistake talk, but I gave in to the updates demand. After all, what are best friends for if not to dish about dreamy guys? Especially the ones you'll never have?

We talked for a few more minutes about Talon and Wesley. I also asked Piper about Oomph and Glo-Glo, the two competing cosmetics companies.

"Meet me at Oodles o' Stuff at nine tomorrow morning," she said. "There's someone down there who should be able to give you all the details."

"See you there."

After we hung up, I grabbed a bottled water and a chocolate granola bar. Then I went over to my desk, tugged a legal pad out of a drawer, and plopped down in my chair. Rascal curled up in the basket Chloe had bought and slept while I worked on themes for the Weston event.

Wesley wanted something hip and young and fresh and cool. Something memorable. Something that would blow Octavia and Oomph away. I tapped my pen against my chin, trying to come up with something I hadn't done a thousand times before. It was tough. I planned more than a hundred events a year, from birthdays to weddings to business conferences. I'd done just about every imaginable theme as well.

As I thought, I sang along with Green Day, and the perfect idea came to me—rock 'n' roll.

Nothing was cooler than that. Rock 'n' roll was the very essence of being hip. Plus, Talon—or rather Wesley—liked it.

And I found myself wanting to please him, even if he would only think I was doing my job.

So, I started to plan.

I'd booked the convention center this morning. With the right decorations and lights, I could transform the space into an upscale rock concert complete with disco balls and neon strobe lights. Maybe even a couple of ice sculptures shaped like guitars.

I'd forgo the usual orchestra and get Melody Masters to do the music. In addition to owning The Blues karaoke bar, Melody fronted Miked, a popular indie rock band. They could play some of their own tunes, mixed in with covers. Classic rock with a contemporary twist—tailored for the rich set. I couldn't go too wild or I'd scare off the society matrons, but it would definitely be hip and cool.

An hour later, I had ten pages of notes and people I needed to call to get the ball rolling. Music, decorations, food, table and chair rentals, all of the usual things to nail down. I looked at the clock. After nine. Tomorrow was going to be another long day. I should crash now and get as much sleep as I could.

I took a quick shower and put on my pajamas, determined to go to bed, but Rascal had other ideas. The puppy waited for me outside the bathroom. He barked once, then bounced over to the front door. He stared at it expectantly, as if he could open it by the sheer force of his mind. When it didn't oblige him, Rascal looked over his shoulder at me—and whined.

I sighed. "Let me guess. You want me to take you for a walk, don't you? So you can go do your business?"

I might have imagined it, but I thought Rascal nodded. So, I threw on my jacket and gloves over my jammies. Unfortunately, Chloe hadn't thought to buy a leash or collar at the pet store, so I had to scoop up Rascal and carry him into the elevator and then outside onto the street. I placed the puppy on the sidewalk next to a snow-covered fire hydrant and stepped back.

"All right, dog," I muttered. "Let's make this quick."

Rascal wandered around, trying to find the *perfect* spot. He sniffed the hydrant. The car parked next to it. The mailbox. The car parked next to that. Finally, just when I was tempted to leave him out in the cold, Rascal did his thing.

When he finished, I reached down to pick him up, but Rascal squirmed out of my gloved grasp. Damn, he was quick. Or maybe I was just getting old and slow. I was twenty-nine now. Unlike Olivia O'Hara, I was saving my mental breakdown and freak-out for later this year, when I turned thirty.

"Rascal! Come here!"

The puppy might have been tiny, but he leapt over the snowdrifts like he was a deer. What had been in that food Chloe had bought? Some radioactive drug like euphoridon? Because Rascal acted like he was on something good.

The puppy bounded across the street, ears pointed sky-high, and I started to panic. I darted after him, my boots skidding on a patch of ice. Piper would never forgive me if I let him get run over by a car. Rascal kept right on going and started climbing up the steps of the brownstone that took up the opposite block—Jasper's brownstone.

Not good.

Rascal made it to the top of the steps, looked up at the door, and wagged his tail. Not a second later, the front door opened, and a woman stepped outside. That in and of itself was strange enough because Jasper didn't have many visitors, but I would have recognized that tall, skinny figure anywhere—Joanne James.

Joanne wore a long, lavender coat with matching gloves and boots, and her black hair spilled down her shoulders. Maybe it was the soft glow from the streetlight, but Joanne looked younger than her forty-something years, her face smooth in the dark night.

Joanne James was the richest woman in the city, having married and divorced several men over the years, getting millions in alimony every time. She had inherited billions more last year when ubervillains murdered her husband, Berkley Brighton.

Rascal barked, and Joanne caught sight of him. She arched an eyebrow, and amusement flashed across her face. She stood there, one hand holding the door open, and stared at the puppy. Rascal, of course, took this as an invitation to gallop inside. It was bad enough he'd dashed across the street. Now he'd invaded someone else's home. That dog was going to be the death of me.

I plodded up the stairs, muttering vague curses at Piper under my breath and wrapping my coat tighter around my body in hopes that Joanne wouldn't notice my blue snowflake jammies peeking out the bottom. Her head whipped around at the sound of my footsteps scuffling in the snow.

"Hi, Joanne. What are you doing here?"

Her violet eyes narrowed. "Just visiting. What are you doing here, Abby?"

I pointed to my building. "I live across the street. My dog just ran inside Jasper's brownstone."

"That puppy is yours?" she asked. "I didn't know you had a dog."

There was that *tone* again. The one intimating it was the shock of a lifetime to learn I had an animal in my care.

"He's not mine. I'm just babysitting until I can find him a good home…" My voice trailed off suggestively.

Joanne cut me off with a laugh. "Oh honey, don't even ask me to take him off your hands. I don't do well with animals unless they're grilled and on my dinner plate."

Joanne was Bigtime's equivalent of a black widow spider. She survived on men, money, and the occasional glass of champagne. I doubted food ever passed through her lips.

We stood there in the cold, staring at each other. Because she was here, I might as well give her the latest information on her event. It would save me a phone call tomorrow.

"Everything's set for the library dedication. I tried to call you earlier today, but Berkley's secretary said you weren't in."

"I was busy," Joanne said in a stiff voice. She batted her eyes, as if blinking back tears.

"Of course."

Seconds ticked by in silence.

"Well, if you need anything or want to know more about the dedication, just call me. You have my number," I said, my voice a little kinder.

Joanne might be a brittle society queen, but she had just lost her husband. I knew she was grieving. I'd planned Berkley's funeral. I'd seen how she'd cried over his grave when she thought everyone else had gone.

Joanne looked at me. "You're such a marshmallow, just like Bella."

"Excuse me? I'm a marshmallow?" Surely I didn't look that fat in this coat.

"Yeah, a toasted marshmallow. All black, tough, and crunchy on the outside, all warm, sweet, and gooey on the inside." She shook her head. "It'll get you into trouble someday."

I started to say I wasn't a marshmallow any more than she was, but Joanne opened the door wider. "Come on. Let's get your dog."

She strolled into the house. I lunged forward to keep the door from closing shut and followed her in.

"Jasper!" Joanne called out. "You've got a visitor!"

"I know," a low voice sounded. "I've got him right here."

Jasper appeared at the end of the hall and walked toward us. He held Rascal in his arms, scratching the puppy's head with obvious affection. I let out a quiet sigh of relief that he hadn't been annoyed at the dog for slipping inside.

I'd first met Jasper a few months ago when I'd moved into my loft. I'd been walking home from work when I'd passed him on the street. He was struggling to pick up some mail he'd dropped. His arm and leg had been in casts at the time, the result of being mugged and beaten. I'd gotten his mail and helped him inside his house. He'd tried to pay me for helping, but I'd refused. Now I said hello to Jasper whenever I passed him on the street, but I still didn't know him very well.

"See, Abby? Your dog is fine," Joanne said.

"I told you, he's not my dog." I turned to Jasper. "I'm so sorry. I was walking him, and he just got away from me. He's very fast for a puppy."

"Yes, he is," Jasper murmured, rubbing one of Rascal's ears between his fingers. "But I suppose that's to be expected."

"It is?"

"Given his breed," he said.

"Oh."

Jasper looked at Rascal, then at me, then at Joanne. The whole situation was strange, but then again, Jasper was a strange sort of guy. Glasses squatted on the end of his nose, while a small diamond twinkled in his ear. His voice was low and soft, and he always wore grayish clothes on his tall, thin frame, as though he wanted to fade into the background. At the moment, Jasper had on what looked like gray coveralls with house slippers. If I'd passed him on the street, I would have thought he was some sort of mechanic.

I didn't even know if Jasper was his first or his last name. Everyone on the block called him *Mr. Jasper* in the respectful, hushed tones you'd use to talk about an ubervillain or mob boss. I'd seen him at some of my events, but like other society folks, he didn't speak to me unless he wanted something. Even then, he seemed to keep mostly to himself, avoiding the limelight whenever possible. Still, he'd always been nice and polite to me.

Rascal started wrestling around, so Jasper put him down. Rascal made a beeline down the hall, stopping in front of a closed door. The puppy sniffed around the door's edges, leaving me standing between Jasper and Joanne. Not exactly where I wanted to be.

"So, how do you two know each other?" I finally asked.

"We're brother and sister," Jasper said. "Joanne and I were having dinner to talk about some old family business."

Joanne's mouth tightened, and she gave Jasper a sharp look, like she wanted to strangle him for revealing state secrets.

I remembered Bella and Joanne talking about Joanne's brother Jasper at the O'Hara party. I just hadn't thought he would be this Jasper. I looked at him, then back at her. They really didn't look much alike. Joanne wore what amounted to a winter power suit, while Jasper looked like he'd be perfectly happy with grease on his ratty coveralls and a monkey wrench in his hand.

Then, I noticed their eyes. Joanne's were a vivid violet color. Jasper's were lighter, but just as intense. Both of them had the same sort of hard wariness in their gaze, as if they expected trouble at any moment. Weird.

Rascal put his paw on the door and barked, like he'd found the entrance to a mine full of dog biscuits. Jasper seemed amused by the puppy's antics. I was not. Every *yip-yap* pounded into my brain, adding to the pain and strangeness of the day.

"Well, I've got to run, Jasper. We'll talk again tomorrow. Good night, Abby." Joanne nodded at us, then sashayed out the front door.

With Joanne gone, I was even more nervous. I went down the hall, scooped up Rascal, and stuffed him back inside my coat. That seemed to calm the puppy, although he kept growling at the closed door, like a drug- or bomb-sniffing dog who'd scored a hit on a major stash.

"Well, thanks, Jasper. I'll let you get back to…whatever you were doing." I kept a firm grip on Rascal and headed for the door, determined to get out of here as quickly as possible.

"Abby?"

"Yes," I said, turning around to look at him, but still backing toward the door.

"You should be careful," he said.

I gave him a puzzled look.

"I've heard about some incidents lately in the neighborhood. Some violence. I just wanted you to keep an eye out."

"Oh. Okay."

His words seemed innocent enough, but there was a strange tone to them, almost like he was warning me about something specific.

"Well, thanks," I said.

He nodded at me. "Be safe."

"You do the same."

Jasper smiled. "Don't worry about me. I'm always safe."

I didn't know about that, because he was the one who'd been mugged, but I didn't know what else to say, so I nodded and left the brownstone. Still pondering Jasper's bizarre words, I headed back to my apartment. I was about halfway across the street when I got the feeling someone was watching me. I stopped and looked up and down the block, but I didn't see anyone.

Still, I felt like I was standing in a long, tall shadow, with someone looking down on me. I raised my head, my eyes scanning the rooftops, but didn't see anyone. No superheroes zooming through the sky. No ubervillains swinging from rooftop to rooftop. Not even a couple of teenagers sneaking out for a quick cigarette. I opened my eyes and ears. *Really* looking. *Really* listening. Nothing.

I shivered, wrapped my arms tighter around Rascal, and hurried back to my building. I didn't stop until I was in my loft with the door locked behind me.

CHAPTER THIRTEEN

The noises woke me.

Fierce, aggressive *yip-yaps* punctuated by squeaky *gr-gr-growls*. Nails clicking on the floor. The slap of a tail against glass.

I smashed my ear into my pillow, flattening the fluffy mound into a fabric pancake beneath my head. Then, I reached over, grabbed my other pillow, and pulled it on top of my exposed ear. I'd stuffed my earplugs in hours ago, determined to get a good night's sleep, but I could *still* hear him.

Rascal, the freaking superdog, was on the prowl.

Evidently, puppies didn't need much sleep, because Rascal had spent the past two hours pacing back and forth in front of the glass windows and door that lined the back wall of the loft. If I didn't know better, I would have thought he was a junkyard dog, trained to bark at the slightest noise. That, or his pea-sized brain thought there was something lurking outside that he could chase.

Of course, I yelled at him. Snapped my fingers. Threatened to leave him out on the cold balcony all night long, even though it was an empty threat and I couldn't bring myself to do something like that. But unlike most of the caterers in the greater

Bigtime area, Rascal wasn't cowed by my sharp tone or harsh words. Instead, the puppy would settle down for a few minutes, seemingly chastised, and I'd lie back down and close my eyes. Then, just as I drifted toward the land of sweet, sweet sleep, Rascal would scramble to his feet and bark at the patio door again.

Finally, after two hours of this chess game, I sat up, smacked the lights on, and marched over to the puppy, who had his nose pressed up against the door.

"What are you doing?" I demanded. "It's after midnight. Puppies should be asleep, and so should I."

Rascal looked up at me, his eyes big and intense, his ears standing straight up like two antennas. He pressed his nose against the door and growled again, as if he wanted me to open the glass so he could sink his teeth into whatever was out there. Except I knew there wasn't anything lurking outside. This was one of the quietest blocks in Bigtime, which was the exact reason I'd moved here. No gangs. No crime. No loud neighbors.

I sighed. "You're not going to shut up until I show you there's nothing out there, are you?"

Rascal looked at me.

"Fine," I muttered.

I yanked a cord, pulling the drapes back. Then, I stepped to one side and pointed out the door. "See? There's nothing out there. Nothing at all."

Rascal let out a low, hoarse growl. He lunged forward, barking like he was a fierce guard dog instead of a couple of pounds of ears and attitude.

A shadow fell on my body. A long, tall shadow, just like the one I'd seen earlier this evening.

I whirled around. Heart pounding. Eyes wide. Nostrils flared—and stared out at my empty balcony.

I put my hands on the glass and looked out—*really* looked. Empty—the balcony was empty.

I took a breath and tried to get my racing heart under control. There was nothing out there. The shadow had probably been a bird, startled by the sudden light and noise inside the loft. I let out an angry breath. Probably another wren, too stupid to seek shelter for the night.

Still, I double-checked and made sure the door was locked. Rascal kept growling, and I massaged my temples. Oh yes, the puppy was definitely going to be the death of me. But I wasn't going alone. Piper was coming too, I thought darkly. She was going to hear *all* about this in the morning.

I pushed the drapes shut and pointed my finger at the puppy's basket in the corner. "You've seen there is absolutely nothing out on the balcony. So lie down and go to sleep. Now!"

Rascal's ears quivered and slowly lowered. His nose twitched, almost like he was sniffling. He looked at his basket, then at me. Tail between his legs, he trotted over to it and curled up inside.

I slapped off the lights, got back into bed, and pulled the covers up to my chin. I sighed into my pillow, more than ready to sink into the darkness until the sunlight slipped through my drapes.

Then Rascal whined—a pitiful, pathetic, *why-don't-you-love-me-anymore?* whine—followed by a whimper of the same caliber and some more sniffling.

"Oh, good grief," I muttered, giving in to the inevitable. "Fine. You can sleep with me. Anything to calm you down. But only for tonight. My bed is *not* going to permanently reek of puppy. Come here, Rascal."

I didn't have to say it twice. He hurdled out of the basket so fast he kicked it into the wall behind him. Rascal bounded over to me. I reached down, picked him up, and deposited him on the foot of the bed. But the puppy wasn't happy there. Oh no. As soon as I put my head on my pillow, the puppy crept up to my chest, squirmed his way under my arm, and put his warm, wet nose next to my cheek.

He grunted with contentment. I rolled my eyes and dug my fingers into his fur. Rascal yawned, and I wrinkled my nose as a wave of puppy chow hit me.

Dog breath—just what I needed to smell all night long. Still, I couldn't help but smile as we both settled down to sleep.

I met Piper the next morning at Oodles o' Stuff, Bigtime's most popular department store. Each of the store's many floors was crammed with every conceivable good in the known universe, from clothes and shoes to computer and printers to exotic spices and gourmet foods. Even though it was just before nine, shoppers crowded into the store, and cash registers rang up sale after sale. Rascal barked, excited by the lights and noise. Nobody batted an eye as I carried the puppy inside. If Yeti Girl could storm through here when she was in one of her rampaging moods, folks weren't going to look twice at Rascal.

I went over to the map inside the front door. I wasn't a big shopper, and I came to Oodles o' Stuff only when absolutely necessary, like when I'd been overseeing the holiday toy drive. The store had rearranged its merchandise since then, so I scanned the table of contents until I spotted the location of the makeup counter—straight back on the first floor. I fell into the flow of traffic and let the shoppers sweep me in that direction.

Piper spotted me and waved. She stood beside a tall woman with cropped blond hair. Everything about the other woman was perfect, from the smart, sharp lines of her ice-blue pantsuit to the subtle makeup that colored her face. I walked over to them, and Piper made the introductions.

"This is Sabrina St. John," Piper said. "She's Oodles o' Stuff's main buyer and color consultant. She also did the makeup for

Fiona's last fashion show, and she's a genius when it comes to color combinations."

We shook hands. Sabrina had a firm, pleasant grip, although her fingers were cool to the touch.

"Piper says you want the lowdown on the lipstick wars in Bigtime," Sabrina said, her pale blue eyes meeting mine.

I nodded. "I just finished an event for Octavia O'Hara announcing Oomph's merger with Polish. Now, Wesley Weston wants me to put one on for Glo-Glo."

"That doesn't surprise me," Sabrina said. "Oomph and Glo-Glo are the two main makeup companies in Bigtime. They've always been competitors. Follow me."

She led us down a long, glass counter. Lipsticks, eye shadows, glosses, blushes, foundations, and concealers lined the area, each one more colorful and in a brighter, prettier tube than the last. Sabrina stopped under a sign that read *Add some Oomph to your look*. Red lips kissed on either side of the word. Another sign a few feet away screamed *Glam. Gorgeous. Glo-Glo!*

Sabrina pulled out products from underneath the counters and started talking about the Oomph and Glo-Glo makeup lines. I picked up some of the pots of color and eyed the glossy packaging. Every product promised to deliver a subtle but different and fabulous look, from the shimmering eye shadow to the matte foundation. I unscrewed two lipsticks that seemed to be the same shade of red and the exact same color as twenty others sitting in the display case, but each one of the tubes had a different name on the bottom, from *Candy Apple* to *Fire Engine* to *Burnt Sienna*. There were lots of colors with the word *sun* in them. *Sunset. Sunbeam. Sunrise.*

I snickered.

"What's so funny?" Sabrina asked.

I shook my head. "Oh, just the fact that somewhere there's a person sitting in an office whose sole responsibility it is to come up with fifty different names for the same color of red. And the fact this person probably makes more money than me."

Sabrina grinned. "I'd say that's more sad than funny, wouldn't you?"

I arched an eyebrow. "Touché."

To look at Sabrina, you'd think she was another puffed-up, self-important, perfectly polished fashionista. But the more she spoke, the more I found myself liking her. She didn't sugarcoat anything, and she didn't talk down to me just because I wasn't wearing the latest design by Fiona Fine or Bella Bulluci.

"So what do you think about Oomph's acquisition of Polish?" I asked.

"I don't think it will help them as much as people think. Although that's not the only thing that Octavia O'Hara is up to these days." Sabrina pulled out a plastic bag embossed with the Oomph red lips logo. "Oomph is set to launch a new line of makeup around Valentine's Day. This is a sample of the products."

I recognized the items inside. The same ones were given away at the O'Hara-Potter dinner. Octavia must have sent them to all the stores in town too.

My eyes flicked down the rest of the counter, and I stared at the rainbow of colors. I hadn't known there were that many shades of red in the world, but Oomph boasted twenty-six of them. Piper dabbed a bit of perfumed lotion on her hand, sniffed it, and started sneezing. Rascal leaned down, trying to bury his nose in a pot of lime-green eye shadow. I pulled him back before he could give himself a clown face.

Sabrina opened the Oomph bag and set a variety of products on the counter. Ivory Tower foundation. Quicksilver eyeliner. Sunrise lipstick. A couple of Black Velvet eye shadows. Everything you needed to turn yourself from drab to glam. At least, that was what the packaging claimed.

"Are those products any better than what they have out right now? Or what Glo-Glo has on the market?" I asked.

"I don't know. I haven't tried them yet," Sabrina said. "Honestly, I don't use the Oomph products much anymore, except for a few old standbys that haven't changed. The company's color palette is too red and orange for my liking, and the quality's really gone downhill since Otto O'Hara died."

"How so?"

"I've had several complaints from customers about allergic reactions, odor problems, gunky residues," Sabrina said. "And it's not just my customers. Oomph has lost a significant amount of their market share in the last six months to Glo-Glo. The truth is Glo-Glo makes the better quality product—at a third of Oomph's price."

"But these Oomph colors look really great, really vibrant," Piper said.

She unscrewed a red lipstick from the kit and showed it to me. My nose twitched, and I caught an acrid whiff of sulfur, a disgusting, noxious smell that left me nauseated.

"Ugh." I wrinkled my nose. "Don't put that on your hand, much less your lips."

"Why not?" Piper asked.

"Because it smells like a rotten egg."

Sabrina leaned over and sniffed the lipstick. "I don't smell anything."

"Trust me," I said. "It reeks. It must be a bad tube or something."

Piper put the lipstick away, and we talked more about the two makeup companies. I opened my mouth to ask Sabrina another question, when she leaned over and grabbed my chin. She had a strong, firm grip, like she could crush my head with her bare hand if she wanted to. It was a little unsettling, as was the critical look she gave me.

Sabrina tilted my head from one side to the other. "You know, you have beautiful skin. What do you use on it?"

"Just soap, water, and sunscreen."

Sabrina raised an eyebrow. "No exfoliators? No moisturizers?"

"Sorry," I said. "Peppermint lip gloss is about as close to makeup as I get."

"That's a damn shame," Sabrina said.

I left Piper and Sabrina and arrived at Wesley Weston's building five minutes before ten. Weston Corp. had its headquarters in one of the downtown area's many skyscrapers, right next to *The Exposé*. One Weston Square was a bit shorter than the other buildings but more than made up for it with its unique architectural design. The outside reminded me of wedding cake—one with square, even layers stacked and twisted at varying angles on top of each other.

I pushed through the revolving doors and looked up. The inside of the building was a hollow oval, with wide, carpeted ramps crisscrossing up to the top floors. A big sign screaming *Get Some Direction Here!* hung over the information desk. I signed in as a visitor and got a plastic pass to clip to my coat. The guard behind the counter directed me to an elevator in the corner of the lobby, marked by a big bronze arrow.

"That goes up to Mr. Weston's private office." The guard fixed his gaze on Rascal, who poked his nose out of my jacket once again. "But I'm afraid you're going to have to leave the dog down here."

"The dog's coming with me," I said. "Believe me, I'm not any happier about it than you are."

After his barking fit, Rascal had settled down, but I'd spent the rest of the night breathing in puppy chow breath. I'd drifted off about two in the morning, only to be awakened by a tongue bath at seven, and Rascal's breath had gotten worse overnight. Ugh.

After meeting with Piper and Sabrina, I'd headed to my office, hoping to leave the puppy with Chloe, but she'd already gone over to the Bigtime Public Library to check on the details for tonight's dedication. I tried to leave Rascal in my office until Chloe came back, but he'd let out another pitiful whine as soon as he realized what I was up to. So, I brought him with me. That way, at least my furniture wouldn't get chewed, peed, or pooped on.

The guard opened his mouth to argue with me, but I cut him off.

"Listen," I said, giving him the cold, hard stare I reserved for Kyle Quicke. "Mr. Weston has hired me to plan a very important shindig for his company. I have to put together the party of the year in less than a week's time. So you can either let me go upstairs with the dog and do my job, or I can turn around and go back to my office. And *you* can explain to Mr. Weston why you wouldn't let me up to see him."

The guard paled at my words, as I knew he would. I'd gotten pretty good at reading folks over the years, learning how much pressure to apply, when to berate, when to cajole, when to just ask nicely. There was nothing an employee feared worse than upsetting his boss, even if that boss was a certifiable angel of hope, faith, and charity.

"Go right on up, ma'am," the guard said, his Adam's apple bobbing up and down.

"That's what I thought."

I got into the elevator and pushed the button marked *Penthouse*. Like most of the city's wealthier citizens, Wesley chose to do business on the very top floor of his building so he could have a commanding view of the significant piece of Bigtime that he owned.

The elevator doors *pinged!* open, the abrupt sound stabbing my brain. I winced and rubbed my temples. It was a good thing the party was being held at the convention center. Hopefully, today would be the only time I had to ride in this noisy elevator.

I stepped outside, expecting to find myself in a hallway or antechamber manned by a secretary. Instead, the elevator opened into a massive room that took up the entire top floor. Thousands of square feet stretched out in front of me, decorated here and there by clusters of plaid couches, leather chairs, and metal tables.

But the waterfall was what caught my attention.

Jagged black rocks made up one entire wall of the penthouse. Water flowed down the rocks and formed a gurgling pool. That pool, in turn, became a stream that cut across the floor, flowing under a bridge. The smooth, round arch contrasted with the sharp points of the rocks. Yin and yang as it were.

I closed my eyes. The steady hiss of the waterfall drowned out the ambient noise from the rest of the building. A bit of spray wafted onto my face, cool and refreshing.

The room also smelled strongly of mint. My eyes flicked to the other side of the bridge, where Wesley Weston sat behind a desk made of silver metal and sleek, blue glass. Today, the businessman wore a pair of gray corduroys topped by a cobalt-blue sweater. He bent over his desk, staring at some papers. Spotlights dangling from the ceiling picked up the dark chestnut streaks in his hair and highlighted the sexy stubble on his chin.

I stood there, staring at Wesley. He must have sensed my gaze because he looked up from his desk.

"Abby," he said. "Right on time."

"It's a bad habit of mine, I'm afraid."

"Please, come in."

I crossed the bridge and walked to the desk. It took several seconds. Wesley's eyes followed my progress, making me feel awkward and self-conscious. I hurried my steps and stumbled over my own feet, having to grab on to the bridge for support. Rascal let out a warning bark, not wanting to be squashed. I righted myself and walked on, trying to ignore the hot, aching blush screaming across my cheeks. Finally, I reached the desk.

"It's nice to see you again, Abby."

"You too, Mr. Weston."

We shook hands, and the familiar, inevitable tingles rushed through my body, tumbling from my hand down into the soles of my feet.

He smiled. "Please, call me Wesley. Everyone does."

"Okay, Wesley."

His gaze fell on my chest, lingering there. Was he checking me out? My heart started to pound—

Until an insistent *yip-yap* reminded me exactly what—or rather who—he was looking at.

"And I see you brought your dog too. How are you today, little fella?" Wesley asked.

Rascal let out a happy bark and squirmed around, trying to leap out of my vest and onto Wesley. I unbuttoned my coat, grabbed the puppy, and put him on the ground. Rascal darted under the glass desk and pounced on the brown tassel on Wesley's loafer.

"Sorry about bringing him," I said, laying my coat on one of the chairs in front of the desk. "I was going to leave him with my assistant, but she'd already gone out to a job site."

"It's not a problem." Wesley shook his foot to make the loafer tassel wiggle back and forth. Rascal growled, his eyes fixed on the waving scrap of leather. "Like I said before, I like animals."

"Well, thank you for understanding."

"No problem."

He leaned down and scratched Rascal's ears. The puppy grunted and leaned into the businessman's leg. I stared at Wesley's fingers as they sank into Rascal's fur. I remembered the feel of those long, hard fingers trailing down my body. The exquisite torture they had wrought in their wake—

I shifted in my chair, an ache building between my thighs.

"Is something wrong?" Wesley asked.

"Of course not. I was just admiring your, um, office."

He quit petting Rascal and took the chair behind his desk. The puppy decided to go exploring, sniffing his way along the carpeted floor.

My eyes flicked to Wesley's desk. Papers and grainy black-and-white photographs of a woman covered the surface, along with what looked like lab reports. Wesley saw me staring at them, picked them up, and flipped them over. The obvious lack of trust didn't bother me. He could have been looking at company secrets. Not exactly something you wanted to share with a woman you thought you'd just met yesterday.

While he shuffled around papers and photos, I latched on to the first thing that popped into my mind to fill the silence. "You know, I haven't been in this building since the city sold it to help pay for the damage done by Morgana Madison and her alter ego, Malefica."

Morgana Madison had been one of Bigtime's richest women and the owner of the newspaper, *The Exposé*. But she'd also had a darker side, moonlighting as Malefica, the leader of the Terrible Triad, the city's most feared ubervillain team. As Malefica, she'd had all sorts of superpowers, including telekinesis, or the ability to move objects with her mind. As Morgana Madison, she wielded almost as much influence. But Malefica, aka Morgana, had disappeared a while back after being in a building-leveling battle with the Fearless Five. At least, that was what the rumor mill kept spouting. Nobody knew exactly what had happened to Morgana, but her assets had been auctioned off to help pay for improvement projects around the city.

"It's been a long, slow job, but we're almost done with the renovations," Wesley said.

"It's very impressive," I admitted, staring at the waterfall. I could close my eyes and listen to the sound of falling water all day long. "Especially the waterfall. It's just gorgeous."

"You like it that much?" he asked.

"Oh yes."

I felt Wesley's eyes on my face, so I kept staring at the waterfall. And I realized there was something strange about it—a pattern hidden in the rocks. It almost looked like two giant cracks cut down the middle of the fall. I squinted harder, trying to bring the jagged rocks into supersharp focus, but the tumbling water obscured whatever benefit my enhanced eyesight might have provided.

"Are you sure your waterfall is structurally sound?" I asked.

"Of course. Why do you ask?"

"I don't know. It sort of looks like it's cracked in the middle."

He hesitated. "Oh, that's just a pipe that goes farther back into the wall. The builder didn't do quite as good a job at hiding it as he said he would. You must have very good eyes. Most people don't even notice it."

His voice was calm and as smooth as the water spilling down the wall, but he'd caught his breath before he'd spoken, almost as if I'd uncovered his greatest secret. I already knew he was Talon. What could he be hiding that was bigger than that?

I cleared my throat. Time to get on with business. I pulled out the thick binder that contained the information on the rock 'n' roll theme I'd dreamed up. I'd converted my notes to glossy pages full of charts, graphs, and seating arrangements. I'd even done some quick mock-ups of what the convention center would look like, should Wesley approve my theme.

I know some folks would have done a fancy display on their laptop or tablet, but I still liked doing paper presentations. I felt like seeing something on paper made it seem more real and helped people better visualize their events. Plus, it just made it easier for folks to flip back and forth to the pages and points that interested them the most. But I'd also e-mail the information to Wesley when I got back to my office, so he could have an electronic copy as well.

"Now, about the party," I said, starting with my usual pitch. "I came up with an idea for the theme that would reflect the hip vibe. If you could review it now, I would appreciate it. Given the amount of time left, I need to start calling people and finalizing orders today. Even then, I have to warn you that I might not be able to get everything you want."

"That's fine," Wesley said. "This was sort of a spur-of-the-moment thing. Usually, I prefer to act rather than react to business problems, but Octavia O'Hara surprised me."

"You didn't think she'd steal Polish away from you?"

Wesley leaned back in his chair and grinned. "You've done your homework."

I smiled back. "Another bad habit of mine, I'm afraid."

"I'm starting to like your bad habits."

His golden eyes met my green ones. He wasn't even touching me, but tingles swept through my body, and I began to ache once more.

"To answer your question, no," Wesley said. "I didn't think Octavia would get Polish considering the generous offer I made Paul Potter and his family. But this isn't the first time she's bested me. I'm sure it won't be the last."

I stared at him. "You seem to be taking it in stride."

He shrugged. "I've made and lost half a dozen fortunes. Another company always comes along. I just like to upset Octavia whenever I can."

"Why?"

"We dated for a few months a couple years ago. But we weren't a good fit, and things didn't end well. Ever since then, Octavia's gone out of her way to meddle in my business affairs, I suppose as payback for my breaking things off. Trying to buy Polish was a bit of revenge on my part."

Wesley had dated Octavia? My heart quit pounding in my chest. It quit beating—period—and whatever foolish hope I'd harbored in the deepest, darkest corner of my soul crumbled to ash and blew away. Because Octavia was everything I was not—wealthy, sophisticated, gorgeous, and elegant. Why would Wesley ever look twice at me when he'd been with someone like her?

"Abby?" he asked, cutting into my thoughts. "I thought you wanted me to look at your proposal."

I'd twisted the folder into a tight cylinder in my hands. "Of course."

I smoothed out the plastic and handed it to him. Wesley opened the folder and looked through the papers. To my surprise, he actually read my proposal, every single page, instead of just flipping through the sheets the way most of my clients did. While he read, I glanced over my shoulder at Rascal. The puppy had wandered over to the waterfall. He sat at the edge of the pool and stared at it, fascinated by the gurgling water.

After about ten minutes of reading, Wesley glanced up at me. "You put all this together in less than twenty-four hours?"

I shrugged. "It's my job. I don't call my business *A+ Events* for nothing."

"Well, the name fits." Wesley studied me. "This is exactly what I was looking for. The rock theme is brilliant. It will really get the local papers and TV stations buzzing."

More than a little pride pulsed through me. This heady sensation, this warm feeling, was the reason I put up with the problems, hassles, and outright crises. The perfectionist in me enjoyed doing a good job for my clients. It gave me a sense of satisfaction as much as it pleased them when everything went off beautifully.

"I thought you might like it."

"Really? Why?" he asked, drawing his brows together.

"Because—" I clamped my mouth shut.

Because you told me how much you liked music in my apartment. That was the real reason. But I couldn't tell him that. Wesley would realize in an instant I was Wren—and that I knew his secret identity as Talon.

"You just seem a little hipper than some of my other business clients," I finished lamely. "I wouldn't exactly present this to somebody like Milton Moore."

He laughed. "I don't know. Old Milton might get into the swing of things."

"If his ninety-year-old hips would let him."

Wesley laughed again. The bass sound rumbled over me, low, deep, and even more soothing than the splash of the waterfall.

"Well, I think these are marvelous ideas," he said. "Run with them, and remember, whatever you need, I'm more than happy to pay for."

He stretched forward and started to hand the folder to me.

"Oh no," I said, gently pushing it back to him. "That's your copy to keep."

Our fingers brushed. Tingles, tingles everywhere. This time, Wesley seemed to feel something too. He frowned and stared at me, like I'd static shocked him or something. I snatched my hand away from his. After a moment, he pulled back and put the folder on his desk.

"Okay," he said. "Thanks for the hard copy."

"Great. You're welcome," I said, nervous once again. "If you're okay with the theme, I should get going so I can spend some time at the convention center, prepping it for the dinner. Do you need anything else?"

"Of course not," Wesley said. "I think our business is concluded. I'm sure you'll do a marvelous job."

Well, he'd certainly been enthusiastic when he'd called out my name a few nights ago. I suppose that counted as one marvelous job.

"I'm looking forward to seeing how everything turns out," he said. "Please feel free to call if you run into any trouble."

I opened my mouth to say something, but his golden eyes had flicked back to his desk, and he started pulling out photos and papers once more.

Business concluded; I was promptly forgotten once again. I was surprised it had taken him this long to start ignoring me. It was time for Wren to fade into the background—just like always.

I collected Rascal from his perch by the waterfall and said good-bye to Wesley. The businessman gave me an absent wave before he picked up a magnifying glass, flipped over the papers on his desk, and returned to examining them. Whatever he was looking at, it must have interested him because he scribbled down notes on a pad.

I sighed and walked over to the elevator. It arrived with a particularly loud *ping!*, fueling the migraine flaring to life in my brain. I stepped inside and turned around, staring back across the vast space at Wesley, but he was totally absorbed in whatever he was doing. He didn't even glance in my direction as the doors slid shut.

Pain pierced my heart. I'd thought Wesley was different, that Talon was different, but he was the same as the other rich people in Bigtime. Just like Ryan. Wesley didn't see the people who made his life easier. Didn't see the people who worked so hard for him. Didn't see the people who wanted to please him so badly. Who wanted him so desperately.

Wesley "Talon" Weston didn't see me—and he never, ever would.

CHAPTER FOURTEEN

I let myself mope until the elevator opened on the ground floor. Then, I straightened my spine and stormed out because I had a job to do—and a party to plan.

I dug my cell phone and headset out of my vest, plugged them together, and slipped the device in my right ear. While I walked to the convention center, I called my usual suppliers, finalizing the orders I'd dumped on them yesterday. It was tough, but I managed to browbeat and badger everyone into meeting my deadlines—at significantly higher prices. Kyle was positively giddy when I got off the phone with him, mainly because I'd agreed to triple his usual catering fee due to the short notice. But Wesley said money was no object, and I was in a mood to spend some of his right now. Maybe he'd finally pay some attention to me when he got the bill. I barked out a short, humorless laugh and kept walking.

By the time I reached the convention center, I'd nailed down just about everything, from the decorations to the food to the music. Melody Masters, in particular, was more than happy to play the Weston shindig. She wanted the exposure for her band—not to mention the hefty fee.

A couple of men wearing gray coveralls, black boots, and gloves blocked the main entrance to the convention center, standing in front of one of the revolving doors. An open toolbox sat against the smooth stone of the building. Hammers, screwdrivers, and tape measures perched in plastic containers inside. As I walked past, the sun glinted on the head of one of the hammers. I grunted in pain as the light stabbed into my eyes, blinding me.

"Sorry, ma'am," one of the men said, mistaking my grunt for some sort of inquiry. "This door is closed. If you need to get into the center, you'll have to use the entrance farther down the block."

I peered around the guy and realized he and his buddy were measuring the empty frame for a new pane of glass. I winced. I'd forgotten about the door I'd broken on my dash out of the convention center when I'd left Talon here. I made a mental note to give an anonymous donation to the Bigtime Symphony Orchestra. I owed Morris Muzicale that much for wrecking a piece of his convention center.

I walked half a block to the other entrance. Instead of revolving, these doors had handles. I opened one of them, stepped into the massive lobby, and headed for my destination.

Eddie Edgars, the regular guard, sat at his perch behind the security desk. At the scuffle of my shoes on the slick floor, Eddie looked up from his comic book, the latest edition created by Confidante. The cover featured a perfect replica of the mock snowball fight between Wynter and Swifte that SNN had aired earlier in the week. Wynter laughed as she pitched a snowball at Swifte. Confidante could sure churn out her comic books quickly. Then again, the superhero's ability to draw at the speed of light certainly helped.

"Hey, Abby." Eddie waved at me. "What's shaking?"

"Not much. Just here to look over a few things for my next event."

Normally, I would have breezed past Eddie, but Rascal started yipping and squirming. So, I decided to let someone else watch the puppy for a while. Unlike the snotty guard at Wesley's building, I trusted Eddie to take care of Rascal. Besides, Eddie owed me for getting him tickets to the upcoming Fiona Fine fashion show. Like most guys, he had a thing for supermodels.

I opened my coat, plucked Rascal out of my vest pocket, and sat him on top of the counter in front of Eddie.

"A dog? When did you get a dog?" Eddie asked, holding his finger out so Rascal could sniff it.

I grunted again. Why did people keep asking me that? It wasn't like I was Frost, the ubervillain who'd liked to experiment on animals before the Fearless Five put the deep freeze on him.

"Do me a favor. Watch him for me for a few minutes."

"Sure," Eddie said. "No problem. I love dogs."

I left Rascal with Eddie, turned the corner, and strode down the carpeted hallway. I yanked open the door to the stairwell and climbed to the second floor. A minute later, I walked out onto the balcony, staring at the vast space below. It wasn't quite noon, but the Bigtime Symphony Orchestra was hard at work. Musicians sat on stage, instruments dangling from their hands, as they chatted and gossiped. A short, thin man with a bald head stood in front of them, rapping on a metal podium with a baton and trying to get their attention.

"People! People! How many times have I said you should always conduct yourselves professionally whenever you're on stage?" Morris Muzicale bellowed at his musicians. "Even when you don't have an audience."

"But we do have an audience," one of the cellists contradicted. "Abby's here. Hi, Abby."

The cellist and his cohorts waved to me. Cellists. Always so cheeky.

I lifted my hand in salute. Most of the musicians knew me because I came by at least once a week to check on arrangements for my latest event. I'd done more than a few of their weddings, anniversaries, and birthday parties too.

Morris, the esteemed director of the orchestra, looked over his shoulder. Even though several hundred feet separated us, I could feel his glare—and see it in remarkable detail thanks to my enhanced eyesight.

"Yes, well, Miss Appleby *hardly* qualifies as an audience."

"So you're saying we don't have to act professionally then?" the same cellist piped up.

A few of his colleagues snickered. I could hear Morris's sigh loud and clear, even up here in the nosebleed section. I'd once suggested to Morris that the orchestra should mix up its repertoire, play some rock operas or something a little livelier than Bach, Beethoven, and other songs by old, dead white guys. His face had turned purple, his eyes had bulged and twitched, and a vein beat like a tambourine in his temple. Morris had been so insulted I'd thought he was going to have a heart attack on the spot.

Morris gave me another hard stare, then turned back to the orchestra. He tapped his long baton on top of the stand. "From the top, ladies and gentlemen…"

While the orchestra played Mozart's "Eine Kleine Nachtmusik," I pulled a notepad and pen out of my vest and paced from one side of the balcony to the other, making crude drawings of where everything would go. I did the same thing for every event, visualizing the decorations, the flowers, the food, the placement of each and every little thing. The rough sketches helped pinpoint potential trouble spots. I had enough crises pop up by themselves. I tried to do everything I could to limit the avoidable ones.

We'd have to pull the auditorium seats out and bring up the hidden parquet floor for the dancing. Standard operating procedure. The long, narrow orchestra pit would be converted into the bar as usual. That was where I'd put the ice sculptures, and let the bartenders use it to cool some of their supplies. It would be fun and functional. Wesley might be free and easy with his money, but I liked to give my clients plenty of bang for their buck.

Water sloshed in a bucket, and the scent of bleach mixed with cigarette smoke drifted over me—a harsh but familiar smell.

I looked over my shoulder. Colt Colton used a long-handled mop to push a yellow bucket along the balcony toward me.

"Hey, Abby. Party planning again already?" Colt asked, yanking his mop out of the water and slapping it against the floor.

"Don't you know it. Big shindig set for Friday night."

There wasn't really anything else to say, and we both quieted. Colt mopped away the sticky film of spilled soda that always seemed to cover the floor, while I continued to plan. After a few minutes, I tuned out the *splash* of his waterlogged mop. I didn't even notice that he'd finished until I felt him staring at me.

"Did you need something, Colt?"

He leaned on his mop. "Actually, I wanted to ask you a question."

"Really? What?" I said, scribbling more notes on the pad. Maybe I should get three ice sculptures, one for each end of the bar and the center, too—

Colt cleared his throat. I kept writing. He cleared it again, and it dawned on me that he wanted my full, complete, and undivided attention. I looked up from my notes.

"I'm sorry. Too much to do, too little time. What did you want to ask me?"

"Well, we've known each other a while now, Abby." Colt stared at me, his eyes dark in the shadows.

"Yeah..." I replied, not sure where he was going. The only thing I could think of was maybe Colt wanted some extra work and was going to ask me to get him a gig as one of Kyle's waiters. I'd be happy to do that for him, given how many times he'd helped me out with various problems at my events.

"Well, I was wondering if you'd like to go out sometime. Get some dinner, watch a movie. Maybe tonight?"

I opened my mouth, but no sound came out. Go out? With Colt Colton? The thought had never crossed my mind. He was just another cog in the Bigtime society wheel like me, a guy I said hello to but didn't think about otherwise. Truth be told, Colt was as invisible to me as I was to the Bigtime society folks.

So I looked at him—*really* looked at him. He was taller than I'd realized, and a pair of faded, gray coveralls covered his body. It was the same uniform the other maintenance personnel at the convention center wore, but he filled it out well, with broad, powerful shoulders and a solid chest. A bit on the long side, his black hair was pulled back into a low ponytail, while his face was pale from spending so much time indoors. He had a perfect, straight nose and lips that would have been more at home on a model than a custodian. Colt wasn't unattractive. Actually, he was rather handsome.

"Abby?" he asked.

I looked at him again—*really* looked at him.

And realized Colt's eyes were dark brown, almost black, instead of golden. His smile full-on, instead of self-mocking and wry. His voice raspy, instead of a deep rumble I could feel in my toes.

Colt Colton wasn't Wesley Weston. He wasn't Talon—and I just wasn't in the mood.

"Um, actually, I'm sort of getting over a bad relationship right now." It wasn't exactly a lie. Getting over one-night stands could be tough, depending on how much you'd had to drink.

"And I have an event tonight. At the library. I'm sorry." I added the last part because it seemed like the thing to do. I didn't want to be cruel. Not like Ryan had been to me.

Not a flicker of emotion showed on Colt's face. No anger flared in his eyes. No embarrassment colored his cheeks. His breathing pattern didn't change. His heart didn't speed up.

Instead, he shrugged. "Suit yourself."

Colt straightened, took hold of his mop, and pushed his bucket over to the service elevator. He stepped inside and turned around. Just before the doors closed, Colt's eyes met mine. He smiled, his teeth flashing like pearls in his face. It was an innocent smile. Just a colleague silently saying good-bye to another.

But for some reason, it made me shiver.

CHAPTER FIFTEEN

I made a few more notes, collected Rascal from Eddie, and headed to the office. Chloe rocketed out of her chair the moment the elevator opened, briefing me on the library dedication. She'd also had the foresight to bring me a cheeseburger and fries from Quicke's. My nose twitched, and my stomach rumbled at the hot, greasy aroma. Maybe I really should consider giving Chloe a promotion.

We chatted for a few minutes about the library dedication. It was the first of many events to be held in Berkley Brighton's honor, and I wanted to make sure everything was perfect. Surprise, surprise.

"It sounds like you've got everything under control. Why don't you see it through to the end?"

Chloe's eyes widened. "You're letting me run point on this?" Her voice hovered dangerously close to squeal territory.

I winced. "Most of the work's already been done. Let's see how you do at handling the last-minute details. That's when you really have to think on your feet. You still want that promotion, don't you?"

She nodded.

"Well then, do a good job tonight, and I'll consider it some more."

Chloe held her arms out wide and started to come around the desk.

I snapped up my hand and stopped her. "No—*no* hugging."

Chloe looked a little put out by my refusal to be all girly-girl affectionate, but she got over it and started making phone calls. I grabbed the bag with the sandwich from Quicke's and went into my office.

I took off my coat and put Rascal on the floor. The puppy trotted over to his water bowl and lapped up half of it. I ripped open the Quicke's bag, unwrapped the cellophane covering the burger, and dumped the fries on the paper next to it. I closed my eyes, leaned over my feast, and breathed in, letting the wonderful aromas assault my senses. Grilled beef. Poppy seed bun. Sharp Cheddar cheese. Extra tomatoes. A dollop of mayonnaise. Blue cheese dressing for my fries.

I was just about to sink my teeth into the burger when a whine sounded. A small, pitiful, *can-I-please-please-please-have-a-bite-of-that?* whine. The one that was like nails shooting into my skull. The one that was like a cheese grinder on my heart. The one that made me feel guilty. The one that was rapidly turning me into spineless mush.

I peered over the side of the desk. Rascal perched next to my shoe. Ears tall. Eyes big. Tiny tail whipping back and forth.

"You cannot possibly be hungry given all the puppy chow you've eaten today."

Rascal whined again and leaned into my leg, pleading with me.

"All right," I muttered. "I'll pet you, but that's it. You're not getting my food."

The puppy barked, knowing he'd gotten the better end of the deal.

That afternoon, I left the office around three to get ready for the Berkley Brighton dedication. Chloe might be in charge, but I was going to be there to supervise. On the way home, I swung by Paw-Paw's Pet Emporium and bought a collar and leash for Rascal. My next stop was Stan's Steamers Dry Cleaners so I could pick up my black coat. Another surprise waited for me besides the exorbitant bill.

"We found this in the pocket. Figured you forgot to take it out." The cashier handed me a silver flash drive.

I frowned and took the drive from him. It couldn't possibly be mine. The ones I used at the office were blue and all had *A+ Events* engraved on them—then I remembered. It was the drive that had fallen out of Talon's belt the night Bandit shot him. The one I'd picked up out of the snow and stuffed into my pocket. I'd forgotten about it. I wondered what was on it, and if Talon even realized he was missing it. Was he looking for it? Maybe I'd slip it on Wesley's desk if I went to his office again.

"Thanks," I said, stuffing the flash drive into my coat pocket once more.

I left Stan's, went to my loft, and took a quick shower. I brushed out my hair, put on some minty lip gloss, and dug through my piles of unpacked clothes until I came up with a sky-blue camisole silk top, navy pants, and matching jacket, not unlike the outfit I'd worn to the O'Hara party. I had a fair number of dark-colored suits in my closet for a variety of occasions. Even I knew better than to wear cargo pants and a flannel shirt to a formal event, even if I stayed behind the scenes most of the time.

Then, it was time to put on my vest of the evening—my

Serious Vest. The black vest looked like the others in my closest, but it contained its own unique set of supplies, ones that came in handy at more somber occasions. Most of the items were of the female persuasion, eye makeup remover, unused tubes of mascara, and tissues. *Lots* of tissues. People usually made with the waterworks at dedications, because nobody in this town got anything dedicated to them unless they were dead, like Berkley. With waterworks came runny mascara and ruined makeup, which the Bigtime society queens always hurried to fix. Folks also tended to be a little more restrained at dedications—at least until the food and booze started flowing.

I looked at my watch. Just after five. The fundraiser wouldn't officially start until six thirty, but I was always the first person at my events. Although Chloe was technically handling things, I wanted to get the lay of the land. Just because I was letting her take the lead didn't mean I wouldn't step in if things got out of hand.

I slipped the new collar and leash on Rascal, flagged down a cab, and hopped inside. The taxi deposited me in front of the Bigtime Public Library just before six. To my surprise, Chloe was already there, supervising a couple of workers stringing a banner above the front entrance that read *Book 'em, Chief! Reading drive kicks off tonight.*

In addition to dedicating part of its space to Berkley, the library was hosting a fundraiser and contest to get patrons to read more. This year, the library decided to partner with the police force to get the word out. The centerpiece of the event was a mock jail where folks could bide their time and drink champagne until one of their buddies paid their *bail.* In other words, wrote the library a hefty check. I thought it was rather ridiculous, but that was what the library's board of directors wanted. The cops, particularly Chief of Police Sean Newman, had loved the idea. Evidently, they relished the chance to slap handcuffs on some of Bigtime's wealthier citizens, something they didn't get to do very often.

The dedication and subsequent fundraiser was one of the smaller events I'd done in recent weeks, which was why I'd decided to let Chloe handle it. Only about two hundred people had been invited, as Joanne had wanted to keep things small and intimate, at least for the dedication. But there were still a hundred details needing attention—like making sure a certain superhero showed up on time.

Once the guys finished hanging the banner, I grabbed Chloe and took her aside. Expecting the grilling, she looked at me calmly and serenely, as though everything was fine. She'd even brought along a clipboard, probably to prove to me that she'd done everything that needed doing.

"Food?" I asked in a tense voice.

"The hors d'oeuvres and champagne will start circulating in thirty minutes, just as the doors officially open."

"Decorations?"

"All of the lights and greenery have been strung up, and the plastic bars for the jail have been erected," Chloe said. "The banner announcing the Brighton dedication should be hung any second now."

"Guests?"

"I've gotten RSVPs from everyone, and we've already had some people show up. They're clustered next to the jail." Chloe gave me a look. "Don't worry, Abby. I know you put me in charge because this wasn't a huge event, but you don't have to worry. I've double- and triple-checked everything. It's going to be fine."

"And Fiera?" I asked, saving the toughest and most important question for last.

Chloe chewed her lip. "Her, I don't know about. She's the only thing I haven't been able to confirm. I haven't seen her anywhere. I was just getting ready to call her."

"Let me."

I whipped out my cell phone and pushed a button, speed-dialing the contact number I'd been given for Fiera and other members of the Fearless Five. In addition to being the city's most powerful superhero team, the Fearless Five were the most popular. *Everybody* wanted the heroes to appear at their events. They got so many requests they'd set up a hot line where people could call and leave messages with dates and details. Even then, the superheroes were always booked weeks, if not months, in advance.

I hit send. Something clicked, and a mechanized voice told me to punch the number that corresponded to the superhero I wished to contact. I punched in 5 for Fiera. A second later, a phone rang just outside the library doors. Chloe couldn't hear it, but I did. "Light My Fire" by The Doors blared out. A good song and a great ring tone. At least I approved of Fiera's taste in music, if not her punctuality. I ended the call without waiting for her to pick up.

"What?" Chloe asked. "What is it? Why did you hang up?"

"Because she's here."

Fiera pulled the front door of the library open so hard I thought she would rip it off its hinges. In addition to having a fiery personality, the superhero was stronger than ten men put together. Sure enough, she clutched a small cell phone in her hand. The metal case looked mushy, like it was slowly melting. Her blue eyes flicked over the entryway, resting on Chloe and me. Fiera flounced over to us, a bit of smoke puffing off her body.

"Did you just try to call me?" she asked.

"Yes," I replied and made a point of looking at my watch. "You're late. You were supposed to be here at six, not six fifteen."

"Well, I would have been on time, but I had to pull a guy out of a wrecked car over on Thirteenth Street. Forgive me for stopping to save someone's life. But I'm here now, so don't get your panties in a wad, Abby."

The fiery superhero crossed her arms over her chest and looked at me. Fiera was a tall woman with the stereotypical superhero physique—long hair, big breasts, and legs that went on forever, all poured into a body-hugging, orange-red spandex suit. Fiera also was the main attraction tonight. The superhero was here to help the cops take people to *jail* and encourage them to read more.

I would have preferred to have Karma Girl, or even Mr. Sage, but Fiera had been the one who'd called me back and said she'd show up. Because they got so many requests, the Fearless Five took turns doing public events, and I'd been unlucky enough to get stuck with her. I was a little nervous at the thought of Fiera around books. Having the library go up in flames would not be good for business. Besides, I'd already had one disastrous run-in with a superhero this week. I wasn't ready for another.

"You know what you're supposed to do?" I asked.

Fiera tossed her blond hair over her shoulder. A few sparks shot out from the ends. "Of course, I know what I'm supposed to do. I *am* a professional superhero, after all. This isn't the first dog-and-pony show I've been to, Abby. Don't worry. I'll make nice with the civilians."

"And," I prompted, "I specifically put it in the contract."

Fiera rolled her blue eyes. "And I won't set anything in the library on fire."

"And?"

She sighed. "Or anything else within a two-block radius until the event is over."

I nodded. "Good."

"Even though everyone would have a lot more fun if I did," she muttered.

If there was one group of people who were even more temperamental and demanding than society debutantes, it was superheroes. I glared at Fiera, and she stared right back at me. Her gaze then dropped to my side, where Rascal sat. The smoky superhero fascinated the pint-sized puppy. Curiosity filled his brown eyes, and his pointy ears perched on high alert.

"Aw! What a cute little dog!" Fiera said, dropping to her knees and holding out her hand.

I winced as her voice pierced my skull. Rascal sniffed her carefully, confused by the smoke drifting up from her body. But once he realized Fiera wasn't going to burn him, he was more than happy to let her scratch his tummy.

"When did you get a dog?" Fiera asked.

I might as well stamp the details on my forehead. Maybe then people would quit asking me *that* particular question in *that* particular tone of voice.

"A few days ago. He's up for adoption, if you want him," I said. "Maybe the Fearless Five could add a mascot to the team. You seem to have everything else already."

Fiera's eyes narrowed at my words, but she kept petting Rascal. I started to open my mouth to say something else catty to her, but Chloe cut me off.

"Ms. O'Hara, how nice to see you again," Chloe said, elbowing me in the side.

Octavia O'Hara strolled over to our group. Octavia might have been all business at the merger dinner a few nights ago, but she was ready to party tonight. She wore a long, green gown accented with crimson trim. The bright colors enhanced the bronze beauty of her flawless skin. A slit ran halfway up her thigh, exposing a very shapely leg, while the neck of the garment dipped into a severe V, showing a healthy amount of cleavage. Octavia's black hair flowed like water around her shoulders, and her dark eyes practically smoldered.

A rare bit of envy stabbed my heart. Octavia looked gorgeous. I could see why she'd caught Wesley's eye. I could just picture the two of them together. They'd be the perfect couple— rich, powerful, beautiful. I fingered the edge of my vest. Octavia was a real nightingale, and I felt more like a wren than ever.

"Abby, Chloe. I wanted to come over and tell you again how wonderful the merger announcement turned out," Octavia said. "It truly was a night to remember—in all sorts of ways."

I wondered what Octavia would say if she knew I was planning a similar event for Wesley and that I was going to outdo what I'd done for her in less than a week. She'd find out soon enough and probably dump me as a client, but I'd cross that bridge when I came to it.

Chloe nudged me in the side again, reminding me that I really should respond when people spoke.

"Thank you, Octavia." I tried to smile. "We appreciate that."

"It was our pleasure, really," Chloe's smile went off a lot better than mine did.

Nice save. Chloe really was serious about getting that promotion, and I just might let her have it if she kept up the good work.

Octavia started to respond, but Rascal barked at her. It wasn't his usual *you're-a-new-person-want-to-pet-pet-pet-me?* bark. No, this time, the dog's voice dropped to a growl. Fiera sank her fingers into his fur, almost like she was keeping him from latching on to Octavia's ankle. I stared at the corgi. I'd never seen Rascal growl at anyone. He might be annoyingly precocious, but he really was a sweet, even-tempered dog. I wondered at the sudden change.

Octavia looked at me, then at Fiera and Rascal, then back at me. Evidently, she wasn't a dog lover, because she didn't squeal and tell Rascal exactly how cute he was. In fact, she took great pains to step around him, not even letting her crimson stilettos come within a foot of the puppy.

"Whose...*animal* is that? And why is it in the library?" Octavia asked, her nostrils twitching in disgust.

Anger surged through me, replacing the hot jealousy. I might be stuck with Rascal, but that didn't give Octavia the right to insult him, especially because I'd busted my ass for her not more than a week ago and had gotten puke all over my shoes for my trouble.

"*His* name is Rascal, and he's *mine*. He's a stray I'm trying to find a home for." My voice could have sharpened knives.

"I see." So could Octavia's.

We stood there toe-to-toe. Octavia sneered down her nose at me. I had to curl my hands into fists to keep from reaching for my stun gun. Chloe looked back and forth between the two of us.

"Well," Octavia said. "I should be getting inside. Abby, Chloe, Fiera. Lovely to see you all again."

"You too, Octavia," I muttered.

Octavia shot one last look at Rascal, who was still growling, before moving into the library.

"I don't think she'll be calling you to plan her next party," Fiera said, letting go of Rascal and getting to her feet.

"Right now, I don't care."

"Abby!" Chloe gasped. "You don't mean that!"

"Yes, I do," I muttered. "Rich types. They're all the same. You do one little thing they don't approve of, and you get on their hit list. How was I supposed to know Octavia doesn't like dogs?"

"But you're Abby Appleby, event planner to the stars," Fiera said. "Isn't it your job to know?"

It was my job to know, just like it was my job to keep everyone happy, just like it was my job to go into the library and make nice with Octavia. But I wasn't in the mood to do any of those things. For some reason, all I wanted to do right now was pet Rascal.

So, I picked up the puppy and snuggled him against my chest. Rascal let out a much happier bark and licked me. For some reason, the gentle scrape of his tongue against my chin comforted me.

"Good boy," I murmured, scratching his ears. "Good boy."

CHAPTER SIXTEEN

More people arrived, including Sam Sloane, Devlin Dash, and Bella Bulluci. Carmen Cole with *The Exposé* and Kelly Caleb from SNN also showed up to cover the event. Making nice with Octavia moved to the bottom of my list of priorities.

I took Rascal to the break room for the library staff. That was where the food was being delivered from Quicke's before being put on silver trays and served to the guests. I tied Rascal to a table in an out-of-the-way spot twenty feet from the platters. Kyle gave the puppy a dish of water and promised to keep an eye on him while I worked the dedication and party.

The main library floor had been largely cleared of bookshelves, and rows of cushioned folding chairs had been set up before a podium. A banner behind the podium read *Bigtime's favorite son—We'll always remember you, Berkley*. Off to the right, plastic bars ringed a fifty-foot-long case of crime books, comprising the *jail* where people would spend their time later tonight. Waiters circulated through the glittering crowd bearing the requisite glasses of champagne so everyone could get a little buzz on to get through the speeches that would make up the dedication.

Everything was perfect except for one thing—Joanne, Berkley's widow, was a no-show. And there were only two minutes, thirteen seconds left until the dedication was supposed to start.

"I'm going to call her again," I said to Chloe and headed to the lobby.

She nodded, her face pale. I felt sorry for her. Everything else had been going so well, and now this. But Chloe had to learn you could never take anything for granted—not even your guest of honor showing up at her own event.

I yanked my cell phone out of my vest and glanced at my watch. Fifty-nine seconds left. I'd just punched in the first number when the door swished open. Joanne strolled inside, a pair of sunglasses masking her eyes, even though it was pitch-black outside. To my surprise, Jasper followed her in. For once, my neighbor wore a snazzy gray trench coat and suit. With his glasses and the diamond twinkling in his ear, he looked quite handsome. I smiled at Jasper, who tipped his head in response.

Then I turned to Joanne. "You're late."

Joanne raised a black eyebrow. She took her time pulling off her lavender coat and glasses.

"Guests of honor are not supposed to be late to their own events."

"I'm not the guest of honor," she snapped. "Berkley is—and he's dead. What are you going to do? Dig him up and wheel him in here?"

Her words and tone were harsh, but the telltale glint of tears gleamed in her eyes. I winced. She had a point. Sometimes, I forgot Joanne still grieved for her husband underneath the hard, brittle, polished exterior. Sometimes, I think everyone forgot.

Jasper put a comforting hand on his sister's shoulder, but she shook it off and lasered him with a hard stare.

"Just because we're speaking again is no reason to get all emotional on me, Jasper. I'm fine."

To prove her point, Joanne tossed back her head, strolled through the rows of chairs and people, and slid into her seat just as the lights dimmed. I checked my watch. Five seconds later, a retrospective of Berkley's life cued up on the film screen behind the podium.

"Sorry about that," Jasper whispered, coming to stand beside me. "She still misses him terribly."

"It's okay," I said. "I'm used to the temper tantrums. Joanne is actually one of my calmer clients."

"Seriously?" he asked.

"Seriously."

Jasper gave me a sympathetic look.

After the film ended, various library officials gushed on about the good they were going to do with Berkley's twenty-five-million-dollar donation. Joanne looked bored by the whole thing, examining her nails through the speeches, but her eyes got misty again when the officials unveiled the solidium plaque engraved with Berkley's name.

Once the tribute ended, it was time to move on to the second part of the evening—the library fundraiser. Fiera did her usual volatile superhero routine, strong-arming men into the faux jail and threatening to smack them around with the long arm of the law if they didn't straighten up. Everyone seemed to enjoy her shtick while they gobbled up spicy chicken and pineapple kebabs and bite-size cucumber-and-cream-cheese sandwiches shaped like books. With all the men and a few of the women clamoring to have Fiera escort them back to jail numerous times, the library received several hefty *bail* donations from Bigtime's wealthier citizens.

Including Wesley Weston.

The rugged businessman showed up just as the dedication ended—and he wasn't alone. A breathtaking brunette who wasn't any bigger around than a kebab skewer stuck to his arm like glue. She wore a glamorous fuchsia dress that showed off every inch of her perfect figure. I stood against the wall and watched them. Wesley murmured something into her ear. The brunette laughed and snuggled closer to him. He took her hand and smiled.

My heart lurched. I would have traded places with her in a second. But she was another nightingale, just like Octavia. And I was nothing but a—no, not a wren. Not even that. Wallpaper. I was wallpaper. Everybody walked by me; nobody noticed me.

For the first time in my life, I wished I wasn't wearing my vest. That I could just enjoy the event. Laugh, talk, drink, and not worry about whether I'd ordered enough food or if the shrimp rolls would make everyone sick. But I couldn't do that. I was the party planner, not a partygoer. This was my event, and I had a responsibility to make sure it was perfect.

So I went into the kitchen and told the caterers to start circulating the cream puffs in the next forty-two seconds, as they were supposed to—or else. Kyle took the brunt of my assault, but yelling at him made me feel a little better.

Once I'd made myself hoarse, I stomped back out onto the library floor. My eyes flicked over the crowd, but I didn't see Wesley anywhere. His brunette date was chatting up Milton Moore at the bar, although she was having a hard time flirting while his two nurses checked the elderly billionaire's oxygen tank.

It was for the best, I decided. I'd done nothing but stare at Wesley all night. It wasn't doing me any good, and I certainly didn't need to start thinking about his alter ego, Talon, again. That would only make me start wishing other things were possible, things that could never be. Like Wesley seeing me for who I really was—and actually liking me. Supersenses, anal retentiveness, freakish tendencies, warts, and all.

Chloe hovered next to a potted palm near the faux jail. I went over to her.

"I'm taking a break."

Her hazel eyes widened. "But you never take breaks during an event," Chloe said, dropping her voice to an awed whisper. "*Never.*"

I shrugged. "Well, this is your event. You can handle the crises for a change."

"Abby, are you okay?" she asked. "You don't sound like yourself. You haven't all week."

My gaze strayed back to Wesley's bombshell brunette. "I'm just a little tired, that's all. I'll be back in a few minutes. Call my cell if you need me."

I could feel Chloe's eyes on my back as I moved through the crowd toward the elevator. I rode it up to the library's top floor, wincing as the doors *pinged!* open. I'd disabled the annoying sound three weeks ago, right before the library's Christmas party. Usually it took the maintenance men at least six weeks to restore the noise, which was why I hadn't bothered to check it before the dedication. Evidently, they'd upped their timetable.

I stepped onto the library floor and walked past the reference section with its movable bookcases and computer stations. Normally, college students clustered up here, reading boring, obscure texts and sneaking off to have sex in the stacks when they thought no one was looking. Because the library had closed early for the fundraiser, the area was deserted. Just the way I wanted it to be.

Spotlights here and there provided a bit of dim illumination. I strolled along the glass wall overlooking the library's indoor garden until I found an easy chair hidden in the shadows. I sank into it, cracked my neck, put my head back, and rubbed my temples. All the laughter, squeals, and commotion had made my head ache, despite the superstrength aspirin I'd taken before the party. The elevator's annoying *ping!* had pushed my typical dull headache into pounding migraine territory. Well that, and seeing Wesley with another woman.

I growled, a low sound that could have come out of Rascal's throat. What did I think was going to happen? That Wesley, that Talon, would swear off all women but me? As if. Wesley was rich, attractive, and single. He wasn't going to stop living his life—or stop seeing the ladies—just because his G-man superhero alter ego had a one-night stand. Just wishing such a thing, daring to dream it was possible, made me more pathetic than I already was.

I sank lower in the chair. I'd told Chloe I'd be back in five minutes, but I was stretching it out to fifteen. Maybe even a full half hour. Maybe by then Wesley and his perfect date would have left.

A whisper of wool caught my ear, and the smell of crisp mint filled my nose. I didn't know whether to howl with frustration or sigh with contentment.

"I see I'm not the only one who needed some quiet time," a deep voice rumbled.

Wesley stepped out of the shadows in front of me. His brown hair gleamed under the dim spotlights. Stubble darkened his face, but his eyes glimmered like pure gold. Tonight, he wore a navy suit that framed his body to perfection. My eyes traced his long torso, pausing at his left shoulder and the bullet wound hidden underneath the thick cloth. I wondered how it was healing—and what his date would think of it and his other scars. Would she be repulsed? Or find them as sexy as I had?

Sexy, I decided. Talon had been right when he'd said chicks dig scars.

"Hello, Abby," Wesley said. "I didn't realize you'd planned this party too."

"I plan every party that's any party in Bigtime." I gave him a wan smile.

He frowned. "Are you okay? You look a bit pale."

"It's nothing. Just a headache. All the noise has gotten to me tonight."

"I know what you mean. Bigtime parties can be rather overwhelming, can't they?"

I caught another whiff of his clean scent. He smelled *so* good. All I wanted to do was bury my face in his neck and drink in his fresh aroma. Wesley was the one overwhelming me, but I couldn't tell him that.

"Yes, they can be."

Desperate for something to do, I unzipped one of the pockets on my vest and fished out some aspirin and my small water bottle.

"I've been meaning to ask you about that vest you wear," Wesley said. "I noticed it the first time we met in your office."

I'd noticed how muscular he was. How wonderful he smelled. How his golden eyes caught the light. He'd noticed my vest. In a way, that was worse than being invisible.

I washed the pills down with the water. "Why's that?"

My vest started quite a few conversations, especially with new clients. It horrified some of them, particularly the fashion designers like Fiona Fine and Bella Bulluci. Others demanded I stock my vest with certain pharmaceutical supplies in case they needed a quick hit of something. One particularly prominent businessman even asked me if I was a professional fly fisherman on the sly.

Piper had been bugging me about my vest for years, insisting that I should let Fiona make me a couple more fashionable versions, but I'd refused. My vest was perfect for what I needed it to do, and I liked it just the way it was.

I stared down at the black fabric with its zippers, pockets, and hidden compartments, comparing it to the fuchsia dress the brunette wore. At least, I used to like my vest just the way it was, before Wesley had swooped in and wreaked havoc on my life.

"I don't know everything you have in there, but I think it's exceedingly clever," Wesley said. "And I very much like clever things, practical things. I imagine you could survive in the jungle for days with just your vest."

His eyes shimmered in his face, and a half smile curved his mouth. I couldn't tell if he was mocking me or not. Somehow, I didn't think he was.

I thought of Wesley's—of Talon's—superhero suit, of his grappling hook gun and electro-shock visor. Maybe we had more in common than I'd thought. Not that it mattered. Because at the end of the night, Wesley and his impeccable business suit would still be going home with a fuchsia dress, not a plain black vest—no matter how clever he thought it was.

Depressed, I wanted to get as far away from Wesley as I could. I leapt out of the chair, and the sudden change in elevation made my head spin. I swayed back and forth, spots flashing in front of my eyes.

"Easy," he said, reaching out a hand to steady me. "Easy, Abby."

I jerked away before he could touch me. My knees hit the chair, and I almost fell back into it before righting myself at the last second. I put my hand against the glass wall to steady myself. Clumsy, clumsy.

"That must be one killer headache," Wesley said. "Can I help you? Get you anything?"

My stomach clenched into a hard knot. What he could get me was another night like the one I'd had with Talon. What he could get me was a guy who listened to me like Talon had. What he could get me was himself. But that wasn't going to happen. The sooner I accepted that, the better.

"I'm fine. In fact, I should be getting back downstairs." The white spots faded to gray, and I pushed away from the wall. "Before something goes wrong."

"What could go wrong?" he asked. "Everything was perfect when I left."

"Perfect," I muttered. "Yeah, everything's always perfect when I'm around."

Wesley cocked his head to one side, as if he didn't quite understand what I was trying to say. I wasn't sure I knew either. All I wanted was to get away from him.

I hurried back to the elevator and pushed the call button. Wesley followed, the fabric of his suit rubbing together as he walked. The doors *pinged!* open. I winced at the sharp noise, stepped inside, and turned to face him.

"Are you coming?" I asked.

Wesley shook his head. He stood there in front of the open doors staring at me. He frowned, and as his eyes darkened, I jabbed the button for the first floor, avoiding his gaze. I didn't look up until the doors closed.

When I was alone again, I slumped against the cold, metal wall and fought the tears forming in my eyes.

I used the elevator ride to pull myself together. By the time the doors opened on the first floor, I'd almost convinced myself everything was fine.

That I wasn't pining for a guy I'd never get. That I didn't want him to look at me, to notice me, and like what he saw more than anything else.

That I wasn't halfway in love with him.

I stepped out of the elevator. The laughter, conversation, and rattle of silverware felt like a drill boring into my skull. If anything, the dedication had gotten louder since I'd been upstairs. I checked my watch. After ten already, and the party was still in full swing, but I was ready to call it a night, no matter how many disasters might be in the making. I found Chloe in the break room, petting Rascal.

"Hey, Abby!" Chloe leapt to her feet as if I'd caught her with her hand in the cookie jar. "I know you said he'd be fine back here, but he looked so pitiful just sitting there and then he started whining..."

I stared at the puppy. Rascal yipped and let his tongue hang out of his mouth. If that wasn't a devilish expression, I didn't know what was.

"Don't worry about it. I'll take care of him from here on out since I'm going home."

"Home?" Chloe looked me up and down. "You're going home?"

I nodded.

"You're leaving?" she squealed. "Now?"

I rubbed my temples. "If you don't shatter my eardrums, I am."

She threw her hands up in the air. "But the benefit isn't even over yet. And you never, *ever* leave before an event is over. That's when disaster strikes. Remember how many times you've told me that?"

I nodded. "I do, and I don't care right now. My head is about to split in two."

"But—but—I've *never* handled an entire event," Chloe sputtered, panic clear in every syllable.

I put my hand on her shoulder. "You'll do fine. Give it another hour, and the party will start winding down. Kyle and his staff will take care of the mess like they always do. Just make sure everyone is sober enough to get into their limo. Okay?"

Chloe let out a breath and nodded.

"All right, then. Good night, and good luck," I said.

I retrieved my black coat, pulled on my gloves, hat, and scarf, and wrapped Rascal's leash around my hand. I didn't want to walk through the boisterous party again, so I slipped out the side door. Rascal huffed with contentment as we stepped into the chilly night air. The puppy seemed to be just as happy to get away from the noise and lights as I was.

After the puppy did his business, I scooped him up and tucked him inside my coat. He licked my chin in thanks. I wrinkled my nose at his bad breath, but it didn't bother me as much as usual.

The snow might have done a disappearing act, but so had the people who'd crowded into the streets earlier today. I relished the quiet darkness after the noise of the party. A few taxis cruised by looking for late-night fares, but I tucked my chin into my coat and kept going. I liked walking. It gave me time to unwind after a long, hard day—and a chance to convince myself that I had to get over this obsession with Wesley. Nothing was ever going to come of it, and I needed to realize that before I did something supremely stupid—like tell him I was the mysterious Wren.

I was so wrapped up in my thoughts I reached my block before I knew it. To my surprise, a black limo idled in front of my building. I'd just stepped onto my street when a shadow detached itself from a doorway up ahead. At first, I thought it was just some guy stopping to have a late-night cigarette.

Then, he turned and walked in my direction.

I slowed my steps, but I didn't stop walking. Instead, I moved to the edge of the sidewalk so I wouldn't have to get within arm's reach of him. I also reached through the slits in my coat and unzipped the pocket holding my stun gun. I might like walking home at night, but I wasn't careless. Granny Cane and Grandpa Pain couldn't apprehend every mugger in the city.

The guy was about fifty feet from me when a car drove by. The glare from its headlights seared my eyes, destroying my night vision. I squinted and kept walking. By the time I blinked the spots away, the guy stood in front of me. Black leather duster, silver-tipped cowboy boots, guns in the holster around his lean waist, a bandana covering the bottom half of his face.

The sight of him made my blood run cold.

"Hello, Abby," Bandit said.

CHAPTER SEVENTEEN

I froze. Bandit on my block. On my street. Talking to me. Calling me by name. Not good. So not good.

"Um, hello," I said in the calmest voice I could muster. One should always avoid being rude to ubervillains if one wanted to keep breathing.

I clutched Rascal to my chest with one hand. With the other, I reached into my vest pocket and curled my fingers around my stun gun. Not that it would do much damage against the ubervillain. If I could somehow manage to use it before he just killed me.

Despite the disasters I'd faced at my events, I'd never been confronted by an ubervillain—not once. I didn't think I had anything that would slow Bandit down, much less save me from getting shot. My vest contained many, many things. Unfortunately, Kevlar was not one of them. But I was definitely splurging for it the next time I went to Oodles o' Stuff.

"You have something that belongs to me," Bandit drawled. He jerked his thumb over his finger, pointing at the limo. "Or rather to my employer, Tycoon. And I want it back. Now."

My eyes flicked to the car. Something red dangled from the rearview mirror, something that seemed to have a familiar, heart-like shape to it, but that was all I could make out. Even with my enhanced vision, I couldn't see who was inside through the metal of the car—and I didn't want to. Tycoon was notorious for keeping his identity a secret. Rumors said only a handful of people knew who the mob boss really was, and his anonymity allowed him to stay in business and avoid being busted by Chief Sean Newman. If I saw Tycoon's face, I might as well just shoot myself instead of waiting for Bandit to do it.

"I have something that belongs to Tycoon?" I said, confused.

Bandit nodded, his dark hair falling forward. The moonlight hit his face, highlighting the black-and-white, paisley pattern in the bandana tied around his face. It only added to his sinister air.

"There must be some mistake. I don't have anything of yours. Or his. I've never met you before. Never even seen you before. Well, not in person anyway."

Like most ubervillains, Bandit occasionally appeared on SNN hawking his latest merchandise. The ubervillain also held illegal camps where people could go play cowboys for a day—complete with real duels using real guns and real bullets. And, of course, Bandit made the news whenever he evaded the police or superheroes during high-speed car chases. A couple of weeks ago, he and Pistol Pete, the gun-loving superhero, shot up the street outside Oodles o' Stuff when they both went in to buy some supplies at the same time.

"That's where you're wrong, Abby." Bandit's voice sounded low, hard, and cold, despite the way he drawled out his words. "I know you have it. It wasn't in your apartment or at the convention center. So, you must have it on you."

My apartment? He'd been in my apartment? My blood congealed a little more.

"What am I supposed to have?" I asked, trying hard to keep my voice from shaking.

"A flash drive," he said, holding his thumb and forefinger about two inches apart. "About this big."

A flash drive? I didn't have any flash drive—

Oh yes, I did. The one that had fallen out of Talon's belt. The one the dry cleaners had found. The flash drive I'd stuffed back into my coat pocket—the same coat I had on right now.

"I don't know what you're talking about." I took a step back. "I don't have any flash drive."

Bandit shook his head. "I'd hoped to do this the easy way. But if you won't give it to me willingly, I guess I'll just have to take it off your body—your dead body."

Bandit stepped toward me, his boots crunching on the snow. Rascal let out a fierce growl, baring his teeth at the approaching ubervillain. Bandit's eyes flicked to the dog. He frowned. I guess he wasn't an animal lover either.

"Actually, let's make that two things of Tycoon's you have," he said.

I shuffled back, ready to turn and run.

"I wouldn't do that if I were you, Abby." Bandit tipped his ten-gallon hat a little lower on his head. "I really hate to chase people. It upsets me. I tend to shoot people when I'm upset."

Upset? Forget that. I didn't want to be this close to him now, when he was just menacing. But I made myself stop. He was right. Running wouldn't help me. He'd just put a bullet in my back.

Bandit opened his mouth to threaten me again when the strangest thing happened—a car exploded.

I screamed and threw my hand up to ward off the intense heat and light. The explosion sounded like a couple of fighter jets doing formations in my head. The pain was so great my vision went white, then black, then white again. I blinked repeatedly, trying to get my sight back. After a minute, I realized it wasn't a car but rather a trash can that had exploded—the one in front of Jasper's brownstone. How bizarre. And the blast seemed to be contained, burning only in the trash can, without spreading to the surrounding cars. A curtain twitched in one of the brownstone's windows. For a moment, I thought I saw Jasper inside, holding a phone in his hand. He must have come home early from the dedication. Then, the curtain fell back into place, and he vanished.

Bandit swore under his breath, and his eyes flicked up to the street signs, as though he wasn't supposed to be here. He looked at the limo, but the car just sat there. The second Bandit's back turned to me, I ran.

I probably could have made it around the corner if Rascal hadn't chosen that moment to let out another growl.

"Bitch!" Bandit screamed behind me. "Come back here!"

Yeah, right. Like *that* was going to happen. I picked up my pace.

Over my pounding footsteps, something *burped* and *zipped!* through the air. Acting on instinct, I threw myself up against the building. A small, silver object zoomed past my head and slammed into the streetlight at the end of the block. The projectile punched through the metal, leaving a hole about the size of a quarter, and kept going until it hit the brick building on the next block. Black gas spewed from the projectile. Red sparks shot out of the streetlight like a sparkler, and the walk sign flashed like a strobe light.

For the first time in my life, I was glad I'd touched that live amp at The Blues. Otherwise, I'd be dead right now, my skull pierced by Bandit's bullet.

I shoved away from the wall, ready to run again. I stepped forward, my foot sliding on a patch of ice. My arms flailed, and my body jerked to one side, but I didn't fall. I made a hard right and raced into the alley stretching between the main streets. Rascal barked and yipped, and I struggled to hold on to the puppy without crushing him.

"Be still!" I yelled at him. "In case you haven't noticed, I'm running for our lives right now!"

Maybe it was the sharp, panicked tone in my voice, but

Rascal seemed to understand what I was saying. He settled down, and I kept running.

The alley led to another street a block over. It was more heavily traveled than my block, with footprints everywhere, so Bandit shouldn't be able to tell which direction I'd gone. I knew I couldn't outrun the ubervillain—or his gun. My eyes flicked over the snowdrifts. But maybe I could hide from him. I dashed across the street and down the block about fifty feet, crouching behind a car still buried up to its tires in snow. I reached up and rattled the door handle. Locked. Damn.

Across the street at the entrance to the alley, spurs jangled, and boots stamped on the snow. The sounds were faint, whispers really, but I could hear them. He was here already. Bandit was here. I went completely still, scarcely daring to breath.

"I told you that I hate chases, Abby." His voice floated across the street. "Now, you've made me upset."

And then—silence.

I strained and strained, but I couldn't hear the ubervillain over my racing heart and quick, frantic breaths. Those sounds drowned out everything else. I couldn't tell where he was, what he was doing, or most importantly, which direction he was walking.

I sank down into the shadows, hoping he'd turn the other direction and walk away from me. There was a police station a few blocks up. If Bandit headed the other way, I just might be able to sprint there before he realized his mistake and caught up with me. I eased forward, ready to take the chance.

And found myself staring at a pair of cowboy boots. I looked up. Bandit towered over me. The wind fluttered his hair and made his duster dance against his legs. The cold, black leather brushed my cheek like the hand of death. I shrank back.

Bandit shook his head, his eyes as black as night. "You shouldn't have run. Now I'm going to kill you and take what's mine."

He reached down and jerked me up by my coat. He must

have smiled, because his breath hit me through the bandanna he wore. Garlic mixed with onions and hot sauce—all of it rancid. I almost gagged.

"Where's the flash drive?" Bandit asked.

"I don't know anything about a flash drive," I said, lying to the end.

He stared into my eyes, as though he could judge the truth of my words just by looking at me. Rascal used the opportunity to sink his needle-sharp teeth into Bandit's hand.

"Ouch!" the ubervillain roared.

He reached out to punch the puppy, but I turned my shoulder, letting him hit me instead. Bandit's fierce, sharp blow penetrated through my layers of clothing. Something in my shoulder popped. Pain shot up my arm, which went tingly and numb. I screamed and fell to my knees in the snow.

Bandit shook his head. "I tried to do this the easy way, Abby, but you just wouldn't play ball."

Why was he talking to me like that? From his tone of voice, you'd think we knew each other, that we were friends or something. I'd think I'd know if I'd been hanging out with an ubervillain. Surely Piper would tell me.

"Get up," Bandit snapped. "Get up!"

He reached down and hauled me to my feet again. Every single part of my body exploded with pain. My head, shoulder, legs. I hadn't felt this much hot, electric agony since I'd gotten zapped by that amp.

He drew back his hand to punch me again. I felt something brush by my face, so close it ruffled my hair. Bandit stopped, surprised by the movement.

"Son of a bitch—"

The ubervillain never got to finish his sentence. A bolt *thwacked!* into the wall beside us, and cobalt-blue smoke spewed out of it. The smoke forced its way into my eyes, my nose, my throat. It smelled minty.

Bandit blinked once, twice. He shook his head, as if trying to clear it. His grip on my jacket loosened, and he went down on his knees.

I took a step back. At least, I tried to. My head felt so strange, like it was floating above my body. My legs trembled, and I couldn't support myself. My knees buckled, and I slid to the icy ground.

Rascal's sharp, worried bark was the last thing I heard before the world went black.

CHAPTER EIGHTEEN

The lump woke me. It pressed into my back like a giant thumb, a hard pressure on my spine. No matter which way I turned, I couldn't get free of it. Couldn't get comfortable. Couldn't sleep.

A few minutes and several turns later, the sleepy fog lifted from my mind—and I realized I wasn't in my bed. The rest of the evening rushed back to me. The library event. Talking with Wesley. Walking home. Running away from Bandit. Being knocked out by that blue gas. After that, someone had come along and done something with me, taken me…somewhere.

But where? And who? And what were they going to do with me now?

I remained as still as a dead body on the sofa, eyes shut, straining with my ears. But I couldn't hear anything. No machines, no whispers of movement, no swirls of air indicating someone else was nearby. Nothing sounded except a steady, low murmur, too faint for even my supersensitive ears to identify. Well, at least it wasn't loud here.

Because I didn't appear to be in immediate danger, I moved my head. Something soft and filmy brushed my cheek, feeling like a spider's web. I jerked away, but it still touched me. I bit back a scream and clawed at my face, ignoring the pain that stabbed through my shoulder with every frantic movement.

I drew in a ragged breath, and a clean, soapy scent filled my nose. It smelled like...fabric softener.

Fabric softener?

I forced myself to relax and reached up. My fingers traced over the thing on my face, and I realized it was a blanket. I moved my legs, confirming my hunch that this blanket was one of several piled on top of me. They'd twisted and tangled together during my thrashing and wrapped around my body like velvet ropes.

I pulled the blanket off my face and opened my eyes a tiny crack. Darkness. Nothing but darkness. I opened my eyes the rest of the way. Using my right hand, I unwound the sheets from my body and sat up.

I sat there, waiting for my eyes to focus. But for once, my enhanced eyesight failed me. No light penetrated this room, and I could make out only what I could hear, feel, smell, and touch. The faint murmur in the background. The lumpy sofa. The shag rug under my socked feet. The stale odor air gets when it's circulated through office buildings over and over again. The sour fear in my throat and mouth.

So, I focused on my body. My left shoulder throbbed with hot, searing pain, a new wave blossoming every second. The pain had spread down into my arm, ending at my fingertips, which felt numb, cold, and useless. My knees ached from where I'd fallen, and the fabric of my pants had glued itself to the cuts that had opened up on them. I could smell my own dried blood, but there didn't seem to be a lot of it.

I wasn't in the best shape of my life, but I could still move. I didn't know where I was, but I wanted to get out of here. Or at least find the light switch.

I stood up and realized that whoever had brought me here

had also done away with my clothes. Some of them, anyway. My coat was gone, along with my heavy boots and vest. All I wore now was my camisole, silk jacket, pants, and wool socks. I patted the sofa and the rug in front of it, but all my fingers touched were blankets and shag carpet. I couldn't find my clothes. Damn. If only they'd left the vest, I could have fished out my miniature flashlight instead of being blind—

It hit me then what else I was missing—or rather who.

"Rascal!" I whispered. "Rascal, are you in here?"

No *yip-yap* or *bark* answered my frantic call. No sudden scurries of happy movement. No tail thumping against my legs. No doggie breath. Rascal wasn't here.

Hot, salty tears welled up in my eyes. I didn't know why. I didn't do well with animals, didn't even really like dogs. The only reason I had Rascal was because Piper had foisted him off on me. But the room seemed so...empty without the puppy. So...still and...quiet. For the first time in a long time, I didn't welcome the silence.

A few tears slid down my cheeks, but I ignored them. Rascal might not be in here, in this room, but maybe he was close. Better yet, maybe he'd escaped during the struggle with Bandit. Maybe he'd even found his way over to Jasper's brownstone. I wasn't going to think about what else could have befallen the puppy. I wasn't going to think about him getting hit by a car or attacked by a bigger dog or shot by Bandit. I just couldn't.

I got to my feet and stumbled to my right, using the sofa as a guide. When I reached the end of the sofa, I put my hand on the wall and kept going. I fumbled around in the dark, sliding my hands along the wall, looking for a light switch, a window, a door, anything. Up, down, left, right.

There wasn't one. No light switch, no door, no window. The wall felt cool and slick like glass, and my fingers squeaked as they moved over the smooth, flat surface. I didn't feel any latches or panes for a window, and I got the impression I wasn't touching the real wall, that there was something behind the glass, some sort of other space.

No lights. A stale smell. Not much noise. The lack of perception, of seeing, feeling, and hearing every little thing, unnerved me. This was the first time in two years I hadn't been aware of everything all at the same time. I didn't know whether to laugh or cry.

I kept feeling along the wall and realized the room was large—several hundred square feet at least. Because I couldn't find a light switch on the wall, I decided to walk out into the middle of the room. Surely, there had to be a lamp of some sort. I took a step forward. Then another, then another—

My knees hit a low table, and I fell on top of it, smacking into the wood, then rolling off. The carpet was thick, but not thick enough to break my fall. I landed hard on my injured shoulder. The steady waves of pain coalesced into an erupting geyser, steaming, burning, and searing my shoulder, my arm, and my fingers. I rocked back and forth, moaning and clutching my good hand to my shoulder, trying not to throw up as the feeling stabbed through my entire body.

I don't know how long I huddled there, curled into a tight ball, but eventually, a sound penetrated the throbbing haze. I focused on it, desperate to pull my mind away from my aching shoulder and bruised knees. The sound came again, a loud, metallic *click*, like a key turning in a lock.

A door opened. White light spilled in, cutting a path across my face and adding to my misery. I squeezed my eyes shut against the sudden influx of brightness.

"Now, you've done it," a voice murmured.

I cracked my eyes open. A figure stood in the doorway. He was nothing more than a tall, backlit shadow, but I would have known that voice anywhere. That deep bass rumble. That sly tone. That rich timbre that made me melt.

Talon.

"Who are you?" I asked, playing dumb.

"Someone who's here to help you." His throaty voice sent chills up my spine.

"Then why can't I see you?"

Careful what you wish for. Something else clicked, and light flooded the room, searing my eyes. A headache erupted in my temples, throbbing in time to the pain in my shoulder. I groaned and buried my face in my uninjured shoulder to shut out the glare. After a few moments, I opened them again, blinking away the white wall that clouded my vision. The room came into focus.

I gasped because those glass walls I'd felt before held gadgets. Dozens and dozens of gadgets. Crossbows, bolts, grappling hooks, swords, staffs. Costumes too. Rows of cobalt-blue leather shirts, pants, and boots. The whole back wall was nothing but a giant display case.

I turned my head, looking at the rest of the room. Monitors took up the right wall, along with banks of computers, a metal desk, and an executive-style chair. Several more chairs clustered around a table in front of me. Papers, pens, and empty coffee cups dirtied the surface of the table. The chairs pointed at the front wall, which was covered with maps, photographs, and dry-erase boards full of squiggly handwriting. I also spotted my coat, gloves, scarf, and hat draped over a chair, along with my vest. My boots sat next to them.

But the most curious thing was the left wall. There was nothing on it. No monitors, no glass cases, no notes or photos. In fact, it looked like it wasn't even really a wall, but a panel that hid something else from view.

I'd heard about places like this. The nooks, crannies, and secret chambers superheroes called home. The safe places where they kept their weapons and assorted costumes. I'd seen them on SNN countless times. But I'd never been in one—especially not Talon's.

Boots squished into the carpet, and a shadow fell over me, blocking the light. Cobalt-blue leather, blue visor, a hint of dark stubble on his chiseled chin.

"Talon?" I asked, trying to pretend like I'd never seen him before—at least, not in person.

"You know who I am?"

"I saw your poster at Quicke's the other day." I didn't add the fact I'd seen the rest of him naked not too ego.

I looked around the room again. "Where are we? Why did you bring me here? What happened to Bandit?"

"You're safe. That's all you need to know," Talon said. "I brought you here because I couldn't very well leave you on the street to freeze to death."

His mouth twisted, and I knew he was thinking about me, about Wren, and how she'd saved him from the cold too.

Talon continued. "I didn't have any problem doing that to Bandit, though. Hopefully, the city workers will find him frozen solid in the morning, although I rather doubt it. He seems to have as many lives as bullets in his guns."

I hoped it too. Probably more than Talon did.

The superhero kept staring at me, and I realized how awkward I must look, sprawled on the floor, legs sticking out, sock-covered toes curled into the carpet. I put my hand on the table to pull myself up. Pain ripped through my injured shoulder, and I fell to the floor, moaning once again.

Talon dropped to his knees beside me. "Are you okay?"

"Bandit...hit me...did something...to my...shoulder," I gasped between waves of pain.

"Here, let me see if I can help."

Talon put his arm under me and eased me into a sitting position with my back against the table. I closed my eyes and inhaled, breathing in his scent. He smelled good—so good. Like danger, sex, leather, and mint all mixed together.

Talon's fingers probed my shoulder. I hissed to keep from screaming with pain—and to drown out the feel of his hard hand on my body again.

"It's dislocated," he announced. "I can put it back into place for you, but it's going to hurt."

It couldn't hurt worse than it already did. "Just do it."

"All right," he said, taking hold of my shoulder again. "On three. One, two—"

Talon pulled my arm forward and wrenched my shoulder back. Bones scraped together. Tendons stretched. Something *popped!*

I screamed and screamed, then slumped over, sweat sliding down my face. Talon gathered me in his arms, and I buried my face in his neck. Another wave of pain hit me. More throbbing. My muscles twitched. And then—I realized I could feel my fingers again. They tingled as if awakened from a long sleep.

"That wasn't three," I muttered against Talon's neck.

He chuckled. "I know, but it's better this way. Trust me. You don't want to know when it's coming."

We sat there on the floor for a while, him holding me, and me trying to get my breath back. I could have stayed in his arms forever, but I kept wondering where Rascal was—and at the fact I missed him so much.

"Where's Rascal?" I asked.

"Rascal?" he echoed.

"The dog. The puppy in my coat. Did Bandit—did he—"

"No, Rascal's fine. I have him in another room. Your dog is just fine."

Some of the tightness in my chest eased. Rascal was all right, and I was counting my lucky stars I'd gotten through the night with only a dislocated shoulder and scraped knees.

Although I didn't want to, I dislodged myself from the superhero's embrace and crabbed across the floor to the sofa. I turned and leaned against it so I faced Talon. The superhero remained by the coffee table, his legs stretched out in front of him—the same pose he'd struck on my bed. For a moment, I couldn't breathe.

Then, I realized I'd shoved my ass in his face when I'd moved to the sofa. I winced. I couldn't make out his eyes behind the blue visor, but he smiled. Maybe the view hadn't been too bad.

"So, what the hell is going on?"

Talon crossed his arms over his chest. "I was hoping you could tell me, Ms. Appleby."

"You know my name?" I knew he did, but it seemed like the right thing to say.

He nodded. "I'm not the only one with a reputation in this town. Now, do you want to tell me what Bandit was after? Why he was harassing you?"

"You don't know?" I asked, surprised.

He shook his head. "No. I couldn't hear what he said to you. I was too far away."

"But why were you even there in the first place? Were you following me?"

Half of me was filled with dread, the other half with excitement. Maybe Wesley had been concerned about me at the library. Maybe he'd decided to make sure I got home safely. Maybe—

"Of course not," Talon said. "I'm not some sort of stalker. I was after Bandit. I lost him for a few minutes, but I got a tip about his location from a guy I know. I spotted the burning trash can and followed the sound of your voices."

A tip from a guy? He must have meant Jasper. I thought I'd seen him holding a phone in his hand through the curtains.

Jasper must have decided to become some sort of superhero informant because of his recent mugging. That was the only reason I could think of for him knowing Talon.

So the superhero had been tracking Bandit, not me. I should have been relieved he hadn't figured out I was his mystery woman. Still, I chose my words carefully. I didn't want to blow my secret identity as Wren when it was still safe. No matter how much part of me just wanted to confess everything to Talon. Did superheroes feel this conflicted when they lied to their loved ones? Maybe I should ask him.

Maybe not.

"I don't know why he was after me," I said. "He must have me confused with someone else. He kept saying I had something that belonged to him. A flash drive."

I thought of something else the ubervillain had said. "He also claimed I had another thing that belonged to him, and he looked at Rascal. It was strange."

"I thought as much."

Talon got to his feet. He held out his hand, and I took it. He pulled me up so fast I stumbled into him, our bodies flush against each other just as they had been that night in my apartment. I stepped back, hoping he wouldn't notice the sudden rush of color in my cheeks.

I shouldn't have worried. Talon had already gone to his computers, sat down in front of them, and started mashing buttons. I was the only other person in the room, and I'd already faded into the background.

Anger surged through me, replacing the usual, bitter disappointment. I wasn't going to be brushed off so easily. Not again. Not by him. I marched over to the computers and stared at the flickering images. Most of the monitors showed news clips of Bandit, hawking his action figures and shooting out tires on police cars with alarming precision.

"What are you doing? What are you looking at?"

Talon swiveled in his chair and faced me. "Do you really want to know? Because if you do, there's no going back."

"What do you mean? You're not going to pull off your mask and reveal your secret identity, are you?"

He laughed. "Of course not, but if Bandit thinks you have the flash drive he wants, you're in danger. The less you know, the better."

"Not really," I pointed out. "He's convinced I know about it. Even if I tell him otherwise, he'd still torture and kill me trying to get me to tell him what I supposedly know."

"Well, yeah," Talon admitted. "But I was trying not to upset you, to get you to look at the bright side of things."

"I'm not really a bright-side kind of gal. Besides, I want to know what's going on. He said he'd been in my apartment looking for it and it wasn't there. What kind of flash drive is Bandit after?"

I couldn't see Talon's eyes through the tall blue visor, but I got the impression he was studying me carefully. "How much do you know about me?"

The change of topic surprised me. "Just what I've read in *The Exposé* or seen on SNN. You're a superhero. You use gadgets to help you fight evil. That's it."

I also knew he liked Green Day and The Pretenders. Secretly listened to John Denver. And that he really liked it when I did that shimmy with my hips—well, I wasn't going to go there. Talon's sexual preferences were not part of this conversation.

"Then you know Bandit is my archenemy. I've been trying to take him down for years."

I nodded.

"But for all his bravado, Bandit is just a hired gun, no pun intended. He works for someone who calls himself Tycoon. Have you heard of him?"

I nodded again. "Sure. Everybody has. He's the big mob boss in Bigtime."

"I managed to pinpoint Tycoon's main headquarters. It took me months, but I finally found where he was hiding," Talon said. "A few nights ago, I broke inside. I was looking for Bandit, but I found something even better—Tycoon's mainframe. The computer that houses all of the information about his organization. The drugs, the gambling, the money laundering, everything. I'd just hacked into the mainframe when someone discovered I had broken in. Before I left, I copied the information onto a flash drive, but Bandit and some of his lieutenants waylaid me in an alley, and Bandit shot me."

I thought back. That would have been Saturday, the night of the O'Hara party, when I'd found Talon blind and bleeding. "How did you get away?" I asked, playing the part of the naïve, innocent civilian.

"Luckily, a woman was there," Talon's voice softened. "Her name is Nightingale. At least, that's what I called her. She helped me get away from Bandit. She took me to her home and patched me up."

"So maybe she has the flash drive Bandit wants." I rubbed my hands together, hoping he wouldn't notice my trembling fingers. "Maybe she swiped it when you weren't looking."

"I think she does have it," Talon said. "But I don't think she took it. At least, not on purpose."

"So, why don't you just go get the drive from her?" My heart hammered in my chest, and my mouth went dry.

His mouth twisted. "Because I don't know who Nightingale really is. We didn't exactly exchange contact information."

No, just bodily fluids.

"She...left me before I could thank her for her help."

Yeah, I drugged you and left you in the convention center so you wouldn't find out who I really was. That sentence dangled on the end of my tongue, but I clamped my mouth shut. I could never tell Talon the truth. He wouldn't understand. Hell, I wasn't sure that *I* understood.

"Oh. So you don't know anything about her?"

His voice dropped to a whisper. "Just that she likes to sing. Nightingale has the most amazing voice I've ever heard."

The heat, the passion, in his tone, made my throat close up. I didn't say anything. I had a hard enough time just breathing.

Talon cleared his throat. "No, I don't know anything about her. Nothing concrete, like her name or age or where she works."

Or the fact that she's standing right in front of you.

I closed my eyes. This was harder than I'd thought it would be. Especially when he talked about Wren, about *me*, like that. Like I was somebody he wanted to see again. Somebody he cared about.

"But I've been looking for her."

My eyes snapped open, and I tried not to stagger back. "You—you have? Why?"

"Lots of reasons," he said. "I want to say thank you, of course. But even more than that, she was...kind to me. Kinder than anyone's been in a long time."

His voice was casual, but there was a sharp undercurrent in it, longing tinged with desperation—or maybe that was me wanting to hear things. Wanting Talon to feel the things I'd felt.

"I've gotten some information on Nightingale, even a photograph, but so far, it hasn't led me anywhere."

I flashed back to the pictures and documents I'd seen on Wesley's desk. The ones he'd been examining so intently. They couldn't possibly be of...me, could they? Where would he have gotten my picture from?

"What I don't understand is why Bandit would confuse you with her," Talon said.

Reality bitch-slapped me in the face again.

"Um...well...I was out late that night at an event. Maybe he saw me walking down the street or something."

A lame excuse at best, but he nodded, accepting it. "Possibly."

"But why would Bandit think Rascal belonged to him?"

"Well, where did you get the dog from?"

I supposed there was no harm in telling him the truth—about this. "My best friend Piper Perez found him in an alley downtown before the blizzard hit. She didn't want to take him to the pound, but she's allergic to dogs. So, she asked me to keep him while she finds him a home."

"I see. Well, that means something."

"What?"

"Before I was discovered at Tycoon's headquarters, I read about a project called *Sunrise*. I didn't read enough to know exactly what's it about, but it looked like Tycoon was experimenting with a radioactive drug—euphoridon. Testing it on cats and dogs. Certain breeds, like corgis."

Euphoridon was Bigtime's radioactive version of crack—only far more addictive and deadly. There was something familiar about the name *Sunrise* too, like I'd seen or heard it somewhere recently, but I focused on the last thing that Talon had said.

"So what are you saying? That Rascal is some kind of superdog?" I asked. "No way. He's just a puppy."

"You haven't noticed anything strange about him? Nothing at all?"

Well, there was his seemingly boundless energy and enormous appetite. But I thought that was because he was a growing puppy rather than a superdog. The only really strange thing about Rascal was the way he seemed to understand exactly what I was saying, but Piper told me corgis were intelligent.

"I don't know. I've never had a dog before."

"You've never had a dog before?" Disbelief colored Talon's voice.

I grimaced. Now, I was getting that tone from a superhero. "No, I've never had a dog. I don't do so well with animals. But what would the drug do to him?"

"I'm not sure," Talon said. "It would depend on the dosage

and various other things. It might make him a little quicker, a little smarter than the average dog. But I'm not sure if Rascal is one of the dogs or not. I'd have to run some tests to find out. With your permission, I'll draw some of his blood."

"Will it hurt him?" I asked, worried.

"No. Just a little prick, and it will be done." He turned back to his monitors. "But even with his blood, it doesn't mean anything without the flash drive. I won't even know what to look for."

"But what about Tycoon's headquarters? Can't you just break in again?"

Talon hit some keys on his computer, and a burned-out warehouse appeared on the monitors. "No. He razed the building that night. There's nothing left."

My eyes flicked to my coat. The flash drive was probably still in there. All I had to do was show it to him, give him the information he needed—and reveal my secret.

I stood there, wrestling with my desire to do the right thing and my need to remain anonymous. Talon hit a button, and the monitors faded to black.

"Enough about this," he said. "You're probably tired and want to go home. Don't worry. I'll find some way to figure it out. I'm just sorry you got mixed up in the middle of it."

He looked at me, and I knew he was dismissing me. He'd done the brave thing, the right thing, the noble thing, and saved me from Bandit. Now, he was going to blindfold me and dump me in my apartment. Just like someone had dumped Rascal in the snow the other night. Just like I'd dumped Talon at the convention center. A vicious cycle, dumping.

"I want to help you," I blurted out, surprising myself as much as I did him.

"Why would you want to do that?" he asked, puzzled. "This has nothing to do with you."

"Yes, it does. I mean, Rascal is sort of my dog, for the moment anyway, and Bandit thinks I have what he wants. I want to help you find the flash drive. That's the only way I'm ever going to be safe. Maybe your mystery woman didn't take it. Maybe you just…dropped it somewhere. I could help you look for it."

"And what would you get out of it?" Talon asked.

The chance to be close to you again. A chance to get you to see me. A chance for you to fall in love with me.

Fall in love with me? Where had that nonsense come from? I was getting as starry-eyed and sentimental as Piper.

I gritted my teeth. "Call me a good Samaritan. I don't like ubervillains. I don't like being threatened, and I hate people who are mean to animals. Besides, if you take out Bandit and Tycoon, those are two less villains I have to worry about crashing my parties."

He leaned back in his chair, measuring my words.

I stuck out my hand before he could think about them too long, because my story had as many holes in it as a piece of Swiss cheese. "What do you say? Partners?"

Talon looked at my hand, then at me. After a moment, he nodded. "Partners."

We shook hands. His hard, calloused fingers covered mine, and I flashed back to that night in my apartment and the marvelous things he'd done with those fingers—things I ached for him to do again.

Evidently, Talon didn't feel anything, because he dropped my hand, reached over, and hit a button on one of his computers. One of the monitors on the wall slid back, revealing a metal nozzle. Something clicked, and the nozzle spewed out blue gas.

"What—what are you doing?" I asked, my voice slurring as the minty sleeping gas seeped into my lungs again.

Talon stood. I tried to step back, but he caught my arms and held me fast.

"I trust you, Abby, but not enough to let you see where you are. Don't worry. I'll take you and your dog to your friend's house where you'll be safe. I won't let Bandit hurt you. I promise. I'll be in touch soon."

"But, the flash drive…" I mumbled, trying to tell him I had it.

"No buts. Sleep, Abby, just sleep," Talon murmured.

His voice was the last thing I heard before my eyes closed once more.

CHAPTER NINETEEN

Something scraped my cheek. Something warm, wet, and sticky. Something that smelled like day-old puppy chow.

I opened my eyes. Rascal stood on the sofa next to me, licking my face.

"Hey, boy," I mumbled, reaching up and scratching his ears.

His tail thumped against my ribs, and he grunted with happiness. More tears gathered in my eyes. I was so happy to see him again, even if he might be a radioactive superpup.

A shadow fell over me. I looked up and blinked. Piper's concerned face came into focus.

"Well, it's about time you woke up," she said.

I sat up the rest of the way and scanned the room. Framed superhero posters brightened the walls. Shelves full of comic books, action figures, and plush toys reached from the floor to the ceiling. Life-size cardboard figures of Swifte, Wynter, and other heroes struck noble poses. I recognized Piper's obscenely neat, clutter-free, superhero-shrine living room.

"How did I get here?" I asked.

We sat on the couch in front of the TV, Rascal snuggled between us. Over some hot chocolate, Piper filled me in on what had happened since Talon knocked me out. The superhero had pounded on her door around two in the morning. She'd peered through the keyhole to find Talon standing outside, holding me in his arms, with Rascal hooked to a leash on Talon's belt. Piper had let him in, and the superhero had put me on the couch before vanishing.

"He said he'd saved you from an ubervillain. That you were fine and you'd wake up in a few hours," Piper said, sipping her hot chocolate. "He was even nice enough to give me his autograph to add to my collection."

I glanced at the TV. Just after seven in the morning. The anchors on SNN did their usual early morning banter before sending things over to the news desk.

"Now, you want to tell me what you did last night, Abby?" Piper asked. "I already know *who* you did."

"Shut up," I growled. "It wasn't like that."

Even though I'd wished it had been.

I told her about Bandit confronting me on the street, then chasing me. How Talon had come to my rescue, taken me to his superhero lair, and agreed to let me help him find the missing flash drive.

Piper's brown eyes grew brighter with every word. "How romantic!" she squealed.

I winced and gave her a pointed look.

"Sorry. And they say chivalry is dead. Not when Talon's around, it's not." Piper stared at me. "So, did you use this opportunity to tell him who you really are? That you're his much-sought-after mystery lady? His one, his only Nightingale?"

"Of course not," I said, horrified she'd even suggest it.

"You're going about this all wrong, Abby."

Rascal rolled over. Piper sneezed and scratched his snow-white belly.

"You should just tell Talon who you really are—and that you know his secret identity too. That way, the two of you can figure out what Bandit is up to together—and see if you have enough chemistry for more than a one-night stand. Besides, it's not good to lie to people. It's just not good karma."

I narrowed my eyes. "You've been looking at your Mr. Sage thought-a-day calendar again."

She shrugged and sniffled into a tissue. "We can all learn a thing or two from superheroes."

Piper lived her life like she was a superhero. She firmly believed in truth, justice, and all that jazz. Lying, fibbing, or telling half truths to make things easier wasn't something Piper approved of, although she'd do it when absolutely necessary.

"You should tell him, Abby," she said, her voice softer. "I know how much you like him. You practically glow whenever you talk about him."

"I know, I know," I muttered. "I do like him, but I just can't bring myself to tell him the truth. That I'm Wren. What if he takes one look at me and wonders what he was thinking the other night? What if he's like Ryan?"

"Then Wesley's not worth your time or energy—leather suit or no leather suit," Piper pronounced.

I bit my lip and looked away. On SNN, men dressed in white protective suits and masks hauled body bags out of an alley and put them into a van bearing the words *Animal Control* on the side.

"Turn the TV up," I said, my eyes fixed on the screen. "Right now."

Piper grabbed the remote and hit the volume button.

"...and we go out to Kelly Caleb, who's on the scene of a

breaking story. Kelly, what's the situation?" the anchor said.

Kelly Caleb stared into the camera, her blue eyes dark and serious. "A city sanitation worker made a gruesome discovery this morning. While collecting trash from this alley, he stumbled across the bodies of about fifty cats and dogs, many of them only a few weeks old. Officials don't know where the animals came from, but Chief Sean Newman of the Bigtime Police Department said they believe the bodies have been here for a few days, hidden by the snow…"

As Kelly provided more background on her story, the screen showed footage from earlier in the morning. The camera zoomed in on the body of a puppy who looked a lot like Rascal. The puppy's eyes were closed, and it almost looked like it was sleeping. The sight sickened me.

"That's right around the block from my office, from Fiona's store," Piper said.

"That's where you found Rascal, isn't it?" I whispered.

The puppy barked at the sound of his name. I picked him up and hugged him to my chest.

"How did you know?"

I told her the rest of the story. How Talon had broken into Tycoon's headquarters. How he'd discovered that the mob boss had been experimenting on animals. The interest Bandit had shown in Rascal and the puppy's vicious reaction to him.

Piper eyed the puppy, who'd decided to go to sleep in my arms. "And Talon thinks Rascal is one of those dogs?"

I nodded. "He said he was going to take some blood to try to confirm it. Although he said he didn't know if he could without the information on the flash drive."

"The drive you picked up in the alley."

I nodded.

"Do you still have it?"

"Let me check."

I handed Rascal to her. Piper sneezed violently three times, but the puppy slept on. I retrieved my coat and dug through the pockets. The silver flash drive was inside, just as I'd left it. I couldn't quite believe that I still had it and that Talon hadn't felt it when he'd put my coat back on my body.

"Is that it?" Piper asked.

I nodded.

"Well, let's see what's on it and why everyone wants it so badly."

Piper flipped on her laptop, stuck the flash drive in the appropriate slot, and hit a few buttons. The computer's gears ground together as the machine tried to read the flash drive. Piper typed in some commands. Numbers, letters, and other coded gibberish flashed on the screen, and a window popped up wanting a login and a password.

She shook her head. "It's encrypted. There's no way I can open it."

I sighed. I'd been dreaming when I thought it would be this easy. That we could just read the information on the drive, find out who Tycoon was, and anonymously give the information to Talon and the police.

Maybe I should just tell Talon who I was. Maybe I should take a chance he was really the great guy he seemed to be. Maybe I should do a lot of things. I wrinkled my nose. Like take a shower. I smelled like sleeping gas and dried blood, and Rascal's tongue bath hadn't helped. Plus, the warm water would help soothe the aches and pains I'd gotten from my adventures last night.

Piper tapped her fingers against her lips. "But I might know someone who could open it for us. Or rather, Fiona does."

"Fiona? What does Fiona know about computers?"

The only things Fiona seemingly cared about were her clothes, food, and her fiancé, Johnny Bulluci. That was all she'd talked about a few weeks ago when she'd come in to discuss plans for her engagement party and upcoming wedding.

"Not much," Piper said. "Although she can break plenty of them. The woman's stronger than she looks. I asked her to unplug a cord for me, and she ripped it right out of the wall—along with the outlet. But Fiona has a friend, Lulu something. She came in the last time our system went down. Our tech guy worked on the problem for two hours and got nowhere, but she had it up and running in ten minutes. It was amazing, especially when Lulu told Fiona the whole system was a piece of junk—and Fiona didn't throw her out of the store."

I raised an eyebrow. "Fiona didn't let her have it?"

Piper shook her head. "Nope. She just let Lulu talk to her like that. I couldn't believe it either."

Fiona never let anyone get the best of her. If you pissed her off, she let you know about it—in a hurry.

"Can you call Fiona and get Lulu's number?"

Piper glanced at her Swifte clock. "Are you kidding? It's not even eight yet. Fiona is *not* a morning person. She usually doesn't roll into the office until after ten. Even then, I normally don't speak to her until lunchtime. At least, not without food in hand."

I tapped my fingers against my knee, more than a little impatient. I wanted to know what was on the flash drive—right *now*. But calling Fiona and bugging her wouldn't do any good. I knew from past experience that the fashion designer did things when she wanted to. Like Kyle Quicke, she had a remarkable ability to tune me out.

"It's just as well," I said. "We need to go by my loft first anyway. I want to see how much damage Bandit did."

CHAPTER TWENTY

I took a shower, threw on some clothes I kept at Piper's, and went over to my building.

Bandit had been telling the truth when he said he'd ransacked my loft. Actually, ransacked wasn't the right word. Decimated was more like it.

Standing in the doorway staring at the mess, I was shocked and horrified. Bandit had ripped the furniture to pieces. Drawers had been yanked out of my desk; their contents upended on the floor. He apparently put his fist through all of them, searching for secret compartments. The couch cushions had been shredded. Down feathers and cotton stuffing covered the floor like soft piles of snow. The light fixtures had been ripped out of their sockets and smashed, and the floorboards pried up. He'd pulled the doors off my closet and rummaged through my clothes and shoes. Several of my vests lay crumpled on the floor, the khaki fabric crisscrossed with cuts where he'd slashed into them, trying to see what was inside.

Bandit had even dug into the boxes I hadn't unpacked, dumping their contents on the floor. Books, papers, dishes, towels. It was a broken, jumbled mess—one Rascal found to be the perfect playground. The puppy grabbed one of my socks and wrestled with it while Piper stood aghast in the middle of the destroyed loft.

I'd sunk almost all of my money into the loft, to have a soundproof oasis shutting out the rest of the world, but Bandit had destroyed my peace, ripped it away from me. I felt sick and violated.

The worst thing was what the ubervillain had done to my music collection. Bandit had tipped over my entertainment center, spilling CDs across the floor. He'd opened every case; I guess to check and make sure they held what they were supposed to and that I hadn't copied the flash drive onto one of them.

Then the bastard had broken the discs—every single one.

All my rock music. My jazz collection. The pop tunes, the disco beats, the classical arrangements. All gone. He'd even smashed my laptop and iPod and the albums I'd collected over the years. The bastard.

"Well, look at the bright side," Piper said, her voice far too cheery for my liking. "Bandit did your unpacking for you."

"Yeah, great," I muttered and kicked a cracked CD case with my boot.

"He actually did you a favor dumping everything out in the open like this. It's no problem. We can have this place clean in a few hours. Sparkling. Spick-and-span. It'll be fun!" Piper chirped.

I gave her a sour look. Neat freak didn't begin to describe the depths of Piper's depravity. She organized her underwear by size, color, and frequency of use.

I, on the other hand, had better things to do, like find out what was on Talon's flash drive and finish planning the event for his alter ego, Wesley Weston. I whipped out my cell phone and called Chloe.

"Hey, Abby," Chloe said.

"How did the party end last night?"

"Everything went fine," she said. "There were a few incidents, but I handled them all."

I gripped the phone tighter. "Incidents? What sort of *incidents?*"

"Well, Fiera started juggling fireballs and accidentally toasted the banner strung up in the jail. But Chief Newman grabbed the fire extinguisher and put it out before it spread, almost like he knew she was going to light it up. Peter Potter got sloshed and had a few words with Octavia, but I broke it up before it got too out of hand, stuffed him in a limo, and sent him home. A few people started saying catty things about Berkley, complaining his name was on everything in the city. Joanne didn't like that. I thought she was going to leap onto one woman and punch her, but this tall guy with an earring pulled her away before too many feelings were hurt."

Out-of-control superheroes. Drunken businessmen. Catfights. Pretty typical stuff. "I'm sure you did just fine."

"Where are you?" Chloe asked. "It's after nine. You didn't call and tell me you were going to be late. I was getting worried."

I couldn't remember the last time I hadn't been at the office by nine, but I figured I'd earned a break after almost getting killed last night. "I've had a bit of a situation."

I told Chloe I'd spent the night at Piper's, and someone had broken into my apartment and made the biggest mess ever. I asked if she could call Clean Dreams and have them send over a crew to help get things straightened up and to haul away what couldn't be salvaged. Chloe agreed to phone them, and we hung up.

Piper was reluctant to leave the cleaning to someone else, but I told her we had a fashion designer to bribe—and a flash drive to decrypt. I grabbed the few clean, undamaged clothes I could find and the two vests that had survived Bandit's rampage. Then, I dropped to my knees and sorted through the broken CDs on the floor, trying to find one that wasn't snapped in two.

Nothing. I sat back on my heels and blew out a breath. I pushed my hair out of my eyes, and my gaze landed on my CD changer. Maybe he hadn't thought to look in there. I scooted forward and hit the button. The drawer slid open, revealing another broken disc. Okay, maybe he hadn't thought to check if there were any more discs. I pushed the button again.

The changer revolved, and a single, intact disc appeared— John Denver's greatest hits. The CD I'd played at Talon's request. A wave of longing hit me. If only I could rewind time to that one perfect moment.

"Are you ready, Abby?" Piper called out from the doorway.

"Yeah, I'm coming."

I slipped the CD in my coat pocket, and we left.

By the time we got to Piper's office at Fiona Fine Fashions, it was after ten. We went through the front of the store. Racks of designer dresses crowded into the white space, each one more brightly colored and boldly embellished than the last. Classical music trilled in the background while models flounced up and down a catwalk, showing off a variety of wedding gowns. Piper moved off to talk to one of the clerks at the front desk. I stood off to the side.

A group of women perched in overstuffed chairs at the end of the catwalk, sipping champagne and eating gourmet chocolates. Octavia and Olivia O'Hara were among them, along with Paul Potter. I waved at Olivia. She smiled, waved back, and started to get up. Then, her eyes fell on Rascal. Olivia froze, half in, half out of her chair. Paul's gaze slid over to me, and he frowned. I don't think I've ever seen him with a happy expression on his face, not even during the engagement party.

Octavia also turned her head at her sister's movement.

Spotting me, Octavia's mouth flattened into a hard line. Not the most pleasant of expressions.

Paul leaned over and whispered something to Octavia. She nodded and put her hand on Olivia's arm, pushing her sister back down in her chair. Octavia got to her feet and walked over to me. Today, she wore a dark green suit with round, white buttons.

"Abby."

"Hi, Octavia. Is Olivia shopping for wedding dresses already?"

"Yes. She and Paul are so in love, they plan to get married on Valentine's Day."

That was less than a month away. "Well, give me a call, and we'll set up a time to talk about the ceremony."

A dark emotion flashed in Octavia's eyes. "We're going to let Katie Connors plan the wedding."

"Katie Connors?" I said in disbelief. "You're going to trust your sister's wedding to Katie Connors? You know, she can barely plan a kid's birthday party and have it turn out well."

"I'm sorry, Abby," Octavia said, her voice cool.

I narrowed my eyes. "Why? Did she offer you a better price?"

"No. We've just decided to go in a different direction."

"But why? You liked what I did for the engagement party, didn't you?"

"Of course," Octavia said. "But it's come to my attention you're planning an event for Wesley Weston, where he'll announce his acquisition of Gelled. I don't appreciate people who stab me in the back, Abby. In under a week, no less. You will not be planning anything else for me—ever again."

Octavia turned on her stiletto and stalked to her chair. Paul stared at his nails, like he could manicure them with his eyes. Olivia gave me a weak smile and returned her gaze to the models, as though ivory lace was the most interesting thing in the world.

"What was that about?" Piper asked, coming to stand beside me.

I shook my head. "Just what I thought would happen. Octavia found out about the Weston party and banned me from planning any more of her events."

"I'm sorry, Abby."

I shrugged. The loss of a customer didn't bother me as much as usual. Maybe it was because it was Octavia, the woman who had dated Wesley and sneered at Rascal.

We walked on. Piper punched in a code on a door, and we stepped into the back of the building. Workers huddled at stations, sewing sequins, feathers, glass beads, and more on clothing, handbags, and other accessories. Piper stopped to chat with some folks before heading to her office.

We also got waylaid by more than a few people who just had to tell me what a cute puppy Rascal was. Rascal, of course, was more than happy to prance around and strut his stuff. I eyed the puppy. Maybe Tycoon's radioactive drugs had made him supercute. That was the only explanation I could come up with for the way people reacted to the corgi—everyone except Octavia.

We reached Piper's office. It was just as neat as her apartment, with everything sorted by size, color, and height. Only a couple of Swifte sticky pads broke up the sterile, professional space. Piper kept her superhero obsession and massive collection of fangirl items mostly at home.

"Piper! There you are!"

Fiona Fine struck a pose in the doorway. The fashion designer was known throughout Bigtime for her outrageous designs, and today was no different. Fiona wore a crimson miniskirt paired with a top covered with black and white geometric patterns. Red go-go boots crawled up to her knees, while white, plastic hoop earrings dangled from her ears. On anyone else, the outfit would have looked ridiculous, but Fiona pulled it off—with plenty of style to spare.

"I was starting to worry," she said. "It's not like you to be late."

"I had to help Abby with something," Piper said in a breezy tone.

Fiona sniffed and tossed her blond hair over her shoulder. "Well, you should have called."

"But if I'd called I wouldn't have had time to get these."

Piper held out a paper bag full of cream cheese-filled doughnuts. She'd insisted we stop by Bryn's Bakery on the way here, even though it made us ten minutes later. She'd wanted to bring Fiona a bribe to help smooth things over.

"Is that a problem?" Piper asked. "If you don't want any, I'm sure Abby and I can take care of them—"

"No!" Fiona said, snatching the bag out of Piper's hands and digging into it with the enthusiasm of a true sugar addict. "Not when you bring me doughnuts to make up for it."

Piper gave me a smug, knowing look before scooting around her desk and flipping on her computer. I leaned against one of the file cabinets and watched Fiona shove a doughnut in her mouth and then proceed to eat the other dozen in under three minutes—without asking us if we wanted a single one. Rascal yipped in protest, but Fiona ignored him, too intent on her food to notice the puppy.

"Actually, I was hoping you could help us with something," Piper said.

"What?" Fiona mumbled through a mouthful of cream cheese.

"Abby's been having some computer problems. I was wondering if you could give me the number for your friend, Lulu. I remembered how she fixed our computers a couple of months ago. I was wondering if she might help Abby."

It might have been my imagination, but Fiona's blue eyes seemed to sharpen at Piper's words. It was sort of hard to tell when she was stuffing food into her mouth at the speed of light.

Fiona swallowed the last doughnut, then licked a few crumbs off her fingers. "What do you need Lulu's help with?"

Piper opened her mouth, but I cut her off. I didn't want her to get into trouble with Fiona over this. I pulled Talon's flash drive out of my pocket and showed it to the fashion designer. "I put some files on here and used the password protection feature. Now, I can't get to them. I don't know what's wrong with the drive, and I need the files. They're for an event I'm planning."

"The Wesley Weston party?" Fiona asked.

I nodded. That lie was just as good as any other.

"I got my invitation this morning. Johnny did too. We'll be there. So I suppose I *should* help you make it as fabulous as possible," Fiona said. "Let me see if I can find Lulu's cell phone number."

She sashayed next door to her office. I followed her, with Piper behind me.

Where Piper's desk was neat-freak clean, Fiona's was a slob's paradise with crumpled papers, uncapped pens, half-used legal pads, crushed soda cans, and empty takeout containers. Fiona hunted through the haphazard mess on her desk while Piper paced back and forth outside the door, growing more and more agitated. Fiona's lack of proper desk maintenance aggravated Piper to no end.

"If Lulu's your friend, shouldn't you have her number in your cell phone?" I asked, trying to speed the process along. "That's where I keep my important contacts."

"I did, but my phone got fried last night," Fiona said.

"That happens quite a bit to you, doesn't it?" Piper asked. "If something's not getting overheated, it's snapping in two."

Fiona put her hands on her hips. "Yeah, it does. Now, do you want Lulu's number or not?"

I looked at Piper. She shrugged, and we both shut up.

"I know I have it here somewhere," Fiona muttered, shoving

a pile of papers off the desk. They hit the reams already carpeting the floor.

Piper closed her eyes and let out a whimper. She looked like she was going to faint.

Fiona wasn't making much progress, so Piper decided to motivate her. She went into her office and brought back another bag she'd gotten at the bakery. Thick, round bagels bulged out of the top of the sack.

"Are those bagels?" Fiona asked, her eyes brightening.

"Blueberry, your favorite," Piper said. "With extra cream cheese."

Fiona leapt into action then, shoving just about everything on her desk off onto the floor as she searched for Lulu's number. Unable to watch the trash piles multiply exponentially, Piper handed me the bag of bagels and went back to her office.

"A-ha!" Fiona cried, holding up a wrinkled business card. "Here it is!"

She handed me the card, and I gave her the bagels. Fiona tore into the bag before I turned to leave. Rascal wandered over to the fashion designer in hopes of scoring a treat. His tail thumped against her boots as he stared at the bag, as if it would magically split in two and shower him with bagels.

Fiona eyed him. "Sorry, dog. No thumbs, no bagels."

"Come on, Rascal," I said. "You had plenty of puppy chow this morning."

Rascal let out a pitiful whine, but I picked him up and carried him back to Piper's office, making sure the door shut behind me.

"I can't believe she eats like that!" I whispered to Piper.

She shrugged. "You get used to it after a while. Although I need to get some more pamphlets about that eating disorder clinic for her. I think if Fiona would just admit she has a problem, that would go a long way toward solving it."

Rascal barked his agreement.

Piper called Fiona's friend, Lulu Lo, and told her about my problem. Lulu agreed to meet us at lunchtime at the coffee bar in the Bigtime Public Library. We dropped Rascal off at my office with Chloe and headed over to the library.

I checked my watch for the fifth time. Lulu Lo was five minutes and forty-nine seconds late. "What does she look like?" I asked Piper. "Is she here? Or just late?"

"Believe me, you'll know who she is when you see her. Lulu is hard to miss. At least, her hair is."

Piper took another sip of her mocha latte and flipped through Confidante's latest comic book. Evidently, Confidante had been lurking around during the library fundraiser, because this issue featured Fiera taking Milton Morris to jail.

My gaze flicked over the other folks slurping coffee, hot chocolate, and apple cider in the library's coffee bar. Nobody met Piper's description of a petite woman who used a cane to get around. All I saw were college students trudging back to the stacks, sad that their winter break was over. An older couple dozed in armchairs in the sunny spots inside the glassed-in garden. A floor above us, children laughed as a librarian read them a funny story. Up on the third floor, someone cursed the copy machine for jamming again.

A steady, solid *thump-thump-thumping* sounded above the hisses, gurgles, and burps of the espresso machine. I turned toward the entrance to the coffee bar.

"Let me guess. You hear her cane hitting the floor," Piper said, not even bothering to look up from her comic book.

"Or something that sounds a lot like it."

More *thumps* sounded, and a woman limped into the coffee

bar. She was around our age—late twenties—and wore fitted jeans, sneakers, and a nice Bulluci pullover jacket. Piper was right. You really couldn't miss seeing Lulu Lo. Because in addition to being very pretty, she sported neon blue streaks in her black hair. Lots of them. Lulu stepped through a patch of sunlight, which the metallic strands caught and threw back in my eyes. I squinted against the sudden glare.

"Hey, Piper," Lulu said, coming over to our table. "How are you?"

"Good," Piper said. "And you?"

Lulu shrugged. "Not bad, although I'm not loving being out in the cold and snow."

"We wouldn't have called if it wasn't important. I'll let Abby explain. Can I get you something to drink? On us, of course."

Piper didn't have to offer twice.

"I'll have a triple espresso with three shots of raspberry syrup, one of vanilla, and whipped cream with chocolate sprinkles on top," Lulu said.

Piper left to place her order. Lulu sat down in Piper's seat and leaned her cane against the table. She shrugged a backpack off her shoulders, put it at her feet, and pulled a slim laptop out of it.

"So, Abby, what's the problem?" Lulu asked, powering up the computer.

"I have this flash drive," I said, pulling it out of my coat pocket and showing it to her. "I put some information on it, and now it's saying it's encrypted and won't let me access my files."

"Encrypted, huh? We'll see about that," Lulu said.

She took the drive and plugged it into her laptop. The same password screen Piper and I had seen this morning popped up, but that didn't faze Lulu. She started typing and muttering to herself about codes, passwords, and firewalls. I didn't understand a word she said, but she seemed to be making progress.

Piper returned with Lulu's espresso, and she reached out and took a big swig of it without taking her eyes off her laptop screen.

If anything, the coffee made her type faster. Piper wandered off to see if she could find a superhero book she hadn't read while I stayed with Lulu.

After about twenty minutes of typing, Lulu sat back in her chair and took another drink of her espresso. Her dark eyes flicked to me. "What sort of information did you put on this drive?"

"Just some client files," I lied.

"Really?" Lulu said. "Nothing important?"

"Well, it's important to me," I said, trying to play along, even though I didn't know where she was going with her questions. "Why do you ask?"

She turned the laptop around so I could see the screen. "Because not only is your flash drive encrypted, but your folders and files are in code as well. I've managed to get around the login encryption, but not the one that unlocks the information in the files. This looks like gibberish to me. Does it mean anything to you?"

Yellow folder icons covered the screen in a long row. They had names like *Ivory Tower*, *Black Velvet*, and *Quicksilver*. The only thing I could think of was superhero and ubervillain names. All of them had strange, colorful names like that. Talon had told me Tycoon was experimenting with radioactive materials. Maybe this was a hit list of superheroes or information on ubervillains Tycoon wanted to hire or even create himself. I didn't know, and it frustrated me.

This was what Talon had risked his life for? This was why Bandit had trashed my apartment and almost killed me? To get a flash drive full of worthless information? How was this supposed to tell Talon who Tycoon really was and what the mob boss was up to? How was this supposed to help me get out of the mess I was in?

"Can you decode the files?" I asked. "I really need the information."

Lulu gave me a sly look. "I can, but it'll probably take me at least a day, maybe two. And it will cost you."

"How much?"

I winced at the figure Lulu quoted me. There went the Weston fee and any chance I had of getting my loft back the way it was before Bandit had destroyed it.

"Or..." Lulu's voice trailed off.

"Or what?"

"You plan parties, right? Weddings and stuff?"

"Yeah." My voice was cautious.

"So do my engagement party and wedding, and we'll call it even."

I sighed. "Let me guess. You want to get the jump on Fiona and all the other brides-to-be in town and get married in some costly, overly elaborate fashion tomorrow night."

"Oh no. Henry and I want a small ceremony. Probably twenty people, tops. And it's still a couple months off, at least. I'm not walking down the aisle while I'm still using that." She pointed to her cane.

Twenty people? That was all she was going to invite to her wedding? I could plan something like that in my sleep.

"Let's do it," I said. "Whatever equipment you need, just let me know, and I'll cover the cost of that too."

"Oh, don't worry about the equipment." Lulu waved her hand at me. An emerald engagement ring sparkled on her finger. "I have some friends who'll give me the hookup. In fact, I think you know one of them—Jasper."

"Jasper? The Jasper who lives across the street from me? You know him?"

Lulu nodded. "We're old friends."

I thought back and realized I'd seen her at the brownstone a time or two. I wondered if Lulu knew about Jasper's role as a superhero informant or his connection to Joanne, but I didn't ask.

Lulu studied me over the rim of her espresso cup, her face serious. I always got uncomfortable when people stared at me, and I tried not to fidget.

She leaned forward and dropped her voice. "Speaking of my friends, you might need their help, Abby. I don't believe this flash drive belongs to you, and I don't think you just have client files on it. I think you're playing with something that doesn't belong to you—and that you're going to get burned by it."

My heart froze in my chest. Did Lulu know? Did she suspect what was really on the drive? Did she know it belonged to Tycoon? Or even worse, did she work for him herself?

I decided to play it cool. "Maybe I should just ask someone else to help me with this, because you don't believe me."

"I wouldn't do that if I were you," Lulu said in a soft voice. "I don't think you want anyone else to know you have this drive. Besides, I'm the best in the business. Nobody else will be able to crack the code but me."

"Really? There's no one else who can decode it?"

"Baby, trust me. I'm the best. But don't tell my fiancé. Henry likes to think he's the best." Lulu grinned. "But I'm going to need to take it with me to see what I can do with it."

I hesitated. I hated letting go of the flash drive. If Lulu took it, what guarantee was there that I'd ever get it back? She might be Fiona's friend, but she wasn't mine. I didn't know anything about her, except that she liked strong coffee and metallic hair dye, and that she was friends with the shady guy on my block. That didn't exactly add up to someone I could trust.

Lulu sensed my hesitation. "Look, I need to make a copy of the drive anyway, just in case I screw something up while I'm trying to decode it. I'll put the copied files on my laptop and let you keep the original drive. Does that sound okay?"

"That'll be fine."

"All right." Lulu's eyes met mine again. "And remember

what I said about my friends. If you're in trouble, they can help you. No matter who or what it is—or how bad it is."

I thought about Bandit and how he'd almost killed me last night. I could still hear that bullet whistling through the air over my head. I tried not to shiver.

"Don't worry, Lulu. I'm not in any trouble."

"Sure," she said in an easy voice, leaning back in her chair. "And I can tap dance."

Chapter Twenty-One

Lulu made a copy of the files on the flash drive and left the library. I found Piper on the third floor, flipping through another Confidante comic book, this one about Swifte. I told her what Lulu said about needing time to decrypt the files.

"Well, I should probably get back to the office," Piper said. "I need to review our latest earnings reports."

"Me too. I still have work to do on the Weston event."

"Call me the second anything changes," Piper said.

I promised her, and we went our separate ways. It was almost two by the time I made it back to my office. Chloe sat at her usual station, throwing a tennis ball to Rascal and working on her computer while he ran after it, wrestled the ball to the ground, and chewed on it.

"There you are," Chloe said. "I just got off the phone with Clean Dreams. They went to your apartment. They said your furniture was a total loss. So were your CDs. Most of the clothes were salvageable, so they took them to clean and repair."

I sighed. Chloe handed me the message, along with a stack of others from clients wanting updates about their events.

Rascal bounded back to Chloe. She gently pried the wet,

sticky tennis ball from his mouth and sent it skipping across the room. The puppy barked and raced after it.

"I also called Lou's Locks and had them change yours. The locksmith dropped off your new keys an hour ago." Chloe handed me an envelope. Then, she gave me a critical once-over. "Are you all right, Abby? You look tired."

I rubbed my head. I was tired. In the past few days, I'd saved a superhero, slept with him, discovered his secret identity, been attacked by an ubervillain, and gotten caught up in some weird conspiracy.

"It's nothing I can't handle." I cleared my throat. "But I wanted to say thanks, Chloe. I appreciate your hard work. I know I haven't been myself lately. You've really picked up the slack around here. I don't know what I would have done without you."

Her face brightened. "That's okay, Abby. I'm just glad you trust me enough to keep things running for you."

"Thanks, Chloe. You've been a big help."

"Oh, Abby!"

Before I could stop her, Chloe leapt up from her desk and threw her arms around me. What was it with her and the hugging? I started to roll my eyes but thought better of it. Instead, I reached up and patted her on the back. I supposed I could suffer through a hug. Chloe had been a lifesaver these past few days.

It was just too bad she couldn't save me from Bandit as well.

I spent the rest of the day working. Calling clients, badgering suppliers, and trying to nail down the details for the Weston event and the others I was juggling. T-minus two days and counting until the party of the week went off, but things were coming along nicely, despite the warp speed with which I'd had to arrange everything.

Chloe left around five o'clock. I dug through the few CDs I had stashed at the office and put in *American Pie* by Don McLean. The singer started the title song, and I kept right on plugging away. It was amazing how much stuff could pile up on my desk in a few hours.

By about nine o'clock, I had finished up everything that absolutely had to get done. Rascal had long ago gone to sleep on one of the couch cushions I'd pulled onto the floor for him. Every once in a while, the puppy let out a squeaky yip and his brown paws twitched. Maybe he was chasing Bandit or some other bad guy in his sleep.

I got up from my desk and stretched, rolling my neck from side to side. It cracked once, twice, three times, and some of the pressure drained from my body. I usually had no problem dealing with stress, but the past week had been a doozy.

I walked over to the door, opened it, and stepped onto the balcony. A spattering of snow crunched under my boots, and a steady, cold breeze ruffled my hair. I crossed my arms over my chest and leaned on the wall that ringed the balcony, staring out into the night. Late evening was my favorite time of day. It had been ever since my accident at The Blues. The Bigtime skyline glowed in the late evening, the buildings transforming into a soft, gunmetal gray around the white lights of the offices. Other beacons around the city added more diluted color, including the flashing red signal on top of *The Exposé's* skyscraper and the blue one over at *The Chronicle*.

The sounds softened too. Street vendors had packed up their carts and headed home, while slowing traffic patterns lessened the rumble of cars and buses. A few people walked on the street, but the frenzied crush of commuters had already trekked to the suburbs to let the city sleep for a few hours.

As I stared down, I thought of how much my life had

changed. This time last week, I'd been worried about pulling the O'Hara-Potter party together. Now I had another event to plan. Not to mention an encrypted flash drive half the city wanted to get their hands on and the unwanted attention of an ubervillain.

Oh yeah, I'd gone and fallen in love with a superhero too.

Maybe it was the hint of a smile that always seemed to be on his lips. Or his self-deprecating sense of humor. Or the fact that he didn't take the whole superhero thing too seriously. But I'd fallen for Talon—and his alter ego, Wesley Weston.

I wondered where Wesley was. If he was out as Talon tonight. If he was any closer to discovering my secret identity as Wren. I hoped not. I didn't know what I'd do if he learned the truth—or more importantly, how he'd react. Despite Piper's assurances that Talon—Wesley—would understand, I wasn't so sure. I'd drugged the man, after all. Dumped him in the convention center. Lied to him time and again.

I sighed. The cold seeped into my body, and I realized how tired I was. Time to go back to Piper's and crash on her sofa for another night. Clean Dreams might have hauled away the damaged furniture and CDs from my apartment, but I wasn't going back there. Not until Lulu decoded that flash drive and I gave it to Talon and the police. Not until I was sure Bandit and the mysterious Tycoon weren't coming to my loft in the middle of the night.

As I turned to go inside, I noticed the bird feeder was empty. Normally, this wouldn't have bothered me, but a solitary bird fluttered down from the sky and pecked at the empty feeder, searching for something to eat.

I stared at the bird. Big, bright eyes. Small body. Dull, brown color. A wren.

The bird hopped around the feeder, twittering a sweet, sad song. It stopped for a moment, shivering. I knew exactly how the wren felt—alone and cold.

So, I grabbed one of the bags of birdseed Chloe kept out here and scooped out enough to fill the feeder. The wren fluttered away at my approach but returned as soon as I stepped away. It dug its beak into the plastic container, snagging seed after seed. I shook my head and turned to go inside.

Thwang!

Something shot into the wall above my head, showering bits of brick everywhere. I ducked, falling into a crouch and pressing my body against the wall. Had Bandit come for the flash drive? Decided to attack me in my office? Was he shooting at me right now?

I held my breath, opened my ears, and listened—*really* listened—but no more *zips*, *zooms*, or *zings* sounded. I heard nothing except the murmur of car horns and distant conversations. I looked up, but my supersensitive eyes couldn't quite tell what had slammed into the building, and I didn't want to stay out here and find out.

I crawled along the ground, staying as close to the balcony wall as I could. Then, I got up into a crouch, balancing on the balls of my feet and ready to leapfrog through the open door back into my office before Bandit put a bullet in my back—

A masked figure dropped out of the sky, landing on the balcony in front of me, like a dark angel falling from the heavens.

I shrieked and rocked back. My right foot lurched sideways, and my knees gave way. I smacked into the ground, almost whacking my head on the bird feeder. I shook off the pain rocketing down my side and scooted back. The icy balcony seared my hands.

The tall figure loomed in the open doorway. Something clicked, like the hammer being drawn back on a gun. The shadow strode toward me. Then—I smelled mint and sighed with relief.

Blue boots stopped in front of me, and Talon crouched down until his face was level with mine. "Sorry about that. I didn't mean to scare you."

"I'm all for this partnership thing, but couldn't you have called first?" I groused. "I thought Bandit was shooting at me."

Talon frowned. "Why would you think that? My grappling hook barely makes a sound."

"Unfortunately, I have excellent hearing."

"Really? How interesting."

I couldn't see his eyes behind the blue visor, but I could feel Talon's gaze sharpening as he studied my face. I dropped my eyes and tried to figure out some way to get back on my feet without overly embarrassing myself—or shoving my ass in Talon's face again. The superhero came to my rescue once more.

Standing, he offered me a gloved hand. I took it, and he pulled me to my feet.

"Why am I always picking you up, Abby?" Talon murmured, his voice low and teasing.

I relished the feel of his hand on mine, even if it was covered by a leather glove. "I suppose because I'm always falling down. Sorry. Being clumsy is a bad habit of mine."

He flashed me a smile. "Don't worry about it. It's my job."

His job. I dropped his hand. He'd given me a hand because it was his *job*. I wanted him to help me because he liked doing it, liked spending time with me. Not because some stupid superhero code of honor made him put clumsy chicks back on their feet.

"How are you, Abby?" Talon asked, failing to notice my darkening mood. "I came by to check on you."

"I'm fine, just a little tired. I suppose I should thank you for taking me to Piper's last night—even if you did knock me out to do it."

He shrugged, not the least bit sorry about gassing me. "It was a necessary precaution, Abby. Surely, you can understand."

I did. More than he'd ever realize.

"So what's going on?" I asked, probing for the real reason behind his visit. He hadn't come just to see me. I wasn't that optimistic—or naïve.

"I uncovered some information that might get me closer to Nightingale, to finding out who she really is. Hopefully, that will lead me to the flash drive."

My heart froze in my chest. "Like what?"

Talon leaned against the edge of the balcony. "I lifted her DNA and a few partial prints off some duct tape she used. I also managed to get my hands on black-and-white surveillance footage of her running away from the Bigtime Convention Center. Unfortunately, the center only has cameras on the front of building, but it should give me a rough idea of what she looks like."

DNA? Fingerprints? Surveillance footage? Who the hell was he? *CSI: Superhero?* Hot, sweaty panic gurgled up in my throat, but I forced it down, squashing it with cold, calm reason. I thought back to that night. Okay, so he'd gotten my DNA and prints off the tape, but it wouldn't help him. I'd never had my DNA tested for anything, and I'd never been fingerprinted.

I'd been wearing a heavy coat, gloves, a toboggan, and a scarf wrapped around my face. More importantly, I didn't remember looking up when I'd rushed out of the convention center, so he shouldn't get much from the surveillance camera. Oh, he'd know I had a black coat, but so did thousands of women in Bigtime. He wouldn't get my hair, eye color, or skin tone. Besides, I had a very average, nondescript sort of face. He wouldn't know it was me. It would be okay, I told myself. It would have to be.

Still, the fact that he was still looking for me, for Nightingale, touched and unnerved me. You'd think he was Prince Charming and I was some fairy princess he was chasing. The fairest woman in all the land, or some such nonsense, instead of a plain Jane, overworked event planner. The equivalent of an ugly stepsister.

"What about you?" he asked. "Did you find out anything?"

"Well, Bandit ransacked my apartment. Not that that's particularly helpful, but I thought you should know."

He nodded. "I don't want you to go back there until this is over with. You shouldn't be alone either or work late by yourself."

"I'll try to remember all that," I said with a wry smile. "Tomorrow."

We stood there, looking at each other.

"Well," I said, "I hate to be a party pooper, but it's late, and I'm tired. I'm going to go back to Piper's and crash for the night. Thanks for dropping by."

Talon hesitated. Damn that thick visor. I couldn't tell what emotions swirled behind the blue lenses. "Would you like a lift?"

"What?" I replied, a little confused. "Are you going to call me a taxi or something? Or do you have your own supervan like the Fearless Five do?"

A slow smile spread across his face. "Nope. I have something even better."

CHAPTER TWENTY-TWO

"I'm not sure this is such a good idea," I said, staring over the edge of the balcony.

We stood on the ledge. When Talon offered to take me home, he meant getting around the way he did—using his grappling hook to swing from rooftop to rooftop. I stared down at the street again. Thirteen stories looked a lot higher and scarier than it had five minutes ago.

"Do you trust me?" Talon asked, using the same cajoling tone I did with my panicked debutantes.

I bit my lip and nodded. Rascal let out an excited bark from the pocket on my vest. Evidently, the puppy knew exactly what was going on and thought the whole thing was going to be a grand adventure. I hated adventures. I'd always thought *adventure* was a polite way of saying *this is a stupid way to die*.

"Then it'll be okay," Talon said. "I promise. Now, hold on to me, and don't let go."

I wrapped my arms around him as tight as I could, not even caring whether it was appropriate. The G-man superhero's right arm cinched around my waist like a steel vise. Talon drew his grappling hook gun out of the harness on his leg and pulled the trigger. The silver hook arched out, carrying a long zip line with it, and clanked onto the building across the street. Talon yanked on the solidium cable, ensuring it was firmly anchored. At least, that was what I hoped he was doing. I couldn't bring myself to look.

"Here we go," he whispered in my ear.

Talon leapt off the roof, taking me and Rascal with him. I closed my eyes, not wanting to see how very high we were. I wasn't necessarily scared of heights, just of falling—and being splattered onto the pavement below. But cutting off my vision didn't help. The rest of my supersenses kicked in, compensating for my blindness. I could feel every part of our descent. The wind pushing against my back. The empty space surrounding us. The sharp tang of terror in my mouth.

We landed on the roof of the building across the street. I didn't move away from Talon for fear my knees would buckle.

"You know, you might enjoy it a little more if you opened your eyes," he teased.

"Maybe next time," I muttered, burying my face against his neck.

Two buildings later, I did manage to open my eyes. We sailed down Talon's zip line, almost like we were flying. The air was clear up here, clean and fresh and free of the hazy smog that sometimes blanketed Bigtime. I drew a deep breath down into my lungs, enjoying the scent. Maybe this wasn't so bad after all.

Rascal liked the sensation too. The puppy let out several happy yips, although he seemed to know enough not to squirm around and fall out of my pocket. Still, I sandwiched him between Talon's body and my own, just in case. We soared from building to building, sailing over the city below. The skyscrapers and office lights twinkled like a carpet of stars beneath us.

Mostly though, I was happy to be with Talon. Even if he was just doing his superhero duty and helping a lost chick get home.

By the time we landed on the roof of Piper's building, I was sorry to see the evening come to an end.

"Thanks for the lift." I forced myself to drop my arms from around his neck and step away. "It was really something."

"Something good or something bad?"

"At first, I would have said something bad, but now I can see why you do it," I replied. "The feel of the wind in your hair, the sense of flying, the thrill of making the perfect landing. It has its charms."

Talon smiled. "You're one of the few people I've met who really understands that."

I gave him a quizzical look. "Why? Don't you have other superhero friends?"

He shrugged. "Sure. We all help each other out, but I'm a pretty solitary guy. Most of the other heroes in Bigtime have a superpower or two. I don't, and that sets me apart."

"So, why do you do it? Why be a superhero if you aren't like everybody else?"

"I'd like to say I'm doing something noble, like avenging the death of my parents at the hands of an ubervillain or making the world a better place for humanity. Being a symbol for justice. Using my superpowers for the greater good. All the usual motivators."

"You're not doing those things?"

"Sorry," Talon said. "My parents are alive and well. I don't have a lot of angst or issues, and I don't consider myself a beacon of hope inspiring others. I just don't like bullies, and that's what so many of the ubervillains are. Schoolyard bullies in spandex costumes, and Bigtime is their playground."

I'd never really thought about it that way before, but I could see his point. "Bullies like Tycoon and Bandit."

He nodded. "They're some of the worst ones. Tycoon thinks his money, power, and anonymity make him untouchable. Bandit just enjoys hurting people. If I never accomplish anything else as a superhero, I'm going to find a way to take them down."

I thought about my shoulder and the way Bandit had hit me. Yeah, the ubervillain liked hurting people.

"It's not easy not being like the other heroes, not having a power to help me, but what can I say? I like a challenge." Talon grinned. "Besides, chicks dig superheroes."

I laughed. "Yeah, they do."

We fell silent. I thought about Talon's words, about how he was a loner. And I thought of the events I'd planned, of all the nights I'd stood along the wall and hovered in a dark corner watching everyone else have fun.

"I know what you mean. It's not easy being different, being an outsider."

Talon nodded. "No, it's not."

"Still, sometimes, it's nice to be alone."

He stared at me. "But sometimes it's even nicer to have someone to share it with."

My brows pulled together in confusion. Was he—did he mean—could he possibly have enjoyed himself tonight? With me? Abby Appleby, not the mysterious Nightingale?

For the first time since this whole thing started, a bit of hope flared up in my chest, a single match sputtering in a cavern of darkness. But before I could open my mouth to ask him what he meant, Talon raised his gun high and shot his cable up into the sky.

He bowed his head, hit a button on the gun, and soared into the darkness. All I could do was stare at the spot where he'd been.

Rascal let out a plaintive whine, wondering where his new friend Talon had gone and desperately wanting him to come back.

"Me too, boy," I whispered. "Me too."

I used my key to let myself into Piper's apartment. She sat at her kitchen table, which was embossed with the Fearless Five logo. Her finger hovered over the buttons on her Hermit phone, as though I'd caught her in mid-dial.

"There you are!" Piper said, getting up and pulling me into a tight hug. "I was getting worried about you. I called your office and your cell, but you didn't answer. I thought something might have happened."

"I'm fine," I said, returning her hug. "I turned the phones off so I could get some work done. I should have told you I would be late. Sorry. But something did happen—Talon showed up at my office."

Piper wanted all the juicy details right away, but I made her order a Pizzazz pizza first. Over slices topped with ham, pineapple, and extra mozzarella, I told her about Talon appearing on my balcony—and taking me on a moonlight ride across the city.

"How romantic! I wish I had a superhero for a boyfriend." Her eyes drifted to the Swifte clock on the wall.

"He's not my boyfriend," I insisted. "He doesn't even like me. He's just letting me help him find the flash drive, humoring me because Bandit tried to put a bullet in my head."

Piper gave me a knowing smirk. "Oh, he's your boyfriend—he just doesn't know it yet."

Pizza forgotten, Piper started talking about how much time we'd been spending together, how he kept showing up wherever I was, and of course, the kicker—the fact that we'd slept together. Piper was so wrapped up in her speech she didn't even notice when Rascal hopped up in a chair, snatched her half-eaten slice, and downed it in two gulps before either one of us could stop him. She sneezed, absently patted him, and prattled on some more about destiny, karma, and true love.

I let her words wash over me as I helped myself to another slice of pizza. No matter what Piper said, no matter what she proclaimed or what her Mr. Sage calendar said, I knew the truth. There was only one woman Talon was interested in, and it wasn't me. At least, it wasn't the *real* me—it was Nightingale.

I sighed. Rascal took the sound as a cue that he could have some more pizza. He put his nose on the table, nudging the white cardboard box toward the edge. I grabbed the box just before it slid over the side and took the last two pieces with it. Rascal whined, upset over the loss of his pizza.

"Sorry, boy," I said, getting another slice. "But I need this a lot more than you do."

I spent the night on Piper's sofa, tossing, turning, and trying not to think about Talon. Rascal awakened me the next morning with a pizza-flavored tongue bath.

"Ugh. You little mutt," I groused, rubbing his ears. "What am I going to do with you? Besides buy you some toothpaste?"

"I might have a solution." Piper sat at the kitchen table drinking apple juice and reading the latest edition of *The Exposé*. "I've been talking to some people about taking him off your hands. Kyle said he'd love to have a dog."

"He did?"

"Yep."

She tried to pretend like it was nothing, but I could have heard the slight catch in her voice even if I didn't have superhearing.

"Wait a minute. Why were you talking to Kyle? What

happened to *I hope the rotten bastard gets an STD and can never have sex again*? Remember? That was your latest diabolical thought."

Piper sighed. "Kyle and I might not be together anymore, but I still care about him. I always will, despite what he did to me. Besides, I should get something out of him dumping me."

I couldn't argue with that. There wasn't much you could do with a broken heart, not even when you were as optimistic as Piper.

"There's a storage room at Quicke's where Rascal could stay during the day while Kyle works," she continued. "I think Kyle wants to make Rascal some sort of mascot. Maybe even dress him up in a little cape. Wouldn't that be cute?"

"Oh yeah. Cute."

Rascal barked, as though he liked the idea. I hugged the puppy to my chest. Over the past few days, I'd gotten attached to the little guy. I wasn't sure how I felt about giving him away. He'd grown on me, wormed his way into my heart as easily as he did everyone else's. Maybe that was his real superpower.

But it would be better for him to be with someone else. Someone who could really be around for him, instead of shuffling him from place to place. Someone who had time to play with him and feed him and love him. Running my own business sucked up most of my time, and it wouldn't be fair to Rascal to be locked in my office or loft all day long, to always be at the bottom of my to-do list instead of at the top. He deserved better than that. I *wanted* him to have better than that.

As much as I would miss Rascal, giving him to Kyle would be for the best. Besides, it would give me another excuse to berate the caterer, if he didn't take good care of my puppy.

Piper left to go to work, and so did I, taking Rascal with me. By ten o'clock, I'd done everything I should have, except for one item—call Wesley and update him on his event. His was the only message I hadn't returned.

I leaned back in my chair and stared at my phone. I should

call him. I shouldn't put it off any longer. Shouldn't wait. And I definitely shouldn't go see him in person.

My hand hovered over the phone. Rascal raised his head off his cushion. Then, he scrambled up, hurtled across the office, and circled around my feet doing the classic, doggie *I-have-to-go-outside-right-now-and-pee-pee-pee* dance.

I smiled. The puppy had just given me the perfect excuse to get out of the office and visit Wesley. Two birds with one stone, and all that. I did so love to multitask.

"Come on, Rascal," I said, grabbing my coat. "We're going out."

I clipped Rascal on his leash—the cobalt-blue one Talon had left behind—and headed to Paradise Park. Normally, I avoided the park because of the constant noise and flashing lights. But I cut through the back side that bordered Bigtime Cemetery and let Rascal do his business on the icy grass. Once the puppy finished, I scooped him up and carried him, wanting to get to Wesley's office building before I lost my nerve.

Ten minutes later, I stepped into the lobby and walked over to the security guard. "Abby Appleby. I'm here to see Mr. Weston."

"Do you have an appointment?" the guard muttered, shooting me a hostile look. It was the same guy I'd faced down before—the one who hadn't wanted to let me take Rascal up to Wesley's office.

"No. But I need to see Mr. Weston and give him this." I held up a folder that contained the final details for the party.

I could have e-mailed the files. Maybe I *should* have e-mailed them, but I wanted to see Wesley—for reasons I didn't want to think too much about right now.

"I can take that for you," the guard replied, holding out his hand.

I pulled the folder back. "I would prefer to personally put it on his desk."

I never left anything with assistants because they had an annoying habit of misplacing things. I certainly wasn't going to leave the folder with Mr. Bad Attitude. He'd chunk it in the trash can before I got out of the building.

The guard looked at me, then at Rascal. "Mr. Weston said he didn't want to be disturbed this morning."

That old excuse? I'd only heard it a thousand times before. "I'll take my chances."

"Fine," the guard muttered. "Go on up."

I rode the elevator up to the penthouse. The doors *pinged!* open, but the sound didn't bother me. I was too intent on seeing Wesley to care about the migraine gathering in the base of my skull. I stepped inside the office. The waterfall gurgled and fell as usual. I admired the rock wall before turning toward the desk.

To my surprise, Wesley wasn't there. My eyes flicked around the office, but he wasn't relaxing on any of the other chairs or couches. I breathed in. I didn't even detect his minty scent in the enormous room.

"Mr. Weston?" I called out. "Wesley?"

No answer.

Maybe he'd gone out for a power brunch or the guard had known he wasn't in the office and lied to me. I pushed away my disappointment and strode over the bridge to his desk. I put the folder on top of the stack of papers. Unlike Fiona's haphazard desk, Wesley's was the very picture of organization, with everything neatly stacked and filed.

Rascal pulled on his leash, wanting to explore, so I let go of the long rope. I reached into my vest and pulled out a notepad, along with a pen. I scribbled down the reason for my visit, asked that Wesley call me, and stuck the note on top of the folder. I also went ahead and e-mailed the files from my phone, so he would have electronic versions as well.

I put my notepad, pen, and phone back in their appropriate pockets, then looked for Rascal. The puppy was sniffing the rocks along the edge of the pool under the waterfall. I walked over and crouched down beside him, running my hands through his silky, sand-colored fur.

"All right, boy. It's time to go back to work."

I started to pick up Rascal, but he wasn't through sniffing. He wiggled away from me and started barking and bouncing around like he was a jackrabbit.

"Rascal!" I snapped. "Come back here!"

The puppy paid no attention to me. He scampered along the pool, running toward the rushing water. He reached the wall, headed left. And then—he disappeared.

I froze. One moment, the puppy had been by the rocks, the next he'd vanished. Had he fallen into the water?

I blinked, sure my eyes were playing tricks on me, but my eyes never did that. Not anymore. Rascal wasn't anywhere in sight.

I hurried to over to the rocks, right up to the edge of the waterfall, where it formed the left wall of the office. I dropped to my knees and peered into the swirling water, hoping to see a wet head bobbing up and down. I wouldn't care how bad he smelled as long as he was all right.

Nothing.

"Rascal? Rascal!"

A tinny bark sounded above the roar of the waterfall. I cocked my ear, listening—*really* listening. He barked again, and something moved off to my left. I ducked my head down and squinted. After a moment, I realized Rascal hadn't fallen into the pool—he'd gone around it. Some sort of tunnel ran behind the waterfall, barely visible from where I was.

I got to my feet and approached the wall, peering through the falling water. Rascal stood in the middle of the hidden walkway and barked again, his feet bouncing off the floor and exposing his white belly.

"Get out of there! Come here! Right now!"

Rascal gave me a silly grin, then turned and loped farther down the tunnel.

I stepped past the cascading water, and the cool mist kissed my face, but the tunnel itself was dry. The three-foot-wide sliver of space ran parallel to the wall. I wondered what it was for. Maintenance?

Rascal galloped ahead of me. Maybe he really was a superdog, as Talon claimed. He could sure move quick enough. I hurried to catch the puppy.

And then—he disappeared. *Again.*

I rushed forward to the spot where he'd been. The walkway came to a dead end ahead, and Rascal hadn't fallen into the pool. I would have heard or seen the splash. So where had he gone?

A strip of white caught my attention, and the faint outline of a door came into focus. He must have gone in there. I pushed on the door, and it swung open. I stepped through, ready to admonish the dog. Just because Rascal was supercute didn't mean he had the right to put himself in danger. He easily could have skidded off the walkway and fallen into the water during his enthusiastic romp. This area was not a playroom—

The thought vanished from my mind.

I found myself staring at three very familiar walls—walls covered with gadgets, maps, photographs, and computer monitors. My eyes flicked to the man sitting in the center of it all—Wesley.

Chapter Twenty-Three

This was the room Talon had taken me to when he'd rescued me from Bandit. The waterfall. Talon's secret lair, Wesley's secret superhero lair, lay behind the waterfall in his office. I should have known.

Wesley stared at me. This time, no visor hid his reaction. Shock and horror flashed in his golden eyes, but it was quickly followed by what looked like relief. Relief? Why would he be relieved I'd discovered his secret?

"Well, I see you found me after all, Abby," Wesley said, rising to his feet.

"I—um—well, you see—"

My voice trailed off under his intense gaze. Finally, I realized that I was supposed to say something, to explain why I'd wandered in here. "I came to drop off some papers for you. Rascal got onto the walkway. I tried to grab him, but he ran away. Then, I saw the door."

"And you just had to push it open."

I winced. "Guilty as charged. I didn't want Rascal to get hurt."

Wesley's gaze went to Rascal, who sprawled in the middle of

the floor, panting. He stared at the puppy, then back at me. He nodded.

"I'm glad you found me, that you know I'm really Talon. It'll make things easier."

I blinked. He wasn't mad? He wasn't going to yell, scream, and try to gas me into oblivion? He wasn't going to shoot me up with some drug to make me forget my discovery? What kind of superhero was he?

"It will?" I asked.

He smiled. "It will. I've made some progress regarding the surveillance footage. I don't recognize the woman, but maybe you will. You seem to know a lot of people in Bigtime."

A queasy feeling settled into the pit of my stomach. "I'll give it my best shot," I said, lying through my teeth.

Wesley shut the door and locked it to make sure no one else would wander in. Then, he leaned over his computer and pulled up the surveillance footage from the convention center the night of the O'Hara party. He hit a few buttons and stepped back.

My picture popped up on a dozen monitors.

The camera had caught me as I fled through the front of the center. My eyes fixed straight ahead, my arms pumping at my sides in mid-run. The still, black-and-white photo was grainy, but I recognized myself. I doubted anyone else would, though, except Piper. With my brown hair, green eyes, and pale skin, I don't have a very memorable face. And I certainly wasn't anywhere close to gorgeous, as Talon had so fervently claimed in my apartment.

"I'm not sure," I said, pretending to contemplate the mystery woman. "It's not a good photo, and you can't see her face. Just a bit of her nose where it sticks out of her scarf."

"I know. I just hoped maybe you might recognize her, that you'd know her from *somewhere*." Frustration tinged his voice. "I ran her DNA and partial prints through every database I could hack into. Nothing. The same thing went for my facial recognition software. All that tells me is she's never been arrested or fingerprinted. Which, I suppose, is a good thing."

I tried to keep my tone light and casual. "Is there another reason you want to find her? Other than just getting the flash drive back?"

He froze for a heartbeat and stared at the monitor. I thought he was going to give me the old song-and-dance about thanking the mystery woman for saving him, but he surprised me.

"I spent some time with Nightingale while I was recuperating from my injury. I know it sounds crazy, but we talked, we laughed, we connected. That kind of feeling, that kind of emotion, is rare."

I had to clear my throat before I could speak. "You sound like you care a lot about her."

He turned his golden eyes to me. "I do care about her. That's why I want to find her. That's why I'm *going* to find her."

There he went with that fierce, princely determination again. That dogged emotion that made me melt. Wesley didn't mention sleeping with the woman, and I couldn't bring it up. In a way, it was like I was a superhero—but I could never, ever tell my civilian lover who I really was. He'd be disappointed and angry I'd lied to him—no matter what Piper said.

"I'm sorry I can't help you. But I'm glad I know who you really are. And—and I wanted to say I had a nice time last night. When you took me home." I forced out the last few words.

Wesley gave me a small smile. "I did too. Once you quit screaming."

My mouth dropped open to protest when I realized he was teasing me. "I didn't scream so much as whimper."

A rumble rose up in Wesley's throat, and he laughed. I joined

247

in, enjoying the sound of us laughing—together. Then, the laughter faded away, and there was nothing left but his eyes on mine, and the tight, hot rush of emotions in my chest.

I looked away. "Well, I should be going. Getting back to work."

"I understand," Wesley murmured. "I should too. Do me a favor, Abby?"

"What?"

"Be careful," he said. "Bandit is still out there. Until we find Nightingale and the flash drive, you're in danger."

"Don't worry. I have no desire to run into him again."

"Good."

He walked over and opened the door for me, and I grabbed Rascal's leash. I started to leave but stopped, not wanting to go. Suddenly, I wanted to confess who I really was to Wesley. Give him the flash drive and tell him everything. He deserved to know, even if I could never measure up to his idea of what his mystery woman was. I moved closer and opened my mouth.

Wesley stared down into my face, his golden eyes tracing my features. He looked at me—*really* looked at me—as if he was seeing me for the first time. His gaze darkened to the color of amber.

The intense scrutiny made me nervous, but I plunged ahead. "Wesley, I need to tell you—"

He leaned in and kissed me. His lips touched mine, and my words were lost, swept away by the tingles zipping through my body—tingles that melted into electric heat.

I couldn't quite believe it. Wesley was kissing me—the *real* me.

Abby. Not Wren. Not Nightingale.

Me. Just me. Only me.

The kiss was soft, gentle, sweet. Nothing like the hard, quick, fevered ones we'd exchanged in my apartment. There was no frenzy here. No hurry. Only his lips and mine—together.

Wesley settled his hands on my hips, his fingers resting on my waist. My hands crept up to his shoulders. I wanted to wrap my arms around his neck, yank him toward me, and kiss him like there was no tomorrow. Kiss him with every ounce of feeling I had for him. But I didn't want to scare him. After all, he really wanted Nightingale. He was probably just kissing me because I was here—because he couldn't have *her*.

The thought broke my heart, but not enough for me to end the kiss.

Wesley's hand went to my cheek, cupping it. He tilted my head and deepened the kiss. I marveled at his gentle touch. How could a man with such rough hands have such an easy way with them? Wesley's tongue found mine, and I opened my senses, imprinting every bit of him onto my mind, my heart.

His hard fingers against my cheek. His clean, minty smell. The scrape of his stubble against my cheek. His body pressed to mine. The quick catch in his breath. The pounding of his heart under my palm.

I knew this would never happen again. Not to Abby Appleby. So, I savored these sensations, these feelings, this one kiss.

Everything was perfect—until Rascal barked.

We froze, lips just touching. Rascal barked again, and we looked down at him. The puppy sat at our feet, wagging his tail. Evidently, he wanted in on the kissing action. I sighed.

Wesley pulled back, dropping his hand from my cheek. I let go of his shoulders. And the perfect moment ended.

His eyes gleamed in his face. "I'm sorry, Abby. I don't know what came over me. Please accept my—"

"Do *not* apologize," I snapped. "Say anything you want but that."

Surprise filled his features, and he looked at me as if he'd spotted something he'd never seen before. As if I were some strange zoo creature he was peering at through metal bars. A freak of nature. If he only knew what a superfreak I really was.

Then, his face cleared and smoothed into an unreadable mask.

"All right," Wesley said. "I won't apologize."

I nodded, not sure what else to say. Not sure I could say anything without telling him everything—including how I felt about him.

"Well, I guess I'll see you tomorrow night at the party," Wesley said. "Unless I find out some more information before then."

"Until then."

"Until then," he murmured.

I gave him a faint smile, then led Rascal through the hidden door as fast as I could.

CHAPTER TWENTY-FOUR

"You have to give him the flash drive, and you have to tell him who you really are," Piper said an hour later. "Not necessarily in that order."

I leaned back in the chair in my office.

"It's obvious the man is attracted to you." Her voice rang with conviction.

I turned down the volume on my headset. "No, he's not. He's attracted to Nightingale. I was just there, a handy pair of lips he could lay into."

Piper sighed. "You are, without a doubt, the most pessimistic person I know, Abby. You need to have more self-confidence."

"Why?" I muttered. "So I can screw up my courage and do something stupid, like bare my soul to Wesley, only to have him tell me thanks, but no thanks?"

"No," she snapped. "So you'll quit thinking of yourself as invisible. As everyone else's problem solver instead of your own. You do so much for everyone else, you never stop and do things for yourself, Abby."

"You're the pretty one," I tried to joke. "I'm the one who gets things done. That's the way it is."

"No, that's just the label you put on me—and yourself."

Piper's sharp tone cut me like broken glass because what she said was true, and we both knew it. I did think of myself as invisible. And not in a joking sort of way. Being an event planner, being a problem solver, blending into the background had become more than just how I made my living—it had seeped into every aspect of my life, like a radioactive goo eroding everything, including my own sense of self-worth.

"Why do you put up with me and my neuroses?" I asked in a soft voice.

"Because I love you, and somebody has to be around to kick your ass every once in a while."

My throat closed up. "I love you too."

"Good," Piper said. "Now that we've got the ass-kicking out of the way, I say we go blow off a little steam. And I know just the thing—karaoke."

"I don't feel like karaoke tonight," I said.

"Of course you do," she replied. "You *always* feel like karaoke. Now, finish up at work and bring Rascal over to my apartment. It's time for some singing and drinking. Not necessarily in that order."

Piper and I arrived at The Blues just after seven. The karaoke bar was housed in a brick building on the outskirts of downtown. A line had already formed outside the door as people waited to get in. Three music notes marking the entrance glowed in the darkening night. Their vivid blue color reminded me of Talon's costume.

Piper and I had discovered The Blues in college. For a five-dollar cover charge, you could drink all the beer you wanted—as long as you sang at least one song. Piper didn't like to sing, but she didn't have to. There was always some guy more than happy to buy her a drink. But I actually enjoyed getting up on stage and belting my heart out. It was the only time when people looked at me—even if they were halfway wasted.

Izzy, the tattoo-covered bouncer, gestured at us. We stepped up, and he let us past the blue velvet rope. Piper and I came to the bar at least once a week, so Izzy knew us well and that I could actually sing a bit. And because this was the place where I'd had my unfortunate accident, they had to let us in.

The inside of The Blues was simple and classy. A long, chrome bar ran along one wall, accented by strings of blue icicle lights. Stairs along either side of the back wall led up to a three-foot-high stage. Sound equipment and racks full of song books crouched in front of the area, while a blue disco ball spun over the top of it. Right now, a college-age girl with pea-green curls warbled out "Hit the Road Jack" by Ray Charles.

"Let's get a drink first," I shouted over the noise. "I need to talk to Melody anyway about tomorrow night."

Piper nodded, and we headed in that direction. We waited until a couple of guys in suits tried unsuccessfully to hit on Piper while ignoring me. After she shot them down, we took their places at the bar. I waved to Melody Masters, the owner, and held up two fingers. She waved back.

About three minutes later, Melody deposited a wine spritzer on the bar in front of Piper and a Bloody Mary for me.

"Hey, Abby. What's up?" Melody asked, her voice a little raspy.

"Same old, same old. You?"

She grinned. "Same old, same old. But it ain't half bad."

Melody's half bad would have been pretty good for anyone else. She was a tall, lithe woman with short, tousled red hair and sparkling blue eyes. She wore a leather miniskirt, a red bustier, and ankle-high biker boots. Melody looked like she'd been born to be a rock star—and she was trying to make the dream come true.

"We all set for the Weston event tomorrow?"

She nodded. "Yep. Me and the gang have been looking over the playlist you gave us. We're definitely ready to rock."

I raised an eyebrow.

"Within reason," she added. "Wouldn't want to give the old guard too much excitement."

"Exactly, I don't need anyone having a heart attack while you're on stage."

Melody laughed, but the sound devolved into a cough.

"Are you okay?" I asked. "You don't sound so good. You're not sick, are you?"

"Nah, I'm fine. Just a little something in my throat."

She grinned again and moved off to take care of a customer at the other end of the bar. I watched her, but Melody laughed and talked with everyone the way she always did.

Piper and I swiveled around on our stools. As we watched the action, I felt myself relaxing. Piper was right. I was in the mood for karaoke. This was my place, and tonight, I wasn't going to think about Talon, Wesley, Bandit, or what could be on the mystery flash drive. Tonight, I was going to drink, sing, and have a good time.

I jerked my head at the stage. Piper smiled and ordered us another round. I moved through the crowd, winding my way around tables and giggling groups of college co-eds, before reaching the steps that led up to the stage. A tall guy wearing an oversized Hawaiian shirt sat at a table in the corner, a headphone held up to his ear. On stage, a skinny guy with a rather large Adam's apple and thick glasses crooned out a decent version of "Come Monday" by Jimmy Buffett. I headed for the guy in the Hawaiian shirt.

"Abby! What's going on, girl?" Stanley Solomon said, grinning.

"Not much."

"You going up on stage tonight?" he asked, sliding controls up and down on the board in front of him.

"You know it."

Stanley had been overseeing the sound system at The Blues for as long as I could remember. He'd been trying to fix that cursed amp the night of my accident, but I'd gotten zapped instead of him. As a result, Stanley never let me touch anything now. I couldn't blame him. Honestly, I wasn't sticking my hand near any amp again—ever.

"What are you in the mood for?" Stanley asked. "Some jazz, some R&B, maybe a little disco?"

"Nah," I said. "I'm in the mood to rock."

He smiled.

For the next half-hour, I sang song after song, pouring my heart out to the drunken patrons and anyone else who was listening. I did some Green Day, a few songs by The Killers, some classics by The Pretenders, all my old favorites.

"'Time After Time'?" Stanley asked when I told him what I wanted to end with. "By Cyndi Lauper?"

I nodded.

A grin spread across his face. "Whatever floats your boat, Abby."

That's what I finished out the night with. More than a few people clapped as I took a short bow and walked off stage. I nodded and smiled, appreciating the applause. Even I thought I'd been pretty good tonight.

More important was how I felt—and the decision I'd made. Somewhere between the first drink and my last song, I'd decided to go for it. To tell Wesley, to tell Talon, who I really was. That I was his mysterious Wren—and see if he thought I could be his Nightingale too.

Piper was right. It was time to quit being invisible. Time to quit blending into the background. Time to make a stand, make some noise. Time to rock. Time to focus on what *I* wanted. And I wanted Wesley.

I just hoped he'd feel the same way too.

"You were awesome, Abby!" Piper said when I rejoined her at the bar. "And I'm not just saying that because I'm your best friend."

I grinned. "I know."

She narrowed her eyes. "You know? Usually, I have to browbeat you before you admit how great you were. So, are you going to tell me what's going on with you? Or do I have to guess?"

"I'll going to tell him. I'm going to tell Wesley everything."

Her lips curved into a satisfied smile. "Well, it's about time."

"But I'm blaming you if he hates me forever for lying to him," I added. "So, be prepared."

"I think I can handle it," Piper replied.

She raised her glass, and I clinked mine against it. The sound was music to my ears.

PART THREE

ABBY

CHAPTER TWENTY-FIVE

The next morning, I left Rascal with Chloe at the office. Then, I spent the rest of the day at the Bigtime Convention Center, ensuring that everything arrived on time and was put in place for the Weston event.

Burly guys hauled in cases of champagne, wine, and other spirits. Three women wearing shockproof gloves plugged strobe lights into hidden wall outlets. Still more men and women carted in tables, chairs, linens, and crystal.

Unlike the O'Hara event, I'd decided to have the business dinner and the after party here in the auditorium instead of serving the food in one of the other rooms. It was easier to oversee everything when it was in one spot. Plus, I'd gone all out for the décor. I didn't want to split the effect by having part of it here and part of it somewhere else. Wesley wanted to wow people, and he was going to get his wish.

Stanley moved from one side of the stage to the other, installing extra amps and wiring in the sound system. Melody clutched a microphone and followed him, doing sound check after sound check. Her voice seemed raspier today, but she gave me a thumbs-up.

I watched from the balcony as five men from Isabella's Exquisite Ice rolled a dolly toward the orchestra pit, which had already been converted into a bar, complete with red vinyl swivel stools. A fifteen-foot-tall ice guitar with flames coming out of its sides perched on top of the dolly.

The movers had almost reached the end of the aisle when one of the men tripped over his own feet and fell against the dolly. The guitar sculpture rocked on its pedestal. I sucked in a breath. The other movers froze. The massive block of ice creaked back, then forth, before settling into its groove once more.

"Hey, buddy!" My voice boomed through the auditorium like thunder.

Everyone turned in my direction. I leaned over the balcony and stabbed my pen at the klutz who'd almost ruined my ten-thousand-dollar ice sculpture.

"You!"

The guy pointed at his chest. I gave him a sharp nod. He swallowed.

"You cause that to tip over, and I'll put you on ice— permanently. You feel me?"

The man nodded and hurried down the aisle to join the rest of his crew. Slowly, carefully, they transferred the frozen block from the dolly onto the air-conditioned, checkerboard stand at the left end of the bar. The matching sculpture was already in place on the right side.

Once they finished, the movers looked up at me. I nodded in approval and checked *ice sculptures* off the three-page-long list on my clipboard.

The smell of bleach and cigarettes assaulted my nose, and Colt Colton moved to stand beside me. The maintenance man wore his usual uniform of gray coveralls and work boots, with his dark hair back in a low ponytail.

"Problems, Abby?" Colt asked.

"No more than usual. Why are you here? I thought you were helping Eddie hang the disco balls."

"I needed a smoke break," he said. "Eddie's doing the last one now."

Smoke break? Yeah, I could have figured that out without my supernose. Colt reeked of tobacco. Filthy habit. Even if Colt had asked me out before I'd met Wesley, I still would have told him no. I didn't date guys who smelled like a smokestack.

A harsh clang of metal caught my ear, and I looked up at the catwalk circling the auditorium. Eddie stood a hundred feet above me. I watched as he lowered a five-foot-wide mirrored, silver sphere over the edge of the railing. The disco ball joined the others that ringed the area. Eddie tugged on the line a couple times. Then, he stepped back and stared at the ball. When he was sure it was secure, he gave me a thumbs-up. I waved back and checked *disco balls* off my list.

"You coming back for the event later tonight?"

I nodded. "Yep, coming back and staying until the bitter end."

"Maybe we could get a drink after you're done," Colt suggested.

I looked up to find him studying me with his dark eyes. "I don't know what to say."

"Say yes."

I couldn't. Not now. Not tonight. In less than twelve hours, I was planning on telling Wesley that I was really Wren. I wasn't going to be stuck in a bar with Colt.

"You know I told you I was getting over a bad relationship?"

He nodded.

"Well, it's back on now."

His eyes darkened.

"I'm sorry—"

"That's okay," he said, cutting me off. "I always seem to be a step behind these days. Later, Abby."

"Later, Colt."

He strolled toward the stairs, opened the door, and disappeared. An uneasy feeling ballooned in my stomach. That was the second time in less than a week Colt had asked me out. I couldn't figure out why. He couldn't think I was that hot. Could he?

I shook my head. Maybe Piper was right. Maybe I only thought I was invisible. Or maybe Colt was just desperate.

The *tinkle-tinkle* of breaking glass caught my ear, and I leaned back over the balcony. One of the workers crouched on her hands and knees, trying to scoop up the shattered remains of a champagne flute. She shot frantic looks over her head, hoping I hadn't noticed the telltale noise. As if. She could have dropped a pin, and I would have heard it like a nail being pounded into a board.

"Hey you!" I yelled. "You with the butter on your fingers! You drop another one of those glasses, and I'll make you eat it for lunch!"

Once everything was in place and I'd yelled at just about every single person on the premises, it was after five and time to change clothes and come back for the event.

Piper called right as I finished up and insisted I meet her at Oodles o' Stuff. Pronto. I checked my watch and muttered. A little more than ninety minutes before the party started. Another few hours after that I was going to tell Wesley everything. I didn't have time for this. I needed to pick up Rascal, go back to Piper's apartment, restock my Party Vest, and try to make myself as presentable as possible.

Usually, I didn't care too much about what I looked like, but tonight, I wanted to be at my best. I'd even resigned myself to wearing a dress—and heels. I figured it wouldn't hurt to show a little cleavage and leg when I bared my soul to Wesley.

Because I was pressed for time, I grabbed a cab and told the driver to make a beeline over to Oodles o' Stuff. He pulled up to the department store about fifteen minutes later. I paid the driver, pulled out my cell phone, and dialed Piper's number as I walked to the entrance. She picked up on the second ring.

"I'm here," I said, pushing through the revolving doors. "Where are you? I have things to do tonight, you know. Like tell the man of my dreams I love him."

Piper laughed. "Relax, Abby. I've taken care of everything. I'm on the first floor next to the evening wear."

I squinted against the glare of the lights. Clothes, clothes, and more clothes crowded the first floor.

"And where would that be?"

"You know your way around that dark, dank, convention center, but you have no idea where the gowns are at Oodles? Your priorities are so skewed," she chided.

"You're not helping."

"About five hundred feet to the left of the front doors," Piper said. "Hurry up."

I walked in the appropriate direction, skirting the shoppers blocking the aisles. I spotted Piper standing next to a tall, blond mannequin that reminded me of Fiona. Piper had been one of the five hundred people on Wesley's guest list, and she was already dressed to the nines in a long-sleeved, shimmering gown made of silver fabric.

"So what's the emergency?" I asked. "What was so important I had to meet you here?"

She beamed. "Your makeover, of course."

I blinked. "Makeover?"

Piper led me into one of the fitting rooms, where a dazzling blue dress hung on a metal rack. Matching shoes, a small purse, and a host of other accessories sat on tables on either side.

"What are you doing?" I asked Piper, staring at the display.

She grabbed my hands. "I'm going to get you ready for your Prince Charming. Or Prince Superhero. Or whatever you want to call him. You want to look great when you tell him who you really are, don't you?"

I hesitated. "But you know that I did the same thing for Ryan. That I tried to turn myself into a different person just to please him. It didn't work with him. What makes you think it will work with Wesley?"

"Because you're not changing yourself," she replied. "You're just looking your best. There's nothing wrong with that. Besides, Wesley already knows you—the *real* you. We're just putting a little icing on the cake tonight. Come on, Abby. Let me help you. Let me do this for you. It'll be fun."

Then she gave me that look—that hopeful, pleading look I could never ignore. I sighed.

"All right, but you know I can't wear that dress," I said. "I have an event tonight. I need my equipment, my supplies. I need my vest."

"I thought you might say that."

Piper sighed and jerked her head. My Party Vest draped over a chair in the corner of the room.

"And before you even ask, yes, I restocked it with your usual gear," she said. "You can wear it during the event, but you are taking it off when you talk to Wesley. Agreed?"

I nodded.

"Good. Now strip."

I went behind a black plastic partition and took off my clothes. Shivering, I crossed my arms over my chest.

"Underwear too," Piper commanded. "You can't wear granny panties under this."

Grumbling, I stepped out of my undies and pulled off the matching camisole. Piper passed me a lacy bra and panties.

"Now the dress," she said, handing it over.

The gown Piper had picked out was short and funky. The fabric was a petal-soft, jersey knit with plenty of stretch. The knee-skimming hemline and long sleeves ended in uneven zigzags, with tatters of fabric layered over the top of them. A wide, patent-leather belt looped around the waist, matching the black velvet trim that piped along the edge of the skirt and sleeves. The dress dazzled me so much it took me a minute before I realized what color it was.

I laughed. "Cobalt blue? Isn't that overkill?"

Piper smiled. "I thought you might like to wear your man's colors. Besides, that shade will rock on you."

I started to pull the dress on. "Um, won't Fiona miss this?" I asked, catching sight of the *FFF* label—and the three-thousand-dollar price tag under one arm.

"Nope," Piper said. "I brought her a dozen hamburgers, twenty hot dogs, five buckets of fries, and enough soda to float a battleship for lunch from Quicke's today. I also stopped by Olé and got her one of those five-pound burritos, three orders of chips and salsa, and fifteen sopapillas with honey. Then, I gave her the fourth-quarter reports, which showed sales rose almost ten percent. She told me to take whatever dress I wanted, along with the shoes and accessories."

I shook my head. Fiona's rampant love of food was going to get her into trouble one day. It was a wonder it hadn't bankrupted her already. I shimmied into the dress and stepped around the partition.

"Nice," Piper said. "Although, it would look better if you'd take your socks off."

I curled my wool-covered toes into the carpet a second before doing as she asked. Piper picked up a pair shoes and held them out. They were more sandals than heels, with long, thin straps that wound up to my knees. They too were cobalt blue.

Piper didn't stop there. She put a black velvet choker with an elegant blue cameo around my neck and handed me a small, boxy purse. I opened the top and looked inside. She'd stuffed essential items in it, like breath mints, tissues, clear nail polish, a small tool kit, and condoms.

I held up one of the foil packets. "Ever the optimist, I see."

She grinned.

I put on the shoes. Piper put her hands on my shoulders, marched me over to the three-sided mirror, and then stepped out of view.

I twirled this way and that, watching the skirt swirl around my legs. Piper was right. The cobalt-blue fabric made my pale skin look delicate and dainty instead of just ordinary, and the deep V-neck maximized what cleavage I had. Overall, I didn't look half-bad, even if the shoes were already starting to squeeze my toes.

"Now," Piper said. "Phase One is complete. On to Phase Two—hair and makeup."

Sabrina St. John waited for us at the cosmetics counter, along with a guy with a short, spiky Mohawk.

"This is Harold," Sabrina said. "He's going to do your hair while I work on your makeup."

I smiled at Harold, my gaze flicking up to the orange streaks in his hair.

The two of them pushed me down into a chair and covered my designer dress with a black smock. Piper settled into a chair and flipped open the latest Confidante comic book, this one featuring the Fearless Five on the front. Harold and Sabrina eyed each other as warriors would on the battlefield. Harold sank a brush into my hair, while Sabrina grabbed the first of the three dozen pots of makeup she had lined up on the glass counter.

And so it began.

Harold snipped, teased, and sprayed my hair, muttering about my split ends. Meanwhile, Sabrina tweezed, exfoliated, and moisturized my face. Harold tilted my head back. Sabrina yanked it forward. Harold brandished his scissors at Sabrina. She made a threatening move with a mascara wand. I was caught in the middle, like a tennis ball whacked to one side of the court, then slammed in the opposite direction. Both kept barking commands at me through the whole, torturous process.

Harold: "Sit up straight."

Sabrina: "Close your eyes."

Harold: "Bend your head down."

Sabrina: "Pucker your lips."

I'd never had so many beauty products on my body at one time. Vanilla-scented hairspray. Raspberry-flavored lip gloss. Styling gel that reeked of jasmine. Blush that smelled exactly like its Apple Blossom name. A migraine tried to pound to life inside my skull at the smelly onslaught, but I took deep breaths and ignored it. Nobody ever said getting beautiful was easy. Besides, I was doing this for Wesley. I could suffer a headache for him.

To amuse myself while I got worked over, I tried to guess the names of the colors of the various cosmetics arranged on the counter, but I was always wrong. What I thought looked like Gunmetal Gray eyeliner turned out to be Quicksilver. The Midnight eye shadow was Black Velvet. The Almond foundation became Ivory Tower. And on and on, with each name more colorful than the last. Something about the names nagged at me, but Sabrina and Harold started working on me once more, and the thought was pushed to the back of my mind.

The bickering beauty consultants worked on me for about thirty minutes before both seemed satisfied. They stepped back and stared at me.

"You good?" Sabrina asked.

Harold nodded. "Yep. You?"

She nodded.

Sabrina whipped off the smock around my neck while Harold spun the chair around so I could see what they'd done. I met my own eyes in the mirror.

Amazing—that was the only word to describe my transformation. Harold had taken my plain, brown hair, given it a bit of volume, and twisted it up into a fancy bun. Curled tendrils framed my face, softening the harsh line of the bun. Two sapphire chopsticks held the updo in place.

My face glowed thanks to the bronzing powder and blush Sabrina had used. She'd painted my eyes a smoky black and lined them with a silver shade, making them seem big and bright. She'd colored my lips a deep raspberry, sealing in the vibrant pink with a layer of clear gloss.

I looked better than ever before. Polished. Put-together. Sophisticated. And dare I say it, sexy. Abby Appleby was gone. So was Wren.

Tonight, I looked like Nightingale.

I just stared into the mirror, awestruck by the change. The consultants took that as a sign of approval.

"You're welcome," Sabrina said, packing up her powder puffs and pots of color.

"Ditto," Harold echoed, grabbing his own gear.

Sabrina handed me a plastic bag full of bottles and brushes. "Here are some trial sizes of everything I used on you tonight, along with Harold's stuff. Try them out. If you like the look, come back next week, and we'll see what other products might work for you."

Both passed me their cards. I palmed the cards and nodded, still too dumbstruck to speak. The consultants moved off into the crowd. I kept staring into the mirror.

"Abby, you look wonderful!" Piper squeezed my hand.

"Wesley is going to take one look at you and wonder where you've been all his life."

I squeezed her hand back, but my answering smile quickly faded.

Underneath the fancy dress, perfect hair, and marvelous skin, I was still the same old Abby—the same woman I'd always been. Was a little color on my lips and cheeks going to be enough to dazzle Wesley? I didn't know.

But I was ready to find out.

CHAPTER TWENTY-SIX

Piper had to return to work to take a late conference call. She promised to swing by my office, pick up Rascal, and bring him to the party. I grabbed another taxi and headed back to the convention center, arriving a little after six. Things weren't officially supposed to get under way until seven, but I wanted to double-check the food and decorations one more time. I wanted—no, *needed*—everything to be perfect tonight.

I pushed through the doors of the center and waved to Eddie at the front desk. He frowned, as if he didn't know who I was, but I kept walking. Well, tottering would have been a better description. The sandals matched my dress perfectly, but they were hell on my feet.

I made my way to the break room. A lone cigarette sat in an ashtray on one of the tables. Colt must have just left. I spun the combination dial on my locker, grabbed my can of air freshener, and doused the whole room.

When the air was somewhat clear, I shrugged out of my coat and stuffed it into the locker, along with the miniscule purse Piper had given me. It might look pretty, but it wasn't big enough to hold my supplies. So, I put on my Party Vest, zipped it up, and checked the pockets. Piper had been more than thorough. She'd restocked every single hidey-hole with the appropriate item, from breath mints to garbage bags. She was a good friend.

I shut the locker and headed down the long hallway that ran through the middle of the center. When I reached a door labeled *Main Kitchen*, I dug my key out of my vest and let myself in.

Kyle and his staff were already there. Strawberries, kiwis, and other fruits painted every visible surface with a rainbow of pinks and greens. An army of apron-clad chefs chopped, peeled, and mashed everything from avocados to zucchinis. The steady *thwacks-thwacks-thwacks* of their flashing knives created a weird harmony. Trays of bread warmed on racks, while more workers filled glasses with ice water and limes. Kyle arranged cream cheese canapés on serving trays. His hands blurred together as he stacked the appetizers on top of each other.

Kyle slowed at the sound of the door slamming behind me. He blinked once and did a double take. He stopped, as if he couldn't quite believe what he was seeing. Then he let out a low whistle. "*Nice* dress, Abby."

"Thanks."

I stalked through the kitchen, my eyes flicking over the pots and pans. Tomato bisque simmered on the stove, while potatoes baked for a second time in the industrial-size ovens. Chefs dumped pounds of pasta into boiling water, while others pan-seared chicken over open flames. Pepper, cinnamon, vanilla, and more spiced the air.

I opened my mouth to launch into my usual tirade about serving times, but Kyle beat me to the punch.

"The hors d'oeuvres will start circulating at seven," he said. "Dinner begins at seven thirty, followed by the speech at eight. We'll roll out the strawberry and chocolate fondue fountain at eight fifteen, and more hors d'oeuvres will be available at eight thirty when folks decide to start dancing. Did I miss anything?"

I gritted my teeth. "No."

"So, relax, Abby." Kyle gave me his usual lazy grin. "Try to have a little fun tonight. Everything will be perfect."

"It better be," I warned. "Or else—"

"Or else you'll chop off my fingers and feed them to me," he finished, still smiling. "I've heard it all before, and I haven't lost my fingers yet, have I?"

I clamped my mouth shut. Damn. I really needed to get some new threats.

I left Kyle to his canapés and walked to the auditorium. The disco balls hanging from the catwalk caught the dim light and reflected it back. Everything shimmered and shined, from the sparkling silverware on the tables to the white and black tiles in the checkerboard dance floor. The two guitar-shaped ice sculptures towered into the air at the foot of the auditorium, creating a perfect frame for the stage behind them. Workers scurried back and forth at the bar, popping corks off champagne bottles and cutting up limes, lemons, and oranges.

Everything looked perfect, but I couldn't relax. I knew from past experience things rarely went off without a hitch—no matter how much I planned. I strolled toward the bar to make sure nobody was being particularly clumsy. Up on the stage, Stanley Solomon talked to Hilary Hoover, a young woman with bright pink hair. Hilary was the drummer for Miked, Melody Masters's band. Stanley played bass guitar. His dark eyes fell on me, and he gestured for me to climb the stairs and join them.

Hilary rushed over as soon as I set foot on the stage. "Abby! Thank goodness you're here!"

"What's wrong?" I asked, sighing on the inside. Nobody ever rushed up to me unless there was a major problem.

"Melody is sick," Stanley rumbled. "Which means we don't have a lead singer for the band tonight."

I closed my eyes. Of all the things that could happen, this was near the top of the list in terms of badness because the event theme revolved around rock 'n' roll. The disco balls, the guitar ice sculptures, the dance floor. What would a rock 'n' roll party be without the actual rock 'n' rollers? *Boring*—not hip or fresh or cool, just a boring letdown. Besides, if I didn't have any music at this thing, people would riot. They had to have something to drink and dance to.

"Where is she?" I asked.

Melody had looked fine when I'd seen her earlier. Maybe if she wasn't too sick, she could do at least one number—

"In the hospital," Stanley replied. "She passed out earlier today at The Blues. Her temp was a hundred and three. Doctors think it's a bad case of the flu. They're giving her fluids and keeping her overnight for observation."

I rubbed my aching head. This was not the end of the world. I wasn't going to let it be. I looked at Hilary. "What about you? You sing backup. Can't you cover for her?"

Hilary shook her head. "Backup, not lead vocals. Besides, I think I'm coming down with what Melody has. My throat is sore, and my voice is really raspy, just like hers."

I ignored the pounding in my head. "All right, this is what we're going to do. You guys will get on stage and play through the opening round of drinks and dinner. Don't sing; just play instrumental versions of whatever you want. Just make it upbeat and snappy."

"What are you doing to do?" Stanley asked.

I pulled out my cell phone and dialed Chloe's number. "I'm going to find you a lead singer."

Chloe picked up on the second ring. "Hello?"

"Where are you?"

"I just parked my car. I should be there in about five minutes."

"Get here faster," I said. "We have a major problem."

I let Chloe oversee the food and drinks while I tried to conjure up a lead singer for the remaining members of Miked. People started arriving around seven. Everyone dashed down to the bar, grabbing drinks and oohing and aahing over the ice sculptures.

Piper was one of the first people through the door, Rascal trotting by her side. Despite my crisis, I laughed when I saw the puppy.

"A doggie tux!" I bent down to pet him. "Where did you get a doggie tux?"

Piper smiled. "Fiona's decided to branch out into petwear. She says there's no excuse for people to dress their dogs in those horrible sweaters now that she's on the job."

Rascal barked and turned around, showing off his designer suit. I scratched his ears, and he leaned into me, his fur tickling my bare legs.

"I'd love to stay with you guys, but I have work to do." I told Piper about my musical crisis.

She nodded. "We'll catch up later then. Come on, Rascal. Let's go get some champagne."

The puppy barked again and followed her.

Wesley Weston made his grand entrance at seven fifteen. Tonight, he wore a navy blue tuxedo and a crisp white shirt. Diamond cufflinks glittered on the ends of his sleeves, while his chestnut hair gleamed underneath the disco balls. He looked every inch the billionaire he was.

Wesley grabbed some champagne and scanned the crowd, as

though he was looking for someone. For a moment, I wondered if it could be me. Then I forced myself to be rational. Wesley wasn't looking for me. He was probably doing a mental inventory, seeing who had showed up and who hadn't. Even if he was searching for me, I didn't have time to say hello. I was too busy trying to avert another crisis. Still, I watched him work the crowd, shaking hands, smiling, and making small talk. His brunette from the library was nowhere to be found. It seemed Wesley was flying solo tonight. That gave me a little bit of hope, even though just about every single woman at the party made it a point to go over and say hello to him.

While Bigtime's elite munched on music-note-shaped canapés, I systematically went through the contacts in my cell phone. I called every single singer, musician, and drummer in the city. Nobody was free. I strong-armed Eddie into bringing me a phone book from the lobby and started going through the yellow pages.

Nothing. I came up with nothing. Every single singer in the greater Bigtime area was already booked for tonight. By seven thirty, I was desperate. By eight, frantic. The lights went down, and Wesley stood up to give his speech about how Gelled was the ultimate lip-care company. I huddled backstage for a conference with Hilary and Stanley. Piper and Rascal were there too.

I checked my watch again. Thirteen minutes, twenty-five seconds left until the band was supposed to start rocking the stage, and I was short one singer. "I couldn't find anybody. Nobody. I'm sorry. You guys will just have to do your best."

Stanley and Hilary stared at each other, then Stanley turned to me.

"Why don't you do it?" he suggested. "We've both heard you down at The Blues. You're good enough to front for Melody this one time, and you know all the songs. All you have to do is one set, just enough to get the crowd rocking. We can take it from there."

The thought made nervous tingles shoot through my body. It was one thing to sing in The Blues in front of drunken frat boys and giggling co-eds. It was quite another to rock out in front of the Bigtime society crowd—my clients. I peeked through the curtains lining the stage. Wesley was well into his speech now. I checked my watch again.

Twelve minutes, twenty-nine seconds, and no rock 'n' roll divas in sight.

"I don't think you really have a choice," Stanley said. "Not if you want a singer tonight."

I looked at him, then Hilary, then Piper. A sigh of acceptance escaped my lips. I pressed a button on my cell phone. "Chloe, can you handle things for the next thirty minutes?"

"Sure," Chloe's voice echoed back to me. "Do you need a break?"

"Not exactly." I closed my eyes. "I'm going to be on stage."

Chloe agreed to take care of any other problems that might pop up. Stanley put a microphone in my trembling hand, while Hilary gave me a quick rundown of the playlist, even though I'd already memorized it. Then, the two of them moved off to see to a few other things before we took to the stage. I unzipped my Party Vest.

"Hold this, and don't let it out of your sight," I said, shoving the vest at Piper.

"You got the mystery flash drive in here?" she whispered.

I nodded. "Yeah. And get the relaxidon ready. I'm going to need it—a lot of it—if this doesn't go well."

"Take a breath, Abby," Piper said. "You're going to do great."

Rascal licked my toes in agreement.

Seven minutes and thirteen seconds later, I found myself standing in the middle of the stage. Stanley flanked me on the left, his guitar heavy in his hands. Hilary sat off to my right surrounded by her drum set.

Everything came into supersharp focus. The smell of the chicken that had been served for dinner. Stanley's sandalwood cologne. Hilary's cherry-scented lip gloss. The faint swirl of air against my cheeks. The knit dress rubbing against my skin. My own frantic heartbeat.

"And now, it's time to get...Miked!" the announcer screamed.

The curtains drew back from the stage, and the crowd went wild. Stanley thumbed out some loud chords. Hilary added a steady beat on her drums. I drew in a deep breath, put the microphone up to my lips, and started to sing.

I sang everything from rock classics to power ballads to a few Miked originals. During the songs, I squinted against the spotlights and looked through the throngs of people, searching for Wesley, but I didn't see him anywhere. So I focused on my singing, letting the music carry me away. Trying to match my voice, my tone, my rhythm to the chords and harmonies filling my ear.

And I found myself getting into it. Throwing my arms out wide. Strutting up and down the stage. Blowing kisses to the crowd. The music turned on something inside me, something that liked the spotlight, that craved the attention.

The first set wound down after about twenty minutes. Stanley took the microphone from me and announced that the band was taking a break. The spotlight went off, and the curtains closed. The heady rush of adrenaline wore off, and tremors shook my body. I doubled over and put my hands on my knees, trying not to throw up.

"That was great, Abby!" Hilary said, coming out from behind her drums. "Melody couldn't have done better herself."

"You did good," Stanley said. "Real good. You wanna do another set?"

I shook my head. "No. I think that was enough for one night. Can you guys handle it from here?"

The musicians nodded.

"Good, because I'm going to get some air."

I stumbled down the steps and out into the auditorium. My eyes fixed on the door that led to the hidden corridor. I walked toward it, not even acknowledging Piper, Rascal, or the people like Carmen Cole who said hello to me.

I went into the corridor and walked about fifty feet down the hallway. I'd just slumped against the cool concrete wall, when steps quickened on the carpet behind me.

I looked up, and there he was—Wesley.

Coming right at me.

CHAPTER TWENTY-SEVEN

Wesley stopped about twenty feet away. His eyes traced my face, my shellacked hair, my blue dress, my ridiculous shoes. Then, he said the one word that made my world start to crumble.

"Nightingale?" he whispered.

Terror roared through my body. No. Oh *no*. He couldn't find out now, not like this. Not when I looked like a sweaty reject from a hair band.

"Nightingale?" he asked again.

I should have protested, should have shook my head as though the name meant nothing to me, but I couldn't. Not after everything that had happened between us.

"Nightingale," Wesley said, his voice harder and more certain.

I bit my lip, whirled around, and walked away from him.

"Hey! Wait!"

By that time, I'd broken into a full-fledged run. I scampered down the corridor, trying to find someplace to hide, someplace where he wouldn't find me. I spotted a broom closet out of the corner of my eye. Hands shaking, I twisted the knob, yanked the door open, and closed it, hoping he hadn't seen me come in here—but he had.

A second later, the door jerked open, and Wesley stepped inside. He scrutinized my hair and makeup. His gaze trailed down my body and over the blue dress. Recognition dawned on his face. "Abby? Abby Appleby?"

"That's my name," I said, laughing and trying to make a joke of things.

Wesley stepped inside, shutting the door behind him. "You're Nightingale? *My* Nightingale?"

I tried to move past him, but he put his hand on the wall, blocking me. "I don't know what you're talking about. Nightingale is your mystery woman. Not me."

I tried to go around him, but he put his other hand on the wall, trapping me between his arms.

"I think you know exactly what I'm talking about, Abby. All this time I've been looking for you, searching for you, and you've been right under my nose. What was this to you? Some kind of sick game?"

My mouth dropped open. Anger surged through me, and I forgot about denying everything. "A game? No, it was *never* a game to me. I'm the one whose life was turned upside down. I'm the one who found you in that alley and put myself in Bandit's line of fire. Rest assured, Wesley, Talon, whatever the hell you call yourself, this was definitely *not* a game to me."

"Then, why did you drug me and leave me here in the center? Why didn't you come forward?" he demanded. "Why didn't you tell me who you really were? Especially after you found out I was Talon?"

I mumbled my response.

"What?"

"Because you wouldn't have cared about me the way you did about Wren, about Nightingale," I said. "She was this great fantasy you created. This wonderful, gorgeous woman who saved you. Look at me. I'm a mess. I'm *always* a mess. I just couldn't live up to that. To your image, your perfect ideal of her. I never can."

Wesley's face softened a bit. "But you didn't even give me a chance."

I shook my head. "I couldn't take the risk. If I'd told Talon who I was that first night, would he, would you have told me your secret identity?"

Wesley didn't answer me.

"I didn't think so."

We stood there, not quite looking at each other. In the silence, my supersenses flared to life. The heat radiating off Wesley's body warmed me from head to toe. His breath slid along my face. I could even hear the roar of his heart. Its frantic beat matched my own.

"So, now you know," I said in a tired voice.

"And what about the flash drive? Do you have it?"

I nodded. "I looked at it, trying to figure out what was on it, but I couldn't get past the encryption. I was going to give it to you tonight."

"So where is it now?"

"In my vest pocket. Piper has it. I'll go get it from her."

"We're not quite done yet," Wesley said in a low voice.

The dark, dangerous light in his golden eyes frightened—and excited—me. He leaned forward, his arms still on either side of my body. I stood straight against the wall, trying to keep as much distance as possible between us. I closed my eyes, trying not to relish his wonderful, minty smell.

"I've been looking for you for days now, wondering if Bandit had gotten to you first, if he'd killed you. Do you know what that did to me? Do you?"

"You're a superhero. Your job is to protect innocents. *Chicks*, as you so eloquently call them. You were worried, and you wanted your flash drive back. I get it," I muttered.

"No, you don't get it *at all*." Fury punctuated every syllable. "Yeah, I'm a superhero. Yeah, I protect innocents. But Nighting—but you were different. We talked. We laughed. We connected. I pretty much bared my soul to you, talking about fairy tales and lightning. Then, there's the fact that we slept together."

"So what? Lots of people have sex with superheroes," I mumbled, trying not to remember how good it had been, how good he had felt next to me. "There's a whole club devoted to it."

"So I cared about *you*, Abby. I thought we were starting something—something that would grow, something that would last. That's why I slept with you. Not because I get some kick out of one-night stands. What kind of superhero, what kind of *man* do you think I am? "

The raw hurt in Wesley's voice made tears gather in my eyes. I couldn't keep the salty drops from spilling down my cheeks, ruining what was left of my makeup.

"Don't cry, Abby. I'm sorry. I didn't mean to yell at you." Wesley brushed a tear off my face. "You're just—you're not—you're not who I thought Nightingale would be."

His words pierced my heart in a way Bandit's bullets never could.

"Of course not. I never am," I whispered. "And that's the problem."

I closed my eyes and turned my head to the side, hoping—needing—him to go away. To leave me alone. To pretend he didn't know the truth. So I could convince myself my worst fear hadn't come true. That he didn't find me to be a disappointment.

Wesley let out a ragged breath. I felt him move, but instead of reaching for the door, his hand cupped my cheek, his hard fingers as soft as ever against my skin. I opened my eyes. His golden gaze met mine. We stared at each other. The seconds ticked by. Still, neither one of us moved—

Wesley kissed me. It wasn't gentle and sweet, as the kiss behind the waterfall had been. This one was hard, rough, and demanding. My supersenses kicked into overdrive. His minty taste. His soft touch. His hot body flush against my own. The sensations overwhelmed me. Frying me just like that amp had done. Melting me from the inside out.

Wesley's tongue plunged into my mouth, and I met it with my own. He poured all of his pent-up frustration, longing, and confusion into the kiss. His emotions matched my own. I grabbed his jacket and pulled him closer. I wanted to be his Nightingale so badly it hurt—even if it was only for tonight.

Wesley's hands went to my breasts, squeezing and kneading the sensitive mounds through the soft fabric of my dress and bra. He flicked his thumbs over my nipples. I groaned and threw my head back. Wesley pressed his lips to my neck, sucking at my skin.

I brought my hands up between us and tore at his shirt. Buttons popped off and bounced away into the darkness of the closet. I ran my fingers over his solid chest, scraping his nipples with my nails. My hands were everywhere, touching him—until they came in contact with something soft and gauzy. I looked down. A bandage still covered his left shoulder where Bandit had shot him.

Wesley grabbed my hand. "It's fine, thanks to you."

He kissed me again, hard. More heat ripped through me, scorching away my doubts. I yanked his shirt up out of his pants and fumbled with his zipper. Wesley reached into his hip pocket and drew out a packet from his wallet just before his pants fell to his ankles.

He wore cobalt-blue boxers underneath, and I slid those down his thighs. I straightened and stroked him with my hand, circling his hard tip with my finger. Wesley put one hand against the wall and leaned into me. His muscles jerked and twitched as he fought for control.

Wesley opened his eyes, those beautiful, beautiful golden eyes, and stared at me. He grabbed my hand and pressed the condom packet into it. With shaking fingers, I tore it open and slid it on him. When I finished, Wesley pushed his hands up the hem of my dress. He hooked his fingers into my panties and slid them down. I stepped out of the wispy fabric.

"Lace," he said. "Nice."

Then, he tossed them aside. Wesley grabbed my hips, lifted me up, and put my back against the wall. He looked at me, *really* looked at me, his golden gaze stripping away all my secrets. I wondered if he could see how much I wanted him. How much I cared about him. How much I loved him.

I couldn't read the swirl of emotions in his eyes, but they glowed with an intensity I hadn't thought possible.

Wesley's hand moved up my thighs, his fingers barely brushing my skin. They tangled in my curls, and he stroked me there, just as I'd done to him moments before. My breath caught in my throat.

"Ahhh," I gasped, digging my nails into his shoulders.

He put a finger inside me, slowing moving it up and down. It was good, so good—but not quite enough.

"More," I pleaded. "*Now.*"

I put my mouth to his for another hot, long, hard kiss. Wesley withdrew his finger.

He pushed up into me, even as I sank down onto him. He pumped into me, over and over again. I buried my face in his neck and cried out with every thrust—and so did he.

"Nightingale," Wesley murmured against my hair. "My Nightingale."

CHAPTER TWENTY-EIGHT

We didn't speak for a long time. Wesley lowered me to the ground. I stared up into his face.

"Nightingale," he said again, smiling.

Nightingale.

Not *Abby.* Not even *Wren.* Still that damned *Nightingale.*

After everything, he still didn't *see* me—not the real me. Wesley could only focus on the person he wanted me to be. His perfect mystery woman. I felt like Bandit had just emptied his gun into my stomach.

"You can get the flash drive from Piper. We're done here. I'm leaving." Somehow I managed to get the words past the knot in my throat. "Chloe can help you if there's a problem with the event."

Wesley brushed my hair off my face. "Abby. I'm sorry—"

"*Don't.* Don't say you're sorry." I stepped around him. "Don't talk to me right now. Just—don't."

I straightened my dress, twisted open the knob to the broom closet, and ran. I ran and ran and ran down the hallway until my lungs and toes screamed for mercy. Then, I sputtered to a stop, rested my head against the concrete wall, and sobbed.

By the time I reached the break room, I'd regained control of myself. Hands shaking, I spun the dial on my locker. I caught a glimpse of myself in the mirror taped to one side. All of the makeup Sabrina had so carefully applied was streaked and smeared from my eyes to my chin. My face resembled a bag of candy left out in the sun—a rainbow of mushy, melted color. I grabbed a tissue out of my locker and scrubbed off what I could. Surprisingly, my hair was mostly in one piece, thanks to the superstrength styling gel and hairspray Harold used.

I yanked out my coat and pulled it on. I closed the locker door and leaned against it, trying to summon up the energy to walk home.

Trying not to think about Wesley.

For a moment in the closet, I'd thought I'd a chance. That maybe he'd take a chance on *me*. But no. Wesley still longed for Nightingale, and I just couldn't be her. All of the makeup and pretty dresses in the world wouldn't change the fact that I was still good ole Abby Appleby. Dependable. Uptight. Invisible.

Footsteps smacked into the floor behind me. Metal jangled together, and cigarette smoke filled the air. I sighed, hoping Colt wasn't going to ask me out again. I just couldn't take it right now. Still, I turned and opened my mouth to say hello.

But Colt wasn't the one standing behind me.

He had Colt's face, with its dark, expressionless eyes. Colt's long hair hung loose around his shoulders. Colt's mocking smile curled his lips. But the black leather duster fluttering around those cowboy boots and the guns strapped to his hips were all Bandit's.

My mouth opened. Closed. Opened again. "Colt? You're really Bandit?"

"Hi, Abby," the ubervillain said.

His gloved fist exploded against my temple, and the world went black.

Something wet dripped on my cheek. The steady *drip-drip-drip* turned into a torrent. A wave of water cascaded over my head, snapping me back to reality. I sputtered and coughed. Rough hands jerked me to my feet. I opened my eyes. Colt's face, Bandit's face, stared back at me.

"It's about time you woke up, Abby," he said.

"What do you want?" My head throbbed from where Bandit had hit me, and I was having trouble focusing on him.

"What I've always wanted—the flash drive," Bandit growled. "Where is it?"

"I don't know what you're talking about."

"Bullshit."

He let me go. My knees buckled, and I hit the floor. I groaned and cradled my head in my hands. Pain stabbed my skull like an ice pick, but I took a deep breath and made myself forget about it, made myself examine my surroundings.

I huddled at the foot of a table in the middle of a large conference room. Chairs surrounded the table, and legal pads covered the shiny surface. Gray carpet stretched over the floor, and matching drapes shuttered the windows at the far end. The water Bandit had doused me with had come out of a crystal carafe sitting on a cart. He'd soaked my head and shoulders, and water dripped from the ends of my hair, spattering onto the floor.

My eyes fixed on the door thirty feet behind the ubervillain—

and I tried to figure out how I could get through it without getting shot.

"Do you think I'm stupid?" Bandit growled. "I know you have the flash drive. You were there in the alley the night I shot Talon. Don't try to deny it."

I gasped. Things had just gone from bad to worse. I didn't think Bandit or any of his goons had spotted me that night. I'd thought I'd had some plausible deniability where the drive was concerned. Now, even that was gone.

"How do you know?"

He smiled. "Because I saw you, Abby. In addition to being pretty handy with these," his hand fell to one of his guns, "I also happen to have supersenses—just like you."

I gasped again. "How do you know I have supersenses?"

"The headaches, the air freshener, the constant wincing at loud noises. All dead giveaways. I did a little checking. Your accident at The Blues was in the newspapers. I got my supersenses when a power line fell on my car. I figured an amp couldn't be much different. But back to the drive." Bandit leaned down until his eyes were even with mine. "If Talon had it, he would have broken the encryption and exposed Tycoon by now. My guess is he lost it in the snow that night. That's when you picked it up. You probably put it in that vest of yours, which is why I couldn't find it when I tore up your loft."

"My coat, actually," I admitted. Had it only been Tuesday since my loft had been destroyed? It seemed longer than that.

An odd thought struck me. "Wait a minute. You didn't ransack my apartment until Tuesday night, a couple days after the fight in the alley."

"I was busy looking for Talon. With that bullet in his shoulder, I'd thought he'd go to the emergency room. When he didn't turn up there or anywhere else, I started staking out your apartment."

I remembered the odd shadow I'd seen and Rascal barking at

the balcony door. Bandit had been watching me even then. Now, I was glad the puppy had kept me awake. I put the rest of the timeline together. "That's why you asked me out, isn't it? So you could get into my apartment and look for the flash drive?"

He shrugged. "You've always been nice to me, never looking down on me just because I'm a glorified janitor. I thought I'd try to be civil about things."

"Why do you even do it? Work as a janitor? Surely, you can make more money doing...this."

"All I do is sit on my ass, smoke, drink coffee, and read magazines," Bandit said. "It's not the most strenuous job, and nobody pays any attention to my comings and goings. It's a good cover."

No, it was a great cover. I'd never looked too closely at Colt. He was another janitor, a guy who cleaned up the messes my parties made. I hadn't thought to look deeper than that, and I'd certainly never dreamed he could be an ubervillain. Maybe if I'd paid a little more attention to him instead of bitching about being invisible all the time, I wouldn't be in this mess.

"After you searched my apartment, why did you confront me on the street? Why just assume I had the flash drive?"

"I couldn't take a chance you didn't," Bandit said.

"You mean Tycoon couldn't take that chance."

The ubervillain shrugged. "He's particular about keeping his identity a secret. Not only would the information on that drive expose him, but it would jeopardize a rather expensive operation he's been working on."

"Sunrise?" I asked, remembering the name Wesley had mentioned.

Bandit's eyes glittered. "You read the flash drive?"

"No. I couldn't get past the second encryption. All I saw were these folders with weird names, like Ivory Tower, Black Velvet, and Quicksilver. I thought they were names for superheroes or ubervillains—"

I flashed back to earlier tonight, when I'd been at the makeup counter at Oodles o' Stuff and Sabrina had been working on my face. I thought of the products she'd used—and their names. Apple Blossom blush. Rocking Raspberry lip gloss. I'd seen the other names there. Ivory Tower foundation. Black Velvet eye shadow. Quicksilver eyeliner. The folders weren't about heroes or villains. They were names for makeup colors.

Makeup? What could a gangster like Tycoon possibly have to do with makeup? He was into drugs and gambling, not lip liners and bronzers.

Bandit's eyes never left my face. "You know, it's a shame you're so smart, Abby. It's going to get you killed."

The ubervillain turned toward the door. "You might as well come in."

The door creaked open. Shadows filled the hallway outside, but I could just see the outline of a dark figure.

"She's figured it out," Bandit said. "Most of it, anyway."

"Well, that's a pity, isn't it?" A soft feminine voice floated into the room.

Octavia O'Hara stepped into the light.

Chapter Twenty-Nine

Octavia walked over to stand beside Bandit. The contrast between the two was striking. Octavia wore a fitted red jacket, a short skirt, and stilettos. Her black hair was up in a tight bun, and her makeup was flawless. Bandit was in black, from the bottoms of his boots to the paisley bandanna tied around his neck.

"Hey, baby," Bandit murmured, putting his arm around Octavia.

She leaned in and gave the ubervillain a slow kiss, raking her teeth across his bottom lip. His hand cupped her breast, and she growled. I cringed and dropped my gaze. I felt like I'd been sucked into some cheesy porn movie, where the rugged cowboy does the uptight businesswoman in the conference room. Or, in Bigtime's case, the ubervillain and the high-society debutante.

They broke apart, each one practically salivating over the other.

Confused, I looked up at Octavia. "What are you doing here?"

Octavia gave me a cool look. "I'm here to make sure this unpleasantness is taken care of once and for all."

It dawned on me why she was here—and who she really was. "You're Tycoon, the gangster?"

Her dark eyes flicked to Bandit. The ubervillain smiled.

"I told you she'd figured it out," he said.

Octavia shrugged. "It doesn't matter that she has, does it?"

Bandit smiled and shook his head. More fear piled onto the hard, cold knot in my stomach.

"But I thought Tycoon was a man," I said. "You're...not."

"My father, Otto, was the original Tycoon," Octavia said. "I took his place last year."

Last year? That was when I planned his funeral. "Your father didn't drown in a boating accident, did he?"

Octavia's smile was all the answer I needed. The cruel curve of her crimson lips frightened me more than Bandit's guns. "I presented my father with a plan that would have made us billions, far more than his penny ante drug and gambling rings, but he didn't want to act on it. So I decided it was time for a management change."

"What plan?" I asked.

"Sunrise, of course," Octavia snapped. "You have the flash drive, don't pretend like you don't know what's on it."

"But I don't know," I said, trying to draw things out so I could keep breathing. "I couldn't open the files."

"But you recognized the names," Octavia said.

"They're just names for different colors of makeup. Who cares about makeup?"

Octavia's eyes darkened, and I realized my mistake. She cared about makeup. A whole hell of a lot—enough to kill me for insulting her.

"You know what, baby?" Octavia turned to Bandit. "Instead of standing here talking in circles, let's show Abby exactly what she's going to die for."

Bandit smiled again.

The two of them exchanged another kiss, then Bandit hauled me to my feet. He let go of me, and I crumpled back to the floor. Bandit dug his boot into my ribs. I gasped and jerked away.

"If you fall again, I'll put a bullet in your spine." His voice was cool and casual.

"Not up here," Octavia admonished. "I just had the carpets cleaned."

Octavia strolled out of the conference room, and Bandit pushed me along behind her. I recognized the hallway. Even if I hadn't, the red lips hanging on the wall would have clued me in—I was in Oomph's corporate headquarters. I'd come up to this floor several times to speak to Octavia while planning the engagement party and dinner for Olivia and Paul Potter.

"What about Olivia?" I asked. "Does she know about you?"

"Olivia does what she's told," Octavia scoffed. "If I hadn't needed her to marry Paul to add the appearance of legitimacy to my takeover of Polish, I would have dumped her overboard with my father."

"What do you mean?"

As we walked, I peered into the offices that branched off the hallway, hoping someone was working late. But the offices were all as dark and empty as Octavia's soul.

She pushed the button to summon the elevator. "Peter Potter likes to drink, and when he's drunk, he likes to gamble. He was into my father for millions."

"And Polish was the payoff?"

Octavia nodded. "We were going to handle the merger quietly, but then Wesley Weston made a play for Polish."

Wesley. My heart twisted. I could still smell him on me, still feel his lips on mine. I should have told him how I felt about him, even if he'd rejected me, because now, I'd never get the chance.

I realized Octavia was staring at me, waiting for a response. "So you forced Olivia and Paul to get engaged so no one would question the merger too much."

She nodded. The elevator *pinged!* its arrival, hurting my ears, and Bandit crowded me inside. Octavia stepped in after him and hit another button, followed by a code on a keypad to one side of the door.

We went down. When the doors opened again, we stepped out into a lab. Everything was white plastic, from the walls and floors to the counters running down either side of the room. Trays sat on the counters, every single one full of eye shadows, lipsticks, blushes, and more. Every inch of space shimmered with color, from soft pinks to aqua blues to plumy purples. There was enough makeup to cover every woman's face in Bigtime.

Bandit shoved me forward. Octavia strolled in front of us and threw her arms out wide.

"This is where the magic happens," she said in a proud voice.

Magic. Right.

We walked about halfway down one of the counters, before Octavia stopped and swept her hand out again.

"And this," she said, "is Sunrise."

A black-and-white cardboard display embossed with Oomph's red lips perched on the counter. The display framed several makeup products, all encased in black plastic—a lipstick, a bottle of liquid foundation, pressed powder compact, eye shadow, eye- and lip-liner pencils, blush, mascara. My eyes caught on the names. Ivory Tower foundation. Black Velvet eye shadow. Quicksilver eyeliner.

I looked at Octavia, who watched me, waiting for a reaction. "But it's just makeup."

What was so sinister about that? The worst thing you could

do was poke your eye out with a mascara wand. What about it was worth killing me for?

"It's not just *any* makeup," Octavia said. "It's a very special blend. New versions of old, beloved products. I called the collection *Sunrise* because that's our signature red lipstick."

She uncapped the lipstick and twisted it up. The Sunrise red shade was pretty enough with a soft, shimmer finish, but it smelled—bad. Like rotten eggs mixed with sweaty gym socks. I realized it was the same lipstick, with the same putrid odor, that had made my nose burn at Oodles o' Stuff when Piper had showed it to me.

"Go ahead, Abby," Octavia said, holding the tube out to me.

I shook my head and backed away as far as I could. I wasn't touching that stuff.

"What's the matter? Don't you want to freshen up?"

"She can smell it," Bandit said. "Just like I can."

"Oh. I forgot she has supersenses."

I stared at the tube. "What's in that?"

"Oh, the usual ingredients. Beeswax, various dyes and pigments, and just a hint of euphoridon."

I blinked. "Euphoridon. But that's—"

"A radioactive drug," Octavia finished. "A very addictive one. Euphoridon is what most of the junkies down on Good Intentions Lane get strung out on."

"And you put it in makeup? Why?"

"To get women hooked on it, of course," she replied, capping the lipstick. "So they crave it. So they buy Oomph makeup and nothing else without even realizing what they're doing or what's happening to them."

"That's why you gave away all those free samples at the engagement party," I accused. "You were trying to get people hooked on it then."

Octavia stared at me. "You really are too smart for your own good, Abby. Actually, those were just trial samples. Primers, if you will, of some of our best-selling products with just a hint of euphoridon in them to whet people's appetites for more. Subconsciously, of course. My market share will double in the first week alone when the Sunrise makeup hits the market. Within a month, I'll have a stranglehold on the industry and be ready to launch a new lip-care line, with the help of Polish."

The way Octavia talked, you would have thought she was discussing the weather, not the massive addiction of every makeup-using woman in Bigtime. There wasn't much I could say. Still, I tried to think of something, because the longer I kept talking, the greater the chances were of me coming up with a brilliant plan to escape. I opened my mouth to respond, when a faint *yip* caught my ear.

My heart froze. Rascal? What would he be doing here? I cocked my head and listened—*really* listened. The yip came again, followed by another, and another, until a whole chorus of dogs yapped together.

"The dogs are howling again," Bandit said.

Octavia rolled her eyes. "Well, we won't need them much longer. One more test, and the lab coats tell me we can start mass-producing the Sunrise makeup. Then, we can sit back and wait for the money to roll in."

"Hopefully I'll have a little more time to deal with the animals," Bandit said. "Instead of dumping them in an alley for the police to find."

"That was your fault," she hissed. "If Talon hadn't slipped past your so-called security team—"

"Wait a minute. You tested your radioactive makeup on animals?" I asked, remembering what Wesley, what Talon had told me, and his suspicions about Rascal. "Those puppies and kittens they showed on SNN? You killed them?"

"I had to test it on something," Octavia said. "The police tend to notice when people go missing."

"And my dog? Rascal, was he one of yours?"

"Unfortunately," Octavia glared at Bandit. "Letting him get away was another one of your slipups."

"What was I supposed to do?" he growled back. "The little bastard bit me, and I dropped him. I took a couple of shots at him, but he was quicker than I thought he'd be, thanks to all that euphoridon your lab coats shot him up with."

The two of them started arguing, but I tuned them out. Red rage colored my vision like the gloss on Octavia's perfect lips. Little bastard? Little *bastard*? Rascal was the best dog in the world. Oh sure, he barked and begged for food and generally thought he was the king of Bigtime and should be treated as such. But Rascal had more humanity in his tail than the two of them did in their entire bodies. Bandit was the bastard, and Octavia was an ice-cold bitch. They had to be stopped. Both of them.

But how? And with what? If I'd had my vest, I at least would have had my stun gun. I might have taken Octavia out with that before Bandit shot me. But I'd left the vest back at the party with Piper. Without my vest, without my supplies, I felt naked, exposed, helpless.

And it wasn't like there were any weapons just lying around in the lab. Just lipsticks, powders, and mascara wands as far as the eye could see. Just makeup. My gaze flicked to the Sunrise display.

Radioactive makeup.

While Octavia and Bandit argued, I palmed a lip pencil with one hand. With the other, I swiped the pot of loose face powder.

"Enough!" Octavia snapped. "None of this is getting us what we really want—the flash drive."

They both turned their attention to me.

"Now you have a choice to make, Abby," Octavia said. "You can tell me where the drive is and who you've told about it, and Bandit can kill you quickly."

The ubervillain pulled out one of his pistols and twirled it in his hand. Light danced off the silver weapon. "Three in the back of the head. You won't feel a thing."

Yeah. Right.

"Or?" I asked, pretty sure I wasn't going to like Option Two any better than Option One.

"Or," Octavia continued, "you can refuse to talk, and Bandit can draw out the process."

He kept spinning his gun. "I'll start with your ankles. Then, your knees. Your hips. Shoulders. You can put quite a few bullets in the human body before irreparable damage is done. Although, you'll wish you were dead after the first shot."

This time I believed him.

"It's your choice," Octavia said. "Now make it."

CHAPTER THIRTY

I drew in a deep breath. "All right. I'll tell you where the flash drive is. There's no need to torture me."

Octavia smiled. "I always thought you were reasonable."

I dropped my head and edged toward her, as if I was totally beaten. It was such a Rascal thing to do, looking defeated and begging for sympathy before springing into action. Octavia smirked at Bandit. I tightened my grip on my flimsy weapons.

"Well?" Octavia demanded. "Where is it? Where have you hidden the drive?"

I raised my head and looked into her cold, merciless eyes. "Up your ass, bitch."

I brought my hand up and rammed the lip pencil into her right shoulder. It wasn't much of a weapon, but I put plenty of force behind it. The pencil punctured her arm, sinking into her flesh. Coppery blood spurted out from the wound, and the odor of sulfur intensified as the euphoridon seeped into Octavia's system.

Octavia screamed. I snapped the pencil off and stabbed her arm again with the broken tip. Bandit cursed and raised his gun. I grabbed Octavia's shoulders, spun her around, and shoved her into the ubervillain. Then, I popped the top off the face powder

I'd swiped and blew into it as hard as I could. A cloud of euphoridon crystals erupted from the container. Bandit cursed as the powder flooded his eyes. He banged into Octavia, and the two of them fell to the floor.

"Get her!" Octavia screamed. "Get that bitch!"

I dropped the face powder, turned, and ran.

I sprinted through the lab as fast as I could. For once, I didn't even think about the sandals pinching my feet. If I did that, I'd slow down, and then, I'd be dead.

A door was at the far end of the room. I sprinted toward it, slammed my hand into the bar, barged through the opening, and kept going. Bullets banged into the closing door. A few pieces of hot lead pierced the metal and *pinged!* down the hall after me. I screamed and kept running.

I went through two more long, narrow rooms, both containing more makeup counters and scientific equipment, before my legs couldn't run anymore. I slowed to a shuffle and listened for jangling, booted footsteps behind me. I didn't hear any, but I kept moving, determined to put as much space between me, Bandit, and Octavia as possible.

I went through another door and found myself in a gray hallway. I went right and came to another branch. I zigged and zagged through the underground maze, going right and right, then left, left, left, trying to take the least logical route possible so Bandit wouldn't find me. I saw another door, went through it, and emerged into what looked like a basement. Lots of metal walls. Lots of concrete beams. Lots of cardboard boxes. No weapons. No way out.

I couldn't go back and risk running into Bandit, so I moved farther into the basement. The *yips* and *yaps* of the animals I'd heard before grew louder. The sounds tugged at my heart, but I pushed the feeling aside. I couldn't help the poor creatures right now. I could barely help myself.

I turned a corner, and my gaze snagged on a red box—a fire alarm. I didn't know if it would do any good, but I yanked the alarm. Sirens blared, reverberating through the building. I winced at the noise. Maybe I could run or hide until the fire department arrived.

I limped along, my eyes sweeping over everything. It was dark here, with only a few weak bulbs flickering on the concrete walls, but the lack of light didn't bother me. With my enhanced eyesight, I could see as clearly as if it were noon. Piper was right. I was going to do great things with my supersenses—like save myself.

I spotted a bit of color ahead and picked up my pace. An *Exit* sign glowed red about two hundred feet away. A sweet, sweet *Exit* sign.

I'd just touched the door when the fire alarm quit blaring. The sudden, abrupt silence made my head spin. Bandit must have told building security it was just a false alarm. He'd probably called the fire department too, which meant no one would be coming to help. Damn.

I shoved open the *Exit* door, and a flight of stairs greeted me. I started climbing. Up, up, up, as fast as I could. My sandals rang on every step, the sound echoing to the top of the stairwell and back down. I didn't care how loud I was being or how much the noise hurt my aching head. Seven flights later, I spotted a door marked *Lobby*.

I didn't barge through this door as I had the others because I had a sneaking suspicion Bandit and Octavia would be waiting for me on the other side. They might have lost me in the labyrinth of underground chambers, but they knew I'd try to find a way out and that I'd head up to the lobby. If I were them, that's where I'd be waiting.

So, I climbed up another flight of stairs to the first floor. I put my ear to the door, but I couldn't hear anything over my own ragged breathing. Bandit could be waiting on the other side, gun pointed, his finger on the trigger. I couldn't tell, not even with my supersenses. I'd just have to risk it.

Putting my hand on the bar, I cracked open the door and winced as it squeaked. I slipped through. The door whispered shut behind me, but it sounded as loud as a drum to my ears. I moved away from it.

Much like the Weston building, the first few floors of Oomph's headquarters wrapped around an open lobby. Three staircases set equidistance apart from each other led to the upper floors. Potted palms, small trees, and other greenery decorated the lobby itself, while a pair of red lips about a hundred feet wide dangled from the ceiling near the elevator bank. The lips swung ever so slightly, the cable holding them to the ceiling groaning with every movement.

I crept through the hallway to the closest set of stairs. My eyes snagged on another fire alarm. I thought about pulling it again but didn't want to give away my position. I had no qualms, though, about opening the glass case and removing the fire extinguisher inside.

Makeshift weapon in hand, I eased over to the left staircase. A frosted glass railing ran between it and the wall. I dropped to my knees and crawled along, stopping as I reached a cut-out lip in the glass. I peered through the clear pane into the lobby below.

Everything seemed to be normal. There was no sign of Octavia, Bandit, or any other goons. Not even a security guard sat at the front desk. Maybe I'd lucked out—

A flash of silver caught my eye, and I looked—*really* looked—at it. Sure enough, Bandit stood half-hidden behind a palm tree in the shadows. I wouldn't have seen him at all except for the gleam bouncing off his gun. I scanned the rest of the lobby but didn't see Octavia. She had to be lurking around somewhere, though.

I bit my lip. There was no way I could get past Bandit without him putting a bullet in my back, but there was no point in going up to another floor. The lobby was the only exit I knew of out of the building. I sure wasn't going back down to the lab again. Maybe I could just hide in one of the bathrooms until morning, then sneak out when the commuters came in—

A faint sound rang out through the lobby. Bandit froze. I cocked my head, listening. It came again. That soft sound of a zipper being drawn down. My breath caught in my throat.

Talon—he was here.

A second later, a thin, black cable fell into the lobby, and a man in a cobalt-blue leather suit slid down it. I would have known him anywhere. Talon's head swiveled back and forth as he unbuckled himself from the line.

In the shadows, Bandit lifted his gun, just as he'd done in the alley. This time, though, I wasn't going to stay quiet.

"Talon! Behind you!" I screamed.

Both men looked up at the sound of my voice. I stood up and chucked the fire extinguisher over the balcony at Bandit. The can clanked against the floor. It didn't come anywhere close to hitting the ubervillain, but it made him flinch, and his bullet went wild. Talon rolled behind a cluster of chairs.

"Abby!" Talon said.

I never got a chance to respond. This time, Bandit raised his gun and fired at me. The glass railing shattered. Jagged, broken pieces cut my arms and hands, and I lost my balance. I bounced down the steps, hitting each and every one, before falling hard onto the lobby floor.

Pain exploded in my body. My hips. Back. Shoulders. Arms. Head. Every single part of me ached and throbbed. Blood filled my mouth.

A hand shoved itself into my hair and pulled me up. White stars burst in front of my eyes. For a moment, I couldn't see, couldn't hear, couldn't breathe. All I could feel was a sharp, stabbing pain in my chest. Somehow, my lungs kept working. I blinked, and the stars faded away, even if the pain didn't.

Bandit shoved me in front of him, using me as a shield. His gun made a cold, round impression against my throbbing temple. Talon slowly stood from his position behind the chairs. He had his crossbow gun up and pointed at Bandit.

"Put the gun down or she dies!" Bandit hissed.

"She dies, you die!" Talon snarled back.

"Bandit!" a third voice cut in. "Bandit, what's your status?"

It took me a minute to realize Bandit was wearing a transmitter in his ear and that Octavia was squawking at him.

"I've got Abby in the lobby. We have a visitor too. Get your ass down here."

Bandit held me in front of him, his gun against my head. Talon stood about fifteen feet away, gun still out, his arm steady. My supersenses kicked into high gear, and I felt, heard, and saw everything amplified a thousand times. The ashy stench of Bandit's sweat. The coppery taste of blood in my mouth. The steadiness of Talon's arm. The cable creaking over our heads. My eyes flicked up.

The cable.

About thirty seconds later, the elevator *pinged!* open. High heels stabbed the floor, and Octavia walked up to Bandit. She also had a gun, but I noticed with no small sense of satisfaction she had to hold it in her left hand. Blood still dripped from the wounds I'd put in her right shoulder. For once, Octavia wasn't the picture of cool perfection. Her black hair hung around her face, plastered to her neck. Dark circles had appeared under her eyes, and her red lipstick had smeared across her cheeks. I wondered if Octavia's haggard appearance was from the blood loss or the euphoridon pumping through her body.

"Well, well, if it isn't Talon, come to save his damsel in distress."

"And if it isn't the mysterious Tycoon," Talon replied. "It seems you're bleeding. What happened to your arm?"

Octavia's eyes cut to me. I smiled.

"I think you need to put your gun down," Bandit replied. "Or I'm going to put a bullet in Abby's head. Right. Now."

Talon didn't lower his weapon. Instead, he raised his other hand. Something silver glittered between his fingers. My breath caught in my throat. The flash drive. He must have gotten it from Piper and broken the encryption. That must have been how he knew to come to Oomph headquarters.

Octavia spotted it too. "Give me that, and I might let you live."

"That's a lie, and we all know it. So, we'll trade," Talon said. "Abby for the drive."

Octavia looked at Bandit. The ubervillain nodded. They were going to double-cross Talon as soon as they got the flash drive and kill us both. I knew it, and so did he. So, why was he trying to bargain with them? To save me? Or to save Nightingale?

"All right," Octavia said. "Bandit, let her go."

The ubervillain lowered his gun and shoved me toward Talon. I stumbled and would have fallen if the superhero hadn't caught me. His arm caused me more pain as it wrapped tightly around my waist, but I wouldn't have traded the feeling of his body against mine for anything in the world.

"Abby—"

"There's no time," I whispered. "The lips. Shoot your crossbow at the lips. At the cable."

"What? Why?"

"Do you trust me?"

Talon nodded.

"You have her. Now, the flash drive," Octavia said. "Slide it over here."

Talon let go of the drive and kicked it away with his boot. It skidded across the floor, and Octavia dropped to her knees, grabbed the drive, and studied it. Bandit kept his guns trained on us.

"This looks like the right drive." Octavia looked at me. Our eyes locked, and her mouth hardened. "Kill them!"

The world went into slow motion. Bandit pulled the trigger on his gun. Talon threw himself to one side, taking me with him. A bullet brushed my cheek, the hot metal stinging my skin. Talon fell to the ground, me on top of him. He raised his arm. The trigger on his crossbow gun clicked, and a bolt shot out. Bandit raised his other revolver, ready to fire again. We were prone on the floor. This time, he wouldn't miss.

But Talon's aim was true too. The bolt zipped through the cable, slicing it in half. Even from my position on the floor, I heard it snap. Air flowed over my skin as it started to fall.

Bandit also heard the sound. His eyes flicked up, but he realized the danger too late. He dived to one side, trying to get out of the way. Octavia was too intent on raising her own gun to move.

Bandit might have been a quick draw, but he wasn't quite quick enough. The neon lips sign crashed down on the ubervillain and Octavia, pinning them. Lights exploded in the glass structure. Sparks hissed everywhere, painting the lobby a brilliant, bloody red. Talon rolled us over so that he was on top. He shielded my body with his, and I buried my face in his neck. Explosion after explosion rocked the room. Metal zinged through the air. Acrid smoke boiled up from the shattering sign.

And then—silence.

Talon rolled off me and up onto his knees. I stayed on the floor. My body ached too much for me to do much more than breathe. Still, I turned my head to look at the damage.

The lips sign lay flat on the floor. Octavia's stilettos peeked out from the middle. Movement caught my eye. A hand holding a gun waved at the left corner of the sign. I watched it move once, twice, a third time. Then, it stilled, and the revolver slipped from Bandit's fingers.

Talon turned his attention to me. "Abby, are you okay?"

"I hurt—everywhere." I coughed, and more blood filled my mouth.

He cupped my cheek with his hand. "Just lie still. I'll call an ambulance—"

He never got to finish his statement. Something, or rather someone, chose that moment to rip the building's front door off its hinges. Metal screeched. Glass shattered. More alarms blared.

Talon snapped up his gun, ready to defend me again. I loved him for it, but he didn't have to—because the Fearless Five strode into the building.

Fiera was first, her fists blazing as orange-red as her costume. Then came Striker in black leather, his twin swords peeping up over his shoulders. Mr. Sage followed in his flowing, green cape. Hermit stepped inside next, his checkerboard goggles catching the light, and finally there was Karma Girl, draped in sparkling, silver spandex.

There was another person with them, someone I never would have dreamed of. She headed for me, along with Mr. Sage. The other heroes went over to the fallen sign to see if Bandit and Octavia were still alive.

"Lulu?" I asked, not quite believing my eyes.

"Hey, Abby." Lulu dropped to her knees beside me. Her neon blue hair gleamed in the light. "I finally decrypted those files you gave me. They were pretty interesting, but I guess you know that already."

Mr. Sage looked at Talon. "I think you can put that away now. It looks like you've done plenty of damage with it already."

Talon nodded and holstered his weapon. Mr. Sage turned his attention to me. He set a bag on the floor and pulled out a stethoscope.

"Hi, Abby. I'm going to take care of you." Mr. Sage's voice was calm and soothing, with an Irish accent.

He put the cold metal against my chest and told me to breathe, but I looked up at Lulu.

"These are your friends? The ones you told me about at the library?" I asked.

She nodded.

"The Fearless Five, the city's best superhero team, are your *personal friends*."

Lulu grinned. "Yeah."

"Some friends," I said.

CHAPTER THIRTY-ONE

The police arrived a short time later. Striker and Hermit stayed behind to help them, while Fiera, Karma Girl, and Mr. Sage tended to me. The superheroes and Lulu loaded Talon and me into their van and took us to their secret headquarters. Mr. Sage worked on me during the ride, checking my blood pressure, pressing on my chest and stomach, asking me where it hurt.

Talon—Wesley—held my hand the whole time.

I faded in and out of consciousness. The van stopped, and someone, probably Fiera, lifted me onto a gurney. The wheels squeaked, adding to my headache. The next thing I felt was someone pressing a cold cloth to my face. After that, the world went black.

Voices woke me sometime later.

"She took a nasty fall. She's got a concussion, cracked ribs, and cuts." Mr. Sage's voice sounded like it was far away.

"But?" Talon asked.

"But she's going to be fine."

"Thank you," Talon said.

A gentle hand cupped my cheek. I tried to reach up to grab it, but I just couldn't move. I just couldn't...move...

I drifted along, not really asleep but not awake either. A loud, angry voice jerked me out of my dreamlike state.

"I'm going to kill Piper!" someone hissed.

Piper? Was Piper here? Was she in trouble?

I opened my eyes. I was lying in a bed in a hospital-type room. Gauze covered my cut arms, while an IV dripped fluid into me. Medical machines beeped and chirped around the bed like songbirds. The lights were turned low, as if it was nighttime outside.

"I'm going to kill her!" Fiera hissed again.

"You can't kill Piper, and you know it," Karma Girl countered.

"Well, I can't kill Abby. At least not before she finishes planning my wedding."

I spotted the two superheroes through the window in front of my bed. They stood outside the room, but I could hear them as if they were right next to me, especially Fiera. Her voice carried.

"I give Piper a three-thousand-dollar dress and what happens? Her friend ruins it!"

Karma Girl crossed her arms over her chest. "And what exactly prompted you to give Piper a free dress? Or do I even have to guess? She brought you food, didn't she?"

"There might have been French fries involved," Fiera admitted.

"Then you have nobody but yourself to blame," Karma Girl said. "Quit letting people bribe you with burritos. Besides, it was for a good cause. Did you see Abby? She looked amazing. I never knew she could sing like that."

Fiera sniffed. "Her voice was great, but a ruined dress is still a ruined dress..."

The two superheroes moved down the hall, and their voices faded away.

The way Fiera was raving about the dress, you would have thought she made it, instead of Fiona. It wasn't like they were the same person or anything—were they? Could Fiona actually be Fiera? That crazy thought was the last thing I remembered before sleep claimed me once again.

The next time I awoke, I felt more like myself. Most of the medicated fog was gone, along with my headache. I opened my eyes a crack, and the overhead light stabbed into them. So, I squeezed them shut and fumbled around, patting the bed, looking for a call button. I wasn't going to open my eyes again until that light was turned down.

"Abby?" Talon whispered. "Are you awake?"

"Yeah, can you turn the light down low, please?"

"Why?"

I sighed. I'd told him everything else. I might as well share my final secret. "Because I have supersenses. Bright lights give me headaches."

His leather costume creaked, and a moment later, the light faded to a low glow. I opened my eyes. I was still in the same hospital room, but now, Talon was here. The superhero dropped into a chair beside my bed. I wondered how long he'd been in here with me.

"Would you like to sit up?" he asked.

I nodded. Talon put his hand under my shoulder and helped me. It still hurt to move, but not as much as it had at Oomph. I didn't have to look under the sheets to know my ribs were taped up. I could feel more bandages on my arms and legs, covering the cuts I'd gotten falling down the stairs.

"How do you feel?" Talon asked.

"Better. How long have I been in here?"

"Two days. You have some broken ribs, but Mr. Sage says you're going to be fine."

"I know. I heard you talking to him."

We sat there. Then, Talon reached up and took off his visor.

"What are you doing?" I asked.

"You know who I am. I feel silly talking to you with my visor on."

"Oh."

More silence.

"So what happened that night after we...talked in the broom closet?"

Wesley cleared his throat. "Well, I went back to the party, heading to the bar to get good and drunk. But your friend Piper cornered me. She wanted to know where you were and what I'd done to you. She said a guy with missing buttons on his shirt had to be up to something."

I smiled. "Piper tends to notice things like that."

"Anyway, she told me she knew I was Talon and that you were Nightingale."

"So, she gave you the flash drive then?"

"No," Wesley shook his head. "We were arguing when Rascal started acting up. He barked and barked and just wouldn't be quiet. He pulled his leash right out of Piper's hand and ran out of the auditorium. We followed him. He managed to push through the revolving doors and get out onto the street. That's when I spotted Bandit putting you into a limo. I tried to catch the car, but it took off. I grabbed Rascal and told Piper what I'd seen. She'd gotten the limo's license plate. She also told me about the file names you'd seen on the drive. I traced the limo to Octavia. Putting two and two together, I grabbed my gear, suited up as Talon, and came looking for you. You know the rest."

I nodded.

Wesley took my hand. His hard fingers gently stroked my sensitive skin. "I want you to know I came for you, Abby. Not for Bandit or Tycoon. Just you."

"Because you save innocents."

"No, because I wanted to save *you*. Because I couldn't have lived with myself if anything had happened to you."

The fervent tone in his voice, the bright light in his eyes, the tightening of his fingers on mine. It almost sounded like he cared about me. About me—Abby.

"I'm so sorry for everything," Wesley said. "I've just been so confused."

"Confused?" I asked. "Why were you confused?"

"That time in your apartment, when Wren, Nightingale, was taking care of me. We really connected."

I nodded.

"I thought we had something—something special. But then, you drugged me and ran away before I could see who you were. I didn't understand why, so I decided to look for you, and then, I ended up hiring you for my event. You were wonderful. Smart, funny, witty. I was attracted to you, and I couldn't figure out why, because I'd already fallen for this other woman."

"That's why you kissed me that day behind the waterfall?" I asked. "Because you were attracted to me?"

Wesley gave me a strange look. "Why did you think I kissed you?"

I shook my head. I wasn't sure what to tell him.

"Then I find out you're really Nightingale, that you've been under my nose the whole time. I'm a superhero. I'm used to lying to people about my real identity. Call me a hypocrite, but I didn't like it when somebody did it to me. Especially somebody I cared about."

I couldn't breathe. *Somebody he cared about.* Dare I hope he still did?

"Can I ask you something?"

"Anything," Wesley said.

"What did you think Nightingale was like? Who did you think she was?"

"I don't know." He shrugged. "Somebody like Fiona Fine, I guess."

My heart broke.

I was about as far away from the tall, blond, gorgeous Fiona as you could get. I'd been right all along. Wesley had been searching for a fairy princess—and that was someone, something I could never, ever be.

"Do you think we could start over?" he asked, his hand still on mine. "As Abby and Wesley?"

I wanted to. Oh, how I wanted to. But so much had happened. We'd told so many lies, hurt each other so much, without even meaning to. Wesley might claim he'd been attracted to me, but Nightingale was the one he'd been searching for. How could I know for sure which one of us he really wanted—his fantasy or my reality? The doubt would eat away at me.

Besides, I'd dated rich guys before. It never worked out. In the end, I really was a Wren, and Wesley was destined for somebody like Fiona, a glittering, beautiful Nightingale. He deserved that. Someday, he'd realize it and leave me. Better to cut my losses now and walk away with some dignity, even if my heart was in shreds.

I pulled my fingers away from his. "I'm sorry, Wesley. I don't think we can. Too much has happened."

"But—"

"No," I rasped, my throat closing up. "Don't say anything else. I appreciate you staying here and looking after me, but I'm sure the Fearless Five can take things from here. Please leave."

Wesley looked at me. I made myself meet his golden gaze. I kept my face smooth, expressionless, the same polite mask I put on at every party I planned.

It worked, just like always.

Wesley stood. He slipped his visor back on, morphing into Talon once more.

"Good-bye, Abby."

"Good-bye," I whispered.

He moved toward the door. I didn't start crying until it shut behind him.

The Fearless Five dropped me off at Piper's apartment the next day. Fiera even carried me up the stairs so I wouldn't have to put too much pressure on my ribs just yet. She put me down on Piper's couch. Rascal hopped up beside me and slathered doggie kisses all over my face.

"I've missed you too," I said, scratching his ears. "So much."

While I got reacquainted with the puppy, Fiera stalked around Piper's apartment, her smoldering eyes taking in all the superhero paraphernalia.

"Wow," Fiera said. "I didn't know you were into superheroes this much."

Piper frowned at the familiar tone in her voice. Fiera stared at a flame-shaped lava lamp in the corner that bore her likeness.

"Nice," the superhero said. "But I would have splurged and gotten the one with the signed collector's plate on the bottom."

"It's in the bedroom," Piper replied. "Right next to my Fiera throw pillows."

Fiera grinned.

The superhero scorched her autograph into Piper's kitchen table and left. I filled my best friend in on everything that had happened. The Fearless Five had called and told her I was okay, but she wanted to hear the details firsthand—especially when it came to Wesley.

"He throws himself at you, and you tell him *no, we can't start over?*" Piper said. "Why would you do that? He's your Wesley, your dream guy, your superhero."

"He's also the guy who wants another woman, a fantasy I can never live up to. I'll only end up disappointing him."

"Those are just excuses, and you know it. You're just scared he'll break your heart," she said.

"Maybe I am. I love him, Piper, but I don't know if he can ever love me for me."

"Wouldn't it be better to take a chance and find out?"

I rubbed my head. "Yes. No. I don't know. I just—I just need to be by myself right now. Everything's been so crazy. I just need some normal for a while."

Piper didn't push me any more. She knew when to kick my ass and when to let me lick my wounds. It was one of many reasons I loved her.

"Well," she said. "I have some good news for you."

"What?"

"Clean Dreams finished fixing your loft, and I finally got Kyle to agree to adopt Rascal."

"Oh no, he's not," I snapped. "Kyle's not taking my dog anywhere."

"Your dog?" Piper asked, arching an eyebrow.

"*My* dog. You think I'm going to give him up after he helped save my life? Not a chance. Besides, Quicke's isn't the only business that could use a mascot." I stared at the puppy curled up between us. "What do you say, boy? You and me forever?"

Rascal barked, jumped up, and licked my chin. I laughed and hugged him closer.

I went back to work a week later. I was still sore and bruised, but I was going crazy sitting on Piper's couch all day watching SNN. Besides, I had events to plan. Parties to oversee. Caterers to berate.

"Abby!" Chloe squealed when I got off the elevator with Rascal. She ricocheted around her desk and caught me in a tight hug. "It's so good to have you back!"

"Not so tight, Chloe," I wheezed. "Cracked ribs, remember?"

"Oops! I'm sorry. How are you?"

"I'm fine. How have you been holding up?"

Chloe had pretty much been running *A+ Events* while I'd been injured. "Well, it's been a lot of work, and I've had more than a few crises, but I've held it together."

She launched into a recap of some of her more memorable catastrophes, like how a star running back for the Bigtime Barracudas football team had hit on the wife of the team's owner at their latest party.

"It sounds like you did fine," I said. "I'm going to go catch up on my messages, and then, we're going to have a long talk about making you a partner."

"Oh, Abby!" Chloe squealed, reaching toward me again.

"No! No more hugging today!"

"Okay, okay." She leaned forward and lowered her voice. "But you need to know that Olivia O'Hara is in your office. She showed up and wouldn't leave. I was going to give her five more minutes before I called the police."

"It's okay. I'll talk to her."

"Are you sure?" Chloe whispered.

"Yeah," I said, handing her the leash. "But keep Rascal out here with you."

I took a deep breath and opened the door to my office. Olivia scrambled to her feet at the sound. She looked as beautiful as ever, but a tight smile creased her face and dark circles ringed her eyes.

"Hello, Abby," she said in a soft voice.

"Olivia."

I walked past her and sat down at my desk. I also unzipped a pocket on my vest, pulled out my stun gun, and set it on my lap—just in case.

Olivia settled back into her chair. "I wanted to say I'm sorry. For everything. I know you probably won't believe me, but I didn't know what Octavia was doing. I didn't know about the radioactive makeup, the animal testing, Bandit, any of it."

"But you knew she was Tycoon," I said. "You knew she killed your father. You had to know that from the beginning."

Olivia bit her lip and looked away. "I suspected, but I couldn't prove it. I tried to go to the police, and Octavia threatened me. She threatened to hurt Paul. His family. I couldn't let her do that."

"So you did nothing instead."

Olivia didn't deny it. Her gaze dropped to her finger, which was missing its diamond solitaire. "The engagement's been called off, and Polish is going back to the Potters."

"Well, that's something."

We sat there, me staring at Olivia, her staring at the floor.

"I came here today because I wanted to ask you—"

"If you're going to ask me to plan some memorial service for Octavia, you can get the hell out of my office right now," I snarled.

Octavia had been killed instantly, her body crushed by the giant lips sign. The coroner said she'd never known what hit her. Bandit hadn't been so lucky, or unlucky, depending on how you looked at it. The sign had landed on his back, severely damaging his spine and putting him into a coma. Doctors said the ubervillain would probably be paralyzed from the waist down for the rest of his life—if he ever woke up.

Olivia's eyes widened. "No! Oh, no. I would never ask you that."

"So what do you want?" I asked, tired of being polite to the woman whose sister had tried to kill me.

"I wanted to ask for your forgiveness," she said. "I know I don't deserve it, that my family doesn't deserve it, but I'm still asking."

Forgiveness? I didn't know if I had it in me, but I didn't want to have hate in me either. That would make me as bad as Octavia and Bandit.

"I hope your future is better than your past," I finally said.

She nodded. "Thank you, Abby."

Olivia walked out of the office and started past Chloe's desk. Rascal spotted her leaving. He barked and wagged his tail, hoping for a tummy rub. Olivia hesitated, then reached down and petted Rascal. Tears gathered in her eyes. Then, she straightened and left the office.

CHAPTER THIRTY-TWO

"Hey! You! You with the giant singing fish! You drop that, and you'll be sleeping with the fishes tonight!"

The mover holding the ten-foot-long plastic fish almost wet himself, but he held the fish steady while his buddy anchored it to the wall. Once the job was done, I checked *singing fish* off my clipboard.

Two weeks had passed since that night at Oomph, and I was back at the convention center, overseeing the annual meeting of the Bigtime Fly Fishermen's Association. The group had been pretty easy to work with. Their only odd request had been that I order fifty battery-operated singing fishes to decorate the auditorium. My watch beeped, reminding me what time it was—and where I had to be.

"I gotta run. I'm meeting Piper over at The Blues. Can you handle things from here?"

"You betcha," Chloe said, pulling a pen out of her vest.

To celebrate her becoming a partner, I'd bought Chloe her very own vest. She wore it only to humor me, but in time she'd realize its value. Chloe still had a lot to learn about how to handle crises in Bigtime.

And I still had a lot to learn about letting go. Making Chloe a partner and giving her more responsibility had been harder than I'd thought, but I was slowly learning. It felt good to let go. Plus, it gave me more time to spend with Rascal. The puppy was growing by leaps and bounds and demanding more attention than ever.

"Have a good time tonight," Chloe said.

"I always have a good time at The Blues."

She smiled. "I know."

I stared at her, wondering at the strange tone in her voice.

Suddenly, Chloe lunged forward and leaned over the balcony. "Hey! You!" she yelled. "You break that wine, you buy it!"

I hid a smile.

I grabbed a taxi and arrived at The Blues at six o'clock. To my surprise, nobody waited outside. Usually on a Friday, you couldn't get near the place, but tonight, the street was deserted, except for Izzy the bouncer. He stood in his usual spot in front of the velvet rope.

"Hey, Izzy, where's the crowd?"

"Private party," Izzy said. "And you're on the guest list."

Party? What party? I planned all the parties in Bigtime. I didn't know of anything going on here tonight.

Curious, I stepped inside. The karaoke bar looked the same as it always did. Bar. Stage. Sound equipment. Except that all but one of the tables had been cleared out. That one table was at the foot of the stage, with two chairs beside it and a single red rose lying across the white tablecloth. An ice bucket stood at one side, chilling a bottle of champagne. It resembled a setup I might do at one of my Valentine's Day events.

"What's going on?" I asked, more confused than ever.

Melody stepped out from behind the bar and handed me a flute filled with champagne. "It seems you have an admirer who wants to serenade you tonight. So sit down, and enjoy the show."

She steered me over to the table. I sank into the seat, still not sure what was going on. Stanley waved to me from his place beside the stage. After a moment, the lights dimmed, and a spotlight fell onto the stage. The curtain parted.

And then—Wesley stepped into the light.

He wore corduroys and a blue suit jacket over a white T-shirt. His golden eyes shimmered. I breathed in, letting his minty scent wash over me.

"Hi, Abby," he said.

"Wesley," I said, trying to ignore how good he looked.

It was a battle I'd been losing for two weeks. Wesley had been at just about every event I'd done since that night at Oomph. My gaze followed him all night long, every night. More than once, I'd found him staring back at me. I definitely wasn't invisible to him anymore, but we never spoke. Never said hello. Never even waved at each other.

Sitting in Piper's apartment, I'd had a lot of time to think about Wesley—and wonder if I was being a fool for not giving him a chance. For not giving *us* a chance. Maybe Piper was right. Maybe a broken heart would be better than always wondering what could have been, because my heart couldn't hurt more than it did right now. Half a dozen times, I'd thought about calling Wesley. Half a dozen times, I'd stopped myself, unable to squash the nagging voice in the back of my head that told me he'd always find me to be a disappointment.

He smiled. "You sang for me once. I thought I'd return the favor."

Wesley nodded at Stanley, who hit a button on his sound board. The opening strains of "Annie's Song" by John Denver filled the bar. Wesley put the microphone to his lips and sang.

Now, if there was one John Denver song that would make any girl cry, it was this one. A beautiful, beautiful song—being terribly, terribly butchered by Wesley.

He might be able to create complicated gadgets, sail over the city on zip lines, and take down ubervillains with a few well-placed punches, but there was one thing he couldn't do—sing. After the first thirty seconds, my ears hurt. After a minute, I was in agony. Finally, around the ninety-second mark, I stood up.

"Okay," I said, waving my hands. "That's enough. Please, please stop."

Wesley winced. "Was I that bad?"

"Honestly? I think I'd rather listen to polka music."

He laughed. I joined in. Now, that was a sound I could get used to.

"Can you guys give us a minute?" Wesley asked.

Melody and Stanley nodded and went into the back. Wesley hopped off the stage and came over to me.

"What's going on? Why are you here? Where's Piper? Why are you…singing?"

"Piper helped me set this up, with Chloe's help," Wesley said. "There was no girls' night out. That was just a story we made up to get you here. I didn't know if you'd come otherwise."

I didn't know if I would have either.

He put his hands over mine. "I lured you here tonight because I wanted to say I'm sorry for being such a jackass. You were right. I was expecting something different from Nightingale."

I nodded, hoping he would hurry up and finish his apology so I could go cry in private. I was right. He'd been disappointed in me—was still disappointed in me.

Wesley's golden eyes locked with mine. "But I found you instead, and you're wonderful, Abby. Better than a fantasy, better than Nightingale could ever be. Because you're the real thing. You're the one I want. Not her. You're the one I fell in love with."

He put my hand on his chest, right over his heart. I felt it *thump* through the fabric of his shirt. "You're the one I fell in love with, Abby. I feel the lightning with you. The passion, the everything. It took me a while to realize it, but I fell in love with you that first night in your apartment. And then again that night I saved you from Bandit. And again that day behind the waterfall. And again that night at the convention center."

"Shut up," I snapped.

"What?"

"Shut up," I repeated. "Shut up and kiss me."

"Yes, ma'am," Wesley murmured.

He lowered his lips to mine—and it was *perfect*.

Better than before. Because this time, I knew he was kissing *me*. Abby Appleby. Wren, Nightingale, they were gone now. I was the only one left—the only one he wanted. Wesley had come to me, not them. He'd done all this for me. He wanted *me*, supersenses, anal retentiveness, freakish tendencies, warts, and all. I couldn't quite believe it, but I wasn't going to ignore destiny's call, as Piper would say. Not this time.

Wesley ended the kiss and leaned his forehead against mine. He stroked my cheek.

"So, does this mean…" His voice trailed off.

"It means I love you too. I have for a long time now." I smiled. "Even if you do like John Denver."

We both laughed.

EPILOGUE

I stood on the balcony at the Bigtime Convention Center. Below me, about a hundred workers strung up balloons shaped like hearts, various superheroes and ubervillains, and certain body parts best left to the imagination. It was time for the big Valentine's Day dance put on by the *Slaves for Superhero Sex* club, and I was overseeing the show, freakish balloons and all.

The doors at the bottom of the stairway opened, and footsteps squeaked on the stairs. A moment later, mint filled the air.

"Did you bring Rascal with you?" I asked without turning around. "Piper had a date or something tonight and couldn't keep him."

A bark answered my question. I turned around to find Wesley standing behind me. Rascal sat at his feet, waiting for one of us to pet him. I leaned down and obliged the puppy.

"I'm still getting used to you having supersenses," he said. "I'm never going to be able to sneak up on you, am I?"

"Probably not," I said, scratching Rascal's ears. "But I can't sail over the rooftops without you, can I?"

"It's not quite as romantic as sailing when your beloved screams her head off," Wesley quipped.

"I don't scream—anymore. Well, not that much."

He raised his eyebrow. He came over and put his arms around me. "Can you get away yet?"

I leaned into him. The past few weeks had gone by in a rosy blur. I wasn't sure where Wesley and I were headed, but I was enjoying the ride so far—and going to do everything I could to keep sailing across the sky with him.

"Give me a few more minutes."

"Well, hurry up. I think there's a broom closet down the hall we haven't explored yet," he murmured in my ear.

I smiled back. "And I just happen to have the master key to all the doors in the building. Imagine that."

"Why use my imagination when the real thing's right here?" Wesley asked, pressing a kiss to the side of my neck.

"Why walk all that way to the broom closet?" I whispered back.

I tied Rascal's leash to the balcony railing and pulled Wesley into the shadows. The puppy barked in protest, wanting to follow us. He strained against his leash and whined and barked.

But it was a very, very long time before we got around to untying him.

FANDEMIC

A BIGTIME NOVEL

NEW YORK TIMES
BESTSELLING AUTHOR

JENNIFER ESTEP

FANDEMIC

by

JENNIFER ESTEP

BOOK FIVE IN THE BIGTIME SERIES

Piper Perez has always wanted to be a superhero. Always wanted to wear a cool costume, have amazing abilities, and save the day. There's just one problem—Piper doesn't have any superpowers.

So she focuses on other things. Facts, figures, memorabilia. Piper knows and collects it all, about both the superheroes and the ubervillains who roam the streets of Bigtime, N.Y. Piper's friends jokingly call her a fandemic—someone who is a superfan of all things superhero. The nickname is truer than anyone knows, especially since Piper can't stop thinking about Swifte, the speedy hero who broke her heart months ago.

But someone has been killing off Bigtime's heroes and villains. When one of Piper's friends is murdered, she vows to do whatever she can to help bring the killer to justice, superpowers or not. All the clues and information she gathers lead her to believe that Swifte is the killer's next target. Piper has always wanted to be a hero, and now she'll have to use all of her fandemic knowledge to save the man she loves—or die trying....

CHAPTER ONE

I've always wanted to be a superhero.

Always wanted to have amazing powers. Wear a cool costume. Be dark, brooding, and mysterious. Say wise, knowing, slightly cheesy lines. Use my powers for the greater good and kick some serious ubervillain ass. You know, the whole superhero shtick.

Over the years, I've done everything in my power to make it happen. I've accidentally-on-purpose put my hands next to scary-looking bugs. Gotten a little too close to some of the more unusual animals at the Bigtime Zoo. Taken multiple tours of the Bigtime Nuclear Power Plant. Actually, I still do that last one at least once a year. Just on the off chance that one of the core reactors will melt down and blast me with radiation that gives me superstrength. Or supersenses. Or superanything. I'm not picky.

"Hey, hey, hot mama! Wanna see my sword?"

At the moment, I would have especially loved the power to make myself invisible.

I looked up to find a guy wearing a Striker costume not-so-subtly leering at my breasts the way he had been ever since I'd come over to the bar to get a glass of Wynter punch. He'd finally decided to make his move and get up close and personal about his leering. Oh, goody.

Black hair, brown eyes, bronze skin. The guy was cute, and he had the broad shoulders and muscled body to pull off the skintight leather he was wearing from head to toe. But instead of admiring just how well he filled out certain areas of that leather, I found myself growing annoyed instead.

Because his costume was *all wrong.*

The outline of two small swords that crisscrossed the guy's chest was backwards and red, instead of dark gray like the ones on the *real* Striker's costume. The swords were located above the *F5* insignia, instead of behind it, like they should have been, and the whole suit was a smoky charcoal, instead of a true, midnight black like the one that the real superhero wore.

Amateur.

I might not be a superhero or have any actual superpowers, but I knew more than enough about the heroes and villains in this town to at least get my costume *right.* And I most definitely did not want to get hit on all night long by guys dressed in knockoff Striker suits. But that's exactly what had been happening for the last two hours. I should have expected as much, since I was at the Valentine's Day dance for the *Slaves for Superhero Sex* club.

More than a thousand people had crowded into the Bigtime Convention Center and Orchestra Hall for the annual event, and almost everyone was wearing some sort of colorful costume, mask, cape, or T-shirt emblazoned with the photo and symbol of their favorite hero or villain.

Striker, Fiera, Mr. Sage, Hermit, Karma Girl. All the members of the Fearless Five, the city's preeminent and most popular superhero team, were well represented among the enthusiastic fangirls and fanboys. So were other iconic heroes like Johnny Angel, Debonair, and Talon.

Many folks had also dressed up like their favorite ubervillains, including everyone from Malefica, Frost, and Scorpion from the Terrible Triad to deceased and comatose villains like Prism, Hangman, and Bandit. One woman had suited up like Intelligal and had even built an exact replica of the dead villain's Intellichair, although the woman's chair just rolled on the floor, instead of flying through the air like Intelligal's had. Still, I had to give her props for getting all the details exactly right. It wasn't her fault she hadn't been able to get her hands on a jet-propulsion system to actually make the chair fly.

Even more colorful than the costumes and capes were the decorations that adorned the convention center's main auditorium. Ten-foot-tall cardboard cutouts of heroes and villains towered above the crowd, along with smaller, life-size versions that you could put your arm around and have your picture taken with. Hero- and villain-shaped balloons filled a white netting that swooped down from the ceiling, while still more balloons drifted freely through the air, many of which were in the form of various body parts that I didn't look too closely at. They didn't call the club *Slaves for Superhero Sex* for nothing.

Balloons shaped like giant candy conversation hearts had been tied at either end of the bar, which was set up in the orchestra pit. Several round tables clustered in front of the bar, where people could sit, drink, and talk, as well as play cards and throw dice in the latest role-playing games. Beyond the tables, dozens of couples were grooving on the dance floor, their colorful capes rippling around their spandex-clad bodies. Vendors hawking everything from imitation swords to replica gadgets to collector-edition toys stalked up and down in front of booths that ringed the dance floor, trying to entice people to ignore the pulsing music, come over, and browse through their wares.

I signaled the bartender that I needed a refill, then dug into one of the glass dishes filled with candy conversation hearts that were spaced along the bar. I grabbed a pink heart and read the saying. *I luv superheroes.* Truer words, never spoken. I popped the candy heart into my mouth and crunched down on it.

The bartender finished with my drink and slid a fresh glass of Wynter punch over to me. I reached for the ice-blue concoction, but the guy in the knockoff Striker suit propped his elbow up on the bar in front of my drink and leaned in closer. I didn't need my best friend Abby Appleby's supersense of smell to tell me that he'd taken a bath in his cologne. The overpowering spicy scent made my eyes water and nose twitch in an all-too-familiar way. I was going to have to get rid of him before my allergies kicked into overdrive. A red, runny nose would so not go with the flame-shaped mask that covered my face.

"I'm talking to you, hot mama," the guy crooned again.

"Really?" I asked. "Hot mama? That's your line?"

The guy frowned. "What's wrong with *hot mama?*"

I shrugged. "For starters, it sounds like some cheesy book title."

His frown deepened. "But you're wearing a Fiera costume. Everybody knows that she has fire-based powers." His eyes dropped to my breasts again. "And that she is smokin' hot. Like, *literally.* Just like you are in that costume. Well, without the actual smoke and fire, of course. But you're still plenty hot enough for me in the figurative sense."

Part of me was impressed that he knew the difference between literal and figurative, but the other part of me was growing more and more annoyed by the excessive leering.

I snapped my fingers in front of his face. "Hey, buddy. I'm up here."

He grinned, evidently thinking the snarky finger snap meant that I was totally into him too. "So what do you say, hot mama? Wanna ditch the party and go have a private one of our own?" He waggled his eyebrows for extra emphasis, as though I didn't already know exactly what he meant.

"Sorry." I sniffed and tossed my black hair back over my

shoulder in my very best Fiera impersonation. "As you pointed out, I'm dressed like Fiera, and you're in a Striker costume. The two don't mix."

He frowned again. "Why not?"

"You seriously don't know?"

He shook his head.

"Because Karma Girl and Striker are an item. I even think they're married in real life, but that's just a theory of mine."

Actually, it was much more than just a theory, since I'd attended the wedding of Carmen "Karma Girl" Cole and Sam "Striker" Sloane last year. Of course, the two of them didn't realize that I knew who they were, alter egos and all. To them, I was just Piper Perez, a business associate and the chief financial officer of Fiona Fine Fashions. But my inner fangirl had been secretly, gushingly, absolutely *thrilled* to attend the wedding of two of my favorite heroes. After all they'd been through battling the Terrible Triad, Carmen and Sam deserved some happiness, and so did their alter egos.

"Theories?" the guy said, an incredulous note creeping into his voice. "You have *theories* about superheroes?"

And that was the official dagger killing any chance he'd had of picking me up. But the guy kept staring at me like he had no idea what I was talking about, so I listed some more reasons we were never going to happen.

"Of course I have theories about superheroes. Who doesn't? Besides, *everybody* knows that Fiera only goes out with Johnny Angel," I said. "If you were a *true* superhero fan, you'd know that too."

"So what?" the guy asked, staring at my breasts again. "What does it matter who dates who? It's not like we're the real heroes. We're just here to party and have a good time."

I snapped my fingers again. "Eyes up top, buddy. And yeah, maybe we are here to party and have a good time, but I also happen to be a superhero fan. A *true* fan. One who knows her heroes and villains forwards and backwards. Which means that I never, ever go home with guys who don't know their basic facts."

"Are you serious?" the guy asked. "You're turning me down just because I didn't know that some hero chick is dating some villain dude?"

"Two chicks and two dudes, and they're all heroes now," I automatically corrected him. "And that's only one reason. Your overpowering cologne is another one, but your main offense is that sad, sad excuse for a costume. I know that Striker updated his suit a few weeks ago, but still, you had plenty of time to tweak your own suit to match his."

Was I being a total bitch right now? Oh, yeah. Normally, I would have let him down nice and easy, but he was the fifth guy to come up to me in the last hour, and the third one to use the cheesy *hot mama* line. Apparently, some guys thought that wearing an orange-red spandex Fiera costume made you ready, willing, and eager to fulfill all of their warped fantasies for the night, since they'd never get close to the real superhero herself.

The guy sputtered like a car engine, trying to come up with some snappy retort. Evidently, he couldn't believe that I was passing up the opportunity to go back to his place and let him paw me.

I didn't give him the chance to make a comeback. Since his elbow was still blocking my glass of Wynter punch, I grabbed a couple more conversation hearts out of the candy dish, popped them in my mouth, and walked away. Unlike his outfit, *my* costume was one-hundred-percent correct, from my flame-shaped mask to my orange-red catsuit to my chunky-heeled boots—the latter of which helped me make a quick getaway.

I strolled past the boisterous vendors, having already examined their goods and picked up a few new collectibles, and headed for the buffet tables lining one wall. Maybe I was channeling Fiera tonight because I felt like I could eat as much as she did. Okay, okay, so I couldn't eat a dozen of anything even at my hungriest, but I'd skipped lunch, and I was starving. Watch out, Caveman Stan mini cheeseburgers and Pimpler pepperoni pizza—

I was so focused on the buffet and my growling stomach that I bumped into a tall woman standing off to one side of the tables. Actually, *bumped* wasn't the right word. I hit her shoulder and bounced off, since I was no match for her superstrength, not even when she was standing still.

The woman turned to stare at me. She was wearing an ice-blue suit that brought out the golden sheen of her cropped hair. Silver sequins were stitched together in the shape of a giant snowflake on the front of her costume, and the symbol flashed like a strobe light with every move she made.

I brightened. "Oh, hi, Sabrina. How are you?"

The woman's ice-blue eyes narrowed behind her snowflake-shaped mask, and she crossed her arms over her chest. Too late, I realized my mistake. I'd just called Wynter, the superhero, by her real name—a name I wasn't supposed to know.

But I'd figured out that Sabrina St. John moonlighted as Wynter, the hero who had superstrength and ice-based powers to match her frosty name. Okay, okay, so I hadn't actually figured it out so much as I'd seen her duck into one of the dressing rooms at Oodles o' Stuff, the department store where she worked, and come out thirty seconds later all decked out in her Wynter costume. But I knew who she was all the same. In fact, I knew the real identities of pretty much every hero in Bigtime, and some of the villains too.

Since, you know, most of them had either saved or threatened me at some point over the years.

"I don't know who you think I am, but I'm Wynter—the *real* Wynter." She tapped the sequined snowflake on her chest for emphasis.

"My mistake. Of course you are," I said. "But what are you doing here? Shouldn't you be out patrolling? Keeping the city safe from villains and the like?"

Wynter huffed. "Believe me, I *wish* I was doing that. But it's my turn to chaperone this year's shindig. I can't believe that I let Abby book me for this."

She muttered the last few words under her breath, but I still caught the reference to Abby, who was the city's premiere event planner, in addition to being my best friend. I knew that Abby had planned the Valentine's Day party, but I hadn't realized that she'd gotten Wynter to be one of the guest superheroes. Then again, I hadn't told Abby that I was coming here tonight. Abby loved me, but she thought that I took my hero worship just a little too seriously. Which I totally did. Not that I would ever admit that to her, though.

"I mean, come on," Wynter said. "I know that parts of the auditorium are dark, but they're not *that* dark."

She gestured at a couple standing in a pool of shadows a few feet away from us who were kissing and fondling each other a little too passionately for such a public place.

I winced and turned away from the PDA. The *Slaves for Superhero Sex* club had a bad reputation because some of the members took the club's name far too literally. All right, *way* too literally. Some folks in the club did stupid, foolish, and life-threatening things like stepping out into traffic during rush hour, climbing out onto ledges thirty stories up, or deliberately capsizing their sailboats in the middle of Bigtime Bay. All so they could get a little face time with whichever hero rescued them. Most of the heroes like Wynter politely turned down everything but autograph requests, but there were a few like Gentleman George who enjoyed the, um, *attention* as much as the club members did.

Most people, Abby included, thought the entire *Slaves for Superhero Sex* club was made up of such rabid fans. But really, the Obsessors, as they were called, were a small minority in the group, as were the Villifiers, the people who worshipped villains and tried to get hired on as henchmen and women. Most folks in the club simply loved all things superhero and ubervillain, just like I did. Still, I couldn't judge either faction. At least, not until I gave up my annual nuclear power plant tour.

During the Valentine's Day party, I'd spotted several giggling couples sneaking off to the darker, quieter, more secluded parts of the auditorium to have some alone time with each other. Instead of chasing after heroes and villains, the couples were pretending that they were the real deals tonight, instead of just regular guys and gals dressed in spandex and leather and sporting whips and chains. But I couldn't fault them for that either, given the orange-red fabric that currently clung to my own body like a second skin—

WHOOSH!

A violent wind swept through the auditorium, hard enough to make my black hair fly around my face. The wind gusted again and again, sending all the comic books on the vendors' tables swirling up into the air, rattling the pink candy conversation hearts in their glass dishes, and making the heart balloons attached to the bar whip back and forth like they were caught in the middle of a tornado. It was a tornado, all right—a superhero-fueled one.

The wind died down as suddenly as it had sprung up, and a tall, lean man appeared on the dance floor, right in the middle of all the grooving couples. He wore an opalescent white costume that shimmered with all the colors of the rainbow, along with matching sneakers from Bella Bulluci's latest collection. A pair of wings outlined in silver, his superhero symbol, stretched across his chest, and a wing-shaped mask covered his face, although it didn't even come close to hiding his wide grin.

I recognized him immediately.

Swifte, one of Bigtime's most popular superheroes.

And the guy who'd broken my heart.

ABOUT THE AUTHOR

Jennifer Estep is a *New York Times*, *USA Today*, and international bestselling author, prowling the streets of her imagination in search of her next fantasy idea.

Jennifer is the author of the **Elemental Assassin** urban fantasy series. The books focus on Gin Blanco, an assassin codenamed the Spider who can control the elements of Ice and Stone. When she's not busy battling bad guys and righting wrongs, Gin runs a barbecue restaurant called the Pork Pit in the fictional Southern metropolis of Ashland. The city is also home to giants, dwarves, vampires, and elementals—Air, Fire, Ice, and Stone.

Jennifer is also the author of the **Mythos Academy** young adult urban fantasy series. The books focus on Gwen Frost, a 17-year-old girl who has the gift of psychometry, or the ability to know an object's history just by touching it. After a serious freak-out with her magic, Gwen is shipped off to Mythos Academy, a school for the descendants of ancient warriors like Spartans, Valkyries, Amazons, and more.

Jennifer is also the author of the **Black Blade** young adult urban fantasy series. The books focus on Lila Merriweather, a 17-year-old thief who lives in Cloudburst Falls, West Virginia, a town dubbed "the most magical place in America." Lila does her best to stay off the grid and avoid the Families—or mobs—who control much of the town. But when she saves a member of the

Sinclair Family during an attack, Lila finds herself caught in the middle of a brewing war between the Sinclairs and the Draconis, the two most powerful Families in town.

Jennifer is also the author of the **Bigtime** paranormal romance series. The books feature sexy superheroes, evil ubervillains, and smart, sassy gals.

For more information on Jennifer and her books, visit her website at www.JenniferEstep.com. You can also follow her on Facebook, Goodreads, and Twitter—@Jennifer_Estep.

Happy reading, everyone!

OTHER BOOKS
BY JENNIFER ESTEP

www.ingramcontent.com/pod-product-compliance
Lightning Source LLC
Chambersburg PA
CBHW050513110726
47899CB00005B/1439